UNITED WE STAND

BAEN BOOKS by JOHN RINGO

BLACK TIDE RISING
Under a Graveyard Sky • *To Sail a Darkling Sea*
Islands of Rage and Hope • *Strands of Sorrow*
The Valley of Shadows (with Mike Massa)
Black Tide Rising (edited with Gary Poole)
Voices of the Fall (edited with Gary Poole)
River of Night (with Mike Massa)
We Shall Rise (edited with Gary Poole)
United We Stand (edited with Gary Poole)

TRANSDIMENSIONAL HUNTER
(with Lydia Sherrer)
Into the Real • *Through the Storm*

TROY RISING
Live Free or Die • *Citadel* • *The Hot Gate*

LEGACY OF THE ALDENATA
A Hymn Before Battle • *Gust Front* • *When the Devil Dances*
Hell's Faire • *The Hero* (with Michael Z. Williamson)
Cally's War (with Julie Cochrane)
Watch on the Rhine (with Tom Kratman)
Sister Time (with Julie Cochrane) • *Yellow Eyes* (with Tom Kratman)
Honor of the Clan (with Julie Cochrane) • *Eye of the Storm*

COUNCIL WARS
There Will Be Dragons • *Emerald Sea*
Against the Tide • *East of the Sun, West of the Moon*

INTO THE LOOKING GLASS
Into the Looking Glass • *Vorpal Blade* (with Travis S. Taylor)
Manxome Foe (with Travis S. Taylor)
Claws that Catch (with Travis S. Taylor)

EMPIRE OF MAN
(with David Weber)
March Upcountry • *March to the Sea* • *March to the Stars* • *We Few*

SPECIAL CIRCUMSTANCES
Princess of Wands • *Queen of Wands*

PALADIN OF SHADOWS
Ghost • *Kildar* • *Choosers of the Slain* • *Unto the Breach*
A Deeper Blue • *Tiger by the Tail* (with Ryan Sear)

STANDALONE TITLES
The Last Centurion • *Citizens* (edited with Brian M. Thomsen)

To purchase any of these titles in e-book form, please go to www.baen.com.

UNITED WE STAND

EDITED BY
JOHN RINGO
& GARY POOLE

A Baen Books Original

Baen Publishing Enterprises
P.O. Box 1403
Riverdale, NY 10471
www.baen.com

ISBN: 978-1-9821-9326-3

Cover art by Kurt Miller

First printing, March 2024

Distributed by Simon & Schuster
1230 Avenue of the Americas
New York, NY 10020

Library of Congress Cataloging-in-Publication Data

Names: Ringo, John, 1963– editor. | Poole, Gary, 1967– editor.
Title: United we stand / edited by John Ringo and Gary Poole.
Description: Riverdale, NY : Baen Publishing Enterprises, 2024. | Series: Black tide rising ; 12
Identifiers: LCCN 2023049235 (print) | LCCN 2023049236 (ebook) | ISBN 9781982193263 (hardcover) | ISBN 9781625799524 (ebook)
Subjects: LCSH: Science fiction, American.
Classification: LCC PS648.S3 U38 2024 (print) | LCC PS648.S3 (ebook) | DDC 813/.0876208—dc23/eng/20231211
LC record available at https://lccn.loc.gov/2023049235
LC ebook record available at https://lccn.loc.gov/2023049236

Printed in the United States of America

10 9 8 7 6 5 4 3 2 1

As always
For Captain Tamara Long, USAF
Born: May 12, 1979
Died: March 23, 2003, Afghanistan
You fly with the angels now.

Dedicated to Kim & Judi
The best sister and sister-in-law a guy could have

CONTENTS

Foreword — Gary Poole — ix

Extraction — John Birmingham — 1

Taking the Next Steps — Jody Lynn Nye — 27

Isle of Masks and Blood — Brian Trent — 63

Things to Do in Denver When It's Dead — Sarah A. Hoyt — 91

For the Triumph of Evil — Jamie Ibson — 117

The Old Bastard — Dave Freer — 147

Let Freedom Ring — Griffin Barber — 175

Maligator Republic — Lydia Sherrer — 201

Do Not Steal — Mel Todd — 239

Gonzo's Gauntlet — Christopher L. Smith — 265

The Bride Wore Camo — Mike Massa — 289

About the Authors — 323

Foreword

GARY POOLE

When John and I first started talking about the idea that ended up becoming the first of the Black Tide novels, neither of us thought that what he was creating would end up becoming so, well, extensive.

What you hold in your hands (or are reading on your reader or listening to someone read aloud) is the fourth collection of stories set in the ever-expanding Black Tide universe. Which goes along with eight novels and a graphic novel adaptation. With, hopefully, more to come.

Which raises the question, why has this series struck such a chord with readers?

Postapocalyptic fiction is hardly a new genre. Writers have been intrigued by the "What happens when civilization falls?" question for decades upon decades. Everything from post-nuclear classics like *On the Beach* and *Alas, Babylon* to more fanciful classics such as *A Canticle for Leibowitz*, and of course the bevy of end-of-the-world novels, television series, films, and games. We, as readers and viewers, have long been attracted to the often very dark worlds portrayed therein and the characters who strive to overcome against long odds. If they overcome at all.

But what makes the Black Tide universe different?

It is a question that John and I have talked about many times over the past few years. And from conversations with fans and other writers, we have come to a simple conclusion: it's all about hope.

Not just Hope, as John so prophetically named one of the most popular characters in the series, but hope as in "even in the darkest times, there will always be someone to light a candle." For as I've written about in previous forewords, the entire core of this series has not been about the infected but about the people who strive to not only survive but try to make the world a better place. Or at least somewhat more survivable. Hope is one of the strongest and most human of all emotions. It is what keeps us going when everything—and everyone—around us is telling us to stop. It's what drives us to build, to create, and yes, even purge when necessary. For without hope, there is nothing to live for, no reason to take another breath.

Each anthology has had an overarching theme: the aftermath, communication, rising above the challenges. For this collection, John and I wanted to go even further. Sure, it's great to survive, it's great to be able to reach out to other survivors, and it's great to start building for a future. But the real challenge is how to keep that future alive. How not just to survive, not just to rebuild, but to actually thrive. To stand united. To tell the universe that mankind can take whatever nature throws against us and not back down.

Even when the enemy is no longer the infected, but ourselves.

I could write more, but, like you, I want to get to the "good stuff." And there's a lot of very good stuff in this anthology.

I hope you enjoy it.

Extraction

JOHN BIRMINGHAM

Night fell on the dead city, and with it, the sounds of things not dead.

Caitlin Monroe leaned against the cold, stone battlements of the old fort and scanned the edges of the forest to the north with the night vision scope fixed to her rifle. The forest had grown wild over there, obscuring all but the roofline of the empty houses beyond.

Well, maybe they were empty, she thought. Maybe not.

Her earpiece crackled with reports from the other lookouts. All of them in French.

"Sector West, clear."

"Sector South, clear."

"Sector East . . . hold on."

A single rifle shot cracked out. The report bounced off the stone walls of the fortress, but she did not turn towards it, staring instead into the darkness to the north, waiting for any sign of movement. But all she saw was the forest; the only movement was the trees swaying gently in the early evening breeze.

"Sector East, clear," the voice said.

The channel went quiet again, and Caitlin gently pivoted, sweeping the tree line one last time.

"Sector North report," a new voice crackled inside her ear. In English this time, but heavily accented. Thierry.

"Sector North...clear," Caitlin said at last. And then repeated herself in French.

"*Secteur Nord...dégagé.*"

Still, she did not stand down.

"You see anything, Doc?" Caitlin asked, taking her eye from the scope at last.

Standing beside her, Dr. Juliette le Marjason scoped out the same length of forest with a large pair of high-powered night vision binoculars.

"Nothing," she said warily, but like Caitlin, she kept looking. Finally, Juliette blew out the breath she had been holding. It steamed in the cold air.

"I think we're good, Caitlin," she said. Her English was accented, but not heavily. She had worked in America for three years before all of...this.

Caitlin nodded and took a moment to survey all of...this.

It might be the last time.

The two women stood at the apex of a massive, graystone bastion, an arrowhead-shaped tower at the northeastern corner of Le Fort de Noisy-le-Sec. Before them, the haunted suburbs of Paris stretched away into the absolute gloom of night. The landscape was a ruin under a clear black sky filled with stars and a waning moon's gunmetal blue light. Caitlin looked down upon streetlamps snuffed out and broken. Telephone poles had snapped and splintered like matchsticks, and weather-worn billboards faded to white slumped over rusted car bodies.

The houses on the far side of the forest stood two and three stories, and there were nights when Caitlin thought she could hear the hushed whisper of monsters shuffling through the dry dust and mold of those crypts.

"We should go inside," Doctor le Marjason said. "Bachelard has outdone himself tonight. A feast is promised."

"Yeah, I can already smell the slow-cooked tins of corn beef from here," Caitlin said. "Nom nom."

"No, no, you are awful, Caitlin," the doctor said, but she was grinning. "Bachelard has made a cassoulet of everything we cannot take tomorrow. He has even done duck legs."

"Wait, what?" Caitlin said. "What about Daffy? What happened to Daffy?"

"We cannot take him with us, Caitlin. We cannot leave him here. The infected will get him."

"Doc, there's not even that many infected left. They died off. Mostly."

"There are enough," Dr. le Marjason said. "Daffy was old and lame. He only had one wing. It was a mercy."

"You're not selling this, Doc."

But the French woman did not have to sell the meal. Caitlin had been working hard all day preparing for the bug-out in the morning, and she hadn't eaten much after breakfast. Just a handful of dried fruit, nuts, and a protein bar so old it had real archaeological significance. As she ducked her head under a low stone lintel, the smells from the kitchen wafted up the spiral staircase from below. What Bachelard was cooking smelled delicious, and her mouth watered.

Pity about old Daffy, though.

Caitlin had liked that grumpy old duck.

Halfway down the stone stairwell, the women had to press themselves against the wall to allow the night watch, Roche and Mercier, to get past them. The young men, a former paratroop sergeant and a Tier One operator from the Bureau were talking and laughing as they climbed the stairs. Roche sucked grease from his fingers, and Mercier chewed on a small drumstick.

Too small for poor Daffy, Caitlin thought, but she greeted the men and wished them well for the night.

The fortress was as secure as anywhere could be in a fallen world. Noisy-le-Sec had been the headquarters of the French Secret Service and, specifically, the military intelligence arm of the French state, the Deuxième Bureau. The layers of security which had once defended the Bureau against enemies foreign and domestic—and once upon a time, Caitlin was very much counted among the former—had allowed a small crew of survivors to hold out here in the first days of the plague. The fort's thick stone walls, well-stocked armory, and two years' worth of provisions meant for dispatch to the Bureau's overseas posts saw them through the worst of the following year.

That and the serum, of course.

Dr. le Marjason had vaccinated everyone who still drew breath in this place in a mad rush by the end of that first horrific week.

"We heard a shot before. Was that you?" Roche, the paratrooper, asked.

Caitlin shook her head.

"Dion, you know when I pull a trigger, you'll never hear it."

Roche snorted, and Doctor le Marjason rolled her eyes.

"You boys stay warm up there tonight," she said. "It's going to get down near freezing."

"But don't cuddle too much," Caitlin teased them. "I'd prefer you kept your eyes out for the biters, not each other."

They did not rise to the bait. Instead, Roche shrugged in a very Gallic fashion.

"I don't think there are many biters left. I haven't seen one in months."

"Dude, come on," Caitlin said. She folded her arms and leaned back against the curving stone wall. It was cold and felt a little damp against her neck. "Remember your classics. It's the character who says things like that at the start of the movie who gets bitten on the ass by a zombie before the end of the first act. And they get specifically ass-bit because they're not looking out for shit. The biters are still out there. And plenty more besides. Stay on it, Sergeant."

Neither man looked particularly chastened. Caitlin had no place in their chain of command. She remained an outsider. It was an accident of history that she was even here. And that accident was sitting at the big common table in the kitchen when she and le Marjason emerged from the stairwell.

Wales Larrison raised a glass of brown liquor, probably cognac, as the women appeared. There had been no bourbon in the fortress stores when everything fell apart, and Wales had been forced to improvise in the years since. More than a dozen people had crowded into the kitchen, and their voices roared even in that comparatively large, open space. Everyone was up, excited for the morning.

Wales's voice boomed out.

"Caitlin! Jules! Get your asses on down here and have a last drink with me. These cheese-eating Asterixes wouldn't know how to get on the outside of a decent drink if it was the last thing they ever did."

Doctor le Marjason frowned at him.

Larrison had been drinking a lot the last few months.

"Wales, this will be the last drink you ever have if you can't evacuate tomorrow. Thierry will leave you here for the biters."

"Don't you worry about me, Doc," he shot back in his big American voice. Larrison swung one leg up on the table, and it crashed down with an almighty bang. Marjason had crafted the artificial limb from an old table leg.

"I'll be ready to hop on down the happy trail the hell out of here, but right now, our liberation calls for a toast."

He banged the wooden leg on the table a couple of times, loud enough that the roar of the small crowd fell away.

Larrison climbed to his feet, or instead to his one good foot. His peg leg, as he called it, he propped up on the seat he had been warming.

"Friends. Countrymen . . . that's you, Monroe. It's just you and me now that Daffy's gone."

Somebody cheered.

Wales patted the air with his free hand, taking a quick hit from his drink with the other.

"My friends, I cannot let this our last night at your marvelous chateau pass without saying what a wonderful time we've had here and how much I'm looking forward to never seeing any of your ugly-ass faces again."

The cheer was louder this time. It sounded somehow drunker to Caitlin. They had been at the fortress a long time. Long enough to reclaim the grounds, plant their own crops, and even source livestock. Chickens, some goats from a nearby petting zoo, and the sadly departed, slow-cooked Daffy. Everyone was used to Wales by now. And to her, of course.

A hell of a thing, really, when you thought about it. The Bureau and Echelon had once fought a shadow war in this city. Caitlin herself had been taken and tortured in the cells below this fortress. But all of that meant nothing now.

No, she corrected herself, fetching a plate and filling it with roasted vegetables and chicken pieces while everybody listened to Wales's speech. No, she thought. She and Wales had been allowed into Noisy-le-Sec after she escaped from that charnel house of a hospital precisely because the station chief here, Thierry, had known them so well as rivals. And even, to be completely honest, as enemies.

Thierry was one of those men who were very good at recognizing when circumstances had changed.

Caitlin caught his eye as he leaned against the mantlepiece which ran over the kitchen hearth. A fire burned in there, and Thierry Duval seemed quite content to warm himself by it, nursing a glass of red wine and smiling at Wales. He nodded to her, and she returned the gesture.

Thierry had overseen her torture when she had been imprisoned here in the before times.

It didn't matter.

He was why she still lived now.

Wales, who had run Overwatch for all of Echelon's field agents in Paris, went on with his speech. His French, unlike hers, was flawless. He worked the room into a small riot of laughter and fake outrage, telling stories of the time before the fall when they had been enemies. Only fifteen souls remained within the ramparts of the fortress, and apart from Wales and Dr. le Marjason, they were all field agents and operators. It made sense that only the strongest, most ruthless had survived. The years had been hard. The small audience cheered Wales through his long and often hilarious retelling of old spy stories, but the biggest cheer came when he had so much to drink that he stumbled on his peg leg and fell over. The doctor rushed forward to help him, summoning a couple of Bureau agents to help her get him back to his room. She grabbed a couple of bottles of water to take with them.

Thierry Duval tapped a small fork against the edge of his wineglass, bringing order and quiet back to the room.

"And that, I think, is enough fun for this evening," he said. "Each your fill, drink no more except for water and get to sleep. We will need all of our energy and focus tomorrow morning."

A couple of people started to clean up, but Duval stopped them.

"No. Do not bother with that," he said. "It is a waste of time now. Leave everything exactly as it is. It will be quite the find for some historian a thousand years from now. It is enough; we're done here."

He clapped his hands twice, making a sound like rifle shots. The party broke up.

Caitlin, who was not finished eating, stayed at the table, piling more food onto her plate. Thierry raised an eyebrow at her, but she kept eating.

"You never did quite fit in here, did you, Caitlin," he said.

Caitlin chewed and swallowed a roasted duck-fat potato. Poor Daffy.

"None of us ever fit anywhere," she said. "That's how we ended up in this life. That's why we're still alive."

He shrugged.

"A fair point, I will concede. But do not be up all night. We must be rested. I fear this will not be an easy journey."

She held up a chicken leg.

"Just getting my protein."

They were up early, but the convoy did not leave until well after dawn, with the sky a dull gray and the moon still visible to the west where the clouds had frayed like the page of an ancient book. Caitlin climbed the tower one last time after waking and took a final look over the sanctuary. The massive stone walls of the fortress glistened dark and gray. The dead world beyond was shrouded in a cloak of early morning fog.

She wondered what waited for them out there.

The only sound was the wind, whistling across the fort's southern walls and over the battlements, stirring the thick soup of cold fog.

Thierry had ordered patrols further into the city over the last six months after the first government radio signals came in from Castle Saint-Ulrich. With cautious patrolling to verify hours of drone cam coverage, the surrounding arrondissements were familiar enough now. They had even begun to imagine they might have an easy time of it, driving to the extraction point. But then bandits shot down one of the fort's two precious drones, and they lost a patrol vehicle to an ambush a few days later.

There was no question of that being the work of the infected. Biters did not use RPGs.

With unknown numbers of *le infecté* still wandering the city's ruins, now joined by armed hostiles of unknown strength and capability, Thierry had ordered a daylight evacuation. They did not have enough night vision equipment to spook their way to the extraction point at Orly Airport, and once they passed into the unknown wilds of Paris, it would be too easy to become lost and separated in the dark.

Caitlin was surprised to find Wales Larrison waiting for her by the vehicle they had been assigned, a Land Rover Defender in light desert tan.

Wales was showered, shaved, and had even dabbed on a spot of cologne. Unlike everyone else, who had dressed in combat fatigues or some civilian analogue, he sported a pair of cream slacks that hid most of his wooden leg, a blue shirt and a dark sports jacket. He looked like a high-tone bookie, off to the races, and Caitlin couldn't help but smile when she saw him.

"How's your head this morning, old man?"

"I have taken more out of strong drink than it has ever taken out of me, young lady," he said.

"I made him drink two liters of water, and I gave him a vitamin B shot," Juliette le Marjason said, appearing from around the other side of the Defender. She wore cargo pants and a photographer's vest over a long-sleeved T-shirt. Every pocket was stuffed with medical supplies. She had a pistol at one hip and carried an FN SCAR rifle slung over one shoulder. If the doc was this tooled up, they really were going on an adventure, Caitlin thought.

She had dressed in plain black coveralls, lace-up boots and a ballistic vest; light body armor protected her at the most common bite sites, on the forearms, shoulders and neck, even though her vaccine was still good. A human bite could still kill you, even if it did not drive you insane. Caitlin carried an M4 as her primary weapon, but the Bureau's armorer had kitted her out with whatever she'd asked for.

"Just gimme the lot, Gaston," she said.

Four vehicles made up the convoy. Two Ford Rangers, her Land Rover and a Panhard VBL armored car. It looked by far the most rugged, but the fort's other VBL had eaten a rocket-propelled grenade in the ambush a month earlier. Caitlin was more familiar with the Land Rover and was glad to have been assigned to it. It offered no protection against anti-armor weapons, but she wasn't likely to crash it into a canal if things got sporty.

Also assigned to travel with her were Roche and Mercier, who arrived shortly after Caitlin, looking none the worse for their night watch. More B12 shots, probably. The doc had offered her one, but Caitlin said no. Noisy le Sec's medical stocks were aging out, and the last thing she wanted was a bad reaction to a jab the morning they were supposed to leave.

There was no ceremony to their departure. Nobody to wave them off. Thierry, in the armored car, signaled to a couple of men at the great iron gates securing the tunnel through the old breastworks and out into the fallen world. The men undid the chains and swung the gates open while a gunner in Thierry's VBL covered them with a heavy, ring-mounted machine gun. The gates screeched open slowly, and Caitlin felt her flesh crawling.

She imagined she could hear the howl of a million *infecté* beneath the rusted metal scream of the hinges. She couldn't, of course. They were mostly gone now, but there were other monsters outside.

The convoy rolled forward.

Mercier and Roche insisted on driving and riding shotgun, respectively. Caitlin and Juliette sat behind them in the second row of seats, with Wales taking the whole back seat for himself and his improvised prosthetic leg.

Even though she had done her fair share of time on the patrols into the surrounding arrondissement, it felt weird to be passing through them in the Land Rover, knowing they would never return to Noisy-le-Sec. The fortress had been their home for a long time now, the world beyond its walls a hostile country.

There was little to be seen from the road, the buildings looming over them on both sides long since fallen to wreck and decay, their rooftops blanketed in ivy and moss. Green tendrils and vines wrapped tightly around every window and door frame. Ivy, thick and heavy, climbed every stone facade and wall, heedless of gravity. Wherever she looked closely at a building, it seemed to be sinking into the earth. Shadowed doorways were black holes in their flanks, waiting to swallow and consume.

Caitlin recalled when she'd first arrived at the fort; she would sometimes climb the battlements in the evening to look down on the gray slate roofs of the old tenements and factories and wonder what lives had been made and unmade there. Now she just looked out the window, scanning for targets among the ruins of what had been. Here and there, they rolled by the desiccated corpse of an *infecté* or two, even bumping over one shot down by a recent patrol. But it was nothing like the mad, horrific race against spreading carnage and collapse that she had run from the hospital to the fort on the first day of the Fall in Paris. Time and decay had worked the magic trick of cleaning much of the city—or at least this part.

Mercier cut the wheel back and forth to weave through a tight barricade at the edge of their patrolled area. An armored truck marked "UN" had turned over in front of a bridge over a small canal, thick with fetid green water and floating rubbish, probably washed into the system by yesterday's brief morning storms. The driver started to say something about having to get out and move the wreckage, but the armored car ahead of them geared down and crashed into the hulk at a low enough speed to push it aside without injuring anybody on board the VBL.

"Goddamn," Wales muttered from the back seat at the crunching, grinding shriek of metal on metal.

The truck toppled into the canal with an almighty splash and a deep belch of dark, rotten water, settling into its watery grave with a series of dull groans and watery farts.

Such a racket would have brought hordes of the infected racing down on them once upon a time. Thousands, even tens of thousands. Now?

Nothing.

The Defender's engine seemed dangerously loud.

The VBL pulled to a stop at the foot of the bridge. Caitlin leaned forward between the two front seats, but Thierry was too good at his job to order anybody out into the open. The ring-mounted machine gun traversed the ground ahead of them.

His voice crackled through the radio.

"Anyone see anything worth shooting?" he asked.

"Negative," Roche replied.

Caitlin held her weapon close, but there was no sign of movement anywhere other than the slow, dreamy wake of the poisoned canal. The sloping concrete sides of the watercourse were painted with streaks of rust. Dead fish bobbed on the surface, disturbed by the roiling waves of the truck's impact. Even with the windows rolled up, it reeked of stagnant water and rot.

A new voice crackled over the radio net.

"*Infecté. Onze heures.*"

They all turned, craning around to eleven o'clock.

A single rifle crack, more of a pop, really, dropped a naked scarecrow shambling out of an alleyway across the canal.

They waited.

Again.

Nothing.

After three minutes, Thierry announced they would push on. The VBL led the way across the canal.

The run to Orly Airport was more of a stuttering crawl. There was an airstrip much closer to the fortress, of course. Charles de Gaulle, a few miles northeast. But the instructions from the Emergency Government at Castle Saint-Ulrich were explicit. They were to convoy overland to Orly, where they would rendezvous with other survivors and await extraction by elements of J-Mops, the Joint Military Operations command improvised by British and French airborne units in the chaos of the Fall.

The chopper flight to Castle Saint-Ulrich from Orly was just a few hours.

It would take longer to get to the rendezvous point twenty-five klicks away than the castle five hundred kilometers away.

If they made it at all.

Sitting in the back of the Land Rover, threading slowly through the chaos of the traffic jams which had strangled the city in her last hours, Caitlin had her doubts. The road network of Paris was choked with vehicles. The main thoroughfares were great frozen rivers of rusted steel, impassable with the skeletal remains of millions of cars, trucks, and bicycles. Duval took them off-piste. Navigating a backstreet path they had plotted over months.

But, of course, that led them to dozens of dead ends, impasses and diversions. Sometimes the VBL was powerful enough to force a way through. More often, they would have to backtrack and work around the delays. By late afternoon they had progressed less than half the way to their objective.

The fog of morning had burned off for an unseasonably warm afternoon, but nobody appreciated the good weather. They could be seen from much further away.

They had just crossed the Marne River, heading south on the Avenue de la Republique, when they got swarmed. Caitlin had been dozing, head propped against the window. She came to in a rush when her ears popped with a heavy, concussive blast. A grenade launcher on the VBL. Instantly she was awake and alert—surrounded by the sporadic crack of gunfire and the deeper rumble of vehicle-mounted weapons.

"The fuck is going on, Roche?" she shouted.

The former paratroop sergeant turned around and stared at her as if she were crazy.

"The fuck do you think, Caitlin? *Infecté.* Fucking everywhere."

The four-vehicle convoy was strung out along a narrow road crowded with breakdowns. The biters, perhaps a hundred, were shambling at speed out of a school building to the east. It had been so long since Caitlin had seen a horde up close that she froze and gawked at all the arms and legs twisted hideously or entirely missing. Some appeared to have limbs knitted back into their bodies with a sickly, pulsing scar flesh. Limbs to replace the ones they had lost, sometimes two or more sets, jutted out of their shoulders or even their hips. They came on with that terrible hive-mind focus, clumped wracks of twisted bone and flesh, human spiders of fleshy ruin moving with dread and stilted determination.

Mercier shouted over the engine and the noise of gunfire.

"There's hundreds of the fuckers!" he cried out.

They had blocked the road ahead of them. A seething mass of *le infecté*, shoulder to shoulder in the middle of the road, stared at the convoy with dead eyes and gaping mouths.

A single gunshot, way too loud, right next to Caitlin shook her out of her reveries.

Doctor le Marjason fired into a crowd of shambling husks coming at them from an avenue to the west. Wales joined her, tossing off round after round from the shotgun he carried.

Violent contrary needs flayed at Caitlin. She wanted to drive. She wanted to shoot. She needed to flee. And she had to fight.

But she had the worst tactical position of everyone in the Land Rover. She was just a passenger in the back on the wrong side of the vehicle.

The machine gun on the VBL hammered out a long burst, a heavy industrial clatter that drowned out the growl of the Defender's engine. She saw the rounds hit home, removing limbs, toppling *infecté*.

Behind them, someone fired a grenade launcher. There was a long, hollow WHUMP and a great cloud of white smoke mushroomed up into the air. A few of the zombies blocking the road ahead of them exploded in a spray of gray, syrupy fluid and pulverized bone. Others fell backwards and struggled to get up again. One of them seemed to have a pair of spade-headed excavator claws grafted onto its torso.

"What is this?" Juliette whispered in horror, over and over. "What the fuck is this?"

The VBL reversed back and forth, muscling aside the burned-out hulk of a minibus. The gun turret swiveled and roared again.

In the brief pause between fire bursts, Caitlin heard the grating scrap of teeth on the metal skin of the Land Rover. She jumped to find an *infecté* at her window, the lines of rot and necrotic flesh running out of the corners of its eyes. Cancers or tumors? Clumps of shriveled black tissue hung from the hairless, shriveled head.

She didn't scream.

She didn't shoot through the window glass.

She checked her primary weapon and waited.

Slowly the convoy organized itself into a mobile fortress with interlocking fields of fire. Even more slowly, they beat back the rotting tide. The biter, chewing at her door handle, went under the wheels of the Defender. A wedge of attackers hit the Land Rover with a sickening thud. Caitlin felt her teeth rattle in her jaw, but shooters in the other vehicles carefully picked them off.

It was a drill they had practiced many times, and it was over a minute later.

Ticking stillness descended on the cabin.

"My god, what were they?" Dr. le Marjason gasped.

"Hungry," Caitlin said.

"No, I mean, did you see them? What had been done to them?"

Caitlin had.

They all had.

The radio crackled again.

"Proceed to the route," Thierry said.

Nobody spoke for a long time. They remained vigilant, on edge. Everyone had seen larger hordes of the infected, naturally. But not for a long time. It was Wales who finally broke the silence.

"Somebody's been playing God," he said.

They had crossed over the Seine at Alfortville and into an industrial neighborhood on the other side of the river.

With fewer people having lived here, the roads were more easily navigated, and the ruins seemed merely bleak and abandoned instead of actively malign. Some of the newer warehouses evoked the neglected foundations of a lost future, a modernist city that had never entirely been born.

Thierry called a five-minute break in the middle of a vast clay field in front of a brick factory. Two giant smokestacks reached high into the late-afternoon sky, casting long shadows east. It would have been a weirdly desolate place even before the Fall. But they had good sight lines, and there was even a small pit where they could take turns relieving themselves in something like privacy.

Or as private as you could be, with a lookout riding shotgun over you while you emptied your bladder.

Caitlin squatted in the pink-red dust while Dr. le Marjason stood watch. Then she returned the favor. A cold wind whipped up dust devils, and the fine particles felt gritty on her tongue and the back of her throat. The earth itself was silent here. No birds, no insects, no living things. Only the wind moving faintly and uncertainly.

Caitlin Monroe licked her lips, tasting grit and gun smoke.

She had a bad feeling about this, but then she'd had a bad feeling since waking up in the Pitié-Salpêtrière hospital just before everything turned to 48 Flavors of shit.

Juliette climbed out of the pit, rubbing her hands with antiseptic gel. She offered the squeeze bottle to Caitlin, who took it and wiped her hands again.

Be pretty fucking funny to escape the city of the dead only to croak from typhus or septicemia.

"They are discussing the attack?" Le Marjason asked, nodding at the others.

The four vehicles had formed a rough circle in the center of the clay field. Three lookouts stood watch with long guns on top of the armored car and the two SUVs. Everyone else had gathered in a loose knot inside the vehicle fort.

"Dunno," Caitlin said. "More likely, they're talking about whether to push through to Orly tonight or find a secure place to make camp."

Dr. le Marjason shuddered.

"Out here?"

She looked at the barren moonscape around them.

"Doubt it," Caitlin said. "Thierry mapped out a bunch of defensible sites between Noisy and the airport. We got ammo, food and water. We could hold off a bigger horde than we met today."

She felt Juliette's hand close around her elbow.

"Caitlin, they were not normal. They had been...changed."

Caitlin breathed out after a long moment.

"Yeah, I know," she said. "But they were as dumb as ever. They went down just as easy as before."

From somewhere, she recalled a fragment of a quote from her studies at the Naval Academy. The Duke of Wellington at Waterloo. *They came on in the same old style, and we met them in the same old way* or something.

It wasn't totes apropos for this audience anyway, so she kept it to herself.

They walked to the edge of the group. Thierry, Wales and Mercier leaned over an old paper map on the hood of the Defender. They were talking among themselves. Nobody else spoke.

Not for the first time was Caitlin glad to have fallen in with professionals.

She did not doubt they would make their rendezvous with J-MOP at Orly. Just as she did not doubt that some of the other survivors' groups meant to meet up there would die on the way if they encountered anything like that infected mass back at the river crossing.

Le Marjason was right to be worried about the weirdness of the *infecté*, though.

Who had done that to them?

And why?

Was it connected to the ambush of their patrols the last few weeks?

None of it made sense.

She shook off her doubts and joined the conference.

"S'up, Wales?"

"We're pushing on," he said.

"We can get to Orly tonight if we stick to the route that skirts the residential districts," Thierry said. His finger traced a line across the map. "We follow the river until the crossing of the rail bridge here"—he stabbed at the map again—"and then track the rail line all the way to Orly. There is a maintenance road that runs parallel to the tracks and no derailments between us and the rendezvous, according to J-MOP."

"According to J-MOP," Caitlin said, leaving the question unspoken.

Could they trust anybody but themselves?

They made good time following Thierry's route to the airport, but even so, the light and warmth were leaking out of the day when they arrived. Of all the desolation and loss they witnessed on that slow trawl to Orly, nothing could match the weird otherness of the airfield itself. The terminals stood dark and silent, with the crunch of their wheels on the tarmac the only sound. The super hangars of Orly's deserted flight depots reminded Caitlin of monoliths on the moon. The whole place seemed less a collection of runways and hangars than a black hole in the howling wastes, an inky absence, riotous with curves and adornments of concrete. The skeletons of fallen, burned-out planes stood in relief against the falling sun and years of wind-blown rubbish had piled up against a chain link fence on the outer edges of the facility.

"You sure our flight was today?" she joked, but nobody laughed.

There was no sign of any other survivors or refugees. No *infecté*. No hostiles.

Nothing.

"This feel good to anyone?" Caitlin asked.

Juliette was about to answer when Mercier suddenly wrenched the wheel hard. Caitlin's head thumped into the window, and she saw stars and a comet tail.

The comet was a small antitank rocket that lanced out of the nearest terminal and speared into the side of the VBL. The armored car exploded in a cloud of orange-and-black flames. The shockwave staggered the Land Rover, and the vehicle slewed across the tarmac, pursued by a storm of grenades and automatic weapon fire.

Mercier shouted at Roche. Roche swore loudly and fired out of the passenger window. A grenade exploded too close, and the cabin suddenly pitched and tilted.

"We're not going to make it!" Juliette cried, but her words were drowned out by the roar of their engine and return fire.

"Nine o'clock," Wales called out from the back. "Shooters on the top deck of the terminal."

Caitlin crawled over Dr. le Marjason to take the position under fire. Juliette squirmed beneath her and attempted to get out of the way. All was chaos and madness as they poured fire into the building, and Mercier tried to avoid the long snaking lines of tracer coming back.

"Drive at them!" Caitlin yelled, but the Frenchman was way ahead of her, slewing around and accelerating into the ambush. Caitlin was relieved to see at least one of the SUVs keeping pace with them. She tasted the coppery tang of blood in her mouth and felt the air turn hot and heavy, like breathing in soup.

The volume of incoming fire died away as they sped towards the terminal. A glass wall loomed ahead of them, and they crashed through, turning the world from the cold yellow light of sunset to darkness, from concrete to dust and rubble, from metal and flame to smoke and fire. The building whirled and tilted, the sky spun, and the ground shook.

Caitlin distinctly heard the odd scream of the Land Rover's tires on the hard tiles of the terminal building just before the loud bang of the heavy steel ram bar slamming into a travelator.

They were inside the terminal. Deep inside.

"Out-out-out!" Roche yelled.

Caitlin was already out, with Juliette half a second behind her.

They hauled Wales from the rear of the Defender and over to a half-collapsed concession stand. It had been a pop-up crêperie. Now it was the best cover they had. Reality flexed and threatened to turn inside out. The terminal looked flat and washed out to Caitlin, like a grainy old black-and-white photograph, but one that had been ripped in half, pasted back together and tinted around the thinnest of edges with garish, unreal colors.

Wales looked sallow and almost permeable.

She checked him for wounds, but he was good on that score.

Juliette le Marjason pushed her aside.

"It is his heart," she said. "Wales! Look at me. Where does it hurt?"

He winced.

"My left arm. Shoulder."

The arm of his ridiculous sports coat was intact. Caitlin swore under her breath.

A burst of small-arms fire chewed into the roofing tiles above them, showering all three with plaster dust.

"Doc," she said, "I'm going to get these fuckers. I need you to see to Wales."

"Just go," Juliette said. She was already unloading equipment and first aid supplies from the five hundred pockets of the photographer's vest she wore.

Caitlin was about to hurry back to the Defender, where Roche and Mercier were hunkered down, returning fire, when her old boss suddenly gripped her arm in a surprisingly strong hold.

"We need some of them alive," he said in a harsh rasping voice.

"I'm not in a very forgiving mood, Wales," Caitlin hissed.

"We need to know," he said, with some difficulty.

"Fine. For you."

He squeezed her arm and smiled weakly.

She smiled back, readied her weapons and took a deep breath before hurrying back to the vehicle and crouching next to Roche.

"How many of them?" she asked in French. Her French was much better than his English.

Roche shook his head.

"About even to begin I would say. But now we are outnumbered and outgunned," he replied.

Caitlin peeked around the edge of cover.

The terminal was a warren of check-in desks, empty security lines and looted souvenir shops. The ceiling was high and painted with faded candy-colored stripes that seemed to dance like ribbons in the dim, dusty light. The floor was sticky, littered with wads of bird shit, scraps of paper and rubbish of every kind.

She edged closer to Mercier, hunkered down at the other end of the Land Rover, sweeping the terminal ahead with his assault rifle. Firing every now and then.

She put her hand on his shoulder and squeezed gently. Twice. Then once.

Mercier nodded understanding, his face grim and determined under its coating of dust and sweat.

Caitlin turned back to Roche, who had pulled a grenade from his vest pocket and was checking the pin.

"Mercier to provide covering fire," she said quietly. *"When I say go, we run like hell for that door over there."* She pointed to a glass door in the nearest wall. The entrance to a United Airlines club lounge.

Neither man questioned her. They all knew the stories about Caitlin Monroe.

She peered around the end of the Land Rover, saw three men dressed in black combat gear, took aim and fired. One of the men fell, clutching his chest, the other two dived for cover, but Caitlin picked them off with shots to the head. She'd had a lot of practice at headshots the last few years. They were dead before their bodies hit the tiles.

"*I thought I was to provide covering fire?*" Mercier said, almost ruefully.

"You snooze, you lose, pal."

She checked her rifle and their surroundings. The coast was clear for now. With a quick nod to Roche, she ran.

They burst into the club lounge and dived for the nearest cover, a reception desk, a cold slab of polished steel, the chairs behind it hard plastic with metal frames.

The space was gloomy rather than dark. Full night had not yet fallen, and the last rays of a blood-orange sunset caught the thick swirl of dust motes in the stale air of the lounge. Her eyes glistened in the dim light.

Mercier joined them a second later.

"*Bachelard is leading the others,*" he said. "*They will assault up the stairwell at the end. Romy is staying to cover Doctor le Marjason and Monsieur Larrison.*"

"Good," Caitlin said. "You boys travel UA out of this place before?"

Neither had.

"*I have,*" she said. "*I all but fucking lived here six or seven years ago. There was a service lift at the other end. It feeds the Air France lounge and the administrative levels above. If they were firing at us from the second floor, they're in that lounge. We can take the high ground and come down on them while Bachelard hits them from the front.*"

The paratrooper and his Bureau colleague assessed the plan and agreed to it in less than two heartbeats.

They moved.

The lounge was deserted. Truly empty save for the desiccated husks of a few corpses here and there. They were so old they didn't even smell anymore. They lay in tatters, and at first glance, it was hard to tell that these shapes were once human.

They looked like the awkward calligraphy of a child scribbling on a pale canvas.

The three killers moved as one, sweeping the space in front of them and around for all threats, human and otherwise.

Caitlin took the lead. Roche and Mercier took turns checking their six. The muted reports of battle reached them from somewhere above. Dust lofted off the rifle shots, briefly executing clumsy pirouettes, then falling back to the ground. Caitlin's trigger finger ever so gingerly caressing the guard of her M4, ready to fire.

The service lift was where it should have been, but the doors were closed, and there was no power.

Caitlin stepped to the brushed metal door and pulled a knife from her tactical harness. She slid it between the access panels and pushed, levering them open. Roche stepped up to help.

They forced open the doors, and Caitlin nodded grimly to find the elevator car waiting for them.

It was full of bodies.

She didn't think. She placed a round into each of them. Making sure.

None moved or made a sound. They were long gone.

"Give me a hand," she said.

Roche bent over and laced his fingers together, improvising a step for her to reach the maintenance panel in the roof. She forced it open with her knife and waited a second.

The sounds of gunfire were louder, but that's not what she was listening for.

Crawlspaces were often, well, crawling with the infected. They could live for years on vermin.

The elevator shaft was empty, however.

Roche boosted her up through the access panel, and she reached down to help both men up after her.

They fitted torches to their weapons. The three beams swayed chaotically in the pitch-dark shaft, and they climbed the steel rungs of an access ladder fixed to the concrete walls.

The stairs were rusted and pitted with age, but they provided sufficient purchase as they climbed.

Caitlin retook the lead, and they moved quickly but quietly, taking care not to slip. As they reached the next landing, she paused briefly before continuing upwards.

She could hear the concentration of fire on this level.

Finally, they reached the top. Caitlin sprung the emergency clasp, and the doors released an inch or two. She put her eye to the gap, looking through into a collection of open-plan workstations.

To one side stood several large crates stacked atop one another, while a row of lockers filled with spare uniforms and coveralls took up the wall on the other side. She forced the gap wider and climbed through.

This floor was quiet, save for the noise coming up from below.

Mercier and Roche joined her.

She looked for a fire escape. It would be near the service core with the elevators.

The darkness up here was more total, but she found the door on the other side of the elevators.

The volume of fire from below seemed to be increasing.

They entered the stairwell.

She was making the first turn when someone cried out behind her.

Roche.

A zombie had emerged from the cubicle farm. A ravaged horror with skin that looked like melted candle wax. Half its face was missing, but it had still fixed its remaining teeth on the neck guard of Roche's body armor. It snarled and chewed as the Frenchman struggled frantically to free himself.

Caitlin slammed her fist down on Mercier's gun arm, not wanting him to shoot in the confined space and give them away. Instead, she smashed the butt of her rifle into the face of the ravenous biter, collapsing skin and bone and whatever the hell was left underneath into a hellish honeycomb crunch of toxic offal.

The thing fell away from Roche, who was shaking and madly checking himself for bites.

"Dude, chill," she said. "You're vaxxed. And that thing bit the ass out of your Kevlar, not your neck. Let's just go. And next time, remember the fucking classics."

Mercier passed his friend a small flask. Caitlin smelled strong liquor when he unscrewed the cap and took a slug.

"Good call," she said, and he passed her the bottle.

She took a swig. Cognac. A nice one too.

It burned going down but settled her nerves.

It had been a long time since she'd gone up against a human enemy, and this one was dialed in.

She had no doubt these were the same bastards who'd ambushed the patrols out of Noisy-le-Sec. She was starting to think they might even have faked up the whole remnant authority J-MOPs thing to lure them out of the fortress.

Where was their extraction force, after all?

And the other survivors?

They had been lured into a killing box. All on their own.

"Let's go," Caitlin said.

They assaulted onto the second floor. Roche grunted and dropped to the ground like a puppet cut loose from its strings. A single round had felled him. Caitlin went down on the carpet under the angry buzz of bullets overhead.

"Son of a bitch!"

She rolled over Roche and grabbed him by his body armor. Strap in hand, Caitlin hauled the young man towards the nearest cover. She didn't pause to think, to examine her surroundings, to question the choices she was already making. Her largest handgun, the Glock 19, had quickly appeared, and it roared, biting huge chunks of wood and masonry from the solid timber furnishing of the Air France lounge.

Roche was gasping and grinding out an arhythmic series of grunts like somebody punched in the stomach trying and failing to draw air into their lungs.

Glass shattered, and rounds cracked past her head to chew up the blonde wood wall panels. Caitlin logged the direction and volume of fire, and part of her mind calculated that they faced maybe seven or eight hostiles. Roche moaned loudly, glancing back over her shoulder; Caitlin saw his legs begin to scythe and kick in reaction to the burning pain that would now be making itself felt. Gut shot by a military assault rifle. There was gore and leakage everywhere.

Caitlin knew exactly the location of a couple of morphine syrettes in one of the bags, but to attend to Roche would mean ceding the initiative to their would-be killers.

He died at her feet, his last breath bubbling out of his lips in a froth of blood.

Mercier was already on the move, pushing forward, and firing.

Caitlin realized then that Roche had probably taken a stray round from Bachelard's group. There just wasn't enough fire coming at them. The enemy hadn't realized they were here yet.

Caitlin holstered her Glock and hauled her Steyr TMPs from the shoulder rigs under her jacket. Safeties flicked off; she held the weapons out around the corner of the desk behind which she hid and unloaded into the free-fire zone of the lounge. The outgoing fire sounded like canvas sheets ripping in the high wind.

After three bursts, she took a quick peek to see what she'd caught.

Impossible to say.

She saw one leg twitching under a desk.

Three shooters in the open.

All white males armed with FAMAS G2 assault rifles. One behind a couch with a possible leg wound. One crouched behind a coffee machine. The last one, aiming from a deeply recessed doorway leading to the bathroom facilities.

She snapped off two quick bursts at the man in the doorway.

The G2 rounds suddenly crashed around her, chewing up her cover and forcing her to fire blind again. Caitlin emptied the rest of the mags with much greater accuracy; however, having sighted her targets, then she turned back into the building and shoulder-charged the first door on the right. It gave way with a crack of splintered wood, and she tumbled into the small meeting room, taking cover below the window ledge, crunching broken glass underfoot.

Caitlin slipped off her backpack and poured half a magazine of 9mm hollow-point from the Glock through the smashed windowpane into the main lounge area in one quicksilver motion.

She opened her oversized pack and pulled out the big artillery. The pistol-grip Benelli shotgun came first, customized twelve gauge, extended mag with a side saddle shell carrier. Next came the deal closer, a specially cut-down Heckler and Koch UMP 45, with an extended box mag housing thirty rounds of .40 caliber Smith & Wesson goodness. She slung the HK over her shoulder.

It was a large, excessive arsenal for just one young lady to haul around Paris, but Caitlin had told Gaston, the armorer, "Just gimme the lot," and Gaston, the armorer, had not disappointed.

She picked up the shotgun, jacked a cartridge into the chamber and poked the muzzle out through the shattered window. The

Benelli was loaded with a buck 'n' ball combo that gave her a nice spread for quick and dirty area clearance but still packed a nasty surprise in the form of one larger brass slug at the center of the load. Unlike softer malleable rounds, it was armor-piercing and would slice through a car door or ballistic vest without slowing down much.

She methodically pumped half a dozen rounds of buck 'n' ball downrange. She briefly heard a few distressed cries, more shouting, and the hammering of boots on polished wooden boards, but then the uproar of her sustained gunfire drowned out everything else.

Bending low, she moved through the line of meeting rooms, blasting through the glass walls between each one, flanking their would-be killers in the dark while they tried to fend off Bachelard from the front and Mercier from behind.

Caitlin dumped the shotgun and swung the Heckler and Koch into action.

She thumbed the selector on the machine gun to full auto. One of the reasons she liked the H&K was its relatively low rate of fire, a modest six hundred rounds per minute, which in the hands of an expert operator, made the burst mode all but redundant.

Caitlin looked out of a window into the lounge area with a black widow's smile.

She had a clear line of fire on five hostile shooters.

"Gentlemen," she said.

Her movements were quick and machinelike.

One sharp pull on the trigger shattered the window, and as the men instinctively looked up, she nailed two of them with short auto bursts, aiming for the center mass and letting the muzzle drift upwards to punch a couple of rounds into their skulls. The first man looked surprised, his eyebrows raised comically and mouth a perfect O before five rounds stitched him up from the sternum to the forehead. His skull disintegrated. The second attacker was fast and well-trained but doomed. He got his muzzle up a few inches and squeezed off one misdirected round before Caitlin nailed him the same way. A fan of blood and brain matter painted the wall behind him.

A sudden surging roar of fire and then...silence.

Six men lay dead on the floor, riddled with bullets, and another three men writhed and groaned in pain. If they weren't dead, they soon would be. She held on for a few seconds longer, readied her weapon and then rose out of cover.

"Sector West, clear," she cried out. Then, remembering, she repeated herself in French. *"Secteur Ouest. Clair."*

The other fire teams called in.

She heard Bachelard and, a second later, Mercier.

She relaxed just a little at the sound of his voice.

Not much. Just a little.

The burning wreckage of the VBL down on the tarmac threw eerie shapes of guttering orange light onto the ceiling of the lounge. Caitlin emerged into the main part of the room, ready to fire on anything that moved. But nothing did.

She thought she could hear the pops and crackling of the fire down below. Smell the burning rubber, the fuel, the plastic and, of course, the men they had lost, including Thierry.

"Search them," she said, *"Fouillez-les."* And two of Bachelard's men set to doing so without question. The others took up positions where they could watch for the approach of follow-on forces and defend the space they had just taken.

And that was that, she thought. They were professionals. They'd deal with this and move on to whatever came next.

Mercier joined her, looking haunted.

"I don't think we're getting extracted today," he said.

"Nope," Caitlin said. "Don't reckon so."

She could tell from the quick, professional way Bachelard's men turned up nothing that they'd learn jack shit from the bodies.

Wales would be pissed, she thought.

If he was still alive.

"Sorry about Roche," she said quietly. "He was a good guy."

"The best," Mercier agreed.

He took out the small flask of cognac and unscrewed the lid.

"To Danton," he said, taking a swig and passing her the flask.

"Danton," she said and took a belt for the fallen paratrooper.

René Bachelard came over to confirm what she already knew.

"They're ghosts," he said.

Caitlin nodded.

"They are now. So, what next?"

"Extraction?" Bachelard asked, looking more hopeful than he should have.

"I don't think so, René," Caitlin answered, almost smiling.

"I don't think there'll be an extraction. I don't think there is an emergency government at Castle Saint-Ulrich. And I know for damn sure those weird fucking biters that tried to swarm us back at the river crossing didn't pimp their own rides."

The two men stared at her. She was about to repeat herself in French when she shrugged.

"We got played."

Caitlin Monroe looked at what she had done, what they had all done.

"But I don't think they knew who they were playing with," she went on. "And now it's our turn. We'll secure a layup point here for tonight. And tomorrow we go to fucking work."

She jacked a new clip into her Glock 19 and went to see if Wales Larrison had survived.

Taking the Next Steps

JODY LYNN NYE

"Just take a look!" Tee Figueroa exclaimed. She wound her arm around her boyfriend Billy Marx's waist and gazed out over the broad, flat Columbus River Valley, the last rays of twilight throwing shadows across the darkened buildings of the distant city.

"Today, Nashville. Tomorrow, the world!"

Billy laughed and gathered her into his arms. Her slight figure hardly made an impression against his sturdier bulk.

"You're setting a lot of store by a shack, an antenna, and a chain link fence."

Since a few months into the lockdown began, Billy had been communicating with fellow ham radio operators worldwide and turned his own reminiscences and stories from those friends into a popular radio show piped over the public address system in the Foresight Genetics compound. He just saw it as a way for survivors of the plague to hear news and realize they weren't alone in the big, wide world. His friends that lived at Foresight, down the hill a few minutes' drive from the new studio building and transmitter tower called him a lifesaver for keeping their spirits up during the dark times. Tee, and many others, thought he should build a real broadcast studio and transmit programs of all kinds over as many frequencies as possible. They had all

27

the fancy gear, now, instead of a digital ham radio attached to a makeshift antenna. The electric and water hadn't been run up the hill to the new facility yet, but they were on the roster waiting for their turn to have the barn-raising crew, as everyone called it.

The U.S. government, now based in Jacksonville, Florida, instead of the Hole in Oklahoma, backed his efforts absolutely. He could legally possess any equipment that he could locate. The idea was to start out as radio and branch into video when they could. The morale boost that a regular entertainment and news channel would provide was worth more than the value of electronics that no one now would ever seek to reclaim. The original owners were all dead or had fled. That didn't stop Billy from leaving IOUs whenever he took something. You never knew. But he must have written ten thousand notes by now. If he and Tee couldn't make a success of their new station, he wouldn't ever be able to pay back the debts he was incurring. Nor was he sure he could collect together enough people to produce programs that filled all the needs of the community. Hardly anyone was left from the entertainment industry, and those who survived felt uneasy about traveling cross-country to a virtually empty city that might still have infecteds hiding out around. His many concerns must have shown on his face. Tee hugged him hard.

Once again, he felt a deep wave of love for her. She was the most amazing woman. Not only was she beautiful, in a kind of slender, wild-haired wood-elf way, but her sheer brilliance dazzled him. Whenever they hit a snag in their plans, she always found a way to keep the project moving forward, all the while keeping him from feeling like an idiot lagging along behind her. Her technical knowledge was far above his own, and she was street-smart on top of it. He kept wondering why she was interested in an awkward small-town boy five years her junior who was nobody's version of handsome. Tee had had plenty of offers from other men in the compound but showed no interest in any of them. If there was any treasure at the end of the rainbow of the nightmare that sprang from the virus, Tee was his.

"This just the beginning," she said, as she always did. "We will do fine. We will make this work. We're together! That's what counts." She gestured behind her at the frame for the structure going up at the rear of the small metal hut. Soon, it would be their home, big enough, as Tee said, for them, and Cindy, Billy's first girlfriend.

Just before the virus had started up, long before he ever met Tee, Cindy and her parents had taken the trip of a lifetime to central Asia. She had sent photographs of soaring, white-topped mountains, and towns and villages thriving at the top of the world. When all communication shut down, he had lost touch with her and feared her lost forever, along with the millions and billions who had succumbed to the virus or become victims of those who caught it. Then, a faint and crackling message over ham radio told them she was all right.

Cindy's mother had died because of the virus, but she and her father had taken shelter in a monastery in Tibet. To Billy's surprise, Tee made friends with her over ham radio, chatting after-hours through bursts of static and unstable power from Cindy's end. Once Cindy would return home again, they said they had plans for Billy, which made him tingle with delight and terror at the same time. They'd be a family, even if it seemed a faint hope for the time being. How Cindy and her dad would get back was still up in the air. So much of the infrastructure that had existed before the plague was gone or nonfunctional. Travel was one of the industries that had little hope of rising again anytime soon. It seemed like decades since the plague broke out, even if it was only two years.

Two years! It had only been two years since he and his mother and sister had fled to the Foresight Genetics facility with anything that they could throw into their small car. The blue Honda Fit had run out of gas for the last time running reconnaissance trips into the nearby communities, then had a load of scavenged batteries installed under the hood by the five remaining plant engineers so it could live again. Maybe like the betas. Maybe like Billy himself. He was looking forward to a new life, one not constrained by the electrified chain link fence that protected the research grounds.

With the disease halted, and the few pockets of infecteds disappearing, everyone was looking outward. Beyond the walls of the compound, a neighborhood had grown up downslope. As time went by, houses on the streets below were being cleaned up and renovated, wiping away any trace that they had ever been broken into and soiled by waves of infecteds and wild animals. Billy spent most free evenings fixing up a little house for his mother. His sister Reena had acquired a boyfriend, Scott, the son of one of his mom's fellow chemists, and moved in with him on the top floor of an abandoned apartment building just on the other side of the river. They had no power or running water, and what lights they had ran on LEDs supplied by solar panels, too, but it was all theirs. Mom and Reena had urged Billy to move on and get his life going, too.

He was working on it. His show got a wider and wider listener base every week. As people around the world were able to go out and about, the reports from his radio friends grew more interesting, but fewer, as they, too, were building new lives with less time to sit huddled over a ham or shortwave radio. His friend Geraint in Wales had taken over the grounds of an old castle and was fixing it up it with the hands of his new wife, Mairi, along with a road engineer, an Anglican vicar, and a handful of people from a medievalist society. A ship had set up deliveries of desperately needed supplies to Dr. Park in Antarctica, and evacuated the scientists who wanted to leave, now that they could. All this was getting broadcast on the increasingly sophisticated equipment that he and Tee had been able to bring back from abandoned radio and television studios and recording facilities all over Nashville. Tee had a dream of booting up the Internet, but that was years away from becoming possible. She had plenty more ideas, each more complicated than the last. He tried to keep up with her aspirations, but he guessed his brain didn't work the same way as hers.

"Who do you think is going to win the election?" Billy asked, packing their tools into the rear of the borrowed pickup truck. Now that things were stabilizing, the government encouraged what populations existed to organize themselves with an eye toward more normal life. That meant figuring out who could do what, and who would be in charge. The people who had taken shelter in the Foresight Genetics compound had pretty much gone with the company chain of command until then. As the population grew, in ones and twos as survivors were located and taken in, the newcomers fell into the established channels, but that couldn't last. Foresight's mission was too important to the United States and the world for the managers to look after such things as construction, road repair, and education. Jacksonville had empowered the folks at Foresight to elect a new governor for the state of Tennessee. Everyone who wanted to run had put their names on a clipboard in the main hallway.

"I'm voting for Melanie," Tee said. "She's the most organized person I know."

"I think I will, too," Billy said. Ms. Melanie Trimble, the general manager of Foresight, had kept everyone from panicking, then killing each other, for the whole duration of the epidemic. "But who will run the lab if she wins?"

"What about your mom?" Tee asked. "She told me she was up for a promotion before—"

The unmistakable sound of a rifle report cracked somewhere far off in the darkness. They both jumped.

"I hope that wasn't an infected trying to break into some-one's house," Billy said. Everybody, including the two of them, was armed with tranq guns in case they ran across an infected, but they carried weapons with stopping power, too. Tee's dark eyes had widened, and she froze in place. He knew what she was afraid of. He and some of the scavengers had pulled her out of the place she had been hiding for weeks all alone, staving off infected attacks and near starvation. This was one of the first times the two of them had been out of the compound without a bunch of others to back them up.

He took her hand. "Come on, it's okay!"

She shook her head. He put his arm around her and led her toward the passenger seat.

"Let's go down, or there will be nothing left from dinner."

Ms. Sharon Tompkinson, the wife of the founder of Foresight, caught them as they drove into the parking lot. For all her long years of marriage to Mr. Jud and six children, she still looked like thirty was a ways ahead of her, still slim, her tan skin smooth and black eyes bright and unlined. She and Lani Sanders were trying to herd the five betas toward the outbuilding that served as their dormitory.

"You're just in time! I need a couple of extra hands," she said. "Olivia, stop chewing on that. It's not good for you." Olivia, a slack-jawed, gaunt female who could have been any age between twenty and sixty, gaped at her as Ms. Sharon stuck a finger into the woman's mouth and dislodged a wad of greenery. Sharon threw it on the ground and wiped her hand on the side of her jeans. "Just when I thought we were making progress with her."

"Good girl, Elsie," Lani said, in a perky voice, the kind usually

reserved for training puppies. The slim young woman, a former
preschool teacher, smoothed back her chestnut curls, and fixed a
beaming smile of approval on her protégé. Elsie held out a handful of bent stems. "See? She's picking weeds and not seedlings.
She'll be a real help to me if we can keep this up."

More than one experiment was going on in the facility. Seeds
from dozens of farms and packets gleaned from stores all over
Nashville as well as minor farm equipment had been put to
use in fields and yards in the new neighborhood downhill from
Foresight. Anyone who had room to plant had tilled up the soil
and were growing "victory gardens" just like in World War II.
Billy had interviewed Lani about the greenhouse at the rear of
the main laboratory building, where anyone with time and even
a faintly green thumb was forcing seedlings. Tomatoes, greens,
beans of every kind, potatoes, corn, and numerous herbs had
been making the canned and dried food a lot more interesting
in the last few months.

The second was causing a lot more controversy, although that
was wearing off as time went by. Most of the infecteds in the
area had died of the disease or exposure, or killed each other, or
starved to death, or been shot when they tried to attack normal
people. Fresh infections were fewer, though they still happened
once in a while, and everyone at Foresight had been double,
triple, and quintuple vaccinated. Of the infecteds remaining
alive, a few were betas, who had a modicum of intelligence left,
but only a modicum. Ms. Sharon had championed a program to
rehabilitate what betas they could that the females—Billy couldn't
bring himself to call them women any longer—would have been
classified as Trainable Mentally Handicapped.

So far, no one had located any betas with higher brain function remaining, such as Educable Mentally Handicapped. The
disease had robbed the victims of all but the basest levels of
intelligence. It also rendered their body temperature, or maybe
their perception of it, too high for them to tolerate clothing.
Despite the chilly spring weather, the five betas stood there as
naked as the day they were born. At first, Billy had done the same
as all the other men and a few of the women, sneaking furtive
and lustful peeks at them. Naked women! On show all the time!
Just watching those bare boobies swaying had set his hormones
on fire. But after a time, he realized there was nothing special

about the betas being unclothed. They weren't sexy or alluring, just sad. He felt he was violating them by staring.

None of the betas could even be relied on to wear safety equipment, so hauling garbage or assisting with the growing construction outside the electrified fence were out of the question. They could barely be relied on to stand still for a shower and howled like wounded dogs when their teeth and hair were brushed. Still, everyone needed to eat, and gardening was one place where the betas could do the least harm. Ms. Sharon thought it was important to help them learn to pull a little of their own weight. Their jerky way of moving and their vacant expressions set Billy on edge. They *looked* wrong, no longer quite human anymore.

One of his ham radio friends had used a term that made sense to him: *the uncanny valley*. It was why no matter how much they might be made to look like people, animated characters or robots were never something he felt comfortable with. Betas, for all that they used to be normal, had crossed to the other side forever. He had to keep reminding himself they were real people, but like his Great-Aunt Lizzy, had lost their senses through no fault of their own. He had never been trapped by them, unlike Tee, who did her best to cope with the constant presence of the betas inside the compound. She wasn't alone in thinking that one day the former infected would flip out and start attacking others.

So, it was hard to find sponsors to work with the betas. Billy completely understood the reluctance. He didn't trust them, even if he was beginning to think of them as unfortunate victims, a little unluckier than the uninfected survivors. He knew Foresight approached the beta question differently than most places. In some places, the normals maintained a shoot-on-sight policy. Others just ignored them unless they tried to attack or steal food. Mr. Jud's feeling was that they were still human beings, and he would give an honest try to rehabilitate them if he could. He didn't discount the uncanny valley but hoped everyone would do their best to work with it.

Elsie grunted, and her nearly toothless mouth writhed as it tried to create a smile at Lani's praise. Tee shuddered. Billy put his arm around her.

"I'm sorry, Ms. Sharon. We've been working uphill all afternoon."

Sharon nodded. "I understand, honey. How's the build coming?"

Tee forced herself to perk up at the question. "It's going to be awesome," she said. "We've laid out two studios and got all the soundproofing up. We ran wires to the control room. The LEDs are in place, so we've got emergency lights. All we need is power, and we can go on the air from there."

"That's fantastic," Lani said, her eyes dancing. "I hope you'll let us all take a snoop through there."

"Of course, ma'am!"

"You're gonna have a story for your show later," Ms. Sharon said. "Angel Velasquez found a pocket of survivors down near Rock City. Seven people!"

"Wow!" Billy said. He reached for the pad of paper and pencil always in his jeans pocket. "Where are they? Can I talk with them?"

"They're getting examined by Doc Butterman. I'm sure they'll be around later."

One of the betas began to moan and claw at her rounded belly. Billy had thought a few months back that Gardenia was just bloated from hunger and parasites, but the women in the compound just shook their heads at him as if he was as simpleminded as the betas.

"Gardenia, are you all right?" Ms. Sharon asked. The female lifted muddy eyes full of pain just as a gush of liquid splashed from between her legs. Everyone jumped back except Ms. Sharon. She'd had six children of her own. "Bless her soul, she's in labor! Help me get her to the infirmary!"

People came running out of the big double glass doors. One of the National Guards looped back inside and came out with a wheelchair. They bundled Gardenia into it and pushed her into the building. The beta fought to get out of the chair. The others talked soothingly but held onto her tightly. Billy gawked after them until Ms. Lani's voice broke the spell.

"Billy, Tee, I need your help right this minute," she said, firmly. "We still got to get these ladies into their rooms right away. Just follow my lead." She took Olivia by the upper arm and steered her toward the dormitory.

"All right," Billy said, though he wasn't happy about it. Though the betas were clean, except for garden soil on their knees and hands, he felt uneasy touching them. He took the arms of two of them and urged them to follow. They stumbled along, as if their bodies and limbs didn't belong to them. Tee bravely escorted Edith, the most docile of the betas.

"Hey, Ms. Lani, have you met the newcomers yet? What are they like?"

The teacher laughed. "Well, Angel Velasquez got word from one of the scouts that they saw fresh garbage on a roadside down in Rock City, and went in to investigate. They've been hiding out in the caves all this time. Can you believe it? It took them several days to get up here. Dieter had to round up enough horses so they didn't have to make the trek on foot." The few vehicles that now ran on alternate fuels or battery packs had become supplemented by feral horses that people caught and re-civilized.

Billy felt excitement rise in his chest. "I've got to talk with them," he said. "Everyone will want to know their story." Interviewing them over the ham radio channel would give all the survivors around the world a lift and give them more hope.

Ms. Lani shook her head. "You better meet them before you decide to let them loose on the rest of humanity."

"You mean they're still in shock?" Tee asked, sympathetically. Like herself, any of the normal humans the scavenging teams brought back to Foresight needed time to adjust. It took them a while to realize they were safe. The mental stress often brought on symptoms like post-traumatic stress disorder, which the few counselors among them did their best to treat.

"I mean they're pains in the you-know-what," Ms. Lani said, her lips thinning with disapproval. She unlocked the door and swung it wide. The narrow room beyond had been a small storage closet, one of several on this floor, and had been cleared and furnished with a mattress with an old blanket, and a heavy metal tub for a toilet. The betas didn't always use those, and the caretakers had to hose out the dormitories every few days. "Come on, Olivia, right in here. We'll bring you supper in a little while."

Olivia grunted. She crouched down on the mattress, ignoring the blanket. Tee guided Elsie to the next small dormitory.

"I don't really like that their rooms are dark all the time," she said.

Miss Lani sighed. "Y'all know we tried leaving lamps in there, but they smashed them up. Same goes for any furniture we let them have. It actually turns out they are calmer in the dark. No matter what you think of them, honey, they're less trouble than our new neighbors are going to be."

∽ ⊖ ∾

Billy didn't have long to wait before encountering the survivors from Rock City. Seven of them, four men and three women, sat at a table by themselves in the cafeteria, as far away from any other diners as they could go. For all that they had been hiding out for almost two years and looked as old as his grandparents, they looked reasonably well-fed and healthy. As he and Tee picked up trays and helped themselves to food, he heard them whispering to one another.

"Come on," he said. "Let's introduce ourselves. Maybe if they're willing to talk about how they got by, we can put them on the show tonight."

Tee glanced at the clock. Although she and Billy checked in on the ham frequency a couple of times during the day, 8:00 P.M. was the usual main broadcast, carried over the airwaves as well as the public address system.

"Mind if we sit down with you?" Billy asked, holding his tray forward. "My name's Billy Marx. This is Tee Figueroa."

Six of the newcomers glanced toward the seventh. He sat at the end of the table. He flattened his hands on the surface and spread out his long fingers as though drawing strength from it.

"You . . . may," the man intoned. Billy estimated that he wasn't much taller than Tee, and at least a decade younger than the rest of the newcomers, probably fifty-something. He had a longish fringe of reddish hair surrounding a domed skull, and prominent eyebrow ridges, under which a pair of surprisingly sharp green eyes lurked. Billy, inclined to be charitable, thought his hesitant way of talking was because he and his group had been holed up so long with only themselves that they were uncomfortable interacting with strangers. They had all seen it before with others that had been rescued. Separation and fear had tamped down civilized responses and, once safe, they had to grow into being people again. He was surprised at the behavior of this contingent because they didn't jump on the food on their trays, though Billy could tell they wanted to. He held back a moment himself, wondering if the leader wanted to say grace.

Instead, their attention turned back to their leader. He waited a moment until all their eyes were on him, then he nodded. Immediately, they started stuffing food into their mouths, fork in one hand, bread in the other. The leader ate at his leisure, keeping an eye on them. Billy understood right away why Ms. Lani felt uneasy about him. He acted like a really stern teacher, or maybe a drill sergeant. No, it went deeper than that. He liked to control things, and they were too shell-shocked to rebel against him.

Maybe it was because of the way they had had to live over the last couple of years. He felt sorry for them. Billy could tell by the look on Tee's face that she understood, too. Well, living in the Foresight compound for a while was going to show them they could take their own initiative.

"How'd you end up in Rock City?" Billy asked. "Were you tourists? Are you from the Chattanooga area?"

"Is that... any of ... *your* business?" the leader asked, his eyes flashing with unexpected hostility.

"Not really," Tee said, her face blank. She stood up and took her tray. "Let's go over there, Billy. We've got a show in twenty minutes."

Billy scrambled up to follow her.

"Who does he think he is?" Tee hissed as they sat down at a table clear across the lunchroom from the newcomers.

"Well, he might feel kind of out of kilter," Billy said. "We've all been together since the beginning. They've had to make their way in a lot harder place."

Tee shook her head. "There's more going on than that."

"I think you're right, but we have to give them the benefit of the doubt."

"My abuela had a saying, Billy. No good deed goes unpunished."

"So, the creature gave birth?" Dr. Park asked from her lab in Antarctica.

"She's still a woman," Tee said, frowning over the big carbon-button microphone. Her indignant voice echoed faintly from the speakers in the hallway behind the storeroom that had become the "show's" studio. Since the ham broadcast was such an important morale booster, not only was it played over the public address system and worldwide by ham radio and shortwave, but the racks of equipment and supplies had been moved out to make way for about thirty chairs. Ten or so were occupied by listeners at any time.

"Yes. It's a boy, and he's perfectly normal. The doctors have been over him and tested him for infection." Tee sighed and exchanged glances with Billy. "One of the mothers is caring for him along with her toddler. I think she'll adopt him. Gardenia isn't showing any interest in him at all. As soon as she felt better, she kept trying to get off the gurney. She's back to picking weeds as though it never happened. I'm not sure she even gets that she *had* a baby."

"Who's the father?" asked Genevieve. She was the girlfriend of Francois, a ham operator in Ocho Rios, Jamaica, and a family court attorney. "Is he willing to help raise up the bebe?"

Billy cleared his throat. "No one is stepping up," he said.

"No one is willing to admit that they took advantage of a woman who cannot think for herself!" Genevieve said, her rich, rolling voice filled with frustration. "It happens here, too. We do not do as you do, taking them in and trying to give them jobs. They live like animals. Some of us put food out on tables in places where they will find it. We try to track the ones who are with child. Sometimes we find the infants..." Her voice trailed off. Billy knew what that meant.

"They are less than animals," Dr. Park said. "They have no normal instincts remaining."

"They are unfortunate victims," argued Father Davies, the vicar in Geraint's new castle. He raised his plummy voice as though he were in the pulpit. "God would want you to accept them as brothers and sisters."

"They're only sisters," Genevieve snapped. "It's your brothers who see them as easy conquests!" Other voices joined in, raising an angry hubbub.

"A lotta men haven't seen a woman in a while," said Kent, call sign Xray Alpha Five Tango Tango Tango, from Idaho.

"And that makes it all right to rape helpless women?" Genevieve demanded.

"Well, ma'am, it's kind of *understandable*..."

Beside Billy, Tee sat up straight. He could tell she was about to dive into the growing argument.

"We've got some new residents," Billy said, cutting her off before she could speak. "They were holed up in a cave near Chattanooga all this time. Seven people, all uninfected." The look on Tee's face said the debate wasn't over. He agreed, but he wanted it to unfold during the late-night conversation, when most people only wanted happy information. "I hear from Ms. Melanie that they're getting a couple of rooms near the showers. It's been a long time since they got to enjoy hot water."

"That's good news-eh," Geraint exclaimed, his soft tones a calming influence. "I will bet they were glad to see you!"

"I dunno," Billy said. "I think they kind of resent us."

He glanced up then and saw the leader of the newcomers standing in the doorway. The man's intense eyes bored into him. He felt his heart sink. He shouldn't have said anything. Tee looked smug, as though she felt the man had it coming.

"With all of the blessings that your group has had during these trying times, someone who has had none could not help but feel envy in his heart," the vicar said, but Billy hardly heard him. He felt ashamed of himself.

The leader stood in the Foresight Cafeteria, refusing to sit down until all of his people were alone at one table right in the center of the room. He'd openly chased off Miss Nora and Mr. Lou, something that wouldn't have been polite under almost any circumstances, but the Foresight people were giving them a little time to get acclimated to their new surroundings. He called himself Mr. Seraphim. It was highly doubtful that was actually his name, but everyone let that go for the time being, too. They certainly weren't making too many friends. Seraphim was the only one who talked to anybody else, even accompanying the women into private medical examinations. And he only spoke to others outside his little group to make demands.

Billy and Tee sat with their friend Orin Feldman near the serving line. Orin and Billy were responsible for wiring the houses downhill as they were renovated enough to become occupied. They marked off each completed building on an unofficial plaque mounted near the entrance to the laboratory compound. The waiting list, though it was kept on a clipboard in the administration office, was also set in stone, but in a different way. Expanding outward was taking time, and there was no way around that. Mr. Jud, usually the calmest of people, had been heard shouting when Seraphim tried to get his request for housing moved up on the roster.

"I bet they're gonna want a place big enough for all of them," Orin said in a low voice, wiping his large nose with a paper napkin. "And some farmland. Did you talk with Angel? They had taken over the whole concessions area in Rock City, except they were sleeping in the Fairyland Caverns with two cows and a *bull.* They must have been in the Grandview for a long time, too. It was a disaster area! Garbage and dung piled up everywhere!"

"They probably had to move in case the infected came looking for them," Billy said. He did his best to see the others' point of view. "The Fairyland Caverns are far enough in that it wouldn't be worth the trouble."

"It'd be cold and damp a lot," Orin said. "All caves are like sixty degrees or so year round, which is great in the winter." He sniffed again. "I'd probably get pneumonia going in and out in the summer. My granddad took us there when I was about six. Did you hear? They threw a whole fit when the beta came into the infirmary to have her baby."

"Not much of a surprise," Billy said. "Lots of people feel that way."

"I mean, a massive throwing-things shit fit! That guy"—Orin tilted his head toward the leader—"said they weren't fit to live, and if the doctors didn't kill the 'spawn of Satan,' he would. They had to lock the door between the wards. They started pounding on the walls."

"That's wrong," Tee said. "The betas are harmless!"

"They're not," Billy said. "Mr. Ellis pinched one of them on the butt, and she went for him like a vampire."

"That was hilarious!" Orin said, his eyes dreamy with the memory. "I mean, they had to bandage his cheek after, and he had to get vaccinated all over again, but it was worth it." He looked at Tee, who wore an expression of outrage. "I mean, she had to defend herself. I get that."

"Did they bring the cattle up here?" Tee asked, burying the hatchet gracefully. "I miss fresh milk."

"They will. It's gonna take a few days because they'll have to recharge the truck a couple of times each way." Orin grinned. "This gives a whole new meaning to 'cattle drive.'"

"I am stealing that joke, Orin." Billy looked at the clock on the wall. "It's almost noon. We're airing an hour each for the candidates for governor every day until the election. You want to come and listen?"

"Hell, no! I'd rather shock myself silly on a live wire. I'll just vote in two weeks. I know everybody on the clipboard already. You think there's even a question as to how it'll go?"

"I...I can't say," Billy said, squirming a little. Tee knew what he thought, but he wasn't talking about it to anyone else. "As the press, I'm supposed to stay neutral."

"That's great as a theory," Orin said, waving a hand. "What'd Mr. Phillips say in History class? 'No plan survives contact with the enemy'?"

"So, Mr. Myron, what will you do if you are elected?" Billy asked, as the second hand on the big clock on the wall swept up to noon. Out of habit, he started to push the microphone toward his guest, then pulled it back. They had microphones and other equipment galore. He could host a whole roomful of people with all the gear they had.

Myron Levy, an architect who had also been a public relations agent in the time before the virus, adjusted the Sennheiser headphones over his ears. He was a short man, about Tee's height, with a round head, a round body, a shock of dark brown hair going gray, and big, round, brown eyes. He looked as though he had been constructed to define the word "jolly." He'd been a big help on the home-raisings that they had done already, especially showing talent for painting and caulking.

"Well, Billy, I can put it into just one word: infrastructure," he said, with an emphatic gesture that no one in his greater audience could see. The leading candidate, Ms. Melanie Trimble, in the front row, grinned. She appreciated the theater. "That's the main thing everyone wants right now. Homes. Running water. Electricity. Insulation. I don't know about you, but I've been sharing a dorm with three of the loudest schnorrers—I mean, snorers—in the county!" That got a laugh, even from Billy, who wasn't sure what "schnorrer" meant, but it sounded funny. "I gotta have my own place. Even a one-room shack with an outhouse behind would be better than listening to a baritone opera every night. But I'm not the priority. People with children should get homes first. What we need is to analyze the places that can be rehabbed, that can be set up for utilities. The government has given the OK to take what we need. And we gotta be practical. Sure, there are mansions that are empty, apartment buildings with lots and lots of room, but they're in bad shape, and we can't run power to them, maybe not for ages. All we've got going right now is the TVA plant down below, and that's limited. It sounds great to live in a big fancy house, sure. I'd like that myself. Maybe one day.

"Right now, let's get this state going forward again. We'll help each other, work together, like people did in the pioneer days. *Infrastructure.* A man who was a lot better with words than me, Sir Winston Churchill, said, 'We shape our buildings, and thereafter they shape us.' Let's build good, and make it good for the people who come after us. All of you guys—and ladies," he added, with a nod to Tee, "have been doing a great job, but the organization is haphazard. We've done our best during the crisis, but that's winding down. I've got an outline of all the departments that we'll need over the coming years, and I want to put a plan in place for the governors who'll come after me. I've got copies of documents from the state house library. I'll be following in a long line of wise people, but I know I'm up for the job."

A row of chairs near the rear of the room was occupied by Seraphim and his people. During each of the candidates' talks, they made disparaging noises. Mr. Myron didn't give a damn about them. He just kept talking. Seraphim cleared his throat noisily, drowning out the speaker. The level on Billy's VU meter pinned in the red zone.

Billy stopped the chess clock on the table and looked out to his audience. "I'm sorry, folks. The candidates are allowed to talk for a whole twenty minutes. You can't interrupt him now. He'll take questions when he's done."

"I don't agree with what he said," Seraphim said. He crossed his arms high on his chest and looked at Billy with his eyebrows lowered. Tee nudged Billy with an elbow. *Ignore him*, her eyes said. Billy nodded.

"Well, sir, he has a right to his say. I'm running this interview. Please don't talk until we're done."

Seraphim frowned, but many of the other listeners turned to glare at him. The rest of the leader's flock looked shocked.

Billy went back to his list of questions. Mr. Myron was a good talker, that was for sure, and he was prepared. The short man waved his hands around a lot, building a new government in the air, sketching his *infrastructure* all over the place, but in a thoughtful way. He didn't act like the last two years hadn't happened, which a couple of the previous speakers had. That was refreshing. Another old saying, "the elephant in the room" couldn't really be ignored.

Mr. Myron was so dynamic that hands began to climb into the air before his speech had ended. Billy began to call on each of the questioners. A couple of them, like Jensen Pike, just wanted to start an argument.

"What are you gonna do about settling differences?" Mr. Pike demanded, stepping up to a microphone set on a stand in the aisle. "I gotta man who's trying to divert water off the property I claimed. Who's gonna stop him? I gotta couple of cows to care for."

"We'll have a court system," Mr. Myron said. "In accordance with the Constitution of the United States. We're under martial law right now, so if you have a dispute, take it up with Jacksonville or with the managers right here in Foresight, who are the interim government. We're gonna have to be a little informal for a while. Talk to Jud Tomkinson if you want a mediator."

"I want justice!"

"You'll have to find a way to work it out, my friend," Levy said with a shrug. "We're all in this together. If you want to be part of the solution, come help us."

Pike grumbled and subsided. A woman stood up next.

"I have grade-school kids. How are they going to get an education?"

"We're starting all over with that, ma'am," Mr. Myron said. "We've got more than a few educators here. We'll work with children at their level as best we can."

The woman nodded and retreated hastily. Seraphim hauled himself to his feet as though he carried tons of unseen weight.

"Mr. Levy, what makes you think that you can be a good leader? You've had it easy all this time, supported by this community. Some of us have held our lives together against monsters with only our wits to save our lives."

"True, I've been lucky," Mr. Myron said, eyeing the newcomer, but keeping his voice level. "I didn't start out up here, though. These good people pulled me out of an office building, where I was living on coffee and vending machine candy bars, maybe one a day after a while. You didn't know that? I'll tell you why I'd be a good leader. I listen to people. I find out about them, and ask them what they need, what they want their lives to look like later on. You should try it."

"What about individual property rights?"

Myron shrugged. "We're the biggest population center in Tennessee right now. You wanna take over a whole county for yourselves? Go right ahead. But if you want to stay here, you have to think of more people than just you."

Seraphim lowered his brows, an expression that threw terror into his followers. Murmurs ran through the audience, and from the speakers beside Billy, most of them approving.

Billy noticed with relief that the clock had moved to the hour mark.

"That's about it, folks," he said. "Thanks for listening. This was Mr. Myron Levy, candidate for governor of Tennessee and surrounding territories. The election is in fourteen days, so come back every day to hear more candidates. Thanks!"

Seraphim led his newcomers out of the room, pushing past everyone.

"Thanks, kids, that was great!" The short man shook hands with both of them and rose. He removed the headphones and set them on the desk. Tee shut off the transmitter. She sighed. Billy sighed.

Ms. Melanie rose from her chair and made her way over to them. Billy stood up at once. She took both of them by the hand. "I know it's hard to deal with someone so prickly. Find sympathy in your heart. They've lost everything that made them the people they were before."

Billy dropped his gaze to the baggy knees of his jeans. Before the plague, he had been kind of pear-shaped, with most of his weight in his belly and rear end, but that all was whittled down by scanty meals and a lot of hard work, so his clothes didn't fit that well.

"I'm trying, Miss Melanie. It's just not easy when they're so rude."

The plant manager wrapped him in a big hug, enveloping him in her comforting curves. "They've suffered, too." She set him back and shook her head. "Billy, you know the war cry of the South!"

"Uh, ma'am?" Billy felt heat rising in his cheeks. He couldn't think of anything except, "The South will rise again," but that had never been his family's creed. Nor could he believe that Ms. Melanie Trimble, an African-American whose own grandparents had been enslaved or impoverished sharecroppers would espouse a return to the time of the Confederacy! "Uh, no, ma'am, I guess I don't."

Her soft brown eyes turned mischievous. "Sure you do. It's 'Bless their hearts.'"

Tee started laughing. "That's what Lou Cook used to say when one of his techs did something really stupid." The late Mr. Cook was the music producer in whose house Billy and the scavenging committee they had found Tee hiding out against the infecteds.

"Exactly," Miss Melanie said. She raised her hands, palms to the sky. "And 'Lord, forgive them, for they know not what they do.' So, bless them, and forgive them for being people who need your help. They're no better and no worse than the betas. I believe in you. Do you need me here earlier tomorrow than noon for my talk? I hope I can come across as well as Mr. Myron. He ought to be a preacher!"

"A few minutes would be enough, ma'am," Billy said.

"I'll be here." She gave them one more luminous smile and departed. Billy felt better.

"Let's go check Myron off the list," Tee said. "After hearing him, I think he'll be a great *lieutenant* governor."

"We gotta stay neutral," Billy reminded her. He shut down the rest of the equipment and turned off the lights before he locked the door.

He felt bad having to secure things, but a lot of people had joined the group over the intervening months. Stuff had begun to go missing, a thing that almost never happened in the early days. Having a common enemy meant that every bite of food, every bullet, every scrap of clothing was a weapon against being wiped out. Nobody stole then. All resources went to the survival of everyone. Money was useless. Sweat equity and trade goods were all the currency that meant anything.

Once the situation began to ease up, people's better angels seemed to desert them. Mr. Jud had quietly dealt with the first couple of cases of hoarding. Vigilance had increased even more as the compound collected stray farm animals to supplement the flocks of chickens and herd of goats that already lived there. Instead of waiting for eggs, some hungry people decided they wanted chicken dinners instead. That had to be nipped in the bud hard. The perpetrators, never named, had to undergo counseling, under threat of being tossed out of the compound. Billy didn't want to have to go scavenging for more equipment to replace what they had amassed, both there and up the hill in the new studio.

The clipboard hung where it had been for the last few weeks, on the bulletin board just outside the management office. Tee brandished a pen and clicked its top. Two names had been crossed off the list of candidates. She drew a line through Myron Levy's name. "Only five to go—no, six! Oh, my God, no!"

She handed him the clipboard and pointed.

"Benedict Seraphim?" Billy said in disbelief, looking at the last name on the list. "Hey, he'll never get elected. No one likes him."

"Never say never," Tee reminded him. "Would you have believed three years ago that humanity would nearly be wiped out by a plague?"

Billy had to admit she was right.

"All right, let's see it!" Ms. Lani said, clapping her hands together. A large group stood gathered outside the chain link fence of the new broadcast facility in the chilly autumn air. "This is the best thing to happen to us in ages!"

"Aw, come on, Ms. Lani!" Billy said, feeling shy all over again. But he had to admit he was proud. With the help of dozens of others, the studio had come together almost completely over the course of a weekend. Even the betas had been brought up to help clear weeds around the two buildings. "We've constructed dozens of houses in the last few months."

"This is special," Ms. Nora said. The half-Choctaw woman didn't talk much, so people listened when she did. "This is the first new community facility since the plague started. It's like we're coming back from a long way down."

Billy exchanged a glance with Tee. Everyone had suffered losses, but Ms. Nora's was especially brutal. She had watched the murder of her first husband and son on her own security camera. He handed her the big shears.

"Will you do the honor of cutting the ribbon, then?" he asked, gesturing at the swathe of crime-scene tape holding the gate shut. She looked surprised. Her husband, Mr. Lou Hammond, smiled at her.

"All right, but don't expect anything neat!" She opened the scissors' jaws and gnawed at the tape a few times. It fluttered away in strips, and everyone cheered. Ms. Nora made a face and handed the shears back.

The visitors oohed and aahed as Billy and Tee showed them

all the features of the small studio building. Most of the lights were clusters of LEDs, with one big battery-packed security light over the heavy exit door.

In the first big room, recording equipment stood out from against the walls with cables coiled up on top of each unit.

"Only the ham radio and the shortwave will go operational tomorrow," Tee explained. "All the rest of the broadcast equipment is waiting for more power, and for the government to give us a frequency to tune to. As soon as we can source more solar panels, we'll be able to put more programming on line. Meera will be offering a daily world music show starting next month." She gestured to a slim woman who worked as a microscopist for Foresight. "We're taking proposals on other shows, so if you have ideas, write them up for us."

"I . . . wish to offer . . . my services," Mr. Seraphim said. His beautiful tones carried and echoed off the painted cinderblock walls. "My program was syndicated nationwide. On Sundays."

"Televangelist," Tee whispered to him. "You can tell by his voice."

"Uh, let me think about it," Billy said. Maybe including him would help get the newcomers to calm down and become part of the community, but he was afraid that Seraphim might preach death and destruction to be rained down on the betas. It was already hard enough to incorporate them into the community. Whatever he thought of them, they were still human beings, and if truth be told, he liked them a lot better than the newcomers. "If you'll just make a note for us on your format, and what you need, we'll discuss it."

Seraphim looked smug, as though it was a done deal. He interrupted Billy most of the way through the tour.

"I will . . . require this room as . . . my personal office," he said, even though Tee had just pointed out the cozy room with the wide window was *her* office. "I will record all public service announcements from here," he said about the small studio to the right of the control room. "Refreshments for me and my flock should be served here, exclusively," was his comment on the tiny kitchenette with one of the few low-power microwave ovens that Billy had been able to source. By now, the rest of the folk touring the facility had clearly had enough of Seraphim's pronouncements.

"Why didn't Angel leave them down in Chattanooga?" Dieter

Vance muttered. Tee shot Billy a sharp glance. He resolved then and there that Seraphim should never have a show on their network.

They gathered again in the middle of the big studio, and Tee lit up the house lights. They were powered by the big diesel generator to the rear of the building. That fuel resource wasn't infinite, but it ought to last them years of judicious use. Everyone let out a sigh of pleasure.

"This looks amazing, Billy and Tee," Ms. Melanie said, beaming at them. "How you managed to pull together such a professional-looking facility is just a wonder!"

"It took us months of searching," Tee said, grinning. "I think we checked out every radio station and television station in all of Nashville and brought back what we thought we would need for the next few years."

"Oh, yeah," Micky Rollins said, with a broad smile on his face. "We know Billy and his endless IOUs."

"IOUs?" Seraphim asked, raising a shaggy eyebrow.

"Oh, yeah," Micky said, ignoring Billy's reddening cheeks. "Every time we took something from a house, he left a note promising to pay the owner. Not that anyone is coming back. Most of it came from Lou Cook's studio, where we found Tee holed up."

"Right," Angel Velasquez said. "It's a little goofy. But he's honorable." She tousled Billy's flyaway brown hair into even more of a mess than it usually would. Billy swatted her hand away.

"So, that's everything in here," he said, uncomfortably. "Our house isn't really set up yet, but we'll have a housewarming when it is."

"When are you two getting married?" Ms. Nora asked, and Billy felt his cheeks burn again.

"Not until Cindy can be in on the ceremony," Tee said, firmly. "She's part of our family, too."

That earned shocked looks from Seraphim and his flock, but this time, Billy refused to let the arrogant bastard get under his skin.

One last touch remained. Billy and Tee brought out a rolling cart that had a white cloth draped over it. In a plastic pail were three bottles of champagne that they had found under a pile of fallen shelves in an abandoned store, a pitcher of grape Kool-Aid for the kids, and a stack of plastic wine cups. Very carefully, he eased the cork out of the first bottle to cheers from the assembled guests. He poured out small servings, with the first one going to his mother. She beamed and lifted it high.

"To better days!"

"To better days!" everyone echoed, and drank.

Billy felt triumphant, as he led everyone out of the studio and locked the door. There were too many guests to ride in what few vehicles they had, so he joined the flock going down the hill toward the compound. Tee got caught up in the crowd, answering questions.

"Young . . . man." The voice caught him by surprise. Billy glanced to his left. Seraphim and his coterie seemed to loom up out of the darkness.

"Yes, sir?"

"I didn't want to . . . embarrass you in front of . . . the others," the shorter man said, his voice carrying a hint of menace. "Those recorders and amplifiers . . . and much else . . . that you took . . . from Lou Cook's studio . . . are *mine*. I . . . paid for them."

Billy peered at him. "Yours? How's that possible?"

"He . . . did some recordings for me. The equipment was . . . payment for episodes . . . never produced. I will . . . take them . . . tomorrow."

Billy felt his heart sink. "But we need them! They're the best ones we found."

Shaking his head, Seraphim frowned. "Then . . . you must pay me back. You left . . . an IOU for them?"

"I always do," Billy said.

"Then . . . I believe you owe me . . . forty-six thousand dollars. That is . . . less than I paid . . . but I will allow for depreciation."

The nightmare Billy always feared had come to pass. "Look, sir, I haven't got the money now. I will pay you back, I swear it. We're about to go on the air! Can I arrange a plan with you to pay overtime?"

"A . . . plan?" Seraphim appeared to consider it. The rest of their neighbors had moved far down the slope, their voices receding in the darkness. Billy had never felt so alone. The smaller man moved closer. "What can you offer . . . of that value?"

"I . . . I don't know," Billy said, helpless in his despair. "I don't have much. What do you want?"

He could almost hear the other's smile in the dark. "Let's begin...with my show."

"Why?" Tee demanded, when they returned to their small room in the compound. "He's awful!"

"Well, we want variety," Billy said, hating himself for even saying such a thing. "We've got a lot of God-fearing people who haven't had a lot of solace for their souls over the last few years."

"And you think he'll make them feel better?" Tee demanded. She stopped when she saw the misery on his face. "This isn't like you. What happened?"

Billy plumped down on the double bed they shared and clenched his hands between his knees. "I owe him."

"You owe him? For what?"

"For a bunch of the equipment we scavenged. Mostly the stuff we took out of your old boss's place. He said he gave it to Mr. Cook to do some work for him. Work that wasn't finished when the plague hit. So it wasn't paid for. It belongs to Mr. Seraphim."

Tee frowned and sat down next to him. "That's bullshit. I don't remember him ever coming to the studio, let alone having recording gear delivered."

"Are you sure? It could have been before you started working for him. Do you think we can find the tapes Mr. Cook made of him?"

Tee grimaced. "I doubt it. I used most of Lou's tapes in the net I knitted. They're ruined. I'm sorry."

Billy put his arm around her shoulders. "Never apologize. You made that net to save your life. Hardly anything from before is worth the same as it was then. Mr. Cook is gone, so he won't care."

"And he can't tell us the truth," Tee said. She sighed. "I'm sure that man is lying, but how do we prove it?"

"Right," Billy said, feeling even more miserable.

"So, we'll put him on the air. What will it matter? Who's out there listening?"

Ms. Sheila Parker, a woman in her nineties whom the scavengers had found sheltering in the back of a grocery store a month into the plague, came to visit them after the first broadcast Seraphim made on a Sunday morning. Her wrinkled face was stretched tight in a smile. Her skinny shanks stuck out from the bottom of a pair of tight, white cotton capri pants. She fastened her bony hands onto Tee's arm.

"God bless you for bringing us such a guide in the wilderness!" she said. "That man is an inspiration! Only he has been brave enough to say what so many of us have been thinking." She reached up and patted Billy on the cheek. "You're a good boy."

Ms. Sheila's feelings weren't universal, to say the least. Ms. Melanie Trimble stopped Billy in the hallway that afternoon. She wore her Sunday best yellow dress, but her kindly face seemed wreathed with worry.

"Honey, can I talk with you a moment?" she asked.

"Sure, ma'am," Billy said, with a warm smile. He really liked Ms. Melanie. "Is this about your interview tomorrow?"

"No. No, it isn't. It's about *that man*." Billy didn't have to ask which one. "His campaign interview for governor held a lot of veiled threats, but this is open prejudice! I know he hates the infecteds, but they are our burden to bear. It doesn't help our constituents, who are already dealing with so many other concerns. Too many of them are listening to him. At least twenty I know of agree with him. I'm getting pushback on some of the social programs I'm trying to institute. Mr. Myron is dealing with the same kind of responses. I'm downright terrified that what little cooperation we have been fostering will disappear into the maelstrom of anger I'm seeing. I have prayed whether to get involved with this, but his kind of racist, ableist hatred is not something that I want spewing out of our facility!"

Billy felt his cheeks grow hot. "I'm sorry, ma'am. I talked with him a little after his show this morning. He said he would tone it down, but he really hates the betas. His flock's experiences down south sound a lot worse than we had up here. They didn't have our resources or our defenses."

"Oh, I understand that! But if he's preaching a message of God's love, I didn't hear a lot of that today."

"I know," Billy said. "I'll keep working on him."

But his efforts at diplomacy seemed to bounce off the preacher's solid brass exterior. No matter how many times he tried to bring it up, Seraphim managed to turn Billy's words around on him.

"So...you say that I should...offer acceptance...to these terrible animals? Have your...fellows not suffered...as we have?"

"Well, yes," Billy said, feeling he was losing the initiative. "But they aren't evil on purpose. I mean, there's hardly any of them left. These people deserve some sympathy, too. We're trying to give them a new life."

The watery hazel eyes fixed on him. "Do they...deserve it?"

Billy had just about had it with the man. He straightened himself up, knowing he didn't make a very impressive figure. "Yes, sir, they do. If I was one of them, I'd be grateful for a second chance. At the bottom of their souls, I'm sure they are. They're willing to work. There aren't too many people left in the world, so we need all the help we can get to start civilization all over!"

Seraphim glared at him. "Just remember...the debt is due."

Billy sagged a little bit inwardly but held himself upright. "Yes, sir, I know it."

"Then you won't interfere with my show. You won't edit a word out of it."

It wasn't until the man strode off down the hall with his entourage in tow that he realized Seraphim hadn't fallen into his usual ponderous way of talking. It was a hoax, like the man himself. But his IOU was real, and Billy knew he had to keep cooperating with the leader to make it good.

The next day, he left the compound after their daily show to help his mother and her new boyfriend move into their new home. The fall air had a snap in it, and he felt refreshed even though he ended up carrying dozens of heavy boxes back and forth. Despite his troubles with Mr. Seraphim, he felt optimistic about the coming election, only five days away. From the scuttlebutt going around the lunchroom and elsewhere that despite a small but vocal minority that agreed with Seraphim, it was a walkaway for Ms. Melanie.

But the mood back in the compound was dark. When he returned in the green Honda Fit, Tee was waiting inside the entrance with her arms folded and an expression that would have dissolved metal.

"What's the matter?" he asked, hoping it wasn't something he'd done.

"That man!" Tee all but snarled. "He threw me out of the studio while I was on with Cindy! His people took over the building and locked it! I can't even get back in!"

"That's not right," Billy said, walking back to the small car.

There ought to be enough power left in the batteries for the ride up the slope. "Get in."

Tee simmered in silence all the way up to the studio.

"Is Cindy all right?" Billy asked, glancing at her. She was mad as hell. He hoped none of it was at him. "Her transmissions have been pretty muddy for a long while. I'm getting worried about her and her dad."

"She's fine," Tee said, curtly. When they reached the gravel pad in front of the studio, she barely waited until the car had stopped before she bounced out and started pounding on the door. Billy followed her. A number of the betas were in the garden, pulling weeds under the supervision of Ms. Sharon. She came over as Billy began rattling the handle.

"I saw what he did," she said. "Isn't there another way in?"

"Yes, ma'am," Billy said, feeling in his jeans pocket for keys. "There's a small security door at the back."

"I tried it," Tee said. "He blocked that one, too!" Billy rattled the handle.

"Mr. Seraphim!" he shouted. "This wasn't part of the deal! Let me in!"

The ponderous voice echoed out from the public address speaker above the main door.

"This is my...headquarters now, boy. You have...proved yourself an...unworthy steward...and are banished! When I am...elected governor, I will nationalize...this station. In the meantime...leave this place!"

"Look, you have a nice place in the compound," Billy wheedled.

"No! Those...things...infiltrate every inch there. We will... not go back! When I...am elected, they will...be banned!" They heard squeals of overmodulation, which meant that he was pulling a live mic too close to the PA. "This is...Benedict Seraphim. Normals have...joined forces with...the zombies that threaten... all good people!" He launched into a rant that surpassed anything that he had said in his previous broadcasts. Billy cringed. Those words were being heard all over the world, and it was his fault!

"He's unhinged," Tee said. "He's going to take over our frequency. Ruin everything we worked for!"

"No, he isn't," Billy said, making his decision. In his mind, he saw Ms. Melanie's sad face. Debt or not, he had to fix this problem, right now. "He's exceeding the time limit on political broadcast. We can't let him do that. Did he take all the tools out of the house?"

Tee's eyes danced. "It hasn't been touched, as far as I could tell."

"Good." Billy marched into their partially finished home and dug through a pile of construction waste until he located the heavy metal toolbox. He hoisted it and marched toward the back of the studio. "Tee, get in the car and get it running."

"Right," Tee said. She retreated around the corner.

"What are you gonna do?" Ms. Sharon asked, shooing the betas away from the building. The naked females huddled together at the edge of the gravel. "And can I help?"

"Stay out of the way of the doors," Billy said. "I think it's gonna get loud in a minute."

Donning heavy gloves, he took out an insulated wrench and disconnected the power lines from the solar panels on the roof as well as the line that led to the main lines down to the TSA generator. Shouting erupted from the studio building as the interior lights blacked out and the emergency lights came on. He didn't have long before they'd undo the locks and come out after him. As quickly as he could, he took a wire cutter and snipped the connectors off the cables. He shouldered the toolbox and ran for it.

The rear door slammed open behind him, and Seraphim erupted out of it.

"Come back here, boy!" he bellowed.

Billy rounded the building and hopped into the open passenger door. Tee tweaked the electric vehicle and steered it down the bumpy slope. Seraphim and the least elderly of his flock followed, but the car soon outdistanced them.

"Aren't you afraid that he's going to attack Sharon and the betas?" Tee asked.

"Nope," Billy said, hauling in deep breaths. "She's got a shotgun in case of zombies. I mean, alphas." He sat back against the upholstery. *What have I done?* he asked himself. *It's all going to fall apart now.*

Tee glanced over at him, then fixed her eyes on the slope. "How much do you owe him?" she asked. "I mean, how much does he *say* you owe?"

"Forty-six thousand dollars," Billy said, misery coloring every syllable. "I've never had a thousand dollars in my life! He's going to go to the others and say I've been favoring him because of it. And I kind of have. I wrote those IOUs."

Tee shook her head. "He's lying. Tell him to stuff it!"

"I can't. I gave him my word." Billy fixed his eyes on the road, a knot of misery in his belly.

"We'll see about that."

As soon as they got back to the compound, they went looking for Mr. Jud. They found him in the cafeteria with Ms. Melanie, Mr. Myron, and the rest of the candidates for governor. It looked, from the number of coffee cups scattered around, that a bigger conference had been going on in their absence.

"We heard all that!" Mr. Jud said, his face like thunder. "This is a serious matter! The election is tomorrow! Seraphim's partisans have already been calling the voting a sham. He's convincing them that the governor will be elected under false pretenses. The more his voice gets out there, the worse things get. Our people don't know what to do. Jacksonville is wondering if they have to step in to run the balloting for us, which will delay getting things done."

"He can't broadcast anymore," Billy said. "The federal broadcast license is in my name. He will never get another chance."

"I hate to ask you, buddy, but why did you put him on the air in the first place?" Mr. Myron asked, his sharp brown eyes boring into him. Billy started to open his mouth, but Tee shook her head slightly.

"It was a mistake, sir," Billy admitted, ashamed.

"The power of the press has to be neutral," Ms. Melanie said. "This election has to be seen to be honest and aboveboard, run according to the constitution and the laws of this state, no matter what condition we've fallen into. We must rise! What everyone hears from now on has to be free from bias and contamination. We can't let people think they're going to fall into the hands of a raving lunatic, not when they've all been through so much."

"Now, now, Melanie," Mr. Jud said. "He'll get the votes he's going to get. If he wins, he got more votes than any of us did. But I don't think that's going to happen."

"I don't want him riling anyone up the way he has been on Sundays!"

"Don't you worry, ma'am," Billy said, thinking hard. "I'm pretty sure he is on his way down here now. I'm not going to let him anywhere near a microphone."

"How you gonna do that?"

"We'll lock ourselves in the storeroom," he said. "We'll use the old ham radio. You can put someone in with us to gather the votes from the outlying areas, but we're not letting anyone else in with us. The only voices going out will be ours. You can tell me who won when it's over, and we'll tell the truth to the state of Tennessee."

Mr. Jud smiled.

"That will do, son." He scanned the others' faces. "Everyone on board with that?"

"What do we do about Seraphim?" Ms. Melanie asked. "His fans are pretty focused on seeing him win."

"I've got an idea about that," Tee said, suddenly. Billy glanced at her in surprise. "You go and get supplies for us for the night," she told him. "Hurry up! We don't know how long we've got until he gets down here."

"All right," Billy said, puzzled. He gathered up packages of food and filtered water bottles on a tray and headed for the storeroom.

Tee joined him a little while later. The two of them went over the ham equipment. All the nice microphones and headsets were at the top of the hill—Billy suspected Seraphim might have trashed the place when the electricity had cut, but he couldn't help that—but the old stuff still worked pretty well. Within a half hour, a soft tapping came at the door. Billy grabbed for a piece of metal shelf support, but Tee waved him down.

"That'll be Lou Hammond," she said. "He's the election judge for the over-the-air votes."

"Hey, kids," the big man said, grinning at them. He had a trio of sleeping bags and a big canvas bag over one shoulder. He raised a growler of beer in the other hand. "I brought supplies."

He could hardly sleep that night. Billy felt like drinking the whole keg of beer once the pounding started about one in the morning. He sat up in his sleeping bag at the sound of the first blow.

"Let me in here, boy!" Seraphim shouted, his resonant voice seeming to fill the room even if he wasn't inside it. Fists, multiple fists, beat a tattoo on the painted metal door. "You won't steal my platform on the eve of my triumph!"

"Go away!" Tee shouted. "You had your shot. No one gets any more airtime until after the polls close. If you're that sure you're going to be elected, what's your problem?"

"Billy Marx, I'm going to tell everyone what you did," Seraphim said, his voice filled with menace. "They'll have to throw out the election results and start all over! Once I am running things, I'll see to it that you are exiled from here! They'll know that you favored me and gave me an edge."

Billy started to get to his feet. Tee grabbed his arm and dragged him down again.

"They already know," she shouted back. "I told them."

"You...you told them?" Billy asked, shocked.

Tee gave him a fond glance. "You're too innocent," she said. "Nobody thinks you did anything underhanded. Now, get some sleep. Tomorrow's a big day. Maybe the biggest of our lives!"

Billy stared at the metal door. Seraphim and his people were still pounding.

"Ignore him, son," Lou Hammond said. "He's not getting in." From his canvas bag, he withdrew his favorite shotgun and broke it to look in the chamber. He nodded. "I promise."

Within an hour, the pounding and shouting stopped. Billy fell into an uneasy sleep.

At six the next morning, he and Tee were at the console. He felt his unshaven chin, wishing he could clean up, but that didn't matter. Mr. Lou, armed with a clipboard and a headset, sat down across from them.

"Good morning, everyone!" Billy announced as soon as Tee signed that they were warmed up and on the air. "It's Election Day! The State of Tennessee will choose its first governor and lieutenant governor since the outbreak and everything went to pieces. This is a major step in bringing us all back together. We're proud to announce that the polls will be opening at 7:00 A.M. Anyone over the age of eighteen can cast a ballot. If you're hearing this, you're already at one of the ham radio locations where you can vote. If you're close to us here, you can come up and vote in person. We'll be glad to see you. Cast your vote for governor of Tennessee and the greater mid-south region! The candidates are Ms. Melanie Trimble, Mr. Jud Tompkinson, Mr. Benedict Seraphim..." He reeled off all seven names and fell back in his chair, smiling. Tee squeezed his forearm.

"...Um, can I vote?" a soft female voice asked. "It's my first election."

Mr. Lou leaned close to his microphone and clicked his pen. "Yes, ma'am! Give me your name, your address, and your choices for governor and lieutenant governor."

Billy and Tee listened with delight as more than a dozen people clamored to be next. Mr. Lou jotted down the votes on separate documents for each voter. Then he glanced up at them.

"You two, get out there and cast your votes."

Billy frowned. "Can't we register ours with you?"

"No, sir, you can't. I'm taking remote voters only. *You* are here on site, so you have to go into the cafeteria." Mr. Lou laughed his big hearty guffaw. He winked at Tee. "It'll be a show worth seeing. Now, go on and git!"

In the cafeteria, it looked as though all three or four hundred people who lived in the compound or the region around it were jammed inside. Even the betas huddled in one corner near the door with Ms. Sharon between them and the rest. It was their state, too.

The candidates sat behind a long table on a dais at one end of the room, looking dignified and nervous. Handmade posters with their names hung on the wall behind them. Everyone was dressed in their best. Ms. Melanie had on her yellow dress and a matching picture hat with a blue band. Mr. Myron had on his usual polo shirt and glad-handed everybody who got close. Somewhere, Mr. Seraphim had scared up a white suit and brushed his thinning red hair into a pompadour. He wore an expression of beatitude. Billy hated him with every fiber of his body. From the cold gaze in the televangelist's eyes, the feeling was mutual. He wondered if he could jump on Mr. Seraphim and knock him unconscious, and if anyone would stop him.

"The polls are open!" Ms. Nora announced, beckoning toward a box with a lock on it that sat on a table next to the candidates. "Y'all got your ballots and pencils?"

Little Ms. Sheila stood at Mr. Seraphim's table. He held one of her scrawny hands in both of his. Her free hand held a paper ballot.

"Yes, ma'am!" she croaked. She beamed at Seraphim, who smirked back. Billy felt sick.

The crowd started to move toward the balloting station.

"One minute!" Tee said, running in front of them and holding up both her hands. The mass of people halted, puzzled. "I've got some information for everyone!"

"What's up, little lady?" Roger Marshall, one of the best of the zombie hunters, inquired.

Tee cleared her throat. "You need to know that one of the candidates is guilty of a number of crimes. Bernard Seraphim—if that is his real name, which I doubt—has been blackmailing Billy Marx! I know, that wouldn't be a crime that would stop an election, but Seraphim has been using the debt to get more airtime and more publicity than any of the other candidates! That would be against election law anytime in the past, and it still ought to be today!"

Murmuring swept through the crowd. A bunch of Seraphim's supporters crowded around the candidates' table. Ms. Melanie looked alarmed.

"What's this debt?" Corporal Chaz Miller asked.

"You all know Billy and his IOUs," Tee continued. Most of the crowd nodded. "Seraphim claims that he owns some of the equipment Billy and I scrounged up around Nashville. But he doesn't! I can prove it. But Billy is too decent to tell the creep off to his face."

"Mr. Seraphim's a good man!" Ms. Sheila shrilled. "He tells us the truth!"

"No, he doesn't," Tee said.

"Now, listen, young lady . . ." Seraphim began.

"Let her talk!" Miller said, holding up a hand. "She can have her say and you can have yours after."

Tee appealed to the crowd. "I haven't lived here long, but I know Billy, and so do all of you. He's as honest as they come. He would pay any debt if he could. He believes he owed *this extortionist*," Tee punctuated her words with sharp jabs of her finger at the goggling candidate, "forty-six thousand dollars! So, here it is!"

At her word, Angel Velasquez and Dieter Vance came in with big baskets on their shoulders and big grins plastered on their faces.

"One thing you have to realize," Tee continued, "is how different things are now. What matters isn't money—in fact, no one has used legal tender for years! But Mr. Seraphim demands cash, so we're going to give it to him. Right?"

"Right!" Angel said. The tall National Guard sergeant unlimbered the big basket and shook it over the candidate's head. "Here you go!" Dollar bills, in every denomination from singles to hundreds, cascaded down over him. Seraphim let go of Ms. Sheila to protect his face.

"And here's the rest!" Dieter said, adding his burden to the cascade. "You better count it. It's forty-six thousand, plus we calculated interest going back to the beginning of the plague."

The room fell into shocked silence. Then, Billy heard the sound of ripping paper. He turned to see Ms. Sheila Parker tear her ballot across.

"Ms. Nora, I wonder if you will favor me with a new paper." Ms. Sheila wore an innocent expression. "I believe I have spoiled mine."

"Dear Ms. Sheila, reconsider!" Mr. Seraphim protested, while still trying to gather the money off the table. His flock stooped, picking up every fallen bill. "I have the . . . best interests of . . . *everyone* in mind!"

"Liar!" The little woman turned her nose up.

"You cheated one of the nicest guys in the world!" a man said, shaking his fist under Seraphim's nose.

"Now, now, folks, it isn't what you think!" Seraphim said, holding up his hands. He was showered by a cascade of torn paper. He stood up and retreated off the dais. His flock followed him.

The betas milled around near the door, staring open-eyed at the activity. Seraphim headed directly for them.

"Get out of my way, monsters!" he bellowed, and tried to shoulder them aside.

The betas might have been fairly placid when being cooed at by their volunteers, but their remaining brain cells rebelled at loud noises or violence. Before Seraphim could escape, the five females sprang at him, biting and scratching. He yelled and shoved, but they were too strong for him. Olivia bit him on the ear. Gardenia went into an especial froth of fury and leaped on him, battering him with both fists. It took a dozen or more strong helpers to pull the betas away and calm them down. By the time they were subdued and tucked back into their corner, Seraphim's white suit was covered in smudges and blood. He puffed himself up with what was left of his dignity and strode out of the cafeteria. Billy laughed out loud.

"Fold up your ballots and put them in the box!" Ms. Nora called, grinning. Billy found a paper and pencil thrust into his hand. He checked off his choices and tucked his ballot through the slot.

"I had hoped we had left people like Seraphim behind in the past," Mr. Jud said. Most of the voters had remained all day, waiting through the counting. To the surprise of few, Ms. Melanie was elected governor, and Mr. Jud was her lieutenant. They insisted on making Mr. Myron a department chair. Tee was congratulated over and over again for her clever handling of the intruders. No one knew where they and a handful of their supporters had gone. Or cared.

He lounged in one of a host of folding chairs in front of Foresight's front door. Mr. Lou had a barbecue going with donations of meat from numerous neighbors, and the last of the sweet corn from the fields out behind the compound. Everyone milled around, eating and drinking and congratulating the two winners on their success. Billy, sitting nearby next to Tee, felt happy for the first time in weeks. He hadn't realized what kind of strain he had been living under. He'd worry later about what kind of a wreck Seraphim and his people had left up in the studio. He took one of Tee's hands and kissed it.

"That was a big surprise," he said. "Thank you."

She grinned. "Seraphim totally deserved everything that happened to him. My favorite part was when the betas gave him a smackdown."

"I feel responsible," Billy said, shaking his head. "I should have asked for help as soon as he started pushing me around. But I never thought about what would happen when someone actually called in my IOUs. I didn't know what to do with a blackmailer."

"You're so straightforward," Tee said, with an indulgent smile. "You never see what's going on right under your nose." She looked down the slope, and her eyes brightened. "Like that! My other surprise. They're too late to vote, but who cares! They're here!" She got to her feet and dragged Billy with her. Mr. Jud and the others near them also stood up. Four riders on horseback were making their way up to the Foresight gates.

"Damn!" said Mr. Jud, peering into the twilight. "Is that Calvin Borstead?"

Calvin Borstead? Cindy's dad? That must mean...

"Cindy!" Billy shouted, and ran down the hill.

It *was* Cindy. She dropped the reins and waved wildly at him. Her father, a rangy man in his middle fifties, grinned at him. The two small women in long robes wearing weird, hornlike hats of yellow silk over shaved heads smiled at him.

Cindy swung off the horse and rushed toward Billy. He almost laughed at her awkward gait. She must have been in the saddle for hours. Her sun-bleached hair was long and braided in a complicated fashion he couldn't begin to describe, and her skin was tanned and crinkled slightly around her brilliant blue eyes. She couldn't look more beautiful. He caught her up and swung her in a circle.

"How...?" he began, hardly able to get words out. "When...?"

"About a year ago," Cindy said, laughing as he set her down. "The monastery thought it was safe to move. We've been making our way home ever since. The abbot sent Zhang Min and Jiao Chu with us," she indicated the two women. "They're *bhikkhuni*, Buddhist monastics. Without them, we would never have gotten here. Tee and I wanted to surprise you, so we made it sound like I was still in Tibet all this time." Cindy turned as Tee approached. The two women fell into each other's arms. "I'm so glad to meet you in real life!"

"Same, sister! You missed all the fun!" Tee said. "I can't wait to tell you all about it!" She gave Cindy a peck on the cheek and kept her arm around the other woman's waist. She turned to Billy, beaming. "What do you think?"

Billy goggled, but no words came out. He'd been thinking about what to say ever since Tee and Cindy had declared they wanted to be a family with him. It wasn't going to come out right, but he was going to say it anyhow. His heart pounded hard as he dropped to his knees in front of his two girlfriends. "Only I'm not worthy of either of you. Will you both marry me?"

"Yes!" Tee and Cindy chorused. They exchanged glances.

"I owe you ten dollars," Cindy said, slapping Tee's palm. "I thought he'd wait a while."

Tee laughed. "Your money's no good here. No one's is."

The voters cheered. Billy knew he was miles behind Tee and Cindy. He'd never catch up, and he was all right with that.

Isle of Masks and Blood

BRIAN TRENT

The last time he was on a boat he had to kill six people.

It had been messy work. Dumping their bodies overboard had filled him with a strange anxiety that remained long after he'd cashed the assignment check. Silvio Cipriano didn't usually remember his dreams, though in the years since he was haunted by a recurring nightmare: he was back on that private yacht, staring down into the Adriatic Sea. Beneath his reflection were the six corpses, gazing up from their watery grave. They were rotted, slimy, all skeletal grins and seaweed hair, pointing bony fingers and saying—

"Papa?" his daughter Caterina tugged at his sleeve, distracting him from his morbid reverie. "Look!"

Sitting beside him in the speeding vaporetto, she pressed her little hands to the window, eyes wide, and pointed.

"Do you see it, Papa?"

"I see it." As their watercraft cut a foaming wake, the city of Venice loomed on the horizon. It was late in the day—just after six o'clock—and the dying sun painted their destination in hues of blood and fire.

Caterina hopped off her seat, scampering past the other passengers—the grim, hardened organizers of Italy's Trade Road—to get a better view. Silvio started after her when a hand touched his knee and stayed him.

"She'll be okay," Anna said beside him. "She's not going to fall overboard, Silvio."

"This is her first experience with the ocean."

"Then let her look."

He sighed and settled back in the vaporetto's seat. "Old habits," he muttered.

"You wanted her to see the world beyond Tuscany."

"Yes."

"You said she needed to know the places on the Trade Road, because one day *she'll* be overseeing it."

"I know."

Anna interlaced her fingers with his. Sunset kissed her face, making her seem a Botticelli statue from an abandoned museum, of which a few still existed on the mainland, overgrown and long-since raided of food and bottled water. "This isn't about Caterina," she guessed. "You've been anxious all day. Is it Venice? There *can't* be any infected there. I'll bet Venice was the first city in Europe to become infection-free."

"It's not that," Silvio insisted.

"The old days, then?"

He said nothing, and she didn't press him.

Anna was a remarkable woman. Since the fall of civilization, she'd consistently proven a resourceful and insightful partner— two qualities that were key in dealing with the survivor enclaves along the Trade Road. She'd seen ugly things since the Fall. She'd seen Silvio do ugly things to bad people who deserved it. Life was tough again, as it had been through most of human history, and people had become tougher as a result.

Yet she also understood that some of Silvio's darkness preceded the Fall. Things haunted him from the past. He never spoke of it openly, and to her credit she never pried.

I can't tell her, he thought. *The world is grisly enough without her knowing what I used to be.*

He hoisted a smile on his face and patted her hand. "It was a long time ago. Doesn't matter now."

Anna kissed his neck and rested her head on his chest. "It's been two years. The zombies"—she used the English word—"are gone. The Trade Road is working. Italy is rebuilding. It's all because of *you.*"

He stared through the window to the floating city that awaited them. The other members of his group leaned forward, murmuring at the sight. They were as much responsible for the Trade Road as he was; he may have conceived of it, but they had trained as a tight-knit force to make it successful. Italy had fractured like a plate when the world ended. The infection overran the peninsula, with major cities burning in its wake. In the bitter aftermath, Silvio's group strove to unite the survivor enclaves. The Trade Road became the lifeline through which commerce and communication renewed. Crops and meats, scavenged goods and medicines, tools old and newly forged . . . it all moved along a network of roads and safe stations stretching from Verona in the north to the southernmost tip of the boot at Reggio di Calabria. Silvio didn't know what the rest of the world was up to, but here at least, a broken land was stitching itself back together.

Venice was the outlier.

No one had been there since the Fall. That wasn't so surprising, really. Only a single road connected Venice to the mainland: when the plague hit, the Venetians demolished a portion of it with shaped charges. After that, the only possible access was by sea.

For that first year, Venice kept its head down. Then, slowly, boats began arriving at the Trade Road's coastal communities on the Adriatic. Even then, the Venetians proved to be a strange, secretive bunch. Tight-lipped and suspicious. Kept to themselves, then fled back across the sea as soon as bartering concluded. Several times, Silvio inquired if his people could visit the floating city. The answer had always been no.

Until now.

"It's been years since I've been to Venice," Anna was saying. "I was in college. It'll be nice to see it again."

"You understand *why* we're going here? You know what we have to do?"

"I do," she whispered.

From the bow of the high-speed craft, Caterina squealed happily. "Papa! It's so beautiful! Come see! Venice is *so* beautiful!"

He sighed and absently touched the SIG Sauer pistol in his pocket. "I've seen it before, my gumdrop. I've been to Venice." He looked uncomfortably at the water racing by their vaporetto.

❧ ⊖ ☙

Venice was sinking.

That had been true for hundreds of years, but since the Fall there were fewer people, fewer resources, to hold back the sea. As Silvio disembarked the vaporetto, he marveled at the sight of Piazza San Marco—once a popular tourist destination—completely submerged. People moved about in ankle-deep water, pushing what seemed to be brooms or shovels. In fact, the entire plaza had been cordoned off with an elaborate network of sandbags. This resulted in hundreds of rectangular seawater pools. Each pool had a large bucket nearby, and...

"We're making salt," a woman called to him from the pier.

Silvio turned to see a group approaching his disembarking retinue. Five people—four bodyguards in crimson cloaks, with Kalashnikov rifles slung at their sides. A woman at their center like a queen bee, dressed in an opulent blue gown with matching elbow-length gloves.

"Welcome to our fair city," the woman said, smiling pleasantly. "My name is Katya."

"Silvio." He shook her hand. "Thank you for receiving us."

She watched his compatriots emerging from the vaporetto. Compared with her spotless entourage, his own people formed a grim portrait. There was Old Man Matteo, the leathery veteran of the Italian Armed Forces, with his service rifle slung over one shoulder. Giuseppe, who towered at nearly six-feet-four and had the physique to match. Even young Salvatore had transformed over the past year from a wide-eyed innocent to a hardened man of the earth, studying the buildings and canals of Venice in steely-eyed appraisal. The only bright spot in the group was little Caterina, whose fascinated expression made Silvio feel a thousand years old.

Katya turned back to him. "I noticed you showing interest in our saltworks."

"Seems an efficient operation," he said, and meant it.

The Trade Road relied on a steady supply of goods. Pigeon meat came from mountaintop communities. High-nutrition crops arrived from country farms. Fresh fruits and vegetables were brought up from the south. Cheeses and meats came from a medieval monastery. Canned goods and paper products trickled in from warehouses in Bologna.

And salt came from Venice.

The electrical grids were dead. That meant no refrigeration. Salt was the new bedrock for achieving food surpluses again.

Katya pointed to the rectangular pools glowing red in the setting sun. "We pump in seawater and let it evaporate. Then our workers shovel out the crystals."

"Your *workers*," Silvio repeated, feeling his skin crawl as he noticed the laborers at the pools. Each of them wore identical black masks with birdlike beaks and eerie goggles. Each wore black robes that covered them from neck to feet. "Can't be comfortable, working while dressed like that."

"Comfort isn't the point. The costumes help us identify them, in case one gets loose."

The truth hit him like a bullet. "They're *infected*?" he cried.

She laughed musically, showing bright teeth. "Technically speaking, no. The infected are all dead. These are what the Americans have been calling 'betas.' Victims of the virus who didn't turn into rabid monsters. Neither dangerous nor contagious. Just hollowed-out husks of their former selves. Barely able to take care of themselves. So we put them to work."

Put them to work. The comment visibly stung Anna, who looked up from the crate she was helping off-load onto the pier. "You've dressed them as medieval plague doctors," she said. "Someone here has a vile sense of humor."

Katya raised an eyebrow. "It wasn't meant to be humorous. It was *my* idea to assign those masks. It helps us distinguish them. They're—"

"Slaves."

"Resources. Let's be honest. Italy was almost entirely depopulated by the plague. If we hope to recover, then everyone must contribute to that effort. Even the betas. Our first instinct was to mercy-kill them. I suggested a better use. There's mutual benefit. They get to live, and our saltworks thrive."

A gunshot rang out from a nearby roof. Caterina shrieked and Silvio nearly drew his concealed pistol, heart racing, but it was only a firework, launched over the Grand Canal by an overeager Venetian.

"Tonight," explained Katya, "we will celebrate Carnival for the first time since the Fall. It will be beautiful! Then you must all join me for dinner. I wish to hear about your Trade Road." Her eyes reflected the sunset and became fiery coins. "And I'm eager to learn more about *you*."

Silvio blinked. "Me?"

"Indeed! Even without the worldwide web, stories about Silvio Cipriano have reached our little island."

"I don't understand."

"No? You aren't the man who last year descended into the bowels of the Earth to kill terrible demons who were lurking there?"

"They weren't demons," he said. "They were wealthy Americans living in a posh survivalist bunker, and who were planning on raiding our storehouses and killing us."

"Like I said, demons." She laughed again, though there was a razor edge to the sound that suggested she wasn't being playful. In fact, the longer she spoke, the more he detected an accent that hadn't been immediately obvious. Italy was full of accents, including a distinctly Venetian one. Hers was different. There was a Slavic roughness to her words. Her stone-cut features seemed to match it.

Silvio's eyes drifted to where her alabaster neck vanished into the blue gown. The edge of a tattooed bird-wing peeked up from there. Maybe an eagle, or falcon, or...

Phoenix?

The word leapt unbidden to his mind.

Caterina tugged on his sleeve. "Papa? Do you see the bird masks? Can I have a mask, too?"

Katya crouched to the girl and said, "Of course you can! Venice is a city of masks! We can all pretend to be something else tonight."

Another firework exploded like a gunshot.

For the next hour, Silvio assisted in unloading crates from the vaporetto, which attracted Venetian merchants as surely as flies to sugar for some good-natured haggling. Salt was the strongest bartering chip for Venice, but the mainland had brought something that leveled the playing field: toilet paper.

"How did you find so much?" a merchant asked.

"We have our sources," Silvio said, not wishing to tip his hand. One of the Trade Road communities had set up camp in a foundered ocean liner on the beaches of Genova. Toilet paper, printer paper, paper towels, tissues and napkins were among the crates that hadn't been swallowed by the Ligurian Sea.

By sunset, the haggling ended. All in all, a successful moot.

Barrels of salt, and salted fish were placed aboard the vaporetto for the return journey.

"Enough for a few months," he noted.

Anna stared at the salt-workers in their creepy bird-masks; with the onset of evening, they were rounded up by guards bearing heavy clubs, and steered down a narrow alley until they were out of sight. It was an ugly thing to behold.

"Like a goddam cattle drive," Anna whispered to him. "Is this really acceptable? What's next—another Roman Empire?"

"I doubt that."

"Why?"

"There aren't enough people around, Anna. You need armies to wage wars of aggression, and commerce is more profitable than conquest."

But she shook her head. "It's not always about what's *profitable*. Some people wage war because they *enjoy waging war*. History's full of examples. These goddam people have seen fit to reinstitute slavery, so who knows what they're planning next—"

"We didn't come here to pass ethical judgments. We came here to trade."

She peered curiously at him. "We came for more than that. How are you going to investigate the—"

"Let's go for a walk," he interrupted, and motioned for the rest of their group to follow.

With evening, the rooftops came alive with lights. A costumed throng gathered, moving back and forth along an impressive network of jury-rigged planks and skyways letting the Venetians bypass the flooded square below.

Caterina stared in astonishment at the crowds, the assorted outfits and masks, and the electric lights festooning the rooftops. It was entirely unlike anything on the mainland. Her awe lifted Silvio's heavy heart, even as he wondered at the power source. Batteries? Generators? It didn't require a lot of juice to run decorative lights; nonetheless, it was a luxury he hadn't seen in a long while, beyond the occasional flashlight.

They ascended a ramp to the nearest roof; Salvatore and Giuseppe carried a gift—a pine-box crate of vodka, rum, grappa, and schnapps—as an offering for the festival. The nexus of the activity was an especially large roof that had been converted into a restaurant, with tables and chairs, well-dressed waiters, and what must have been the costumed cream of Venetian society. Salvatore and Giuseppe brought their crate to the bar, glancing back only once to give Silvio a meaningful nod.

Silvio barely had time to soak in the details of his airy surroundings when he was accosted by a vendor pushing a cart. The fellow wore the jingling cap and checkered livery of a court jester. His cart was decorated with masks.

"A crime!" the vendor crooned. "A crime to have anyone here without a mask tonight! Tell me, what can I get you? Everyone must wear a mask on Carnival!"

"*You* don't have one," Silvio observed.

The man's smile burned on his face. "Don't I?"

The two men regarded each other in silent recognition—the look of rivals reunited after an absence of years. Caterina flitted around the cart like a moth encircling a lamp; Anna trailed her, smiling in spite of herself.

"Mr. Cipriano," the mask peddler whispered.

Silvio nodded. "Detective."

"You received my letter?"

"That's why I'm here."

Fireworks exploded in the sky, reflecting in the pools below. The rooftop crowd milled about, talking and laughing—laughing!—as if the world hadn't been thrown into a new Dark Age. Of course, there was something to be said for not dwelling on tragedy, and more to be said for focusing on present circumstances. Nonetheless, Silvio detected a haughtiness about the Venetians. A decadence. An air of superiority so unlike the grounded attitudes on the mainland.

"Papa!" Caterina cried. "Aren't the masks beautiful?" She'd pulled the hair stick from her golden curls and was using it like a wand, touching the masks as if sprinkling fairy dust on them.

"They are, my gumdrop. You pick any you like."

The peddler said, "She's gotten big."

"It's been two years," Silvio reminded him.

Indeed, it had been more than two years since the peddler had seen Caterina. Back then, he hadn't been a seller of masks. He had been Detective Gaetano Farina with the Polizia di Stato. And he'd made a career out of hunting the Sicilian and Croatian mobs...

... as surely as Silvio had made a career working for the Sicilian and Croatian mobs.

It was the secret he fervently kept from Anna. From everyone on the Trade Road. Before the world ended, he'd made his living in the grisly vocation of contract killer-for-hire.

It had been a quick way out of the slums. He did his morbid work and went home. Killed his targets efficiently. Used the money to build a life for his mother, his wife Maria, and his daughter. Silvio was a meticulous planner—a skill that would later serve him with the Trade Road—and so he'd executed more than three dozen assassinations across Europe without ever coming to the attention of law enforcement.

Until the morning of his wife's murder.

Sitting at the kitchen table of their Milanese apartment. His wife Maria by the window, aglow in morning light. The kettle shrieking on the stove. She pours two cups of tea as she relates what she's been hearing on the news: that a strange virus has broken out in America. She brings the teacups to the table. The window behind her cracks. A bullet blows out her skull.

Presumably it was the work of a rival syndicate exacting revenge. Maybe even a multinational corporation sending a message to the Cosa Nostra (conflicts between the two were part of a longtime invisible war). But there were problems with both hypotheses. Silvio didn't hobnob with his employers. Didn't hang at mob-owned clubs. He kept off the radar. Played the part of insurance salesman. Stayed far away from the neon and glitz, the drugs and flashy cars and whores. No one knew his real identity.

So who had put the hit out on him? And why bother killing his wife, when the sniper could have easily assassinated him at the kitchen table, instead of her. Silvio never learned the truth.

When Detective Farina showed up at the scene, the man made no effort to conceal his suspicion that Maria's death was somehow tied to illegal business that involved Silvio. It was obvious that this had been a professional hit.

Yet the murder investigation came to nothing, as the "American pandemic" became a "global pandemic" and then an outright global collapse. The infected were everywhere. Cities burned, and society followed.

Then—two years later—a letter traveled along the Trade Road. It was addressed to him. It was unsigned. And it was worded in such a way that only he would know the scribe's identity.

Silvio Cipriano,

We met under terrible circumstances some twenty months ago. The morning of your wife's murder. As I did that day, I offer you my sympathies. Despite all that has happened, I still think back on the scene in your kitchen. The instincts of my profession run deep, I suppose. I don't like unsolved mysteries.

Allow me to congratulate you on the success of the Trade Road. Word of it has reached me all the way here in Venice. People talk fondly of it, and of the person behind it. This is how I heard your name again after all this time.

I'll come right to the point:

I know that your trade stations are being attacked. Your supplies are stolen, your people have gone missing. I know that you have struggled to learn who is responsible for these crimes.

Venice is responsible. My city is in the hands of criminals, and if I am correct, they are planning a far larger crime than ransacking your coastal outposts.

If you want proof, I have it. Come to Venice on the night of Carnival, and I will supply you all the proof you need. You remain a mystery to me, but I know at least that you are a man of action. Even in the apocalypse, criminals must not go unpunished. We must stand united on this. Lives depend on our cooperation.

Go to Piazza San Marco. I will keep watch.

I pray this letter finds you. We don't have much time.

"Papa!" Caterina shouted, pointing with her hair stick "wand" to a particularly scintillating mask. "I like the gold one! Don't you like the gold one, Papa?"

"I think it's perfect for my little princess," Silvio said, and to the detective, whispered, "Tell me what you know."

Detective Farina glanced around worriedly, making sure there were no eavesdroppers. He'd certainly changed in the past couple years. He was grayer, thinner, and (like many men nowadays) wore a short beard, no doubt as the convenience of shaving equipment dried up with the rest of the supply chain. "Life has been hard here since the Fall," he said.

Silvio indicated the plentiful food and wine circulating among the crowd of costumed revelers, and the fireworks blossoming in the sky. "Doesn't seem so hard."

"Appearances are deceiving."

"Truer words have never been spoken."

"For the first few months, this was a nightmare town," the detective explained. "The plague hit us hard. Infected were eating people in the streets."

"I thought you had been spared that," Silvio said, genuinely surprised. "You demolished the only road to the mainland."

"Not right away. When the plague hit Europe, lots of people flocked here, assuming it would be safe. It was a stampede, and the infection came with them. A bunch of engineers got together and blew up the road, but the disease already had a foothold. I'm sure you experienced something similar."

Silvio nodded. When the plague hit Italy, he'd hightailed it out of Milan for the rural countryside. Lots of others had the same idea, and the infection chased them.

The detective was interrupted by a young man wanting a mask, and who paid for it with a nipper of rum—alcohol had become the default currency in many places, as its application ranged from medicinal to recreational. With the transaction done, Farina continued, "Six months into the plague, we received a new visitor."

He pointed across the skyway to the rooftop bar. Amid the revelers, it was easy to single out Lady Katya in her blue gown and mask. She drank from a fluted glass, intently watching the celebration. Her retinue of crimson bodyguards surrounded her like protective hawks.

Silvio's eyes narrowed. "Who is she?"

"No one knows for certain. Most of her people don't even speak our tongue."

"What *do* they speak?"

"With us? Simple words in English or Italian. Truth is that they keep mostly to themselves. Katya deputized a number of Venetians to serve as go-betweens. The rest of the population is kept at arm's length."

At this, Anna laughed coldly—she had remained in earshot. "Even in the apocalypse, there's first-class and steerage," she scoffed.

Silvio's gaze swept along the neighboring rooftops, picking out other men in similar crimson attire. "The locals are okay with foreigners ruling their city?"

"Lady Katya arrived by boat with some fifty people. They were armed to the teeth. Fiercely loyal to each other. The Venetians were desperate, frightened, and running out of supplies. Katya directed her men to comb the streets and eliminate every hostile. She purged the city of infected. And from her boat, she off-loaded food and water for the locals. She was the savior of Venice. Is it any surprise that she's in charge?"

He considered that. "How did *you* end up in Venice? You were operating out of Milan last we met."

"I came to Milan to investigate *you*, Silvio," Farina said. "But Venice was my main base of operations. I'd been working a case here for a year before your wife's murder."

Silvio glanced quickly to Anna. She was helping Caterina try on the gold mask, but at the detective's words she stiffened. He felt a pang of fear.

God in Heaven, he thought. *Let the past stay buried! Don't let her know what I used to do. What I used to be.*

"So I returned here," the detective continued, "to my earlier investigation, when the plague hit."

Silvio drew the man a distance away from the cart where they could talk in greater secrecy. "What were you investigating in Venice?"

"A smuggling operation."

"What smuggling operation?"

"The Russian mob."

Silvio felt a chill snap through his limbs. "You...you're sure?"

The detective's eyes burned. "I'm sure."

Before the Fall, there'd been numerous crime syndicates with international aspirations. Unsurprisingly, lines of control were always in flux. Since the late '90s, the Russian mob had rapidly expanded across Europe and the United States. Known popularly as the *Bratva*. Run by former KGB and FSB. Had their hands in everything—drugs, weapons, extortion, racketeering, prostitution, even human trafficking. As with any enterprise of global ambition, they'd set up regional hubs for distribution and enforcement. That included Venice.

"They made use of private boats to conduct their business," Farina explained. "Smart, really. It made them difficult to track."

Letting the pieces assemble in his mind, Silvio said, "So when the virus hit, they simply sailed off to where the infected couldn't reach them. A year passes. Local military and law enforcement are destroyed. When the dust settles, they return and take possession of the city." He shuddered. "Mother of God."

"That's only half the story. In the past six months, I've learned their ambitions are not confined to Venice."

"You mean..."

The detective nodded grimly.

Silvio looked to Anna; she was gazing directly at him. "I'll need proof," he said quietly.

"The proof is at my apartment."

"Where's that?"

"It's northeast of here. The only mask shop on C. de Mezzo."

"Google Earth is off-line. How the hell do I find your place?"

Detective Farina led the way back to his cart. There, he rummaged in a cabinet, exhumed a skull mask, and handed it to him. "Here you are, sir! I think this one is appropriate for you, yes?"

Silvio inspected the mask and found a slip of paper taped to the interior—a hand-drawn map of nearby streets and canals. His route was outlined in red, zigzagging marker like a jagged scar.

Evening folded into the cloak of night, and stars hatched like twinkling diamonds. In response, the festival of Carnival increased to vertiginous levels of revelry and drunkenness. There was even a string quartet, though instead of Mozart and Beethoven they played music from the lost days of radio, mostly '80s and '90s pop songs. Silvio, Anna, and Caterina seated themselves and dined on fresh seafood—octopus, fish, and eel. Throughout, fireworks seared the heavens, and gondolas threaded the canals below.

Anna clinked her wineglass against his. "To new beginnings."

Silvio indicated the incandescent sky. "You don't find this all a little much?"

"People need to cut loose. It's not enough to survive—life must have joy in it, too."

He glanced to his daughter. She wore her new gold mask, lifting it only to take small bites of her food. Every once in a while, she put down the fork and took up her wand, running around the rooftop with the random energy that is the exclusive domain of young children. He'd never seen her so excited. It made him sad, actually. She'd been three years old when she saw her mother die. Barely a week later, Milan was overrun by zombies. Even when they fled to the Umbrian countryside, there were new traumas to contend with—a year into the Fall, she'd been kidnapped by a rich American family living underground in a survivalist bunker.

Now, she was getting to be a child at last. Giggling, twirling around in her mask. Scampering about with her fairy wand, as if she was the princess of a fabled Atlantis. This carefree spirit had seemingly transmitted to the rest of their group, too; at the bar, Salvatore had managed to become one of the bartenders, shaking mixers and pouring drinks with a skill that suggested he'd done his share of mixology in college. Even the famously sour-tempered Giuseppe had gone over to the fireworks station and was chatting happily with the crew. Old Man Matteo was slurping oysters with gusto.

"You were right to insist that we bring her," Silvio conceded. "I've been so focused on protecting her... on training her to survive... I hadn't thought about the need for... you know..."

"Happiness," Anna said, chuckling. "It's not a difficult word to say."

"It's a difficult word to trust."

"You're a good father, Silvio."

He stared into his wine. "I wasn't always a good person. And now that you mention it, I'm not sure I'm even a good father."

She touched his hand across the table. "Silvio, I've seen you with Caterina. You're a wonderful father."

"Am I? Do you know what I taught her last week?"

"Self-defense, wasn't it?"

He shook his head. "That's one way to put it."

"Silvio—"

"I taught her how to use a knife. Not for whittling or dicing tomatoes. I showed her what to do if anyone put their hands on her. I taught her how to be brutal, Anna. How to inflict the kinds of injury that people don't come back from. Is that the stuff good fathers are made of?"

Anna squeezed his hand. "Yes."

"Don't be ridiculous!"

"What do you think ancient mammoth hunters taught *their* children? Or Spartan fathers taught *theirs*? Society isn't a universal fixture, Silvio. It changes according to the needs of the time, and our time is—"

"Monstrous." He finished his wine in one gulp, hoping it would suppress the cold revulsion in his stomach. Then he stood and said, "Keep an eye on Caterina."

"Of course."

"If things go bad..."

"Maybe they won't." She stared at him with tenderness—their blossoming love had been a slow and tricky development. As Silvio struggled to nurture the Trade Road, he struggled equally with conflicted feelings. Maria had been dead only a couple of years. Every intimate moment with Anna felt like infidelity to the memory of his wife.

And how could a woman like her truly love a monster like me? At the end of the day, apocalypses and zombies aside, I'm a monster and always have been.

He cut across the rooftop, finding a stairwell that led down the building's side. On the next landing, electric lights blinked around signs for lavatories. Silvio went there, ducking into a stall, where he donned his skull mask and shed his white shirt for the black one beneath. He didn't know if his group was under surveillance, but he'd survived the years by always assuming so.

He exited the lavatory, descending quickly to the Venetian streets.

They were not the tourist-clogged paths he'd known before the Fall. The new Venice was a ghost town—the music and laughter from Carnival dissipated as he followed the zigzagging illustration the detective had given him. Almost immediately, he was alone. The alleys were deserted.

It set his instincts thrumming. What if he ran into infected hordes in these lonely streets? Detective Farina had insisted that Venice was purged of zombies, that Katya's people had eliminated all threats. Yet was that true? The slave labor force he'd seen at the salt pools certainly qualified as a species of infected. The so-called "betas" weren't dangerous. Hell, they supposedly weren't even contagious. Silvio wasn't a microbiologist. He only knew that they made his skin crawl, and honestly, who was to say that every beta specimen was harmless? What if the virus's more cannibalistic effects had merely gone dormant? Chickenpox never truly disappeared from those it infected. What if that was true of the zombie plague? What if the bird-masked workers still had the virus in their cells, and one day it would reemerge as a more dreadful Gamma variant?

Silvio touched the SIG Sauer in his pocket. He thumbed the safety off.

It was a half hour before he found the detective's apartment. Drawing open the door, he entered into a mask shop—no surprise there. Hollow-eyed faces leered from the walls. Costumes hung from hooks. He wondered if this had been a formalized police front during Farina's pre-apocalypse investigations, or if the man had claimed the place in the aftermath. Neither option would have been surprising.

Society isn't a universal fixture. It changes according to the needs of the time.

The shop was deserted. Silvio crept to the back of the shop, passing through a curtain, and finding a small office and staircase. Anxiety gnawing at him, he drew his pistol and advanced up the ancient wooden steps. They creaked and popped from his weight.

The stairs led to a second-floor landing with a single door. He pushed it open and considered the view.

A small, gloomy apartment. Kitchen, bed, bookcase and Detective Farina sitting at a desk by the window. A strange glowing object lay before him. It took Silvio a moment to realize what it was.

A smartphone.

He hadn't seen one in more than a year. The cell towers were gone, after all. So were the power grids. CB radios had become the go-to replacement; they facilitated smooth operations along the Trade Road, allowing security to call ahead to the next station, explaining *which* trade caravan was en route, *what* they were bringing, and how many people comprised their group. Smartphones were a bygone marvel that newer generations like Caterina's would never know.

"I know you're not checking email," Silvio said, approaching the detective. The phone was open to a picture in its camera roll. It showed a canal-side warehouse. A vaporetto was tied to the dock. Men armed with Kalashnikovs milled about.

Frowning, Silvio said, "Is this what you summoned me to Venice for? What does this prove?" When the man didn't answer, he took the phone and scrolled to the next photo, and the next.

Apparently, the detective had been staking out the warehouse. He'd used the smartphone to create a kind of digital documentary. One picture showed naked men and women—the beta slaves, almost certainly—laboring to unload crates from the vaporetto. Another showed them opening those crates and sorting the contents. The detective had taken his pics from high above—presumably the warehouse rafters—so it was difficult to see precise details. Nonetheless, it was obvious that the crates contained things Venice couldn't produce. Red meats. Paper products. Clothing. Grain. Vegetables. These were goods from the mainland, and there was a *lot* of them...a lot more than could be obtained from a trade moot.

"They're raiding us," Silvio said. "For six months we've had stations and caravans attacked...always in the dead of night. The attackers vanish without a trace. We figured it was the work of bandits...we've had unpleasant encounters with a few. But this? Venice is launching coordinated raids on the rest of Italy! This is war, Detective. This is...holy shit!"

He was scrolling through photos when a flash of understanding came to him. Something the photos were showing. Something his mind had refused to accept at first. It sent a chill of horror through him.

Outside the window, a firework burst in the sky. Silvio instinctively glanced there. Reflected on the glass, he saw himself, the detective, and...

...a stranger creeping out of the room behind him.

Silvio moved with reflexes honed from a lifetime of dealing with dangerous adversaries. Leaping aside, he narrowly avoided a swipe from a wooden club—a skull-cracker of a blow if it landed. Jerking his SIG Sauer, Silvio fired twice, center of mass.

His assailant went down hard. Another firework lit the room, revealing what the gloom had concealed: Detective Gaetano Farina was dead in his chair—had *been* dead. By the look of things, he'd had his neck broken while waiting for Silvio to arrive.

Jesus Christ.

We were being watched on the skyway, Silvio thought. *Despite our precautions, we were being monitored and shadowed. They'd followed Farina home. Executed him. But why, dammit?*

His question fled as he heard footsteps thundering up the stairs. A backup team, waiting in the street. Responding to the sound of his gunfire.

Shit.

The door kicked open, and two men—both clad in red cloaks—fanned into the apartment, Kalashnikovs raised in their hands.

Silvio dove into the next room as the weapons chattered. Bullet holes stitched a macabre constellation in the wall.

With his free hand, Silvio peeled off his skull mask and flung it across the room. One of his attackers took the bait and fired wildly. Silvio peeked out from the wall, aimed at the muzzle flash, and fired four times. The man dropped.

His remaining opponent kicked over the kitchen table and sprayed bullets across the rim. It was undisciplined behavior—more than that, it was foolish. For one thing, a Kalashnikov had a standard clip of thirty rounds. Shoot recklessly and you'd empty the clip in seconds... which was exactly what his gung-ho attacker did.

Secondly, a kitchen table was not Kevlar.

As the man fumbled for a spare clip, Silvio rounded the corner and fired twice into the table. The bullets tore through like a hole-puncher through paper. His assailant slumped over, and Silvio rushed forward to make sure the fight was over.

It was over.

The man was dead—he just didn't know it yet. One round had blown out half his skull. Bone gleamed through bloody tissue. A pool of dark fluid the same shade as his cloak spread out behind him. He blinked. His lips quivered.

Silvio held the smartphone to his face. "Do you see this photo? Where was it taken?"

"I...I..."

"Is it on the Grand Canal?"

"I..."

The man spasmed. His eyes rolled white, bearded mouth expelling a final breath.

Cursing, Silvio returned to the detective. Farina had been a good man. He could have kept his head down in these brutal days; instead, he'd risked his life to inform the mainland of a sinister plot. He deserved a better fate than this.

Silvio retrieved his skull mask and made for the door, concerned that the gunshots might have carried despite the fireworks. Pistol out, ready for more trouble, he stepped onto the stairs.

Then he heard the dead gunman speak behind him.

"Is it done? What's taking so long?"

The words were in Russian. Whirling around, Silvio shone the smartphone's light on the corpse. The man was dead—both gunmen were dead. Yet the voice came again even though his mouth didn't move: *"Vitaly? She wants to know if it's done."*

Silvio patted down the cloak and, discovering a walkie-talkie, he considered his options. He knew a smattering of Russian, as it was useful in his line of work. But he didn't know enough to engage in a lengthy conversation.

"Vitaly?"

Silvio took a breath. Lifted the radio to his lips.

"Yes," he grunted.

"You captured him alive, right? The mask-seller can die, but the other guy—she wants him alive!"

"He's alive."

"Good," the device crackled. *"Bring him to the palace, and be quick about it. She's got something interesting planned."*

The palace could only refer to the doge's palace, which overlooked the sea. For centuries it had been the seat of Venetian power. It was typically the first thing tourists saw when they visited. Not surprising that the Russian mafia had co-opted the place. Hell, there were actual dungeons beneath it.

Burying the smartphone in his pocket, Silvio fled down the stairs. The street appeared deserted. Fireworks stretched like bright spiders. Warily studying the windows and rooftops, he sprinted back the way he'd come. The air smelled of a pending storm.

He was placing his skull mask on his face when he rounded a corner and walked right into a rabid crowd of the infected.

They were on him with customary savagery. Clawing hands, pulling him into their midst. Faces set in a freakish rictus of hunger. Someone grabbed his arm. A mouth lunged for his neck. The sheer weight of so many attackers dragged him into their nexus.

It wasn't the first time he'd been attacked by alphas. Six days after Maria's death. The American virus had reached Europe and exploded across the continent. Silvio fled Milan with his only surviving family—his daughter and mother—and drove straight to his Umbrian safehouse.

It had been no scenic exodus, unless the scene was out of Dante or the lurid paintings of Hieronymus Bosch. The roads were gridlocked. Everyone was trying to flee the cities, partly from the infected and partly from the fires that burned unchecked in their wake. Fighter jets streaked overhead.

It wasn't long before a tide of alphas caught up to the traffic jam. People were dragged from their cars. Terrified, Silvio escaped into the hills with his mother and daughter. Several alphas caught up to them—he shot them until his clip was empty, and then used his trusty knife—his preferred means of assassination—to brain the ones who remained. It had been a raw, primal fight.

Now, in a Venetian street two years later, he found himself reliving that terror. His mask was torn away. He reached for his SIG; someone wrenched his arm backwards.

"Kiss me!" a woman cried, her mouth still questing for his neck.

"Dance with us!" another cried. "Everyone has to dance!"

Silvio twisted and pulled free. The crowd churned around him, laughing and clapping. His panic subsided, leaving only a bitter taste of adrenaline.

They're not infected, he realized. *They're drunk.*

Not just on wine, but on wild abandon. He'd never seen anything like it, not even in the seedier nightclubs of Europe. Silvio found himself in the midst of a barely clothed bacchanalia. Men and women, men and men, women and women . . . part dance, part copulation. A fellow in a domino mask stumbled towards him, lurched sideways, and vomited on the street.

Silvio retreated from them and climbed back to the rooftop. He spotted Anna at once. Caterina still zipped around like an errant moth, wand in hand.

Anna spotted him and saw immediately that something was wrong. Crossing to him, she said, "You okay?"

"Never better. Where is everyone else?"

"Right where you left them."

He looked around for his troop. Salvatore was at the bar. Matteo was plowing through another plate of oysters and had added octopus to his feast. Giuseppe managed to ingratiate himself with the fireworks crew and was participating in the lighting of fuses.

"Silvio?" Anna prompted. "What's wrong?"

"You were a tour director here, yes?"

"Years ago. Why?"

"I need you to look at some pictures and identify a location for me."

"I'll try."

Mindful of eavesdroppers, he steered her toward the stairs.

Caterina came running by, gleeful in her gold mask, and pointed with her wand to the sea. "Papa? There is a huge boat on the water!"

"That's nice," he said absently.

"Can I go watch the boat?"

"Sure, but stay where I can see you."

"Yes, Papa!" She scurried away, and Silvio slung his arms around Anna's waist and kissed her.

She was so shocked by the kiss that she gasped. He knew his anxiety must be evident—it hung around him like a cloud of electrically charged particles. She surely understood they were in trouble. Nonetheless, she kissed him back fiercely, indulging in the moment.

His lips went to her ear. "I just placed a phone in your pocket. Go into one of the bathroom stalls. Look at the pictures. I need to know the location of the building shown in the photos. It's by a canal. A warehouse of some kind."

"Of course," she murmured, cheeks flush.

"It can prove that Venice is behind the attacks on the Trade Road."

She stared into his eyes, fireworks crackling and sizzling in the sudden flurry of a grand finale. "I was hoping..."

He touched her face. "So was I."

The unsaid words hovered. They'd been hoping that the mysterious midnight raids were the work of random thieves and marauders. But the raids seemed too organized, too perfectly executed. Whoever was attacking them had an intimate knowledge of the Trade Road: how many people manned the stations, what the defenses were, where the best angle of attack could be achieved. They were inexplicably well-informed.

Silvio had concluded that there were only two possibilities. The first was that it was an inside job. He dismissed that notion immediately. The Trade Road was a close-knit community. All participants understood that survival depended on collaboration. There was nothing to be gained by betrayal.

The other possibility was that it was a rival community. Someone not immediately local. Someone who could strike fast, and disappear...

...by sea.

Even before the detective's letter, Silvio's suspicions gravitated to Venice. They participated in the Trade Road, sending merchants across the sea with salt and fish and potassium chloride (cooked down from seaweed). They traded for what they needed and departed over the sea when done. And yet... it wasn't difficult to imagine they were conducting reconnaissance for darker purposes. That they were assessing local resistance. Noting the landmarks and topographical features. Memorizing the patrols. Counting the personnel. Reporting this intel to a hidden group of maritime raiders...

Anna kissed him again. "If you're right, what do we do?"

"Do you trust me?"

"With my life, Silvio."

"Good, because what we do next is... is..."

She raised an eyebrow. "Is... what?"

But he wasn't paying attention to her anymore. He crossed the rooftop to where Caterina leaned at a guardrail. Out at sea, a massive yacht had glided into view. It was practically an island unto itself. Farina had told him that Venice's ruling cabal had survived the plague by staying at sea; he hadn't said that it had been aboard a mega-yacht. Hadn't told him that the name of the boat was...

"*Phoenix*," Silvio muttered, reading the hull's black lettering. "God Almighty..."

The memory possessed him.

Two years earlier.

The Venice job.

Sicily's Cosa Nostra had tolerated a limited number of foreign mobs working in-country; after all, it could be good for business. The problem was that the Russians had crossed a line. They were running a human trafficking racket in Venice, and it was attracting Interpol's attention. The Sicilians asked the Russians to halt their operations. The Russians had flatly refused, and so Silvio was hired to send a message.

You don't have to be clean with this one, his handler said. *Make it messy. We want those fucks in Moscow to understand they can't do whatever the fuck they please.*

I don't do messy, Silvio replied.

Yet in the end, the job *had* been messy. The Russians were making bimonthly runs to neighboring Croatia in a luxury yacht—a forty-foot cabin cruiser. Silvio snuck aboard the ship. Strangled one Russian when the man went to use the bathroom and went to find the others.

Three of them were in the hold.

Amusing themselves.

With several bound women.

Silvio killed them, and it was messy indeed. He lost his temper. He'd never lost his temper before. By the time he was through, the hold was full of blood, brains and bullet casings. He set the women free and hunted the remaining Russians on the top deck.

It was then he discovered the ship was bearing down on a mega-yacht. The fucking thing dwarfed the forty-footer by an order of magnitude. Like a goddamn whale compared to a bluegill. And Silvio suddenly understood: the Russians had been handing off their abductees at sea, where prying eyes couldn't see.

He managed to kill his remaining targets. Took control of the cabin cruiser. Swung the boat around and caught a glimpse of the mega-yacht's name.

Phoenix.

The larger ship didn't give chase, but they must have known something was wrong. Silvio was anxious during the return voyage. He dumped the bodies into the Adriatic. Killed the engine within view of Venice. Jumped overboard. Swam to safety. By morning he was on the train from Santa Lucia, while news of a "thwarted kidnapping" broke on social media; for a whole hour it was the top story, until bumped off by the bigger news of a Hollywood engagement and release of a new iPhone.

Now, Silvio gaped at the mega-yacht—the same goddam ship!—gliding offshore of the salt pools.

Should I be so surprised? he thought. *They'd already been operating in the area when the plague hit. They just sat it out, and swooped in to conquer a desperate city.*

Instinctively, he grabbed for his daughter's hand. His fingers closed on empty air.

Silvio spun around. Caterina hadn't gone far, but she now had company. The Lady Katya stood behind her, clutching the girl's shoulders in a possessive threat. The woman wasn't wearing her mask anymore, and she grinned coldly at him.

"You disappeared on me, Silvio Cipriano," Katya chastised, eyes flashing a malefic gleam. "You're supposed to be my guest of honor."

"Sorry. I had to use the bathroom."

"Are you feeling better?"

"I am, thank you. Caterina, leave the nice woman alone now. Come to Papa."

The girl started forward. Katya drew her back.

"Now, now," the woman chided, her gaze never leaving his. "You wanted to see the boat, yes? Look at it, Caterina!" She pointed to the *Phoenix*. "Do you know what's onboard? I'll tell you! It's filled with my people. Men with lots of guns. Do you know *why?*"

Caterina's voice was tinny in her mask. She fidgeted with her wand. "I don't know."

"They're going to visit your daddy's precious Trade Road."

Silvio glowered. "As if they haven't been visiting it, right?"

Katya laughed wickedly. "*Visiting* it, yes. This time it's different. We're going to claim the outposts for ourselves. Put *our* people there. It's been my plan for more than a year. Should have been easy! You know the plague killed off ninety percent of the population, yes? The Italian Army was obliterated. Conquering Italy should have been simple because who could possibly oppose us?"

"*We* could."

The rising crescendo of fireworks detonated over the salt pools, and it had the effect of transforming Piazza San Marco into a vision of hell. Molten light glimmered in the pools, glinted off windows, and shimmered in Katya's eyes; in that ghastly moment, Silvio imagined that she was not human but an infernal demoness risen to torture Earth's survivors.

"We started hearing the stories," she hissed. "Armed outposts. Communication relays. Farmland and warehouses under protection. Instead of easy pickings, we discovered a well-oiled network of survivors. And that, my dear Silvio, is how I heard *your* name . . . the man I'd been hunting *before* the Fall!"

His fury melted into confusion. "We never met before the Fall."

Katya hooked one hand around Caterina's throat. Her bodyguards spread out like wings on either side of her. "That's not true. We were never *formally* introduced, but we saw each other once, Silvio. During the last time you were in Venice."

"I've never been to Venice."

"Not even to kill my brother?"

He stiffened. Turned to see if Anna was still there, but she had disappeared.

Katya tried to smile—he could see that she'd rehearsed this moment in her head—but the expression wouldn't come. Instead, a rictus of fury distorted her features. Her hand gripped Caterina's throat hard enough to cause the girl to choke and sputter.

"You murdered my brother aboard his yacht!" Spit flew from her teeth.

"Your brother," he muttered, the truth clicking into place with the precision of bullets loaded into a revolver.

The man behind the human trafficking ring. The strutting brigadier of the Bratva, who Silvio had executed aboard a luxury yacht, and dumped overboard with the rest of his crew.

"We knew the Italian mob was behind the hit," she said. "And there was little we could do about it—no one wanted a war. But *I* wanted to know who the triggerman was. I put out feelers for you. Took me months. I burned through a lot of money in the effort. You're good, Silvio—you kept your head down. But eventually I tracked you. To that apartment in Milan."

Something cold burst in Silvio's chest. He remembered his kitchen window cracking from the mysterious sniper shot. Maria's head blowing apart. The blood gushing over his arms as he cradled her body.

"Your brother deserved to die," Silvio hissed, and he looked directly at Caterina. "You know exactly what to do, don't you?"

His daughter stiffened in the woman's grip. For a moment, Silvio worried that she didn't understand.

But it was only for a moment.

Moving with the speed and efficiency that he'd taught her, Caterina unsheathed the hidden blade from within her wand... a blade Silvio had given her, had trained her with. And as the steel emerged, the fear in her eyes dissipated. The muscles in her face went rigid. She didn't look six years old anymore. In a flash, Silvio glimpsed the woman she'd one day become.

Katya opened her mouth to say something more, but the words were cut off as Caterina whirled about and plunged the knife into her throat.

Several things happened at once.

The Lady Katya recoiled from his daughter, the blade still protruding from her throat. Silvio saw immediately that it wasn't the fatal blow he'd hoped for—Caterina had missed the jugular. Nonetheless, Katya didn't know that. She choked, blood weeping around the hilt.

Her bodyguards were clearly unprepared for this unexpected turn of events; some attempted to help their leader, others stared in shocked fascination. Some reached for their Kalashnikovs. Then a stream of fireworks streaked into them like meteors. Men were hit in the face, chests, and legs; gunpowder flared and exploded in a hellish danse macabre. Silvio looked toward the nearby rooftop to see that Giuseppe had commandeered the evening's entertainment and was aiming firework tubes at Katya's gang. Caterina threw herself to the floor, screaming and covering her face.

The fireworks were followed by the staccato pop of handguns. Salvatore was using one; no longer mixing drinks but firing over the counter at Katya's men. Old Man Matteo wielded the other one, having flipped his table of oysters and unloading with deadly accuracy.

A pair of Russian guards sitting at a nearby table leapt to their feet; Silvio rammed his body into the table, bowling them over. He drew his SIG and killed them both where they lay.

The crowd screamed and scattered. In a blink, Katya stood abandoned. Her bodyguards were wounded or dead around her. The *Phoenix* continued to glide away, its hidden soldiers too far off to realize anything was amiss.

Silvio moved his gunsight a few inches, aiming between Katya's eyes.

If there was one thing he could say for her, it was that she had the feral instincts of a natural-born predator. She saw the danger and, without hesitation, vaulted over the rooftop rails to the salt pools below.

Caterina lay curled on the floor, eyes red and miserable. "Papa!"

"Stay down!" he shouted and rushed to peer over the side of the building. He expected to see his enemy's broken body down there; instead, he was amazed to discover that his enemy had survived her suicidal leap. Katya was limping—she'd clearly broken her leg—yet that wasn't stopping her. The salt pools sloshed as she hobbled toward the *Phoenix*'s retreating silhouette. "*Zhdat!*" she screamed. "*Podozdhi menya!*"

Silvio aimed again at the woman, lining up the fatal shot.

For you, Maria. This is for you, and it's far better than your murderer deserves...

His fingers slackened from the trigger, however, when he heard a bizarre cacophony. It was so strange, so inexplicable, that he lowered the pistol and gazed at the far end of the plaza.

The last time Silvio had been in Venice, Piazza San Marco was its timeless portrait of tourist crowds. Now, it seemed as if he was reliving the past, because there was indeed a crowd surging across it. Men and women, dressed in black robes... and without the bird-masks they'd been forced to wear.

And he saw the awful truth for himself.

The truth he'd gleaned from the detective's photos.

They weren't beta zombies. Even in these postapocalyptic days, the Russian mob had continued its human trafficking. They'd abducted people from the Trade Road and elsewhere. Forced them into slavery. Told the Venetians a lie that no one had bothered questioning.

At the back of the crowd, Anna appeared. She looked triumphant.

Silvio called out to her, "I told you to *look* at the pictures!"

"You told me to *find* where the warehouse was," she countered. "I found it and did something about it!"

The liberated crowd spotted the Lady Katya. They gave chase, a fearsome tide of vengeance closing the distance to her.

Katya saw them coming and went wild in terror. "No!" she shrieked, waving her arms wildly at the departing mega-yacht. "*Podozdhi menya! Pozhaluysta!*"

Then the crowd was on her. They grabbed her, pulled her into their rabid fray. Katya vanished beneath fists and boots. Silvio had witnessed lots of death in his life. Never before had he seen someone literally torn limb from limb.

His group settled into the vaporetto, and he personally took the controls, speeding away from the Venetian pier. Moments later he zipped past the mega-yacht, not interested in boarding her as much as in beating it to the mainland.

To warn the Trade Road that an invasion was coming.

"Papa?" a small voice said behind him.

He glanced back to see his daughter in the cabin doorway. Anna stood with her. In the distance, the lights of Venice dwindled like a dream lost upon awakening.

Caterina Cipriano didn't look like a princess anymore. Her mask was gone, her wand with it. She still wore the little dress he'd gotten her, though now it was blood-spattered, seared and torn.

She looked like a warrior.

"What is it, my gumdrop?" he asked, heart twisting at the lost innocence in her eyes.

She pointed to the mega-yacht they'd already left behind. "Those bad people want to hurt our friends?"

"Yes."

"We're going to stop them."

It was less a question than a statement of fact. He glanced to Giuseppe and Salvatore and Matteo. He stared at Anna, whose decisive action had changed the fate of Venice. He studied the crowd of abductees they'd freed from bondage and were bringing home.

Home, he thought, realizing suddenly that for all his devotion to the Trade Road, he'd never really thought of it as home. He'd begun it through necessity. Organized it for the sake of survival. Maintained it as a way of working through his grief. Yet it *was* home, and homes were to be defended for the sake of everyone and everything you loved.

"Yes," he told his daughter, gazing into a horizon he couldn't see but knew was there. "We're going to stop them together."

Things to Do in Denver When It's Dead

SARAH A. HOYT

Climbing up the once-glimmering glass-fronted building on Seventeenth Street in Denver shouldn't have been a problem. Well, it shouldn't have been a problem any other day.

But the cold, snow-laden wind blowing from the West stung his face and hands and sixteen floors up it howled like something in pain. Next pair of headphones he came across, he was going to grab, because screw that, he didn't want his ears to freeze and fall off. Colton should have listened to the weather report, he thought. And grinned to himself because there were no weather reports, anyway. Not that they had ever been much use. Colorado meteorologists before the Fall had all gone insane. Predict ninety-degree weather, get snowstorm. And vice versa.

"Hey, slow poke," Mike shouted from above him, her voice taunting. "Are you coming?"

He didn't answer. He'd get a mouthful of cold air and not much else. He could only decode Mike's words in retrospect.

And yeah, she was climbing up faster than he could. That was because Mike—Michaela Argyris—was a tiny young woman, maybe five two, and weighed eighty-five pounds soaking wet, with lead in her pockets. So, once the climbing rope was thrown, she could climb up with very little concern that a badly placed foot would crash into the window she balanced against, or cause a cascade of falling glass.

As his foot did just that and caused three of the glass plates in the warped frames to drop straight down, raining glass fragments on Joss and Mira below. Colton heard them yell something, though too far to hear words, and flinched a bit. Maybe he should diet or something. Not that it made much difference when you were six three.

And frankly, Mike was just better at climbing. She'd been better when they were college students and climbing over at Garden of the Gods in the Springs on weekends, and she remained better now that climbing was deadly serious business for the Colorado Reaper Club.

But he thought, as he balanced and climbed up the rope by the force of his well-gloved hands, at least he got a full-on view of Mike's rounded, muscled rear as she scrambled up ahead of him.

As he looked, said rear disappeared through the window to which they'd secured their rope. They'd used a drone to both break the window and secure the rope to frame, but that was a minor refinement that Joss had come up with to climb these glass monsters.

After a while he heard her give a shout. Since it seemed to be glee, not fear, he grinned and hurried up.

By the time he got there, Mike was fleeting around happily. There were desks and computers. Good, even if it was going to be a pure bitch to secure those to send down. But the components would come in handy. There were people, down in the Springs and Monument trying to build server farms, trying to get an Internet backbone back up that could be used by people desperately in need of information on how to rebuild, well, everything, from computers to farms, from raising livestock to growing corn, from how to get oil out of the ground to how to refine it. Yeah, yeah, experts in all this had survived, somewhere. The problem was often getting the expert together with the need.

So, they'd crate these computers with found materials and get them down. Some might be used as was, but mostly—if he understood rightly, and he had a couple of friends doing it—they were breaking the machines down to component parts then building smaller, less energy-hungry computers that would function on battery most of the time since energy was still hit or miss.

Sure, the powerplant in the Springs mostly worked on coal. Getting the right shipments of coal was like getting the right experts. You could get them, just not often in the right place.

The armed services, of which Colorado had a surplus, had tried to restore order and supply lines for the last six months, by sending people out to look for specific things and send them back to specific places. It worked, sort of. Except that it worked a lot like Soviet requisitioning. Someone at the top thought they needed something, sent out exact specifications, and the people looking passed over a lot of things that might have worked, because they wanted that other thing. So, if the computer was not green, they might ignore it rather than take the purple computer.

Not that Colton had ever told the few armed forces searching parties they were being Soviet. For one, he liked to live. For another it wouldn't change anything. It was the way they were set up to work. Requisition and fulfillment, though he's seen some amazing improvisation over the last two years. Eh. Heard about it on the radio. Or rumors around the campfire.

On the other hand, the Reapers made their living from the in-between. Climb these abandoned buildings—the bottom floors were likely to be burned out, destroyed and otherwise hazardous, including increasingly rare appearances of dangerous infected—find whatever could be crated and rope-and-pulleyed down and barter it to the people who needed it. Or to one of a dozen distributors who could get it places across the country.

He was trying to figure out if they could use one of the desks—upside down, and sides protected with the screwed-off tops of other desks—to pack full of computers and rope-and-pulley down, when Michaela gave another whoop of delight. He looked up.

She was fiddling with something she'd found in a desk drawer, and suddenly a voice sounded, loudly, "This is Radio Free Colorado, bringing you things to do in Denver when it's dead. Go to the zoo. Identify the animals by the skeletons." There was the self-conscious laugh of a DJ who thought he was too clever by half, and then, "No, seriously, folks, wherever you are in our beautiful state, I hope you're doing something worth doing. Far as we can tell from our mountain fastness in beautiful Monument, your day is going to get much colder faster, and there might be a few eruptions of zombies, so be prepared."

"Great," Colton said, as the radio broke into a rendition of "Rocky Mountain High," the state's unofficial anthem, "now we can work to music."

Mike laughed. "No, you're missing the point. We're hearing it all the way from Monument. I wonder who has set up a repeater—" She stopped and reached for the little transistor radio, turned it off.

"Wha—?" Colton started.

Mike took her finger to her lips. "Shhh."

Then grabbed Colton and pulled him behind a cube wall in the corner.

Colton still hadn't heard anything, and was about to fight free, when the floor shook. Then there was the sound of footsteps as if heavy men were jogging across the floor.

Mike and Colton exchanged a look, the kind of look that said without words *Are they going to bring the whole thing down?*

Because that was the thing with these buildings: you never knew. You never knew when or where a decisive impact would bring the whole thing crashing down. The bottom floors had been burned, probably multiple times, in the firestorms caused by the infected, they had sustained explosions of cars parked in front of them, and it wouldn't be the first time that one of them went down, suddenly, without provocation. So far none of it had happened near Colton, much less a building they were on, but it was one of the reasons they harvested the contents very carefully and pushed them out the window, lowering them down with extreme care.

Whoever these people were, they had no care. By the sound of it there were two of them, running, and for a moment Colton wondered if they were infected. It was rare to find them in the upper floors. Well, it was rare to find them period, except for a rare beta here and there being looked after by some order or nuns or other, but not the aggressive ones.

It had happened, though. Three months ago, he and Lillian had been going through a building where there should've been no life left, when suddenly an infected came charging out of the dark. Lillian had nailed it with a shot from the Glock she carried, but damn, it had been scary and close.

But just as he thought maybe these were two large infected chasing each other, a voice sounded, "So, they're here? Shouldn't important paintings be in the art museum?" The voice had a marked foreign accent.

"No," another male voice answered. "Here in the building, there's an art shipper tied to an auction house, and there is a portrait from—" The words became fuzzy. Colton looked at Mike, who squeezed his wrist and said, "No."

But Colton was not in the mood to hear that no, and he guessed it showed in his face. He shook his head at her, and then got up, tiptoeing.

The inside of the building, outside the office doors, had the once common structure of a balcony-hallway that allowed a view of escalators. The escalators were burned here and there, and the men must have been carrying a telescopic ladder because it was set up between the floor directly below and this one, where the escalator had collapsed in on itself.

He heard noise of voices from further down the hallway and knit himself to the wall, following it. The door at the end of the hallway was open, and he heard talk coming from there, but before he got close enough to hear words, two men came out at a semi-jog.

He ducked quickly into the recessed entrance to the bathroom. As two men came trotting past, he saw that one of them was a powerfully built maybe fifty-year-old man, and the other a tall, dark Mediterranean type. The second was carrying a maybe three-by-four parcel. "See," he told the other man. "I figure he will pay well for this, and then there's the museums we can go through, though that's dicier. I understand the art museum is unstable, structurally—"

They walked towards the telescopic ladder, climbed down, then must have collapsed it by some mechanism, and he heard them set it up to go down another level.

When he came back, Mike was packing stuff into the desk, her mouth set in a grim line. She didn't say anything, so he didn't either.

Over the last few months they had improvised and learned to arrange for ropes to lower things with. Even quite heavy things. Colton carried the ropes, and they usually arranged them on office furniture or structures, so they could lower loads of salvaged material slowly.

In this case the ropes were wound around two columns,

deflecting enough of the weight, so Colton could lower the desk-loaded-with-computers slowly enough.

Not that there hadn't been mishaps in the past, like the time he'd lost his grip on the rope, and the whole load of paper had dropped on the street, spraying printer paper all around. He'd not heard the end of that one for a while.

Not that paper was a high-return merchandise, but it was needed by practically everyone, and there were no manufacturing processes for it going on anywhere near. He wasn't going to say there wasn't manufacturing going on anywhere in the country, but it wasn't nearby. Part of what they were fighting against was a lack of information.

Computers would bring in more, and he and Mike lowered two desks full of computers and components before they left the building via the rope ladders. They didn't talk. They ignored the next few buildings. The brewery had burned, which was a pity, not just for the finished product, but because some of the equipment might come in handy to someone trying to start up brewing again.

The Reapers had found there were all sorts of opportunities in stuff like that, from restaurant equipment being used to feed large groups of people, to car parts, to other stuff. They'd cleared up the top floor of a bookstore. The bottom had burned and there was nothing of value there, but the top was intact, and was mostly reference books. A broker from Greeley had given them top dollar on it—well, top military script, anyway, which was what most of them were using for trade—and if Colton had understood correctly a lot of that truckload was now being distributed up and down the Eastern Seaboard, both as information and as entertainment, because so much of the printed word had burned.

It wasn't until they had picked up a load of canned goods, from a warehouse distribution point that Joss had found—working with Denver-area phone books—that Colton figured out why the guys retrieving the painting with the intention of selling it, presumably, had bothered him, or the idea that they intended to hit up the museums next.

He was driving the expedition, with Mike riding shotgun, while the other couple drove the truck full of computers. It had started to snow, a fine, powdering of the kind that didn't stick, not yet, but made visibility shit in the darkened streets.

The city looked dead. He and the original Reapers had been going to college in Colorado Springs when the apocalypse had started.

For a long while their lives had consisted of shoot or be eaten, run or be eaten, move, move, move. They'd lost Zed and John, then. They'd zombed out early and had to be killed. Colton still had nightmares about strangling Zed, while Zed chomped, trying to bite him.

The group had started in the beforetime as a climbing club with a spicy-food problem. There had been ten guys and six girls who spent their weekends climbing, and then found out the local restaurants with the hottest food. Both the climbing and the food were uploaded to the Internet, where they'd gathered a bunch of fans for their fun, fast banter during both activities. They'd named themselves Colorado Reapers because Mira had thought it was a hot pepper. She was a bit of a ditz and Colorado and Carolina were obviously the same to her.

Now it seemed more appropriate to the work they did. And the fourteen survivors had been joined by friends, and girlfriends— Joss was living with five women—and moved to Castle Rock to the south of Denver, to an oddly untouched mansion up on one of the ridges, with all approaches clearly visible.

Though they still did most of the reaping—and selling—in Denver or the Springs. Or Monument, where the Air Force had secured the town and setup a sort of trading post that took a lot of things and found someone to distribute them. That's where this load was headed, which made the snow bothersome.

Every little storm became magnified in Monument Pass.

But he wasn't even thinking about the snow. He'd grown up in Colorado, unlike a lot of other Reapers—lucky them, who didn't know what had happened to their families, or not for sure—so driving in blowing snow was automatic.

Instead, he was thinking of all the books that had burned or been destroyed, and of electronic books which might or might not still exist in some database. And then of art. "You know," he said, "I bet in the future this will be like those historical periods when all the books disappeared or burned, or something, and there's only a handful of works left, from which people try to guess what the rest must have been like. Like...like the Library of Alexandria or something."

Mike gave him a dark look. "That was never true. Well, not really. There were many libraries of Alexandria, and many of them burned, but there's no reason to think—"

"Yeah, yeah," he said. "It was just an example."

But Mike was glaring at him, and then it occurred to Colton she'd been unusually quiet all this way. Of course, this occurred to him just as she stopped being quiet and cut loose. The fact that she spoke in a really low voice made everything worse, "Don't you ever," she said. "Do anything like that again."

He was so surprised, he crossed the road, not that it mattered much because there was no traffic coming the other way. There was no traffic practically anywhere.

Partly because fuel was hard to get on a regular basis. A lot of the people that used to live in the city had escaped to more sparsely populated and more defensible places. Though it was suspected that most of the ones in the big cities had died, which made sense. Pretty hard to avoid contagion when you were all packed in and eating at the same restaurants.

Which was why Denver was dead. The Springs had a few more people, at least in the suburbs that had forted up and where someone had been ruthless enough to kill any infected who turned up within the perimeter.

Castle Rock had come through relatively well. The downtown had burned, but the rest of it, all ridges and broken terrain, had seemed to escape much of the problem. Some people who worked in Denver had never made it back, which was why the Reapers had found themselves an abandoned mansion.

But other than that, it was almost back to what it had been. Except that few people drove, commerce took place in military credit notes or outright barter, and there were patrols of citizens down the main streets at night.

They'd pulled the Reapers over, the first time they'd come back to the compound—which they'd just claimed—at night, and asked way too many questions. But in the end they seemed to decide the Reapers were harmless, and that the house they'd taken over was better occupied than not.

"The books," Colton said, confused, after he got the expedition back on track on the bouncy slopes of 85.

"No. Going off where those guys were talking. You didn't know who they were, and the way they were galloping around,

I got this feeling they were as likely to shoot us as not. I sat there, wondering if I'd ever see you again."

He gave Mike a look out of the corner of his eye. A lot of the Reapers were sleeping with each other. And a lot were sleeping with people who had joined in the last few months. They weren't exactly a commune. For one, none of them believed in sharing everything. They might have, once, when they were college students, but now any of them who didn't pull their weight would find him or herself cast out to figure out their own way.

There was no give in the group. There was no lovingkindness. They'd all survived tough times by doing what they had to do. There was probably no one there who hadn't lost someone. He'd lost his parents, and from something Mike said, she was sure she'd lost hers.

The one thing they were like a commune on was . . . well, people slept around. A lot. Partly because they had been through enough in their mid-twenties to know that life was short and the unspeakable could happen at any time. *Carpe diem* and all that. A couple of the original reapers had dropped out to go work for a guy with a cattle farm down near Rocky Ford, because they had a couple of kids, and thought what they did was no way to raise them. And there were other women who were pregnant or had infants. But he and Mike—

He'd had a crush on Mike from the beginning. The curly-haired girl, first generation born in America from Greek parents, was funny and cute, and full of life, but she'd been pretty traditional, and she'd said early on when time came to marry her parents would probably arrange something with someone from Greece.

So, American-mutt-stock Colton had put her out of reach from the beginning. And never revised it. Never taken much interest in anyone else, either. Instead, he'd spent his days planning places they'd hit next, driving out to see if they were solid enough to climb and—

Now he looked at Mike. "You'd have been okay," he said. "They might have shot me but they had no reason to know you were there. You'd have been okay."

"Not if you'd got shot. I'd never have been okay."

She did that thing she did when she grabbed his arm. It was both dorky and super intense, because the way she did it was as if it had all kinds of meanings. "I don't want to lose you, okay? I've lost too many people already."

"Uh. I'm sorry. I didn't know—" He almost said he didn't know she cared, but the fact was he still didn't know. She might just be trying to avoid another tragedy. "It's just, I had a bad feeling about them. And I was right."

He got a silent look and raised eyebrow and he related the conversation to Mike.

She was silent a long time. "Yeah, that bothers me too," she said. "But I'm not even sure why. Not quite, you know?"

"Because," Colton said. "I don't know what they intend to do with it. And . . . it felt wrong. Like. Like . . ." They passed a car headed the other way. The snow had intensified to the point that he wasn't absolutely sure where they were on the road, and sometimes he felt like he was just following the taillights of Joss and Mira's truck. "Look, what if we'd taken that load of books we got, and instead of passing them to a reseller, we'd locked them away somewhere in a basement?"

"Well, they'd be okay in a basement. . . ." Mike said thoughtfully.

"They should be okay. But what if they weren't. What if something happened. It would be like losing part of the past forever."

"My roommate, when . . . you know, in the beforetime. She used to go out and topple statues, because she said they were white supremacy and a sign of the times when women weren't free."

Colton spared her a look, but she was looking ahead, her forehead wrinkled as though in deep thought.

"I don't think it was right. I didn't think it was right then, mind you. I mean if you want to fight for something fight things that can fight back. Statues can't. But more than that, I thought it was stupid to destroy things you couldn't build. I guess—" Mike shrugged. "Hey, she was one of the first to zomb out and I bashed her head in with a piece of a chair, before running out and finding you guys."

"Yeah," Colton said. "But I think that's it. Something like it. It . . . it doesn't seem right. I got a feeling—I know it makes no sense— that these people are getting art from various places and taking it somewhere, perhaps Europe and . . ." He shrugged. "If we're going to rebuild, we should have that stuff here, where people can see it in the future. You know. All the kids being born now."

"Cultural patrimony," Mike said. "My dad used to talk about a lot of that, in Greece and how it had got destroyed with invasions and stuff. I wonder if any of that is left?"

After that he had to concentrate on the drive, and then, when they got to Monument, and emptied the trucks, and got their scrip, it was time to rush back, to grab some food at the house.

The house had started out massive. Ten bedrooms with en suite. But it housed even more people, as people had staked out corners of the great room and there was a family living in the solarium.

They all put money in the pot for the food, and took turns on a strict rotation, cooking and doing dishes.

There was dinner being held for them when they came in, and the others listened to both the finds and the amount they'd received, and some guys sat in the corner, mapping out the next few hits.

Joss and Mira grabbed bowls of pasta with meat sauce—that night's fare—and sat across from them. "It still feels a bit like robbing graves. I was an anthropology major, you know, and we used to talk about how much more we'd know if over time it hadn't all been robbed and the graves despoiled."

"They're not graves," Joss said. One of his girlfriends came and sat next to him, as he spoke. "And besides, we can use the stuff."

"Yeah, well, the Egyptian robbers probably could use it more than the dead pharaohs too," Mira said. She took her empty bowl, gave either a disgusted or resentful look at Joss—Colton was never sure if she was interested in Joss or just annoyed by him—and wandered off. She and Joss had been an item in the beforetime, but they didn't seem that close now.

Mike plucked at Colton's sleeve. "It's not the slightest bit like robbing graves," she said. "It's more like what happened after the Black Plague in Europe when suddenly there was a need to find new owners for things that would otherwise decay and become of no value to anyone. I mean, probably a bunch of livestock died because no one took them over, and we know a lot of farms returned to forest. But what people could find, and use, propelled the largest expansion in wealth and lead to the greatest scientific knowledge and population explosion our kind has seen."

Colton looked at her for a while. "You were majoring in history?" He felt like he'd known her major once upon a time, but it seemed like it had been another life altogether, and anyway they'd been too busy climbing rocks and trying out new restaurants.

She laughed. "No, economics. But I like history."

He nodded. "So, you don't think we're hurting anything?"

"Uh. No. There are things that lost value precipitously overnight. I mean, I hear that most of the cars they hauled off from the highways were probably junked by the time anyone got to them. And that was the ones where the owners hadn't rotted in there. But—" She shrugged. "You know, a lot of the houses will lose value. That's why no one minded we claimed this place. It's better for it to be lived in, even above occupancy, because we keep it heated and cooled, even if it's heated with kerosene sometime, and we'll fix it if it needs fixing. Modern houses aren't built to be unlived in for long times. Some of them are already collapsing. Burst pipes in the walls, the roof gets a leak, and next thing you know, it's all back to nature."

"I remember there was some kind of program about how long it took. Never watched it."

"Me neither, but it's obvious. Even the roads are becoming all ruts. We're in a harsh climate, you know? And most of the stuff we take will be lost when those buildings collapse. The structures are unstable already and will get more so over a few cycles of freezing and thawing. The cities will pretty much disappear in a few decades. What we're saving is stuff that we don't need to produce."

Colton frowned. "Shouldn't we produce it, though? Make our own stuff?"

She sighed. "What, from some kind of moral point of view? Why? We have a surplus of most things, except one: labor. There aren't enough people left, and there isn't enough to restore worldwide commerce. And a lot of things need it. Well, for now. Things like paper we can make, but there isn't a pipeline for wood pulp and spending fuel to carry it will make it short elsewhere."

"The frackers in Weld County are hiring," Colton said. "Joss keeps talking about going and working out there."

"Joss talks a lot of talk," Mike said. "But he doesn't have enough interest in life to do it. Here's the thing... the things we need, and we need to make anew, are the consumables. Food, fuel. Not even because we don't have enough food—there's probably enough canned to keep the entire population alive for a year or two, even if we didn't grow anything—but because in the long run we have to keep the farmer animals alive. And we have to know how to grow food and keep the fields going. And we need fuel. We need a lot of fuel. Modern civilization runs on fuel, and if we want to live like we used to, we need energy."

"Yeah, renewables aren't gonna make it," Colton said. "They told us they would, but it was obvious even then..."

"Right. Most of the wind farms are stopped and broken. So, food, fuel. Clothes? Parts? Computers? Hell, we have all that. Which is where we come through. We're gleaners. That's what they used to call the people who went through harvested fields and picked what had been left behind. Because if we don't pick it, it will go to waste."

"Like art. And books."

She looked at him and frowned but didn't say anything.

And he went to bed, still not sure what bothered him. He had a room for himself, in the basement, which must have been one of the kids' rooms, because it was small, with a single bed.

He'd grabbed the little battery radio that Mike had found in the first office. He turned it on, very low, in the dark room.

"Radio Free Colorado rocks you through the night," a female voice said. "Whatever you did today, we hope it leads to restoring a better life for everyone around you."

The people running this must have come of age in the nineties, because they plunged into a selection of music that had since become the fodder of easy listening. Other than their obsession with John Denver—which was a thing of post-Fall Colorado—it was all Green Day and Spice Girls, and other blasts from the past in eclectic profusion that told him they were running whatever they could find.

Whatever they could find.

He woke with Mike pounding on his door. Only he didn't know it was Mike, of course, and only found out once he'd rasped, "What?" and she answered, "Mike. I wanna talk."

He'd looked at the window high up on the north wall, through which streaky thin light shone, then pulled the sheets up and bunched them on his lap, because he wasn't sure what she'd do if confronted with a morning glory. "Yeah, come in."

She came in in sweats, her curls adorably mussed, and he thought she'd come straight from bed, which did not make things easier at all. "Yeah?" he said, as she sat on the edge of his bed.

"I was thinking about what you said. About something being wrong. And I think something is, though not...perhaps? With what those people were doing?"

He ran his hand across his face. "What?"

"The people who picked up the painting. You thought there was something they were doing wrong. And mind you, I think there was. I mean, they were running in a building that might fall at any minute. I don't think they're the sanest or most careful people around, but what they're doing isn't wrong. Not that."

"What?" he said again, furious at himself that he couldn't find a better way to express himself. But the thing was, he was tired, and none of it made sense, not really.

She grinned. "Hold on." And left. He realized she was barefoot, and she walked with a little wiggle, and no one had the right to look that good in baggy gray sweats. But there it was.

She came back, with a smell of coffee, and handed him a big mug. "Black, with sugar," she said. "Like you take it."

Which was true. He sipped at it.

"So you know what Mira said, yesterday, about all the stuff we don't have? Like . . ."

"The Library of Alexandria," Colton said, and in the next minute realized that wasn't right and could have kicked himself.

Mike laughed. "No, it was you who said that. But right. The library burned several times, and even if we probably have copies of most of the stuff in it, there were probably things we don't have copies of. But more what Mira was saying. Grave robbers robbed the graves, but . . . but they went down into a long time of darkness and ignorance, so things weren't kept, and we only have a fraction of the knowledge lost then."

"Like the books," he said.

"Right, and the art. And you know . . . it hit me. It's not that they're doing something wrong. It's that we are."

"Uh? You said—"

"Oh, not the stuff we take," she said. "The stuff we leave behind. It occurs to me that there's art, in abandoned mansions in Denver. All of it can't have burned. And there's books. And there's stuff that will be lost forever, as the city gets eaten by the wilderness. And it will be."

He shuddered. "Maybe not. I mean, the military and . . . and people from government are talking of rebuilding and—"

"Oh, the military will try," Mike said. "But they can't do everything. Their primary need is to restore their own ranks and make sure they can defend us, and . . . and lend what aid they can to people who are in real trouble. Then there is that republic thing."

"Uh?"

"They're supposed to defend and uphold the republic according to the Constitution which guarantees everyone in the territory of the United States a republican form of government. I've heard stories, and you have too. I don't know how long we are from those elections they keep promising us, but I know that there are places in this country right now that are fiefdoms and tyrannies. And the military has to deal with those first. I heard there are slave auctions in New York, and even if that's not true, I bet you there's slave auctions somewhere. Even if the slaves are just beta females that someone wants to use for the sex trade." She shuddered. "The military is dealing with all that and restoring communication. Which means restoring power, which means restoring energy supplies, and they have to coordinate all that. Do you really expect them to go house to house and door to door, and get all works of art, and all books?"

Colton finished his coffee. Slowly, his brain was coming together like a puzzle, and he was trying to follow Mike's silvery intellectual trails in the fog-benumbed darkness of his brain. "Do you mean that we need to? Do you want to leave the Reapers?"

He felt a vague surge of alarm, but his heart thumped wildly. If she wanted to leave the Reapers and undertake doing something just with him, surely that meant that—

"Nah," she laughed. Then her face became grave. "Well, not yet. I want to start doing something about those books and paintings in our free days. Like today."

He nodded. "Right. Give me half an hour." He stopped, half out of bed, conscious that he probably looked obscene in his underwear. Or at least he became conscious of it, when he saw her blush. But she looked up at his eyes and grinned. "Hey, I need to get dressed too."

"We're going to need to pay for fuel," he said.

They'd paid for fuel from their store of scrip. They'd taken a map of Denver, though it was still easy to get utterly lost because so many buildings had burned to nothing and so many were lost.

They'd tried to find the homes of the richest people in the area, on the assumption they'd have art. After three of the intact mansions had been gone through, they regrouped, sitting in the truck.

"Nothing," he said.

"Well, those funny woven things were probably considered art," she said. "The problem is that I don't know much about art to know what will be considered art, now or in the future."

"Don't ask me," Colton said. "I was in mechanical engineering." He sighed. "And it's not what we're after, is it? Things that might be considered art, maybe?"

This time, it was Mike who looked like he'd left her completely behind. She frowned at him. "Uh?"

"Well, it's not, you know, art. Not real art. Collectors might have paid a great price for this funny woven cloth, and some professors might have said a bunch of things about how great and innovative it was, but does that really matter? Will our kids or grandkids think it's great?" He started digging through the glove compartment until he found a bag of candy he'd stowed there when they'd cleaned out a food warehouse. "Take this candy. It's perhaps a little stale." He opened the bag and grabbed a mini-Snickers, one that had probably been headed to the stores for Halloween before the zombies. "But it's edible, and we can eat it and appreciate it."

She dug in, and grabbed a peanut butter cup, which she unwrapped carefully. Like it was a precious and rare pleasure. Which it was these days.

"Imagine, though, that instead we'd found a gourmet food store, one of those weird ones that sprouted in places like New York City and they had...I don't know...candy-coated rhinoceros poop."

"No one coated rhinoceros poop in candy," Mike protested, laughing.

"Maybe not, but I heard of things that were almost that weird, and so did you. And I often heard of it when people who had a ton more money than I even ever dreamed of talked about how amazing it was. But if we found it now, without all the hype, do you think it would be amazing?"

She took little bites of the chocolate peanut butter cup and sighed. "My dad used to say that art had gone to hell when it started needing a card with an explanation to know it was art."

"That," he said. "Your dad had it exactly right."

"He did about a lot of things," she said. "So, what you're saying is that we should get art, real art. Like the older stuff, and stuff that's obviously art? Not funny woven bits of cloth. But neither of us know anything about art. What if what we pick are bad reproductions?"

He laughed. "Well, I don't know. I know that what we have now might very well have been the dogs playing poker of Classical Greece. But it survived, and it was better than anything that came after." He made a face. "I grant you it would help if we could find a good book on art. But you know what's more important? Finding things people will buy and want. Because the more art that's out there and sold, the more chance that some of it will survive."

She looked at him a long while, and it pulled some sense from him, some need to explain. "Look, I think we're going to go through very tough times. Maybe half a century of tough times, maybe more. When it's done, a lot will be lost. Let's save what we can." He looked at her face, starkly beautiful and reminiscent of Greek sculpture. She had a face like a thousand caryatids holding up the ancient temples of civilization. "People will need beauty to survive," he said.

"Yeah," she said. "Yeah."

They went back. They went to a few more houses, then decided to risk the Denver Art Museum.

It was . . . falling apart. He had some memory of having read a lot of blather about it, in the time before the zombies. It was a modern building, and the architecture was all sorts of innovative.

He had a vague memory—all memories before the Fall were now vague, like a dream from long, long ago—of having gone there once with some girl whose name he no longer remembered, and who had probably died in the great zombing. He remembered walking up a glimmering staircase with strategically placed lights.

Now . . . well, the entire entrance area was filled with dirt and ashes and shits. There was someone in what looked like the remnants of a uniform rotting in a corner. Mike slipped her hand into his and clung near him. Neither of them went near the human remains, or the other piles of stuff that might also be human remains. Things scrambled in the piles of refuse, either mice or squirrels or whatever, and Colton didn't want to know which. His hand came to rest on the Glock strapped at his side.

The Reapers mostly packed Glocks which were light and convenient when climbing buildings the wrong way, but also because they were easy to find at every single—now abandoned—police station, as was the 9mm ammo, found in bunches and handfuls everywhere including at the sports and fishing stores that had long since been forgotten and were falling to ruin.

He'd not fired a gun before the Fall except once, for Joss's birthday, when they'd gone to some outdoor range, and notably failed to hit the target.

But after the first shock of the zombies and the attacks, Mira had said, "You know how you can't hug every cat? You can't strangle every zombie. Sooner or later one of them is going to get a bite in when you're doing close-in work."

So, someone, he no longer remembered who, had said they should go to the police stations and get guns, and then they'd practiced.

Until the last six months, all their—ah, what had Mike called it?—gleaning work in the ruins of civilization had involved shooting an infected before it could get you. And they'd got pretty good at it.

Colton put his arm around Mike and pulled her close, as they walked up the staircase, picking the part with fewest debris. His free hand rested on the Glock. He had a strong feeling that the Colton from before the Fall would have been shocked as hell at him. He remembered his mother saying she'd never enter a place where people had a gun. And his dad had said that one of the advantages of civilization was that a man didn't need to be armed.

Well, Dad might have been right at that, though Colton had an inkling of a suspicion that he wasn't. That even before the Fall, guns were just as they were now, just a way to defend yourself. And if you could defend yourself, you were more likely to survive whatever came your way. A zombie apocalypse, for example.

He was thinking about it, which was good, because when the infected came running from the dark area above them, headed for them, teeth clacking, he pulled and shot without thinking. Mike's shot echoed his, and the infected's head exploded all over the hallway.

"Damn," he said. "What has it been living on?"

Mike grimaced and gestured at the piles around. "All this."

They proceeded twice as cautiously, but other than a corner

that the infected must have colonized, a mess of soft furnishings and blankets not even a coherent nest as betas were supposed to build, the upper floor was clear of infected and debris. There was what looked like a human skeleton in a corner, but for all Colton knew it might have been some weird art installation.

They walked through the area where he vaguely remembered there used to be installations, including one that looked like the twisted remains of someone's kitchen drawer, with a plaque that called it something like "Drudgery" and talked about how it represented female domestic slavery.

"This way," Mike said. She'd got her flashlight out and lit a plaque that said "Western Art."

The gallery was untouched. Someone had managed to close it off before it could be fouled by the infected.

They walked, like kids at an art show, from a painting of a cowboy on a horse, to paintings of wild prairie, to paintings of men who'd conquered the West, or Native Americans in barbaric finery.

"This is us," Mike said.

"Uh, not noticeably."

"No, think about it. They faced an untamed land and they had to fight like hell, sometimes against each other, to make it civilized and plentiful for the people who came after."

"Oh," he said.

They took the Western gallery first. Mike had found some kind of packing paper in one of the back rooms. Cushiony stuff. They'd wrapped the pieces reverently and taken them out with a dolly.

"Where do we take them?" he said, as they headed out of dead Denver, listening to Radio Free Colorado play "Unwell" by Matchbox 20.

"Let's see if the military wants them," she said. "Let's go to Monument and see if anyone bites. All except one. That one of the guy on the horse, with the untamed West all around. We're going to keep that for our living room, eventually."

And he was so shocked she'd said our living room that he buzzed with happiness all the way to Monument.

Weirdly, no one gave them guff over taking the art, and no one told them that this was already owned by the people of Colorado. They'd been prepared to defend their actions, to explain that they were trying to save things before "nature" brown and black in mold and mildew ate them.

Instead, they were thanked for having rescued the paintings, given a finder's fee—not of course what the paintings were worth in the time before the Fall, but a very nice fee that would keep them in food for many years—if they chose not to glean anymore.

Then the guy in charge had taken them to one of their experts. "Because Tommy here can tell you what we'd like you to rescue."

Tommy, who looked fifty or sixty, a suave, gray-haired man, whose face bore marks of grief and tiredness, and who wore a uniform with markings that meant nothing to Colton or Mike, had sat with them at a table, offered them coffee, and said, "I thought most places in Denver were still too dangerous to go to. Not infected, though I hear there are some still around, but—"

"Yeah. There are, other people trying to get things," Mike said.

"And I hear the buildings aren't safe," he said. "Mostly that."

Colton shrugged. "No, sir, they're not. Which is why we've gone in and tried to save what we could. We figured the armed forces couldn't do it all. And I know there's been talk of the government—"

The man made a face at the mention of government. "Yeah," he said. "If we're lucky we maybe might have an election again before I die. I'm almost afraid of what kind of politician will come out of these times." He sighed. "But the two of you, why art?"

So they'd explained. All about the guy with the German accent and the other guy, and how it had seemed really wrong, until they realized that everything might be lost if the buildings collapsed, or another firestorm swept the area.

He'd choked on sudden laughter when they explained the rhinoceros-poop-covered-in-chocolate theory of art.

And then he'd sat with them and a map of Denver and circled the places they might expect to find things worth saving.

"Get what you can out of there before it all goes down. And we'll pay you. You're risking your lives. You should be paid."

That night, Mike had come to his bed, as though it were the most natural thing in the world. As if they'd been living together and making love for all the time since they'd first met.

Their first coupling was like predestined eternity, like they'd been lovers forever and would be lovers forever. And even though Colton was a geek with nearly no experience, and Mike told him he was her first, there had been no awkwardness, no embarrassment.

In the morning, Mike brought him coffee and said, "We're

going to have to leave the Reapers, if we are going to make this art salvage thing a go."

"Yeah, I'd figured that out sometime in the night," he said, and then stopped because it was a pretty uncouth thing to say and she might be offended.

But she laughed. "And now I know what you think about during sex." She kissed him, her mouth sweet and tasting of coffee. "Next time I'll have to make sure you can't even think."

Hours later, they were driving back to Denver. They'd bought an old blue Expedition off the Reapers. It had enough room for a lot of art in the back, and a tendency to just keep on trucking, no matter what got in its way.

Mike had, solemnly, painted on the door DOGS PLAYING POKER ART SALVAGE.

But that wasn't what they got. Of course it wasn't.

They collected art from museums and private homes: pictures of women in beautiful gowns, of rugged men sitting atop horses, and beautifully groomed men in dinner jackets. Books too, when they found them. Those went to the distributors who were always hungry for fiction and nonfiction.

Along the way they found a house, behind the old botanic gardens now wild and overgrown, the fountains silenced, the statues verdigrised.

"I thought we would end up settling in a farm or something," Colton said, as they walked hand in hand through the home which was inexplicably—or perhaps explicably—pristine. Perhaps explicably because it had been surrounded by a wrought iron fence that turned out to be electrified. Which had probably been illegal in Denver before the Fall. And also probably needed to keep the feral homeless—almost as bad as the infected—out.

"Later, we can take down the wall to the botanic gardens, and we'll have a spread. They even have vegetable gardens in there somewhere." She squeezed his hand. "Remember how I told you this was like the wild, untamed West? The city is too. It's mostly empty, and someone should recolonize, and save what we can. Eventually people will want cities again, and to see the things that were important. Not the downtown, and all the skyscrapers. I don't think they'll hold. But these old mansions are part of history, part of the gold rush and all that, and we should keep all of them we can going. Maybe get some people, over time, to take the others around here."

They'd set up there, behind the electrical fence, and fanned out.

They ran into the art salvagers with the German accent only once more, in the Denver Museum of Nature and Science, where Tommy told them there were some carved Russian gems and other gems worth preserving.

They'd taken the gem carvings and come back for the preserved butterflies and insects under glass. Not because they were art, but because it might be many years, perhaps a century, before people gathered such a collection again, and because frankly Mike thought they'd look good on their new bedroom walls.

They were in the semi-darkened niche, methodically removing the cases from the wall, or the insects from cages, when they heard the same running feet they'd heard before.

"Are you sure this is worth our time?" the German accented voice said.

"Yes," the darker man answered. "I hear they have some Egyptian mummies. No one is going to Egypt for a long time. My people in Italy will give us good money for them."

Mike and Colton stayed very quiet, in their corner, in the dark, while the men went back and forth, with loaded dollies and platforms.

"Now," the German guy said. "We'll go to the art museum. I hear they have some very fine Western paintings."

Mike saluted silently as they left. She looked very cute, in a tight little T-shirt that showed off the baby bump. Colton was going to have to talk to some of the people in Monument about obstetrics. He heard there was a bit of a baby boom, and the armed services baby catchers were all subsisting on two hours of sleep and pulling babies out and slapping baby bottoms around the clock.

Except he didn't even know if it was true that anyone slapped baby bottoms when they were born, and whether they were—as Mike said—new pioneers or not, he had no intention of delivering their kids. He'd read enough of history and even Western books now to know that a lot of those births ended with Mommy or baby or both under a slab. And he was not willing to lose Mike or their kid.

When they left there with the stuff for the guys in Monument, and the stuff they intended to keep—mostly the insects and some trilobites and ammonites—Mike drove. She didn't take the normal route back, but instead plunged into the narrow little labyrinth of streets, radiating from Colfax. These were mostly working-man Victorians, though by the early twenty-first century they'd come to be worth close to a million each, as the city gentrified, cleaned up and became very refined indeed—and sold out to the Californians. Colton remembered a bumper sticker: *Don't Californicate Colorado*. He felt an almost unbearable loss, a longing for those days. Even Californians were better than infected.

"Where are we going?" he asked.

"To a place I haven't had the courage to go for a long time."

They parked, and she held his hand as she guided him up a dozen steps to a garden raised from the street. It must once have had a very nice garden, because early in spring, it showed a profusion of bulbs in every flower bed, and what must have been a very nice handkerchief-sized lawn, even if it was now completely overtaken by dandelions.

The front door was locked, though it opened relatively easily, and the inside was remarkably clean, if covered in an inch of dust. The walls had paintings that were obviously reproductions of classical works representing Greek gods. The furniture was good and old-fashioned. There were black splatter stains on the kitchen cabinets, and a huge dark stain in front of the cold, abandoned fireplace.

And Mike's eyes held all the sorrow of the zombie apocalypse, all the sadness of the collapse of civilization under a virus that made people mindless, destructive animals.

She looked out the window at the overgrown garden in the back.

When she spoke, her voice was low and raspy. "When I had beaten the brains out of the roommate, I was surprised to find it did in fact have some. I didn't go in search of the Reapers. Not right away. I came here. I came home to Mom and Dad."

Colton put his hand on her shoulder then, but she didn't turn around. "I found them dead, you know? The story was easy to figure out. Mom zombed, and Dad beheaded her by the fireplace. Then he blew his brains out in the kitchen. Mom had been sick with that flu thing. She caught it after traveling to Greece. Those bathroom air fresheners." Mike sighed. "I dug a grave out back and dragged them out and put them in together. I haven't dared come back here since. First, because it was too dangerous to come out, with all the zombies, unless there was a group of us, and I didn't want to bring a group here. And then because I was afraid to find that the place had been torched, their graves desecrated."

They opened the back door, and Mike found the graves. "I planted the rose," she said. He nodded and wondered if she realized there were tears falling down her cheeks. She didn't seem to react to them or try to clean them off. "They came here in the mid-nineties, you know? Dad was hired by an engineering firm, and they moved to Denver, where we had some kind of cousins. They loved it here. Dad always said that like Greece was the finest flourishing of ancient civilization, America was the pinnacle of the Western civilization."

"We'll be again," Colton said. "We'll be again." And he kissed away the cold tears on her warm cheeks.

She smiled wanly as she led him back in the house and led him by the hand to the basement. "Let me show you why I named our salvage operations what I did."

Down in the basement there was what had obviously been a man cave, or perhaps a rec room.

There was a huge television, which didn't matter much, since electricity and broadcasts were both sporadic. But he could imagine Mike's father sitting there and watching sports.

There was a billiards table. And on the wall there were two things: a picture of Elvis on velvet and a giant, gold-framed picture of dogs playing poker.

Mike turned to him, laughing through her tears. "He said if he could find a picture of a big-eyed crying toddler, he'd put it down here too."

"We'll keep this place," Colton said. "We'll keep the house from getting hurt in storms. We'll check in on it. We'll keep the roses over the grave out back. We'll tell the children about them."

And then she'd leaned on his shoulder and cried. She cried for all they'd lost. And perhaps, just a little, she cried with joy for their future together.

Later, in the car, he told her about his parents, dead from a zombie attack and torn to pieces in their car, as they'd been trying to load it to escape the city. "I know how you feel," he told her. "I too never got to say goodbye."

The carved gems brought them much scrip, and since they were helping the armed forces to "preserve the cultural patrimony of these United States" while remaining civilians, they were given access to the food supplies the armed forces were starting to organize. The Air Force had this thing they called "Farmer Flights" where they were mapping who was growing what, and matching farmers to places that needed tending and had no one to take them. Colorado ranches were coming back, and cowboys . . . well, mostly fed the cows, but it was something.

It was the Air Force that had figured out, somehow, that Joss came from a farming family in Texas, and after he and Mira married in a ceremony for which all the—admittedly bewildered—Reapers got together once more, Joss and Mira had headed out to run a dairy ranch in the flatter portion of the state.

The DJs from Radio Free Colorado—Steve and Melissa Green—had come out for the ceremony, as celebrity guests, and Rocky Mountain Suite had played as the bride and groom left in an old truck for their new destiny.

A couple of the other Reapers moved in to deserted mansions near the Botanic Gardens. Over time, their work morphed from mere gleaning to keeping the places around them livable, and to making Denver what it had once been, a crossroads of commerce and culture.

Andreas Argyris Johnson made his entry into the world at a makeshift medical center in Monument, Colorado. Named for his maternal grandfather, he entered into the land his grandparents had loved, and the wild untamed frontier it had become once more.

Colton and Mike hung the picture of dogs playing poker in his bedroom and told him, often, about the wealth and luxury that used to be that allowed people to make and collect whimsical art like that and reproduce it by the thousands.

Because they wanted him to know that Western civilization had been a thing of wild beauty and unbelievable abundance.

And would be again.

For the Triumph of Evil

JAMIE IBSON

When they turned into the farmhouse, Avery Todd's heart sank.

Two bushels of corn, *maybe*, lay heaped in the dirt outside the home. They hadn't been shucked; they'd barely been trimmed of their stalks. Not nearly enough.

"Fink, take Charlie team around back."

His second-in-command did so, and they faded into the tree line that defined the homestead's front yard. Todd went to the front door and knocked on it sharply, three times.

"*It's all out front in th'dooryard*," a man's voice shouted.

"No, it isn't, and you know it, John," Todd replied. He stepped back down off the porch. "You've got better than five acres here, all prime farmland. You and I surveyed it a month ago. Even by hand, you had fifty bushels, and we were taking five."

The door slammed open and John Hudson, a skinny, red-faced man in tattered plaid and jeans, stormed out. "Yeah? That was before bandits from La Belle Province came and stole half in the night. Where were you then, *militia*?" The man's voice dripped with venom. "We hid in the crawlspace, had to listen to them as they eyeballed the laundry on the line, and joked about what they'd do to Hazel. What they'd make me *watch* them do to her."

Todd sighed. "I know ammunition's scarce, John, but—"

117

"But nothing!" he shouted. "It was all we could do to keep the babies quiet. Two bushels! That's all. More than you thieves deserve, running a protection racket like this."

A woman emerged from the house, an infant cradled in one arm and a toddler holding her other hand. "John, getting mad at them isn't going to help. They didn't steal the corn—"

"What does it look like they're doing right now?" he snapped.

Fink came around the corner. "There's more out back, Sarge. A lot more."

Todd shot Hudson a glare and followed his second around behind the house. Old plastic rain barrels had been tucked under a threadbare tarp. He counted twenty-three barrels, and ears of corn stuck out the top of each one. One barrel generally held three bushels of corn, more or less.

"This looks like a helluva lot more than just twenty bushels, John," Avery called. "You lying to me?"

The back door burst open, and John stormed out holding a Remington 870. He pumped the action and pointed it at Fink. "You had to go snooping, didn't you? Get off my property, thief."

Finkenzeller raised his hands. Todd swore and brought his rifle up, but Hudson was on the far side of his second, and he didn't have a shot. He'd gotten complacent, and now someone was going to die.

"This isn't helping anyone, John. Lower the gun."

"Not until you thugs are off my property!"

"Everyone, back off. John, we'll just take what's out front and go—"

"No, you won't," the man snarled. "You had your chance." He descended the steps from the back porch and cross-checked Fink in the chest with the shotgun. Craig Finkenzeller was a tall man who'd been doing this long enough to know why no one had lit the homesteader up yet. Fink let the cross-check knock him over backward; Hudson lowered the shotgun barrel, and realized his error too late.

The recoil on the C7 rifle was light, and adrenaline meant Todd barely felt the kick. He stroked the trigger twice—*tak tak!*—and Hudson's chest blossomed red. Other members of One-Three-Charlie fired, and the man collapsed under the fusillade.

As abruptly as the gunfire started, it was over. The gunshots rang in Todd's ear—his tinnitus was getting worse—but worse than the ringing was Hazel Hudson's shrieks.

She rushed out of the farmhouse to her husband's side with nothing but a wordless wail. Todd kept his rifle at the low ready, but the danger wasn't past. "McCain! Get that shotgun clear!"

"Sarg'nt!" he acknowledged, and the young rifleman moved up and pulled the shotgun clear. Hazel ignored him completely, and from within the farmhouse, a baby started to cry.

"Fink, you all right?"

"Yeah." The junior NCO got to his feet. He knelt next to the homesteader and reached to feel for a pulse, but Hazel slapped his hand away.

"You've done enough already, bastard," she hissed. "I suppose you'll moralize to me about defending yourselves next? So was he!"

"Sarge?" McCain said. "Gun was unloaded."

"'Course it was unloaded!" Hazel snapped. "He used the last of our shells scaring off those bandits what came raiding a few weeks back. They's the bastards what came back again and stole *your* thievin' share of the crop. S'not our fault you assholes suck at your job! Get the fuck off my property. Don't ever come back."

Fink looked to Todd in confirmation. He nodded. Without a word, the section moved back to the front yard and down the lane to the road. "Hey, uh, Sarge?" Brooke Pelletier said. "We leaving the corn?"

"Yeah, Brooke. We're leaving it," Todd replied. Pelletier and her fireteam partner kept an eye on the house as the rest of the section left the property, then fell back to join them. Todd made it all the way out to the road before he sank to his knees and vomited.

The roar of the falls hid his section's footsteps as they headed for the barracks—what had once been the visitor's museum. Todd leaned on the railing and watched the St. John River churn and foam below the dam that kept an ever-shrinking portion of Grand Falls and the surrounding area powered. Parts were scarce, mostly cannibalized from a smaller station downriver, and one day something vital would break. Until then, Grand Falls' command post was as close to their generating station as they could manage.

"Stu's ready for us, A-T," Finkenzeller said.

Todd leaned back from the railing and let out a deep breath he'd been holding. He unloaded his rifle's magazine, ejected the chambered round, caught it midair, and replaced it at the top of the magazine. He locked the bolt back and stuffed the magazine in a pouch. No loaded weapons allowed in the command post, Superintendent's orders. The old tourist info center, now a command post for the militia, looked directly at the falls that gave the town its name and inside, Inspector Kris Stuart waited for them. The info center had once had a pool-table-sized 3D map of the area, to show tourists how the Grand Falls hydroelectric dam operated. Now it was their deployment map.

"Sergeant Todd, how very good of you to join us," he said. Stuart oozed smarm. He was the only member of the platoon who'd managed to keep himself freshly shaven, per regulations, and treated himself to a trip to the barber at least once a week. He was one of those political animals that would suck ass to the higher ups and insult you to your face. He'd smile when he did and took great offense whenever someone called him on it. Maybe Todd's platoon was unusually rebellious, but it seemed Stuart spent half his time sucking up to Superintendent Reynolds, and the other half having a tantrum because one troop or another had called him out on his crap.

Other than Todd's troops, Stuart was the only one in the ops center. The regular staff had evidently found somewhere else to be, as they often did whenever he was around. "I'd hoped to catch the afternoon wagon south, Sergeant, but missed it on account of needing to meet with you."

"Sorry to be an inconvenience," Todd said. "It's a six-and-a-half-hour hike from Sisson Ridge, sir."

"I know how far it is to Sisson Ridge, Sergeant, but you'd just had a UIS. You had horses, did you not?"

"UIS, sir? Is that some new TLA I'm not familiar with?"

"TLA?" Stuart replied. "What's a TLA?"

"Three letter acronym."

"Oh. Oh, I see. Yes, very, um, clever. I'm surprised you don't know the proper terminology, Sergeant, you really ought to keep up on reporting standards better. A UIS is an uninfected-involved shooting. As you know, ever since the CAF came under civil control, it's not just kicking doors and grenading the room anymore. Any time you shoot someone not affected by the H7D3 virus, you need to report in immediately, by radio preferably, on foot ASAP if not."

"Understood, Inspector. The batteries on the handhelds aren't holding a charge like they did, and these longer-distance patrols you've been sending us on mean the charge is gone by the time we're coming back in. We had horses, yes, but they're draft horses pulling wagons laden with the harvest tax. They lack saddles, reins, and everything else necessary to ride them. Never mind the wagon needs both of them to pull it, can't be done with just one."

Stuart rolled his eyes. "Excuses. Not impressed, Sergeant. Now, explain to me why you and your troops shot an unarmed man?"

Todd clenched his jaw until the fury passed and narrowed his eyes tight. In short, clipped phrases, he explained what had gone wrong at the Hudson homestead.

"Unacceptable, Sergeant. You let some country bumpkin get the drop on your men, and couldn't even tell if the rifle was loaded?"

"Riley?" Todd called.

"Sergeant!" the corporal responded and handed over the pump-action twelve-gauge. Todd pumped the action aggressively and lowered the barrel.

"Can you tell? *Sir*?"

"Excuse me?"

"You're a trained cop, you guys get way more time with shot-guns than a mere infanteer. Is this shotgun—and it's a shotgun, sir, not a rifle—loaded? Or no? If you're convinced it's unloaded, just say the word and I'll pull the trigger and prove you right or wrong. Better be sure, though."

"Sergeant Todd, put that rifle on the ground this instant."

Todd glared at him, then shrugged his shoulder to let his C7 slip free, and he let the rifle clatter to the floor.

"You know what I mean!"

"Loaded or unloaded, sir? Fifty-fifty. Make the call."

Stuart glanced around the command center and realized, perhaps for the first time, that he really was alone in there with Todd's team. "Unloaded!" he blurted.

Todd shook his head, hit the bar release, and pumped the action. A red-hulled twelve-gauge buckshot shell flew clear and clattered to the ground. "Wrong. Boom, Fink's dead."

He laid the shotgun on the map of the area, barrel pointed safely out the window. "My section is done for the week, sir. The wagon's been dropped off at the old Walmart and we are heading home. See you next Tuesday."

Todd scooped up his C7 from where it had fallen and left without looking back.

His troops fell in behind him, and once they were clear of the parking lot, Todd stopped and faced them. "Bring it in, guys." He looked over their shoulder, to be certain no one from the command center had followed. "Okay, that went immediately to shit. That's on me. Don't think for an instant you can, or should, ever treat a civvy oversight officer like that. I should be cut loose for that. But I'll be damned if I'm going to let him second-guess us over whether a gun's loaded or not, not when Fink's life was at risk."

"I'm confused about that, Sarge," McCain said. "It *was* unloaded. I cleared it at the site and cleared it again when we went into the CP."

"I palmed a shell from my pocket and slipped it into the ejection port when I pumped the action. Emergency reload. I may have a little more time with smoothbores than Stuart realizes. Obviously, there's no way to tell whether a weapon's readied just by looking at it, but Stuart needed a reminder."

"The hell good are the COOs doing, anyways?" Pelletier groused. "All they do is shit all over our work."

"You know the answer to that," Finkenzeller said. "They're what makes what we're doing legitimate. As legit as anyone is. Stuart's boss is Reynolds. Reynolds is in touch with the government types in North Bay. Otherwise, we're just a well-armed street gang—and that would mean John Hudson was right."

McCain looked like he wanted to object, but he kept his mouth shut. Todd told them to expect to report in, in the morning, despite what he'd told Stuart. He dismissed them and went home.

The old house was way too empty, but he wasn't about to open the ancestral Todd family home for anyone else to move in. Family roots went deep in New Brunswick, and the house had been built one hundred twenty years earlier by a great-great uncle, some kind of local magnate in the lumber biz. It was old, creaky, the floors were uneven, and the plumbing didn't work anymore, but it was the home he'd grown up in. It was the home he'd retired to after getting a little too intimate with a Kandahar IED, and the home where he'd buried his family. Before the collapse, a shrink might have told him staying in the house after interring his wife and sons in the yard was unhealthy.

Fuck healthy, he thought. *Ain't no one alive today who hasn't lost loved ones to the plague; stress injuries are the new normal.*

He'd only just lit a fire in the basement wood furnace when a knock came at the door. He staggered his way up the stairs. Finkenzeller stood at the door, with a bottle in his hand. "Come in," he called.

Finkenzeller knew his way around the old place and went directly to the kitchen while Todd made his way out front, to the library. He sank into his favorite chair and when Fink returned from the kitchen, Todd accepted a glass. He drained it and placed the glass down.

"Give me that, you're not done yet," Fink said, and refilled the whiskey tumbler again.

Todd eyed the bottle. The label was scratched and faded. "What is it?"

"Only the finest from the Finkenzeller liquor cabinet. Writer's Tears. The last bottle of real whiskey I've got left, to toast you for saving my ass. Again."

"You know that gun was empty just as well as I do," Todd said. The second glass, he sipped, and appreciated the real honest-to-God whiskey, vastly better than what passed for local hooch.

"I believe you just finished explaining to His Lordship, Inspector Screw-up, that we did not know it was at the time."

"Dammit, Craig, you know there's a difference between what's just, what's legal, and what's right."

"Fuck that. What's *right* in this world died of plague."

"I don't believe that. Not for a second. Grab that book, there. Second shelf, left-hand side, third one in."

Finkenzeller went to the bookshelf and searched the titles until he found the one Todd meant. "Edmund Burke?"

"That's the one. *Thoughts on the Cause of the Present Discontents.* Check the inside cover."

"*All that is necessary for the triumph of evil, is that good men do nothing*," Finkenzeller read aloud.

"Correct. He didn't actually say that, but a lot of people thought he did, and I wrote it in that cover before I learned he'd been misquoted. What he actually says is *When bad men combine, the good must associate; else they will fall one by one, an unpitied sacrifice in a contemptible struggle.*"

"And what the hell does that mean?"

"I'm sure some zombie somewhere that used to be an English prof could give you the official interpretation, but I take it to mean we can't lose sight of our moral compass and we have to do what we know is right. We need to stick together, maintain the standards. We can't let pragmatism justify harm or let circumstances excuse evil. I'm not feeling that, right now. I feel like John Hudson was, if not right, at least justified in trying to keep what he'd grown to feed his family. If we were in the medical profession, I'd say we'd violated the hell out of First, Do No Harm. There's never been a military in history that did double duty as local tax collectors that didn't go to hell with a real sense of urgency. We should be protecting people, not rolling up and down the road seizing corn and potatoes at gunpoint."

"How very philosophical," Fink replied, a mocking grin on his face.

It might have been the whiskey hitting his system, but Todd felt his heart quicken its pace. "Damn right! What else is there? Either we're the good guys, or we're thugs. Either we're scum, or we're the goddamn Royal Canadian Regiment. There's no middle ground here. And I'm steadily coming to believe Stuart, Vander Goof or whatever his name is, Reynolds, and all these Civil Oversight Officers are scum that's poisoning the well."

"From philosophy to treason, in twenty seconds, that's gotta be a record." Finkenzeller got to his feet and collected Todd's empty tumbler. "Inspector Stuart here, Thought Police," he mimicked. "Looks like you've had a little too much to think, there, Sergeant. Fifty lashes with a wet noodle!"

"Oh God, not the noodle!" Todd chuckled. Finkenzeller's impression was spot on.

"And no more reading!"

While Todd feigned horror, the junior NCO returned to the kitchen, and quickly rinsed the glasses with water from the rain barrel outside. He returned to the library and leaned against the doorway. "In all seriousness, A-T, I'm not thrilled with Stuart or Reynolds either. But we'll get through it. The military's had shitty PMs, shitty CDSs, and shitty generals before. We've always managed."

"We've never had to manage with the near-total collapse of Western civilization before, Craig."

"You may have a point. Until we've got a solution, Stuart

wants us back at it tomorrow morning. I imagine he thinks being posted to the Hub for a few days is some kind of punishment."

Todd stood. "Of course he does. Better hit the rack, then. Sleep in tomorrow, I'll send someone for you before lunch."

"Appreciated."

The section, less Master Corporal Finkenzeller, marched along the old 108 Highway until the overpass came into view. Todd searched the tree line two kilometers south and shook his head. "Doesn't it just give you the warm fuzzies, knowing we're being watched by a troop of Leopard 2s and Coyotes?"

"So long as they're on our side," McCain replied, and waved to the Royal Canadian Dragoons, whose armored vehicles covered the Hub from a distant ridge to their south. Between the Coyote's 25mm Bushmaster chain guns and the Leopard 2's 120mm Rheinmetall cannons, they were the *actual* security for the Hub—the infantry were merely an ablative tripwire. Todd left the roadway and crossed to a tree line by the rail. "Hello, the Hub! One-Three-Charlie's come to visit!"

"The hell does Charlie want?" a voice called back. Sergeant Oliver Wood, section commander for One-Three-Alpha, emerged from the camouflaged OP and tipped back the brim of his bush cap. He was the height and breadth of a Morian Dwarf, with an accent and ginger beard to match.

"Sergeant Wood," Todd greeted him, and threaded his way through a cordon of camouflaged sandbags. The soldier frowned, and Todd allowed himself to smile. "Per Inspector Stuart's orders, I relieve you."

"I stand relieved—but we're not due to rotate off for another three days," Wood scowled. "What gives?"

"Ordinarily, yes. But we had a shooting yesterday out near Sisson Ridge, and so His Magnanimousness is punishing us by giving us extra duty. You're being granted a few extra days off."

Wood cocked his head quizzically. "Because you tagged an infected? The hell is his—"

"No, because I let an angry farmer get the drop on us with an unloaded twelve-gauge. Fink'll be along later; he's the one who was looking down the barrel, he mighta tied one on last night. Medicinal, of course."

"Medicinal or not, looks like he's not too far behind you, A-T."

The shorter man pointed back down Highway 108 to Finkenzeller, only a hundred meters back or so and marching quickly. Wood handed over a battered pair of binoculars hanging from a braided string around his neck. "It's been quiet. Nothing to see except the occasional fox, coyote, porcupine, or raccoon. Hotel-One-One spotted a moose last week, but nobody had anything large enough to take it down. The Dragoons wanted to have a go at hitting it with their Bushmaster, but their commander wimped out."

"Wimped out?"

"Oh sure," Wood replied. "Maybe you were out on patrol, didn't get the orders. No more using 'inappropriate' calibers for hunting. The only rifles we can use for deer or moose are the C3 or the C14. No more M2, no more twenty-five mil. The Dragoon commander had this enormous bull moose dead to rights but he punked out, didn't want to piss off His Magnanimousness."

"We don't *have* C3s or C14s," Todd protested. "The only .308 we have is for the C6s, and .338 is rarer than a COO with time on a trigger."

"As you say. But them's the orders. Stuart said it came from Reynolds, and Reynolds got it from Paul McIvor himself, direct from North Bay."

"McIvor?" Finkenzeller replied as he approached. "The defense minister? He have another visit from the good idea fairy?"

Wood nodded. "He must've. Terribly helpful he is, governing from a thousand klicks away, six hundred feet down."

Todd rolled his eyes. "Fink, so long as you've joined us, get the troops out into their OPs to relieve One Section and figure out a relief rotation."

Fink nodded and assigned Three Section's fireteams to OPs. Each observation post had a clear view of the primary command trench, where Wood had been and where Todd would remain. One OP surveyed the Trans-Canada Highway as it went north and west towards Quebec. A second OP watched Highway 108 to the west, and the third was elevated to keep an eye on the only rail line that connected the Maritimes to the rest of Canada.

Pelletier and McCain were making their way down the rail overpass when an unfamiliar voice shouted, "STAND TO!"

Wood's head snapped around, searching the three OPs for the one who called out. Pelletier and McCain froze in place, halfway across the bridge, looked back at where they'd come from, then

Pelletier smacked her fireteam partner on the arm and dashed forward. Wood pointed to the rail line OP, where one of his troops waved a yellow signal flag. "Yellow! Shit! Flags, where are the... there!" Wood seized a .50cal ammo can, threw the lid open, and pulled out one of their signaling flags. He unfurled the yellow banner and waved it madly overhead.

Finkenzeller passed Todd the binoculars. "There, about three hundred meters out," he pointed.

Todd lifted the scarred binocs to his eyes, and yes, there was indeed someone—multiple someones—approaching down the rail.

They might have been pickup trucks, once, but had been skeletonized down to the frame and approached backwards, with the truck's tailgate and a canopy at the leading edge. Those created a strange kind of enclosure at what would have been the bed of the truck, above small train wheels that kept it on the rails. At the rear, where the cab of the truck should have been, someone wearing green CADPAT pedaled... a bicycle?

It took a moment for Todd to discern its function. There was no rear wheel on the bike, it had been fixed in place somehow, and the rear sprocket turned a second chain that disappeared beneath the deck. Todd had a brief flashback to Bugs Bunny cartoons when he was young, and the pump trolleys Wile E. Coyote favored. He supposed a bike would be far less tiring to use than one of the armatures. However the approaching strangers had done it, it worked. They were still at distance, but even that far out he could tell they were moving at a pretty good clip.

Two more trucks, more or less identical, followed the first. Pelletier and McCain stayed low and dove into the OP. A muted *thud* came from the embankment to their left and a moment later, the staccato *crack* of a single Bushmaster 25mm chain gun blast followed. The Dragoons had spotted Wood's flag and were ready to support.

"Let the first one pass the OP, then smoke the bridge off. If they're smart, they'll stop and do as they're told. If they're not, we light 'em up and wait for the Coyotes to do the same."

Finkenzeller unslung his Ruger Mini-14 and pulled an all-too-rare colored smoke grenade from his load-bearing vest. He eyed it critically.

"We're not saving them for a rainy day, Fink, get ready."

Fink unscrewed the lid of the grenade, yanked it away from the grenade's body, and threw it as far down the tracks as he could manage. It hissed, puffed, and red smoke began billowing from the device. It briefly obscured the lead vehicle, but the screech of steel train wheels on rails made it clear the occupants were stopping. Todd went to one of the preestablished firing positions and looked down the scope of his C7.

The grenade hissed red smoke that obscured the vehicles but as it finished, it appeared the occupants of the lead vehicle had dismounted. Three occupants had taken cover kneeling against the concrete edges of the railway overpass. The canopy window had flipped up, the tailgate was down, and Todd spotted a fourth still in the shadows of the canopy, lying prone in the truck.

The dismounts wore CADPAT and hunter camouflage, while the one in the bed of the rail-truck thing appeared to be in navy blue that blended into the shadow. They were all armed with a rifle Todd was well acquainted with.

"They're carrying C7s," Fink whispered. "They might be friendlies."

"YOU! ON THE RAILS! ADVANCE ONE TO BE RECOGNIZED!" Todd shouted.

The three who'd dismounted exchanged glances. One of the men wearing Canadian Army camouflage came forward, holding his C7 barrel down in his off hand. He let the stranger advance until he stepped clear of the overpass. Todd ducked low and went to one of the side entrances to the OP that looked south at the rails as it passed. From there, he would be wholly hidden from the others on the bridge, and able to see the man more clearly.

"Halt there, stranger," Todd ordered. The man turned to face him. A long-faded memory floated to the surface. "Who are—wait. Holy shit! *Jim*? Is that you?"

Recognition crossed the man's face, and he broke into a smile. "Avery Todd, you sonofabitch! How the hell are you?" Warrant Jim Kolar asked.

His mustache was more salt, and less pepper and he'd slimmed down some—but then, everyone had. Todd had served with Kolar years earlier, and though it was a relief, he eyed Kolar warily. "Well as can be expected. Not to be too blunt but *what the hell are you doing here, and who do you have with you?*"

∞ ⊖ ℮

The sun crept ever closer to the horizon, and Avery Todd's heart was thudding so hard in his chest he thought Two Section's commander, Master Corporal Danielle Shearer, might hear it. He hadn't been this nervous since—well, he couldn't remember a time being this fearful.

"Hello, the Hub!" she called as her section approached. "One-Three-Bravo approaching."

"Come on up," Todd called back. She would have been given the update by Stuart by now and would know he was being rotated into the daytime guard spot for the time being. Shearer led her section of militia up the trail and pulled up short when the trench came into view. She counted the bodies present in the dugout bunker in an instant, and her hand went to the pistol grip of her rifle.

"What the hell is this, A-T?" she asked.

"This," Todd replied, "is an introduction. To some friends from points west of here. Far west of here. Make weapons safe and bring everyone in. It's been an unusual day."

Shearer frowned but ushered her section forward. Her lone C9 machine-gunner, Corporal Vince Keegan, led the way in. He paused a moment to clear the belt off his gun's feed tray, slammed the cover back down, and took a seat. Her junior-most private, Alexandra Fox, came second, and the rest of the section followed.

The command OP was built to be a fighting position for the whole section, if need be, with additional slots dug and revetted in case they ever got ammunition for one of their recoilless rifles again or brought up a C6 medium machine gun. As such, there was sufficient room for Todd, Fink, Wood, Shearer's section, and their guests. Even more strangely, everyone was sitting on fresh ammo crates.

"Danielle Shearer, meet Warrant Jim Kolar. Jim, this is Danielle and Duke's Company, Three Platoon, Two Section. Danielle, I know Jim from years back. We did CIMIC projects in Afghanistan together, before I got blown up way back when. We lost touch after they gave me the medical discharge. Apparently, Jim rode out the end of the world in North Bay. He's just arrived, hauling party favors." Todd gestured to the ammo crates. "We've practically got enough to clear Halifax, and there's more where it came from."

"That so?" Shearer said. "The question is, are you better or worse than our current batch of bunker bastards?"

"Better, I hope," Jim said with a confident smile. "That's why we're meeting here, instead of your command post downtown."

"I don't follow."

Todd took a deep breath. "What would you say if I told you, Stuart, Reynolds, and the rest of those supposed Civil Oversight Officers have been lying to us since day one?"

Danielle frowned. "I'd say, convince me."

Todd opened a scrap of paper where he'd written some notes and read it aloud. "Danielle Shearer, originally joined the CAF Reserves as Danielle Boarmain in 1998. Service number Echo-3-2, 1-9-0, 8-6-9. Qualified LS and ML driver in 2000, Comms in '02. Passed PLQ phase one first attempt, did not finish PLQ phase two due to an ankle injury. Reattempted PLQ phase 2 in '05, passed. Promoted to Master Corporal in '07. Transferred to regular force in '08. Busted back down to corporal, went through all the same shit a second time, passed in '10, promoted to Master Jack shortly before the plague kicked off."

Shearer had been nodding along unconsciously as he recited a very brief overview of her service history. "Your point?"

"My point is, Jim's people have satcoms with CFB North Bay, where our government is still trying to function but with very limited contacts. They gave up on radio ages ago—it doesn't have the range and we don't have radio rebroadcast centers anywhere in Canada. Yet. They do have access to certain databases, though, including military records. Here's the problem. Stuart, Reynolds, and the rest of the COOs have supposedly been in radio contact with North Bay. That's why they've been ordering us to collect 'taxes' for them—Ottawa's orders. That's why they've decided to limit what we can hunt with."

"Ottawa's orders," Shearer repeated.

"Right. Do you remember whose, specifically?"

"D-Min McIvor."

Kolar nodded. "Defense Minister McIvor was indeed our senior minister when Reynolds and his group left North Bay. He had a heart condition, and with no blood pressure meds, he died of a heart attack in his sleep a year ago."

"Who's in charge, then?" Shearer asked.

"General Nadarzinski is chief of defense staff. He's advising Prime Minister Singer directly," Kolar said.

"You're building up to something," Shearer said, "and I'm afraid I know what it might be. Out with it."

Kolar stood. "You're right to be skeptical. Even with Todd

vouching for me, Sergeant Wood still needed to have my bona fides confirmed as well. The truth of the matter is this. Reynolds isn't a Superintendent, never was. He was a Staff Sergeant in Ottawa Police's traffic section. Stuart was a sergeant in Emergency Planning. Morris was in Professional Standards. De Groot was a drug investigator who got busted *by* Morris for trafficking in bogus vaccine. He was literally in custody the day Cabinet got airlifted out to North Bay, and they brought him along rather than leave him to starve to death in a cell."

"Jim was part of a group called Task Force Sunset," Todd continued. "After that first winter froze most of our infected to death, they spent the first year and a half making their way west to the Pacific. They reconnected communities, reconnected supply routes, got Camp Dundurn active again, and distributed ammunition to anyone who needed it for clearance. When they made their way back to North Bay, they learned Task Force Sunrise—Reynolds and his team—only made it as far as Montreal before going comms dark. North Bay's theory was that Sunrise hit a heavy pocket of infected there and died, until Jim's team arrived here this morning. Assuming they're really them—and not some shitheads who killed them and assumed their identities—they've been falsely pretending to have North Bay's authority this whole time."

Shearer glanced around the trench, then pulled out a notebook and a pencil. "Fox, come here." She whispered into Fox's ear and handed her the notebook. Fox looked at her quizzically for a moment, then nodded and wrote something down. Shearer turned back to Kolar. "You have satcoms with North Bay? And they can pull up a soldier's service record?"

"I do, and I can."

"Okay. Contact them and get the last three of Private Alexandra Fox's service number. Born 1996."

Kolar looked to a blonde woman with him, and she retrieved a satphone from her pack. She powered it up, entered an encryption sequence, and placed a call.

"Sergeant Cavanaugh, Tango-Fox Sunset, for Colonel Anderson," she said. She waited a moment, then requested Fox's service record details. She paused a moment. Then, "Are you sure? Okay, thank you, Colonel. More to follow soon, we hope. Out here."

She stabbed the button to end the call. "North Bay says, no record of an Alexandra Fox on file from 1996."

Shearer smiled. "Good. There shouldn't be one, Alex joined us last summer. She doesn't have an official record."

"That was a test?"

"It was. And you passed. You must have some sort of plan?"

At oh-dark-thirty, Wood knocked on Todd's rear door. The only people who could really keep time anymore were those whose watches' batteries hadn't died yet. Todd hadn't worn a watch in the years prior to the plague. He'd bought one of the new Samsung Galaxy S's, and used its clock, calendar, and alarm for anything specific he needed to remember.

Then the plague hit, the power grid started to fail, and they began cannibalizing parts and cutting off power lines to maintain what little they could. With no way to keep his phone powered outside of the CP, the best he could do was keep time "ish." Wood, meanwhile, still used his ruggedized G-SHOCK watch, which had taken a beating but kept on beeping. Todd had made sure to light his evening fire and extinguish his candles as he "went to bed," but rather than hitting the rack he'd gone up to his attic and dug out his old hunting gear.

His duty uniform, a threadbare old pair of CADPAT fatigues sized for someone better fed than he, got left at home. The benefits of blending in with anyone not read-in on the plan to remove Stuart and his ilk also meant it would be harder to identify friendlies at a distance. By now, most of the survivors had hunting garb that would do in a pinch and were just as good if not better for inclement weather. That would be the new "uniform."

His C7 stayed at home too. He didn't want to have to shoot anyone—in fact, he'd be happy if he never shot anyone ever again—but C7 mags were few and far between and they'd left them with the troops in case the whole op went to hell and the militia went full fratricide.

It was his .308 RFB he picked up instead and slid out the back door. They followed a long-beaten footpath back out to the main road. They moved from backyard to backyard, until Stuart's house, across the street from the tourist center, came into view.

Where Todd's heart had hammered against his chest before, as they hoped to convince Shearer to if not join in on the plan, at least accept it, he was calm now. It was rebellion, certainly, but against an unlawful authority who'd deceived the whole region.

He'd strayed entirely too close to "just following orders," and that shit was over. They crept up to the front of the house, staying to the shadows until the very end. Wood handed his bolt-action Ruger over and produced a flask from a pocket.

"To hell: may the stay be as much fun as the road to get there," he said, and took a swig. He let the moonshine swirl in his mouth for a moment, then he grimaced, swallowed, and belched. With his breath suitably tainted, he affected a drunken gait and stumbled up to Stuart's front door. Wood pounded on it for a moment, then took a few steps back and leaned against the railing.

Stuart came to the door a moment later. His normally slick blond hair was free of whatever oil he used to keep it that way and was an unkempt mess. He wore a thick, baby blue dressing gown, flannel pants, and slippers. His right hand was buried in the pocket of the dressing gown and that side of the gown sagged sharply, as though something heavy and pistol-shaped was concealed within. Wood feigned drunkenness and waved.

"Oh, shir, oh, sho good yer 'ome. There'sh been an, an ack-shident!" He pointed across the road to the tourism center, lost his balance, and stumbled clear of the porch.

Stuart frowned, unlocked his door, and stepped onto the porch. "What is it, Wood? An accident?"

Todd raised his rifle to his shoulder. "Not yet, Sergeant, but the night is young." Stuart jumped at the ambush and stumbled backward, almost toppling over the railing. Todd continued, keeping his voice clear and even. "Show me your hands, slowly. Up above your head. If steel comes out of that pocket, you die."

Stuart's eyes bulged but he did as he was told and raised his hands—empty—until they were fully outstretched. "I'll have you banished for this, Avery," he snarled. "If not executed outright."

"You and what army?" Todd snapped back. "Pistol, right side pocket, grab it, Oliver."

Wood ascended the steps and patted Stuart down thoroughly. The .44 revolver—unloaded—went into Wood's cargo pocket, as did a knife he'd found tucked into the waistband of Stuart's pajama pants. Woods pulled out a length of paracord and slipped a prepared loop over one wrist, tied it around the other, and then looped the whole thing around Stuart's waist, cinching it tight.

"We are going to the command post," Todd said. "Move. Now."

Wood shoved him forward, and Stuart stumbled off his steps. Todd returned Wood's rifle to him, and shoved Stuart forward with the body of his rifle. The COO sullenly marched across the street, slippers and all, until they went inside.

"Oh...Oh shit," Stuart said.

"Evening, Kris," Jim Kolar said. He got up from behind the ops table and gestured for Stuart to have a seat. "Been a long time."

"I—I—it's not what it looks like," he stammered. Shearer was present, as was her gunner Keegan, Finkenzeller, and Wood's second-in-command, Kulveer Singh.

Todd scoffed. "It is *exactly* what it looks like. I notice you didn't react when I called you Sergeant, just a few minutes ago. Sergeant Stuart, from OPS Emergency Ops, is it?" He gestured to an always locked door, with a "Communications, Keep Out" sign stuck to it. "You've claimed you're North Bay's mouthpiece since you got here. Prove it."

"But—I..."

Shearer let out a growl of frustration and buried her hand in his hair. She took hold and dragged him headfirst over to the door.

"Open it!"

The door was secured with a mechanical combination lock, and Stuart let out a deep sign of resignation. He punched in the code—1-3-5-2-4—and pulled the door open.

"Are you fucking kidding me?" Shearer gasped. "A *broom closet*?"

It could have been a comms shack, Todd supposed. It was narrow, just wide enough he couldn't have touched both walls at the same time. With some imagination, a desk with radio equipment, a mic, a headset and some notebooks could have gone against one wall with room for a chair.

Instead, there were metal racks with old, unused cleaning products in plastic jugs, a shaggy dust broom, and a yellow mop bucket with a "Caution—Wet Floor" sign hanging off one side.

"Boy, that's awkward," Kolar said, shaking his head sadly. "Bring the prisoner over and sit his ass down, would you please, Danielle?"

Stuart yelped as she dragged him over to an empty folding chair and forced him into it. Jim turned to face him. "In case it wasn't clear, you are relieved of command. One, you and yours have all been lying to these people ever since you got here. Two, as far as North Bay knew, you were dead and dead people don't have a position in the chain of command. And three, you're outranked. Questions?"

"What...what're you gonna do?" Stuart whimpered.

"That's a good question, Kris. Maybe we ought to ask North Bay what their intentions are? Sergeant Cavanaugh?"

Cavanaugh stepped forward and put her satphone down on the table next to Stuart and punched in her codes. "Sergeant Cavanaugh, Tango-Fox Sunset, for Colonel Anderson, please. Good evening, sir. Yes. We have him here. No, nothing like that, meek as a beta with performance anxiety. One moment."

She pressed the speakerphone button and replaced the handset in its cradle. "Colonel Anderson, present is Kris Stuart, Warrant Kolar, myself, retired Sergeant Avery Todd and his 2i/c, Master Corporal Craig Finkenzeller. Master Corporal Danielle Shearer, her 2i/c Corporal Vince Keegan, Sergeant Oliver Wood, and his 2i/c, Corporal Singh. Go ahead, sir."

Anderson's voice was digitized and scratchy, but it came through clear enough. *"Please hold for the prime minister."*

Eyes around the room widened at that. Todd had been present when Kolar and Cavanaugh discussed the situation with Anderson, and gave the Colonel a frank, no-bullshit update that started from the moment 911 wasn't answering anymore. At no point did Anderson suggest they'd be speaking with Singer himself.

"Sergeant Stuart, this is Joe Singer. It's been almost two years; do you recognize my voice?"

Stuart swallowed hard. "I do, sir."

"Good. I'm going to be blunt, because the battery packs for those satphones don't last very long and we've got a very convoluted situation to unfuck, thanks largely to you, Tanner Reynolds, and the rest of Sunrise. By my authority, you and the rest of Sunrise are being held for Personation, Fraud, Sedition, Mutiny, and a number of other offenses. Once Sunset has done their work, yourself, Reynolds, and anyone else originally part of Task Force Sunrise will be transported back to North Bay. There, you will be granted access to legal counsel, answering to Major General Carhardt, and eventually, tried. If we are to begin rebuilding this country, we must recognize the powers and the limitations of our government. Might does not make right, and even the most heinous accused is guaranteed some protection from the State. There will be no

summary executions, no extrajudicial sanctions, and no violations of our Charter, by anyone. Do you understand?"

"I do, sir."

"Does everyone else present understand?"

"We do, sir," Kolar replied.

"Good. That said, Mr. Stuart, Sunset and everyone else there serving in the militia are wholly entitled to use force in the defense of themselves or others. I'd strongly urge you not to test their resolve."

"Understood, sir," Stuart whispered.

"Good. As you were, Warrant Kolar. Singer, out."

Todd closed the door to the "communications room" and slid a chair under the doorknob. "He won't be going anywhere soon like that; one down, three to go. Next?"

"We have to bring the Dragoons in on this too," Wood said. "I tend to forget about them, off on the ridge like they usually are."

"I'll get them read in," Danielle said. "One of their troop commanders is an old boyfriend. Do you think Three Section and your new Sunset friends can go handle the other COOs, A-T?"

Avery looked at Kolar, who nodded. "Between my section and Jim's guys, we'd be twenty. Four DMRs, three MGs and thirteen rifles. Not that we want to shoot anyone at all, but I think if we rolled up what's his name, the asshole overseeing One Platoon in Woodstock, then we stand a chance of resolving this without a shot fired. They can't have any more love for their guy than we have for ours."

"How do we get there?" Kolar asked. "The only maps we've got of the rails show this railway cuts straight across the province to Moncton. Hell, we weren't expecting to encounter anyone yet; we were aiming for Halifax. You mentioned the Dragoons: do you guys still have diesel somehow?"

"No, when all the fuel started to go bad, that first summer, they brought up a troop of Leopard 2s, a troop of Coyotes, and parked them to function more or less like direct-fire artillery bunkers. They're running off ethanol, for very short periods of time."

"G-Wagons will run on ethanol," Shearer said abruptly. "I'd totally forgotten. We don't see the RCDs a lot; they've mostly just established their own camp up on the ridgeline and communicated directly with Stuart. But they have G-Wagons they converted to run on ethanol too. They used them to bring ammo up from Gagetown last spring. It's a pain in the ass to distill ethanol in mass quantities, so they try not to run the vehicles any more than necessary."

"I'd say this is pretty necessary," Kolar said. "Can you arrange us a meet?"

"Asshole!" Leftenant Campbell shouted, and he pounded a fist on the cleaning closet door. "Lying prick!"

"Evan, ya big dumb zipperhead!" Danielle shouted. "Rein it in!"

Campbell gave the door one more quick boot, then turned away. His face was flushed and eyes wild. Cavanaugh smirked. "Evan?" she echoed. "Zipperhead? First time I've ever seen a junior NCO jack up an officer, by his first name no less. Old boyfriend, you said?"

"Ex," Campbell admitted. Getting called out like that appeared to have brought him back to calm, somewhat, and the flush in his cheeks had shifted from fury to embarrassment.

"Ex-*fiancé*," Shearer said. "Right up until the plague hit. After that, we kinda figured maybe getting hitched in the middle of the end of the world was overly optimistic."

"Fair," Kolar allowed. "I take it you share our concerns with Mr. Reynolds and his merry band of lying liars?"

"I do, very much," Campbell said. "It will deplete most of our reserves, but I've got seven G-Wagons that still function. With their adapted fuel tanks, they have the range to reach Mactaquac if you don't put the hammer down. Alcohol engines guzzle their fuel like you wouldn't believe. Driving most of the way to Freddie is a one-way trip unless they've been distilling fuel down that way too. I'd feel a lot better about it if you'd let my troops drive."

"They're your wheels, sir. Master Corporal Shearer might get to order you around, but this humble Warrant isn't about to," Kolar grinned.

"Excellent, I'm glad we understand each other. I'll head out now and get the troops doing their primary DIs and fuel up. Dani can show you guys the way once you've got things sorted here."

Todd found it strange to be back in a vehicle again, to have the klicks tick by with little to no effort on his part. He'd gotten used to hiking just about everywhere, in the years since the plague. They'd had one moderately disastrous attempt at training up the infantry to ride on horseback and make them Dragoons in earnest, but without proper veterinarian support, tracts of actively farmed grains, winter fodder storage, and leathercrafting equipment, it was just too difficult. Premodern cavalry was going to remain premodern.

The sun broke over the hills to the east, on the far side of the Saint John River, illuminating the mists that drifted over the water's surface. Todd rode up front, with Corporal Prinsloo driving. Pelletier rode in the back with one of Kolar's Sunset members, a slim, dark-haired woman in her early twenties whose nametag read KALISZEWSKA. "How was it, living in that bunker underground, Private?" Todd asked. "I can't imagine being that far down, with no sunlight, for so long."

"Oh, I wasn't in North Bay, Sergeant," she replied. "I was holed up in the Moose Jaw Armories. Stone walls, plenty of IMPs to eat, but had a rapist scumbag for a boss, so it was still pretty awful."

Pelletier, who was taking a sip from her canteen, choked and coughed a mouthful of water all over the inside of the SUV. "A what?" she gasped.

"He was a piece of shit, a stolen-valor asshole who slid into our chain of command as everything was falling apart. Had been dishonorably discharged but showed up with forged, bogus orders. I guess he imagined he'd be some kind of zombie apocalypse warlord with a harem. Almost worked, too. Sergeant Cavanaugh vented his cranium all over the drill hall floor. Then she and Warrant Kolar invited we survivors to join up with Sunset. Rylie Hamilton and I stayed on with Sunset after we got Camp Dundurn functional again, the others stayed behind to start distributing ammo all over the prairies."

"Do you know where whatsisname lives?" Todd asked their driver. "Or what the Woodstock CP is? I haven't been this far south in a year or more."

Prinsloo nodded. "I haven't been here, but the LT knows the route. It's on the far side of the Meduh—Meducks—hell, far side of a little river that joins the Saint John. The CP is a great big warehouse-looking building by where, and I quote, 'the old train station used to be.'"

"That's helpful," Todd grumbled. "I assume they'll see us coming?"

"Maybe, maybe not. We'll get off the road before we get to town. They've got a vehicle checkpoint at the north end of town with wrecks and sandbags. Locals, however, know there's a water-front trail that used to be a rail line. It's more than wide enough for a G-Wagon and will take us exactly where we need to go."

"...to where the old train station used to be."

"Correct. Looks like we're at the turnoff."

The lead jeep turned off the main road, down a short side street. Todd's was second in line and followed it onto a poorly maintained, overgrown path with weeds doing their best to break through the gravel. Overgrown limbs scraped the roof of the G-Wagon, but the ground itself was clear enough that the militarized SUVs had no trouble.

Up ahead, a pair of CADPAT-clad militia troops armed with rifles stepped out of the bush. One put his hand up, as if ordering them to halt. Prinsloo tightened his grip on the steering wheel. "Ready on the doors?"

Kaliszewska reached up to unlatch the roof hatch and unbuckled her seatbelt.

"Top, ready."

"Right, ready," Todd said, and unbuckled his belt as well. So did Pelletier.

"Left, ready,"

"Stopping...now."

Prinsloo threw the wheel over to the right just as the G-Wagon came even with the guards. Ahead, Campbell and Kolar goosed the throttle and sped up. Todd threw his door open before the SUV came to a halt, and the Dragoon from Moose Jaw threw the turret hatch open, leading the way with her C7.

"What the hell is—" the guard started, but Todd moved with unanticipated aggression. He clamped both hands on the guard's bolt-action rifle, shoved, and twisted to disarm him. His victim fell on his ass with an *oof* and the second guard panically tried to work the bolt on his rifle. Todd drove the barrel of the first guard's rifle barrel down in the dirt, burying it a handspan deep and rendering it useless. He moved to the second guard, who backpedaled, still trying to work the bolt, but Todd advanced quicker than he could back up. He pushed the gun away and shoved, sending the guard off-balance. He crashed into the brush and Todd pounced.

"STOP! FIGHTING!" he shouted, and jammed the rifle's receiver under his arm, pinning it between his tricep and ribcage. "WE DON'T WANT TO HURT YOU!"

"Funny—ugh—fucking way to show it!" the guard snarled and yelped as Todd jammed a thumb into his cheek and leaned on the pressure point in the man's jaw. Todd forced the man's face over sideways and kept it there.

"Brooke? Rifle!"

"On it!" she replied and approached cautiously. She slung her own weapon and carefully disarmed the soldier.

"A .22?" She gasped in surprise when she cleared the magazine.

"...Yeah," the man said. "De Groot won't let us carry anything heavier."

Todd eased up on the pressure he was applying to the man's face, then backed off and got up. "A .22 isn't good for anything but putting holes in paper and shooting squirrels. Is De Groot your COO? Who are you?"

"Yeah," the man said. "Geoff MacGrath. Who the fuck are you guys?"

"Three Platoon. Here to remove De Groot and put the *actual* government back in charge. They've been lying to us; it's complicated. Stay here, stay out of the way, and everything will make sense soon."

Pelletier stripped the bolt from the man's rifle and held up the bolt. "I'll leave this for you at the CP." She pocketed it and leaned the rifle against a tree. "Keep your heads down."

"Covering," Kaliszewska barked from the turret hatch.

"Moving," Todd and Pelletier replied, and in seconds they were back in the SUV and peeling out after the rest of the convoy, leaving the bewildered guards in their dust.

The trail passed beneath a bridge that crossed the Saint John River and emerged from the woods behind what must have been "downtown" Woodstock. Todd spotted an old Legion building, a farmer's market that still advertised *Buffalo Burgers every Friday*, and then they were up onto an old train bridge. It thumped and rattled as the G-Wagon crossed. Todd chuckled when he saw the old sign. "Meh-ducks-neh-kag? Meduxnekeag? Is that how you say it?"

"You see why I gave up trying to pronounce it," Prinsloo

said. A gunshot report washed over them, followed by a flurry of more shots. "Shit!"

Their driver accelerated to clear the bridge faster. "Everyone okay?" Todd asked, searching for whoever was shooting. Kaliszewska kneeled down from the turret hatch. "It came from up ahead, I don't think it was intended for us." She stood back up and continued scanning.

More gunshots.

The woods to their left gave way to open lawns, houses, and the river. A minor avenue paralleled their trail, and up ahead the G-Wagons were parked, their occupants ducking behind the vehicles for cover. The warehouse came into view on their left and the instant it did, another flurry of shots rang out. Impacts on their windshield quickly rendered it opaque, and Kaliszewska let out a shrill scream. She fell into the body of the G-Wagon, clutching a bloodied arm. Pelletier cursed and reached for the trauma pack in the trunk. "Get us stopped, Prinsloo; Brooke, take care of her!"

The moment the vehicle stopped moving, Todd threw his door open and rolled clear. The shooting prompted a return salvo from the Sunset members, but no one seemed willing to commit to a full assault. Soldiers fired occasional, individual rounds, but years of being cautious with ammo made them reluctant to commit to winning the firefight.

Todd low-crawled to Kolar's vehicle where the Warrant was sitting with his back to the engine block. "I take it we lost the element of surprise?"

"You could say that." Kolar grimaced. "No plan survives contact with the enemy."

"Where's Campbell?"

Kolar pointed a thumb over his shoulder. "Silly idiot threw the door open and marched out, ordering De Groot to surrender. They chose violence."

"He alive?"

"Can't say."

Todd got very low and scanned under the G-Wagon. Campbell's body lay motionless, halfway between the warehouse and the line of G-Wagons. Someone wearing a camouflage hoodie and jeans lay prone, just outside the door, a C7 trapped under his body. Above, the last inch of a rifle barrel poked out from the edge of the overhead door. Although the warehouse walls were corrugated tin, odds were good they were reinforced with concrete cinder blocks for the first eight feet or so, otherwise Sunset's salvos would have punched right through and taken out the shooter.

The barrel of the rifle, though . . .

His RFB had always been a tack driver. He was maybe fifty meters away, but the RFB was zeroed for two hundred, so he'd have to hold over a bit high. It was a tiny target—but he'd hit smaller before. Once.

"I'm going for his gun," Todd said.

"You're *what*?"

He'd figure it out. Todd's heart pounded in his chest, and he took a breath to calm himself. He placed the dot of his scope over the exposed barrel and lifted the dot an inch or so. Took another breath. Took up the slack in his trigger. Let the breath half out.

Squeezed.

Missed.

The muzzle blast kicked up grass, dirt, and leaves all in front of him, but the exposed barrel remained right where it had been. The shooter leaned out and fired a couple more rounds in their direction. One struck the side window of Kolar's G-Wagon, nudging the vehicle on its shocks. The shooter returned to his previous waiting position, apparently unaware that the rifle's muzzle was exposed. Todd took another breath and repeated the process. He lifted his point of aim another inch and fired again.

The impact tore the rifleman's weapon from his grasp and sent it clattering across the warehouse door. Whether the copper-jacketed round had actually damaged the rifle, Todd had no idea, but "disarmed" was infinitely better than "actively shooting" any day of the week. That was the moment the rest of Sunset had been waiting for. Cavanaugh began shouting orders, and her section began a steady staccato beat, pinning the shooter down behind cover, preventing him from retrieving the weapon.

Todd groaned as he got his feet back under him. "FINK! YOUR SHOW!" he shouted.

"Charlie team!" Fink called. "Assault that building!" He emptied his magazine into the side door in one salvo of rapid, aimed fire, dumped his magazine, and reloaded. "Covering!"

McCain and his new fireteam partner, a redheaded South African from TF Sunset named Rowe, raced out from behind their G-Wagon and sprinted for the door. They took positions on either flank of the door, rifles up. "Covering!"

"Moving!" Finkenzeller raced forward with the rest of his assault group. The door handle had taken some hits and rather than move to the side, Fink used the rush to front-kick the door handle, slamming it open. He threw himself aside, and McCain rushed in, followed by Rowe and Finkenzeller.

No gunshots.

Fink returned to the door long enough to call "Building clear!" before disappearing back inside. Todd got up from behind his G-Wagon and was first to the door while Kolar saw to their casualties.

Inside, McCain covered the gunman—a private from One Platoon—while Rowe had her rifle on a trio of unarmed soldiers who cowered in the corner.

"Well, how about that," Todd said. "I guess we don't need to roll down to Mactaquac after all. It's been a while, Tanner."

"What the hell is the meaning of this, Sergeant?" Tanner Reynolds demanded. "Is this some sort of coup?"

"Oh this? This is you, out of a job and destined for prison. You three know the man commanding the troops outside, it seems."

"Gentlemen," Kolar said from the overhead door. "Been a long time. Prime Minister Singer is *very* displeased."

"The . . . who?" the young private stammered. "But—"

"McCain, disarm him, search him, and get him outside," Todd ordered. "He did what he thought was right but was working for the wrong people. Sit him next to the LT."

"Sergeant," McCain said, and hustled the private out the door. Todd looked back to Reynolds, Morris, and De Groot, who'd gone pale.

"Awkward, am I right? Seems North Bay's thought you lot were dead for two years now. Making bogus calls to 'your bosses' and making up bullshit to keep all the peasants under your boot. *Our* boot. Duping us into believing your orders were legit. Had the PM not made it explicitly clear what he plans to do with you—arrest, charges, trial, the works—I'd execute you both, here and now. But that's not how we roll anymore. So stand up, march outside, and take a good look at dead Lieutenant Campbell and everyone else who's been wounded by good people who honestly believed they were on the right side of things."

Todd lowered his rifle and turned to Kolar. "How's Kali...whatsername? The Dragoon from Moose Jaw?"

Kolar frowned. "Not good. She might lose that arm."

"Dammit."

Todd's eyes snapped right at a sudden movement. Tanner Reynolds, rather than marching peacefully outside into custody, dove across the floor for the private's abandoned rifle. "GUN!" Todd shouted and brought his RFB up. Reynolds didn't turn, though; he just presented his bare back—and Todd knew he couldn't shoot him from behind. No threat. Not yet.

"You think I don't know what Singer's got waiting for us?" the bogus Superintendent growled. "You think I want to go back in that hole? Just to be condemned to life in another one?" Slowly, he turned. He had the rifle vertical, with the muzzle just below his chin, like he was presenting arms, but his thumb rested on the trigger. "See you in hell."

"DON'T!" Todd shouted, but too late. Reynolds pressed the trigger.

Rather than painting the ceiling with his brains, though, the report of the shot was muted, and the side of the rifle blew out. Reynolds screamed in pain as his hand was shredded by flying fragments; he dropped the weapon, and clutched his hand under his armpit. Todd tackled Reynolds to the ground and brought his uninjured hand around in a chicken-wing. Rowe came forward with paracord handcuffs and secured both hands behind his back. The wounds to Reynolds's hand were numerous, but superficial and bloody. Todd spared a look at the rifle.

The muzzle was deformed from where he'd hit it with his rifle round, bending the last few inches of what had been a hot barrel and pinching it shut.

"Coward," he spat at Reynolds. "You don't get off that easy. Fink, get him out of here, and post a guard."

"You got it, Sarge."

As Finkenzeller and Rowe took their prisoners outside, Todd groaned and stretched. "I'm getting too old for this shit," he complained.

Kolar laughed. "I'd been meaning to talk to you about that. You ever consider, you know, retirement?"

∽ ⊙ ⌁

"...Yes, Mister Prime Minister, it would be an honor."

"*Very good. Director of Restoration Operations has a good ring to it. May I call you Avery?*"

"Of course, sir."

"*Thank you. Warrant Kolar was an absolutely fundamental member of our team, here in the bunker. I came to rely on his judgment just as much as General Nadarzinski's or any of the other cabinet ministers. I'm pleased you've accepted his proposal.*"

"It'll be a bit strange, sir, not wearing a uniform again, for the second time. We took some casualties bringing in Reynolds, good people who aren't combat effective anymore, but they can still help. We'll do our best."

"*That's all anyone can do, these days. New Brunswick still needs its militia, but as a constructive force for rebuilding, not coercion and tax collecting. Trust is a hard thing these days, but you've more than earned it and I expect you will demand nothing but the highest standards from your charges. Sunset's rail riders will be slow in coming, but we will provide you with all the ammunition you can handle to keep clearing east, all the way to Charlottetown and Halifax. We need those cities back, Avery, and if they're anything like every other city we've seen, they're still hives of infected that need to be tracked down and cleared. Getting the Halifax port functional again is our next major objective, so we can better manage shipping and trade all up and down the St. Lawrence, the Great Lakes, and even down into the U.S. I understand they've got a sizeable lash-up down there that has been more or less restoring the government's capabilities faster than anyone would think possible.*"

"We'll do our part, sir."

"*Very good. Good luck in your new role, Director.*"

The Old Bastard

DAVE FREER

They landed on the far side of the island a bit before dawn, with the wind easterly so the outboard couldn't be heard. Might have worked too, if that old bastard and young Mick hadn't gone to set a dawn net in one of the small bays on the lee of the island. If the old bastard hadn't gone and taken his rifle with him it might have worked out different too. But he always did.

Anyway, it was a rough awakening for the rest of the people in the camp. A shot, a scream and a few more shots, and some running, and frantic panicky looking for guns. The last part, for Jim, had been his role in the entire process. By the time he'd had his shotgun in hand, there was nothing to shoot at, just the old bastard up in the rocks telling him not to shoot him.

"Don't tempt me," said Jim. "What the hell is going on, you old bastard?"

"Three fellers thought they'd sneak up on us. So, I give one a new hole in his ear. Thems still running, but you better see 'em off. Keep a distance, because they're shooting back. I left young Mick watching their boat. They landed in the cove next to Hippo Rock."

Jim had gone off with three of the others, legging it along the upper track. Their "visitors" had run along the beach. You

147

had to know the bush-track to the far side of the island was there. By the time they got to above the cove, the three were scrambling into the boat they had anchored just off the rocks. Lizzie, panting—she was maybe the fittest of all of them, but at five months pregnant, had less lung capacity than she was used to—took a bead.

"Save it," said Jim. "They'd be lousy eating."

She looked at him with a scowl. "You probably would." Liz had been a vegetarian...before this all started. In the first month of survival out here, with nothing much but fish to eat, she'd changed her ideas. Wallaby, wombat, muttonbirds came onto the diet list a little later. It had been five months before the first vegetables, per se, could be said to have been part of their diet. There'd been a little bush-tucker, thanks to the old bastard knowing what you could eat, but mostly it was fish, shellfish and meat.

"It'd make a change," said Jim, stirring a bit. You didn't want to stir her up too much, though. Liz had had to kill a few of the infected to get this far. She was capable, especially if scared. It was more than his abilities, he suspected. He was just a lines-man, a new emigrant who had been having a kayaking holiday and gone off to the islands when things went wrong. Australia was strange to him, as strange as their way of saying his name, so he'd settled on "Jim."

"Unless you told me they tasted like white bread and their blood was coke, I'm not having any. What's that?" she said, shifting the rifle she carried, peering through the scope. "That" proved to be young Mick, emerging from some tea tree and tumbled boulders. They called out to him, and the youngster grinned and waved back. He was a long way from the scared thirteen-year-old kid who had stayed home to play computer games...and whose family never came back. Like all of them, he'd never be quite the same again. But he'd found stand-in parents, and a nightmare of a grandfather in the old bastard...and maybe a bit more. There were more women than men on the island, and, well, old taboos had seemed a bit silly when you were hoping to survive.

"He's calling us to come down," said Liz. The vessel was now some distance off. "Think it is safe?"

Jim nodded. "I reckon."

They soon found out just why.

"The old bastard told me he was going back, and I was to

see what I could nick off their boat as soon as they was gone," said Mick, meeting them, looking pleased with himself. "It's back in the rocks."

The boy had been busy. There were several boxes, and a fuel tank!

"They had a spare. And they must have found a house the zombies didn't trash. There was a bit more, but I heard the shooting and got out. I was coming back, when I saw them running on the beach and hid out."

The loot, when they got back to the camp, was, in Liz's words, "exquisite." One wouldn't have described tinned tomato, a packet of weevil-infested flour, and a twelve-pound bag of sugar, gone hard, but still sugar, as that, two years back. Some of the other bits were more precious still—toothpaste, soap, half a brick of .22 and, most importantly, the fuel.

It called for a celebratory meal...and afterwards, introspection. The biggest problem, in a way—besides the five graves behind the little hut that had once been a shelter for visiting biologists, was that they had no idea what was left of the world. No working radio. No communications. All they knew was what had been known when they fled to Roydon Island. There were three little "tinnies"—aluminum boats, with outboards—two of which were a whole fifteen horsepower, and the third, twenty-five, a single-seater sea kayak that belonged to Jim, and the one Hobie 16 catamaran from the beach. Fine to cross the eight-hundred-yard channel, not so good for exploring, especially in light of not having fuel—years had passed and petrol didn't like it. There had to be other survivors—there were fifty-two islands in the group. Sometimes they could see smoke. But no one had come driving or walking along the shore. No boats either—not since the twins had showed up in the tinnie from up North, scared and warily waving from the water, maybe twenty months back.

They'd waited. A few quick careful trips to loot the holiday houses and few permanent residences on the close shore when things got too scarce and hard after the first month. The bag of sprouting potatoes had been a lifesaver—because the old man had insisted on planting them. That trip had nearly ended in disaster because the zombies had been sleeping in one ruined house, hadn't left to go hunting food yet. It had taken another five months to find the courage to go again, and it was only because of the death of one of the children. Still, that had brought little food, but two plastic five-thousand-gallon rainwater tanks, emptied and rolled down to the beach and towed across. Corrugated iron and fasteners and tools from the houses—and then a retreat.

"The authorities are going to be along eventually. As soon as it is over." Jim remembered it being said, like it was some kind of holy mantra.

It was a very urban Australian attitude, and of the ten adults that had taken refuge on Roydon Island, eight had been blow-ins, sea-changers come to live on a remote set of islands...that was very much part of Australia. It had always seemed like a perfect place to ride out the end of the world...which was of course why it hadn't been. One could not expect that no one else would think that, and when the end of the world came rolling relatively slowly towards them, that they too would not flee there, and bring it with them. They were an odd group, three men, old Mick, the old bastard, and himself, and the seven women. None with surviving partners. And, of course, young Mick, who was growing to be a man, fast. It hadn't been quite that unbalanced originally...but, well, graves. The women worked it out between them it seemed. There was five of them pregnant, and two toddlers.

Next time, Jim decided, he'd pick a faster apocalypse to wreck his holiday with. One where the Internet worked and you didn't run out of coffee before you died. The virus had spread just slowly enough to reach here too. On the positive side, relatively few of the infected made it here. On the negative side, there was lots for them to eat, and, well, Australians mostly didn't think defensively. So, then there were more infected. Not a lot more, because the big island only had a population of a thousand odd people, in more than five hundred square miles. But that meant the little towns went down pretty fast. And then there had been the infected roaming around—could be anywhere. There was lots of cover, millions of wallaby, wombats, sheep and cows for food.

And here they were, two years on. With a flourishing potato patch, and all the fish you could eat—and precious little else. Well, no, that wasn't true. They'd contrived a lot. But clothes were wearing out, and there was no fuel for the outboards, and there was no coffee left. The last part seemed as good a reason as any to go looking: to find more supplies, if not to find more people.

"Look, you can see smoke, sometimes. They must have dealt with it all," said Liz. "We've got fuel now. We should go looking."

"And find it's that bunch that come sneaking in here," said the old bastard, quietly and methodically cleaning his rifle. One of them, anyway. He'd been the first to move across to the island and had stashed a lot of his gear in the caves between the rocks. He could have sat up in those rocks and shot anyone who tried to land... instead he'd gone to the next island, the low-lying Inner Pascoe and watched. When he was sure it was okay, he came back. He'd been born on the islands, spent his life as a farm laborer and a deckhand. In Australia, guns had been hard to come by with a sea of permits and "reasons" required. But farming and vermin control on those farms was one of those reasons. So was shooting zombies—but that wasn't on the application form. By Australian standards—no one else's, there'd been lots of guns and lots of shooters on the islands. I never got any straight answers about how the old guy—and he was over seventy, and creaked and wheezed a lot—ended up with his collection. I was just glad he had.

"We'd have to be careful," conceded Liz. "But winter is coming and we can't go on like this."

"Seem to be doing pretty well to me," said the old bastard. "We can go and fetch a bunch more roofing tin and stuff. Let them come to us." He stood up. "I better pull that net or it'll be too late on the tide. Anyone coming along?"

Of course, young Mick was keen. I went along just to get out of the argument that I knew was coming. We got a good haul—the effect of minimal fishing pressure and the old bastard knowing exactly when and where to put the net. We had to do four trips, carrying baskets. It would have been easier using a boat, but it was a long row, and we were saving fuel. "Bloody fish," said Kayley, looking up from the basket she was weaving when we got back. Someone was always at it. The baskets wore out.

"You just love filleting so much," said young Mick—sticking his tongue out at her. A little exchange of courtesy followed involving her chasing him and hitting him with a bunch of rushes. Courtship, I guess, but pretty soon they were all filleting except for the three who were still busy banking potatoes.

Filleting, salting, and then hanging in the smoker to dry. It might be tedious—which was why we took turns to read aloud while it was being done—but it meant we'd not have another hungry time when the weather was foul for days. It was the old bastard again—he might be the wrong side of seventy, but he knew how to do all this sort of thing.

"I am just so sick of the same books," said Bethany, and Jim had to agree. This one was a murder story—and they all knew who had done it. And they all knew that urban world had vanished for them. Maybe it wasn't ever coming back. Talk soon fell to the idea of going searching for others. Liz was like water dripping on stone, Jim thought. He wondered how long it would take. The old bastard wasn't listening. In fact, Jim realized, he wasn't there.

Later, after they had buried the guts and heads in the potatoes, he came in, with a new axe handle he was whittling. Jim asked him where he'd been.

"Keeping lookout. I guess we're going to have to do it. Them fellers this morning...they wasn't up to any good. I know, 'cause, seeing as I wasn't up to any good myself a lot."

"You reckon they'll come back?"

He shrugged. "Not the same way, maybe. Might try for softer pickings. There was only three of them, and they got shot at."

"What do you think of going looking for people?" Jim asked.

"The smoke from the fire out on Prime Seal stopped." That was a big island, a few miles long, much further out to sea, that had had quite a substantial house.

"So?"

"So, they either left or got killed. I thought about us going out there, only this is nearer to the shore. Run out of fuel there, and we're stuck."

"We can't go on like this. We need to know what is happening."

He tugged his beard. "I reckon mostly they're all dead, but for people like us."

"Maybe we need to get together with people like us then."

"We don't have it bad right now. We got enough to eat. There'd be people who don't have that. Who are still livin' off what they can scavenge."

"We need more. We need medicine, and things are wearing out. I could use shoes that aren't held together with bailing twine," said Jim, looking ruefully at his feet.

"What makes you so sure they're gunna have shoes or anything?" he said grumpily.

"What makes you so damn sure they won't?" said Liz.

"Seventy years of experience," said the old bastard.

It was plainly going to be an uphill struggle to convince him.

So, Jim was glad that decision was taken out of his hands the next day by the old bastard coming down to where they were working on cutting firewood. The old bastard was never idle himself. No one was, unless you wanted to catch an earful from the entire crew. There were few enough of them, that it stood out. Besides... what the hell else was there to do? It wasn't exactly like you could surf the 'net or catch something on Netflix or even sit and drink a few beers. The brew made from potatoes had made them all puke.

"You got your wish," he said. "Boat coming around Bun Beetons Point. Looks like an old cray boat. She's got an Australian flag flying." Even he sounded impressed by that.

They all rushed to look. After all this time it was good to feel that they had not been forgotten after all. By the time she came past the Pascoes everyone was down on the beach, waving.

Well, not quite everyone. Jim noticed the old bastard wasn't there. Jim hadn't spent two years with the old guy without getting to know how he thought. He'd be up in the rocks above the bay, with the boat under his 'scope. He suddenly wondered if they were all being too trusting. He tried to say so, but, honestly, Jim thought, he might as well have been trying to stop the tide with his feet. Everyone was just so excited, the women especially. He saw Liz trying to comb her hair with her fingers.

The boat stopped some hundred yards offshore, and someone used a bullhorn to call out that they were from the Australian government, sent to assist. Could they come ashore?

And of course, they said yes. The words "where have you been for the last two years?" never crossed anyone's lips, honest. They were just that glad to see them. And the woman and the guy who came in on the dingy with a little outboard chugging were something they never thought they'd see again. Yes, their clothes were good... which was weird, and the guy was clean-shaven, wearing a woolly beany on his head. But the odd thing about them was that they were... well, fat. By Roydon Island standards anyway. They were smiling and waving, kind of like rock stars, and that was the sort of greeting they got.

"Glad to see you all so welcoming," said the man as they

stepped ashore. "Now, we had a report that there were some raiders up here. Bandits. You don't know anything about this? I am sorry, but we have to make sure you're not harboring them."

"They tried a few days ago, but we saw them off," Bethany volunteered. "We're really glad to see someone from the government! What has happened out there?"

"Things have collapsed quite badly, but we're rebuilding," said the chunky man. "Now let me introduce myself and the mayor of New Hobart. So: this is Mayor Swinner and I am Fred Burroughs. I am the surviving senior representative of the Tasmanian Government, acting as the manager of the Bass Region. We'll be happy to answer any questions, but we need you to join us in our growing settlement of New Hobart." He looked up at our camp. "Oddly, not everyone wants rescue, but if we're to rebuild Australia, we need you to join us."

"Just try stopping me," said Liz. "I can't wait to get out of here."

It seemed that everyone felt that way. Except for the old bastard. He didn't say, because he wasn't there. Well, young Mick didn't say much, just looked confused by it all. Burroughs and the Mayor, however, were in a hurry to get back.

"The tide will be a problem if we get back later than midday," explained Burroughs, when we wanted to give them a meal, and talk. We all had so many questions.

"If we don't go now it may be some months before we can do this again. We don't have a lot of spare diesel. So: basically, if you're going, you need to come with us now. Collect anything you might want to bring with you. Extra food is always welcome, but it doesn't look like you have a lot of clothes to pack," he said, laughing.

People rushed back to the camp. Soon we were carrying down baskets full of potatoes, dried fish.

"I don't suppose you will want dried fish. It's awful," said Liz.

"Oh, we don't get a lot of fish," said the mayor. "You seem to have done well on the potatoes."

"The old bastard sees we get enough fish," Jim said.

And then Liz said, "No, Jim. You're not bringing those jars of muttonbird oil. It stinks."

Jim noticed that the boxes of food that young Mick had pinched from the raider boat were missing. So was the fuel can. He nearly said something, but Mick nudged him.

"The old bastard took 'em," he said quietly. "Said he is not

going nowhere. Just to leave him alone. He said don't say nothing about him. I don't like it, Jim."

Neither did Jim. The old bastard was a pain in the butt at
times, but he was the one who knew how to do things. He'd
grown up poor, without a fridge as a kid, and with the sea for
a larder. But if that was the way he wanted it...well...it was
difficult. But it all got taken out of his hands. They were on the
beach, getting people into the dingy to go across to the cray boat,
when Kayley said, "Where is the old bastard?"

"Who?" asked Burroughs.

"The old man," explained Liz. "He's about seventy. A bit out
of it at times."

"Anyone seen him?" asked Sally. "We'd better go and look
for him."

"We don't really have time," said Burroughs. "We'll miss the
tide, and there is weather brewing."

But most of our mob was bellowing for him. Well, except
me and young Mick.

"We have to go looking," Liz announced. "We can't just leave
him here."

She wasn't all bad.

"It's what he wants. He doesn't want to go. And you'll never
find him if he doesn't want to be found," Jim said. "I hate it but
it is what he wants."

"He told me to go. To leave him," said young Mick, looking
seriously unhappy about it. Jim thought he was going to burst
into tears, and found he felt the same way.

Burroughs stared at his watch. "Look, we'll be back in a week
or two, if the weather allows. We really don't have the resources
for aged care. We need the young and strong for this."

"He's not needing care. Much," said Sally.

That was true. He mostly didn't. "He doesn't want to leave,"
said young Mick.

"Well, see how he feels in a week or two," said Burroughs.

Jim wondered what had happened to the "won't be up this
way for months."

"He's been on his own for weeks," admitted one of the others.
"But we can't just leave him."

"You must if you are to come with us. Come on, it's not for
long," said the mayor woman.

So: they went.

Jim stood on the stern, looking back at the few acres that had been their home. Young Mick was there too. He didn't want anyone to see he was crying. He waved at the island.

"He's watching through that scope of his," Jim said quietly. "We would battle another winter out there, Mick. Knowing him, he'll probably follow us in his own time. He's got boats and fuel." The government people had not been interested in the vessels. Well, the island probably had one for every four people before this, and tinnies don't rot.

Eventually, when Roydon Island was out of sight Jim went forward to where most of the rest of the group were trying to find out just what was going on in the world, how the Australian government was trying to put things back together. What they all knew, that we didn't. He was in time to hear old Mick—who was in his forties, but it separated him from young Mick—say: "So you reckon the Australian government is getting back in charge. You took your sweet time. Where did you spring from? You're not a local. I know the people what was in the council offices. They give me a lot of strife."

Burroughs gave us a kind of sideways answer to that: "I've been in local government a long time. Not here, of course. The Planning Office and then General Manager of Johnstown. Things were a bit of a mess when I arrived here. Fortunately, I have the experience to manage the complexities of setting up a new administration. You'll be glad to have the government back in charge of your lives, I am sure."

Quite a few people nodded. The uncertainty had got to all of them, Jim knew. There was a comfort in having someone in charge.

New Hobart, it turned out, was a lot closer than old Hobart—the state capital—was. Maybe twenty miles away, just further south on the same main island our refuge had been off the shore of. They could have gone ashore and just walked south. The big island's main little town had been about a mile further south, but that had been badly hit when things went pear-shaped with the initial spread. The cray boat scraped into a very shallow little bay. "Bluff road," said Bethany. It had been a single-road sort of suburb, before.

"It's New Hobart now. The city is at the old showgrounds," the mayor informed them.

They had to wade the last bit ashore. Jim was surprised to

see there were no other boats moored there. Even the dingy was winched onto a trailer and hauled up to the road. But there was a truck parked at the shore. A truck! And they had fuel and it was in going order. They loaded baskets of potatoes and fish onto it and then themselves and were driven to the gates of the "city." It had...people. And the oval where the kids had once played sport was cultivated. A tractor stood there, people behind it who looked up, as they were brought into the fenced area.

As cities went, it wasn't up to much. After living in what was basically an A-frame kitchen common room and bedrooms made of scavenged wood and tin, it was quite large. It was a series of big sheds and smaller buildings, with a fenced area and guard towers on the corners.

"Right," said Swinner, getting out. "Welcome to being citizens of New Hobart. We run a cooperative society here, where everyone is cared for. I'll have a word with the kitchen staff and we'll have some lunch for you. You must be hungry after your sea journey and after living in such primitive conditions. Then we'll have Mr. Burroughs and his assistants talk you through the city ordinances and how we work together for a new Australia."

The food part sounded good. And it was. Much of it came out of tins, but we'd had precious little like that. And there was crockery, and knives and forks, sufficient for everyone, and not carved out of wood by the old bastard.

Then we went through to what we were told was the administrative block—a smaller shed, but well fitted out with comfortable couches and a lovely long wooden table, as well as having sections partitioned off, behind closed doors. It looked pretty civilized, after Roydon Island. You could almost believe you were back in the pre-plague days.

The mayor made a speech about us all working together, and how we'd be rebuilding Australia. Then she handed us over to Burroughs who said, with a smile: "Firstly, I am going to have to ask you to turn in your weapons to the armory. We have a strict no-firearms policy in New Hobart."

Jim saw he wasn't the only one who looked a bit taken aback at this. Not all of them had guns—but it had been the insurance against any attack by the infected. He said as much.

Mayor Swinner shook her head. "Goodness. This is Australia, not some savage place. You're safe here. And honestly, we have a problem if you don't hand them over. Our citizens are not armed. You are quite a large group. You might decide to attack them. This is for everyone's good and comfort and security. Firearms and ammunition are scarce resources. We can't just have everyone armed. That would be against the law! We need the weapons for hunting for the group and for defense, and to control any individuals who break the law. You can apply to get a rifle or shotgun, of course. It's all done according to Australian law, under permit, and we assess your capability and suitability, and decide."

Jim didn't like it, at all. Yes, that was how it was in the old Australia. And yes, he missed a lot about it. But what if they got attacked? Or there were more infected that got here somehow?

"We have fences and guards. You'll be quite safe," Burroughs assured them. "Really, it is nothing to worry yourself about. You're here now. You're much better off than you were. You'll just have to fit in. Honestly, I can't see what the fuss is about. You never needed them in Australia before. The government took care of you, and we will again. You can trust us."

It seemed most of the others were willing to do so. A man in a police uniform—somewhat the worse for wear, but still a police uniform, took the guns, and made them fill out paperwork. It all seemed very normal bureaucracy.

"They'll be safely locked away," said Burroughs. "Now, let's record your names and assign you to the various work groups. You'll get a chance to meet the other citizens that way. Young mothers will join the childcare group. Older children help with pulling weeds. We'll be starting school soon."

Jim found himself assigned to those carrying water from Pat's River, about five hundred yards away from the "city." It was backbreaking work, carrying a pair of five-gallon plastic drums from the freezing beer-brown frothy river, up the slope next to the bridge and then back, and then up a ladder and into a tank. It was like filling a bucket with a teaspoon. He was also sure it was unnecessary. The old bastard would have either moved the camp to the water or the water to the camp, he thought, grumpily. They only had rainwater on Roydon, but the tanks filled from sheets of corrugated iron sat against the cliff, making a store for all the bits they used occasionally, as well as the fish which was smelly enough to want to keep there.

He was shocked to see Liz carrying drums of water too. "She's pregnant!" he protested to one of the guards—supposedly there to keep them from being attacked.

"Shut up. If she loses it we'll give her another, soon enough," said the guard, sitting, smoking a joint, shotgun over his knees. Jim weighed up his chances.

They weren't that good. "Careful," said one of the others, quietly, "Shady shot someone about a week ago."

"How the hell do you guys put up with this?" asked Jim. "They just sit and do nothing. He's fat and you look half starved."

His fellow water-carrier grimaced. "They're armed. We aren't. My mob hid out on Prime Seal. When things got too hard, we headed back here. We could see smoke, we knew there were people. There was a bit of a settlement, maybe twenty people, around the old town. It was...a bit chaotic. Some fights about the food we found, about grog, about one of the women—and a few people got hurt. And then Fred Burroughs, Shady Johnson and Linda Swinner showed up on the old cray boat, said they were from the government and were here to help us get things organized. They aren't from the island, and I reckon people wanted to believe. Things did get a little better. We had a meeting, and elected Swinner as Mayor—she had Burroughs backing, and well"—he pulled a face—"the other three who stood sort of split the vote. She made Burroughs Manager, and he made Shady Johnson the police officer and Smythe into captain of the town guard. They got Belcher, Ferny and Morgen in with them as guards too. Anyway, about two months later someone got on the piss, and took a shot at someone else. Nearly hit one of the kids. Next thing we had another meeting, and Swinner said guns were too dangerous, and we needed to keep them locked up unless needed."

He sucked between his teeth. "And it went downhill from there. More groups and people come in—but they made sure they got disarmed, pretty quick."

"But surely—I mean they can't watch you all the time? You could make a run for it," said Jim.

The Prime Seal refugee shuddered. "They say there's still infected outside the fence. And there's guards on the watchtowers. They say they're for the infected, but they'd likely shoot you if you tried to go over it. There's a bunch of bandits out there too, even if you got a boat. They attacked the Wybalenna Island lot. Shot someone, raped a couple of women, stole their stuff. They weren't gonna come in, but after that, they came running. It happened on Tin Kettle Island too, or so I heard. But they killed everyone there."

Jim had taken a good look at that fence. He wasn't sure what it could keep out. But he held his tongue, wishing like hell they'd been less pot-sure about being rescued. He was even less happy about it when he discovered the accommodation. The group had taken over the showgrounds where the islanders had held their local agricultural show for many years. On the positive side, the buildings kept out the rain, and the fire in the middle of the floor of the biggest shed provided heat and light. But that was the point where "positive" ended.

The meal that evening was...a stew of potatoes and salted, smoked fish—prepared by someone who had no idea how to deal with fish preserved by salt and smoke. Rather than the "government" providing for them, they had provided for the "government," it seemed. And the "government" had made a mess out of it. But, by the way their fellow citizens were tucking in, the food was welcome.

"Not much compared to food we got for lunch," he said.

That got a laugh. "Oh, they always give new people a good first feed. That way you think you're coming to the good time. Which it is, of course. Much better than out there."

"I don't bloody think so," said Liz. She got up. "I think I made a mistake. I think I'm going home. Anyone with me?"

The little Roydon group got up. Some slower than others, but everyone got up. That is...except for the three mums with young kids. Jim realized they weren't there. He'd been too tired when he came in to realize it, but no kids were.

One of the others said: "Sit down. You'll get into trouble. You can't leave."

"Why not?" asked Liz, belligerently.

"Because they won't let you. And it isn't safe out there."

In answer Liz just marched out, across to the "administrative block"—where they found the mayor and her manager and various parts of "government" and several young women enjoying drinks and lounging after their hard day at the office.

Liz cut to the chase. "Look, I think we'll just go back to our old settlement. We don't like this setup. We don't fit in here. We don't want to be here. Give us our stuff back and we'll take ourselves back home. This was a big mistake."

Burroughs puffed at his joint. "Sorry. You are not going anywhere. Go back to your quarters."

Mayor Swinner tried a different tack. "We can't let you do that. You didn't have permission to be there. It was an illegal building in a conservation area. You're lucky we didn't press charges."

"Press charges? Are you insane? We'd have died if we hadn't stayed there! You can't stop us going back," said Liz, angrily.

"We can," said Burroughs—waving at two of the guards—who now had shotguns pointed at them. "We can't afford to let people go off and do their own thing, even if it wasn't illegal. We've got rebuilding work to do and we need labor. We'll make an example of you if you try."

"You could do some labor yourself," said Sally. "I haven't seen any of you lift a finger."

"We do the planning. Without us you'd be in dire trouble," Burroughs informed them. "Without us this group would be starving and fighting. Someone has to organize. And anyway, if you went out there tonight, you'll be unarmed and in the dark, easy meat for the infected and without weapons easy prey for the bandits out there. Because no, we're not giving your guns back, and we're not going to let you take the children. It's not safe out there for them. Now get out of here. Shady. Smythe. Take them back. Note down who they are. It'll be on your records."

"On our records! It sounds like we're in a prison, not Australia," exclaimed Bethany.

Jim looked at the fence in the moonlight as the two guards herded them back. "I suppose Australia started that way. Only I don't think I wanted to go back to that Australia."

"Shut up," said the guard, backhanding him across the head. "And get a move on."

Later that night, Jim discovered they were also locked in. The problem was not just getting away. It would be how to get all of them away. Water-carrying seemed the one chance to make a break for it, but their group was divided up. And anyway—fleeing with children and pregnant women was going to be hard. The boat would be the best answer—but getting out to it without swimming, when it was not sitting on the sand at low tide, would be tricky. That was obviously why no boats were left on the beach. Talking was difficult, there was no real privacy, and they could plainly be overheard. It seemed probable that at least some of their fellow citizens were likely to inform. Jim was no closer to an answer by the time he got to sleep.

The next day saw them split into different work groups, Jim and young Mick and Liz and old Mick on water-carrying again. Jim had been shocked to discover that much of that water went into the two still-working flushing toilets. There were no showers or even a bath available. They had done better than that back on Roydon! It wasn't that hard. Walking down to the river young Mick edged to get next to him and said: "I'm going to try and escape. Go back to the old bastard. Maybe he can help us."

It was an idea Jim had kind of had himself. But if anyone could, it would be the kid. He'd learned a lot from the old bastard. And the old bastard had learned a lot from being a poacher. "I'll create a distraction," Jim said quietly.

Young Mick nodded. "I'll get into the water. I think I can swim a bit underwater and get away."

"I'll start something when you're at the river," said Jim.

Jim had collected his water drums and started back up the slope. The two guards were sitting on the edge of the muddy path down and he got between them as young Mick arrived at the water. At that point Jim screamed, "SNAKE!" and peered wide-eyed at the guard with the rifle, and backed off a step.

"Where?" demanded the guard, looking at the ground instead of the "citizens" at the river.

"Behind you!" said Jim.

The guard turned hastily, and his attention—and his fellow guard's attention—was just where Jim wanted it. And then some rat down next to the river yelled: "He's jumped in the water!"

As the rifleman swung around, Jim hit him with the water can. It only had about a gallon in it, as Jim had realized, yesterday, that that was the wheeze all the others were pulling. The Roydon crowd were carrying full cans, the others were just carrying a little. The guards didn't check, or slither down to the river and watch them fill.

The guard fell over, and Jim grabbed for the rifle, as the other guard's shotgun boomed behind him. He was still struggling when there was another rifle shot. Jim almost lost his grip on the rifle barrel, and then managed to kick the guard in the face, and wrench the rifle away from him, and roll and try to get away from the shotgun blast he felt sure was coming.

Only it wasn't. The shotgun-wielding guard was suffering from a serious dose of dead. Liz was scrambling to grab his shotgun. And the old bastard yelled from the far side of the river: "You better fish Micky out before he drowns."

Jim slithered down the slope, and ran along the bank, to where the boy had just surfaced and...was struggling to swim. He could swim like a fish, Jim knew. Jim dropped the rifle and went to haul him out—and damn near drowned himself. The water was that icy it half sucked the breath out of him. Anyway, Jim managed to haul the kid to the bank. The fellow from Prime Seal gave them a hand up. Liz had come slithering down too.

The old bastard walked across the bridge to us. "That bloke you knocked down took off, Jim. I'm too bloody old for all this. I should have shot him too. Leave off pounding that fellow, Mick."

Old Mick had a hold of one of the other "citizens" and was busy punching him. "Him what told them the boy was getting away," he said, indignantly.

"We're probably going to need you to do some shooting instead, Mick," said the old bastard. "You all right kid?" he asked of young Mick. "Sorry. I wasn't expecting that bastard to shoot you. I could see you was going to jump."

Liz was examining young Mick's back, pulling the torn, wet shirt up. There were a couple of tiny holes, but not much blood, because of the cold. She squeezed one and a bit of shot popped out. "Ouch!" said young Mick. "That hurt."

"Just under the skin! I thought you were dead, you young fool," said Liz crossly.

"The water caught most of it," said the old bastard. "Water stops bullets quite remarkable. We used to try shooting the seals when they was robbing the nets. Never had much luck unless they were on the surface. Now, where is the rest of you? Don't look like the 'government' is treating you too well," he said sardonically.

"Back in the camp...they call it New Hobart. But it's just the old showgrounds. You were right," Jim said.

"Excuse me," said one of the other water-carrying "citizens." "What are you going to do with us?"

"Do with you?" said the old bastard. "What the hell should

I do with you? You're grown up, aren't you? Do whatever you want with yourselves."

"But...you just killed that man. That's a crime. Manager Burroughs is not going to like it," said one of the women, plaintively.

"Oh, shut up," said Liz. "He tried to kill Mick. And Burroughs and that lot are making you work like a slave, while they do nothing."

"I'd like to join you, if you'll have me," said the Prime Seal fellow. "I want out of here."

"Maybe getting into there, rather, son," said the old bastard. "And the rest of you? Choose. Run back or stay? Or run away."

Of the water party of fifteen, four chose to bolt up the bank and start running back to the camp. The Roydon party made up four of those who stayed. "Good," said the old bastard. "I only got another six guns. Yer better fetch 'em, Mick and Mick. They're just next to the bridge. I've had enough of walking for one day. My feet are killing me. And you better get a move on, because they'll be coming after us soon."

"You mad old bastard," said Liz. "It's good to see you."

"Well, check that feller's pockets and see if he's got any more shells," said the old bastard, "instead of complimenting me on my beauty." He'd seated himself at the top of the slope. The road to the showgrounds curved a little, giving him a clear view to the fence. "Now, how many of these jokers are there? Didn't recognize the one that run, but that dead one is one of the blokes that come and sneak up on the camp."

"The same people?" exclaimed Liz.

"Too right," said the old bastard. "Good wheeze, getting you to all run to them and give 'em what they came for in the first place."

Mick and Mick came running, carrying a bunch of firearms.

"Where did that come from?" said the Prime Seal islander. "That's my shotty!"

"Their boat," said the old man. "The one they got moored at Long Point. The one they use for being raiders, not the cray boat. They must have access to the big fuel tanks at the wharf."

Long Point, Jim knew, was perhaps a half a mile back north from where they'd landed.

"Can any of you shoot worth a damn?" asked the old bastard. "'Cause it looks like they're coming, and I am too old to run. How many of them are there? I can just see a mob coming this way."

"Nine," said the Prime Seal guy. "But Whitey is dead now. So, eight if you include Swinner. There's a bunch of women who hang around them too."

"The food was better and you don't get crap duties," said one of the women who had remained, who now held a rifle. It was only a .22, but it plainly was a comfort.

"Looks like six of them," said young Mick, squinting through the scope of the .223. "I can drop one." The old bastard had made sure that everyone on Roydon knew their way around firearms. They'd had to be careful about ammunition, but they at least had some idea what they were doing. He always said it was for the infected, but, well if you could shoot, you could shoot.

"Wait up," said the old bastard.

"You going to shoot them all?" asked one of those who had joined them. He sounded doubtful.

"Not unless they start it," said the old bastard. "You reckon they ain't gonna shoot us?"

"They...they could," he admitted. "But they are the government, I suppose."

"Government, my arse," said Liz.

"Yes, that about describes government," said the old bastard. "But we'll give 'em a warning shot, first, if we has to. Waste of ammunition in my opinion, but we give them a chance, right? We don't want to shoot no one, just get our people back."

"And mine," said the Prime Seal Island guy. "I got a brother in there."

The mob advanced, well, as a mob, set to sort out uppity citizens.

"Right, you lot," the old bastard yelled. "That's far enough."

The lead member of the mob loosed off a shot. He wasn't trying to give chances or engage in discussion. His little crew did much the same. The rebels were all down over the lip of the ravine that the river ran through, and it didn't take the old bastard saying "Down" to get everyone to duck. Jim found being shot at—even ducked behind a good solid bank—something he could happily avoid. It was maybe why instead of nine rebels shooting back, perhaps four did. And they were not combat veterans, so it wasn't much of an effort.

The advancing mob were not soldiers either, and they were out in the open, maybe eighty yards off, and the last thing they'd been expecting was anyone to shoot back. They'd been out to chase down runaways, not fight. Two were down, one screaming. And two had run—one dropping his weapon. The remaining two stood like rabbits in the headlights, firearms raised.

"Drop the guns, raise your hands, and you get to live," yelled the old bastard.

The one thing you could say about the man they'd made a guard was that he wasn't a coward. The other thing you could say was that he wasn't very bright. He had a pistol, perhaps that had once belonged to a real policeman, because they were rare elsewhere in Australia. He loosed off another shot ... with a pistol at eighty yards. It spat dirt next to Jim, showing that distance and accuracy at range didn't alter the fact that being shot at was never safe. At which point the "guard" discovered that a 'roo shooter with a rifle and a telescopic sight and dead-rest was more accurate. He spun around and fell like a ragdoll. His companion had dropped his gun and raised his hands.

"Cover me," said Liz. She'd been a nurse once.

"Stay down," said the old bastard. Then he yelled at the standing man. "Kick the guns away. I've got you on my scope. Make any wrong move and I'll drop you. We'll come and give some first aid if you cooperate."

"You shot them," said one of the new people in horror, as the man under the old bastard's sights did exactly what he was told.

"They tried to shoot us. What did you want us to do, kiss them?" said Liz getting up. "Come and help me, if you feel they need help."

"Don't get between me and him, Liz," said the old bastard.

"Tell him to move away from his chums, then."

The fellow edged away, nervously, and Liz went to the fallen, shotgun ready. Jim, after a second, followed her. She was looking at the wounded—or as it turned out, one dead. Jim was looking to the camp, to make sure nothing threatened from there. It was about four hundred yards, but with his tepid knowledge of firearms—he'd never even held one, before coming to the island—he had no idea if that was far enough to be safe.

One of men had a bullet through his calf. The leg could well be broken. The other fellow got hit twice: once through the shoulder exiting under the armpit, another inch toward the center of mass—and if he hadn't been partly side-on he'd have been dead, not, as Liz pronounced, lucky to be alive—and once grazed across his head. The third one—the pistol-wielder, was dead.

"You can tell the old bastard's shooting," she said with a grimace. "The rest of us are pretty useless."

She ripped the shirt from the dead man to make a pad to stop the bleeding on the shoulder wound. One thing you had to say about Liz: in a crisis she was brutally practical. She could sound off about the causes she'd spent her life on before the plague, but when it came down to it, she actually did, when others panicked.

Jim realized the others had emerged from the riverbank and were now—at the yelled instructions of the old man, in a scattered skirmish line, advancing on the camp. He picked up weapons—one shotgun and a cartridge belt, and a bolt-action rifle—and left Liz to the injured, or them to her. She had shoved the pistol into her waistband. He had to wonder if she had any idea how to use it. Well, being Liz, she'd probably work it out. The "prisoner," if you could call him that, was being chivvied along in front of them.

Jim caught up with the stragglers, who, fair enough, were unarmed stragglers, and altered that situation. Heaven knew if they could use the weapons, but it looked threatening. What good that would do if it came to a fight, he didn't know. He was also glad they didn't have to find out. The gate was open and there was no sign of armed resistance. Some panic and flight from the "citizens" of New Hobart, but then of course someone from Roydon recognized the old bastard and started cheering.

"We've not come to cause trouble. Just to get our own back," Old Mick yelled out. That was about the longest speech he'd ever made.

"They're in the Administration block," called out Sally.

So, they went over to the shed they called the Administration block. "It's got two doors," said someone.

"They have blocked the other one," the Prime Seal man informed them.

"Do we need to go in there?" said Sally, who had joined us, holding her child.

"Do yer reckon if we left them alone, they wouldn't come after us? Besides, I hear you gave them your guns. We're going to need them because this lot won't be the last," said the old bastard.

"But if we go in there, well, someone is going to get shot.

Probably us," said Jim. "Probably you. And we need you. We didn't know we needed you until we didn't have you, you old bastard."

"It ain't me you need. It's less like them. But you're right. Let's get them out of there. They'll shoot at the door, likely."

Just then someone from inside yelled: "This is illegal! Put down the guns. You're breaking the law. You're going to be in a lot of trouble when the authorities get here."

Jim started to laugh but realized that quite a few of the band had actually lowered their weapons, and looked uncomfortable. A glance at who it was told him the story—Australian, urban. Had grown up accepting this. Not like where he came from.

For a moment he was worried. But the old bastard's laughter broke that, and then the laughter spread. "It's been two years, sonny," said the old bastard. "They ain't come before, and I reckon most of them that wasn't zombies already got et by their friends, 'cause you parasites can't feed yourselves. Now, we'll burn you out of there if we have to, but our people want their guns back."

"And everything else you stole," said one of the people who had been there from before the Roydon group arrived. "You told us you were going to see we all got a fair share, but you just kept it all!"

An angry rumble came from the crowd. Plainly that had struck a chord of resentment.

"Burn them!" shouted someone.

And the crowd took up the chorus, some hitting the corrugated iron walls with sticks and fists.

"Give 'em five and they'll unblock the other door and bolt out of it," said the old bastard. So, he and Jim—and a few others moved around quietly as people beat on the main door.

Sure enough, they came sneaking out, the three of them. Shady, Swinner and Burroughs, all trying to hide behind each other. All armed to the teeth.

"All right," said the old bastard. "Drop the guns and you can go."

"I'll drop you first," snarled Burroughs. "Shady, cover them."

Shady had, however, fallen over Swinner, while trying to get behind her.

But Burroughs had his rifle to his shoulder, muzzle raised. "You must be the one we left behind. We should have hunted you down."

"Yeah," said the old bastard. "And I should have shot you instead of notching your ear when you come sneaking around the first time. I used to work on that cray boat, once. You must have killed old man Harrison to get it, 'cause he'd never part with it. What happened? Did he rescue you—and you and your friends killed him for the boat?"

Burroughs flushed. "He was dead. We found the boat."

"Liar," said the old bastard. "I should have shot you."

"And I should have had my men hunt you down. We were going to. But I can make up for it by shooting you now." He was plainly working himself up to it.

The old bastard grinned his skew grin. "I don't miss at this range. You shoot me, we both end up dead. I'm an old man. And my medication run out a while back. I'm dead, pretty much anyway. My family and my kids are dead. This ugly lot are all I have got. I got nothing to lose, shooting you. But if you drop it you might get to live."

"And if you shoot him," said Liz, from the side, shotgun raised. "You're going to die, even if he doesn't kill you. I can't miss from this range either."

"But if you drop it, you get to walk away. You can go to your boat at Long Point," said the old bastard, reasonably. "Go anywhere you please. Take your friends along. Or you can die right here."

"Fred. Please. Let's just go," said the "mayor," looking terrified.

"This is illegal," said Shady, sitting up and trying to look like a police officer, albeit one with brown trousers and wild eyes.

"So was what you did to Buzz Pasloe. You shot him," said one of the crowd, which had rapidly come around.

"Go while the going's possible," said the old bastard, persuasively.

"I'll drive them to their boat," said old Mick. "Give me an excuse to drive the truck."

"Like you need an excuse," said Liz. Mick had been a trucker, once, who had come across to drive cattle to the ferry.

"You'll let us go?" said Burroughs, wavering.

"My word on it," said the old bastard. "Your boat is ready to launch, on the trailer. Mick will push it out for you. Just drop the guns, and you can go."

"Could we take the cray-boat?" asked Swinner. "It's bigger."

"It's on the sand with the tide," said the old bastard. "Now drop that gun, Burroughs. It's over. Take yourself, your friends and get on the boat."

Reluctantly, Burroughs put the rifle down.

"Walk away from them. Hands in the air," said the old bastard.

They did as they were told, and the old bastard got Jim to search them. He found two handguns, one in a concealed shoulder holster, and one tucked into a waistband and hidden under a shirt.

"Interesting," said the old bastard, evenly. We all knew that, given the laws in Australia, those were either illegal or police weapons.

"I am a police officer. I have a permit," said Shady.

"You're a weed merchant who came to the island to sell speed for weed," said someone, tersely. "And that's not the make or model the cops carry."

"Whatever he was, he's out of here now," said the old bastard. "Anyone else want to go with them had better go to the truck. Liz...you and Jim and Sal. You watch their stash of stuff. We want our guns and food back, and we'll try and see everyone else gets a fair shake."

He set off with the former mayor, chief of police and manager of New Hobart—and two others that survived uninjured sitting on the back end of the six-ton truck, with young Mick and the old bastard sitting backs to the cab, keeping shotguns pointed at them, while old Mick drove.

It didn't take long before they were back. In the meanwhile, Jim found himself doing quite a lot of talking. Everyone wanted to know who the old bastard was. After a couple of years...Jim found he knew a lot and a little. He could—and did—tell them that the old bastard had taught them how to live off the land sea, that he never stopped doing something with his hands—even when he was sitting with his feet up.

"We got lucky. We'd all have died without him. And I don't know his name. He just said to call him 'that old bastard,' and in time for tucker."

"So...he was your leader?" asked someone.

"Um. No," said Jim. "He just did stuff and expected you to keep up. And we did, because, I don't know, we had to. I don't think we really had a leader...there were only a few of us. We all worked. The old bastard would tell us when we were being dumb, or how we should do things. We'd argue, but mostly we ended up doing things his way. See, he knew how to do a lot of what we needed. He's old, done a lot, and grew up poor and needing to grow, preserve, hunt. He was a fisherman, a farmhand."

"I thought he must be a soldier. Or have been one," said someone.

Jim shrugged. "He went to Vietnam, but he reckons he was a storeman, and a driver. A REMF. Says someone had not to have been a hero. I suppose he must have learned something."

They asked about how they lived on their little island.

Jim was proud to explain. "We . . . we were actually better off than you seem to be. We piped our water, and we have a solar panel and a battery. It only does lights, but we always had someone reading aloud to us while we worked. We had fourteen gardens in case something happened to one. You seem to be growing half the potatoes we did. We had lots of food stocked, and spare time to work on projects. I guess because we were all working. Not carrying water a gallon at a time."

"Have you got space for more people?" asked one of the women.

Jim took a deep breath. "Honestly. Maybe a few. But you'd have to ask him."

But when the old bastard got back, he short-circuited that question. "Nope. Well, you can go. But I am not going back. Maybe to fetch stuff." He scowled at Liz. "You're right. We need more people. It seems like winter pretty well killed the infected, and we can run bait traps until we're sure."

He took a deep breath. "Them lot we just got rid of . . . well, that woman said something. About the mainland and getting radio messages." There was a sudden silence. "Seems like other people are coming together. We're going to need more than ten, if you're not going to end up as slaves. We need more land, more people, and a lot more guns. There's gonna be people with better than our rifles. But if every man and woman and child can shoot back, they'll pick on a softer target, or trade instead of raiding."

"You mean . . . there might really be an Australian government trying to get things back together? And they didn't tell us?" exclaimed one of the crowd.

The old bastard shrugged. "Why would they? But forget this 'Australian government' story. That's the past. No one is coming to look after you. You got to look after yourself. Anyway. We'll try the radio on the cray boat. If anyone is broadcasting, we'll be able to find out more."

They did. The people of the settlement of New Hobart... discovered they were not alone. No, no one was coming to rescue them, but there were other people out there, some flourishing, some taking in new refugees. It was going to take a while to process it all, but somehow with it came the realization they'd moved from merely surviving to rebuilding.

That night they ate as a huge group. Some people contributed tinned luxuries from the divvied up loot the "government" had kept—but mostly they ate roasted meat—wallaby. And fish. And squid. It turned out that some of the New Hobart "citizens" could fish, and a few had done some hunting, but the "government" had had them confined to the farm area, growing crops on a field too small to feed everyone. When turned loose—and knowing there was a real future to be built, there was a great deal of knowledge and expertise there. You could literally see the idea that they could do more than survive; they could do quite well, germinate... and begin to grow like a weed. There was no one making the decision for them, but it seemed that most people wanted to stay close, even if they didn't have to.

Later that evening, Liz handed a bottle over to the old bastard. "There are more. I've got a stock now. Half the old people on the island were on some kind of blood-pressure treatment, you silly old bastard. They're dead, but you are not and we need you. I went into the remains of the town this afternoon. The pharmacy was looted—but they were looking for exciting drugs, not blood-pressure treatment. The diet on Roydon probably helped, but you won't eat sensibly. So, take pills. I need you alive."

"So do we all," said Jim. "They might come back."

The old bastard shook his head. "You're going to say I'm a bastard, but it's easterly blowing—offshore, and they got maybe half an hour's fuel. Remember, I went over that boat on my way down." He threw two bungs on the table. "They thought they had guns on the boat and could come back tonight. But you need to remember to check your bungs and fuel before you go to sea."

Jim stared at him. "You're a bastard."

The old man nodded. "Yep. Told you that. But killing them

here would have caused more problems. And they weren't just going away. So, I dealt with it, rather than you. So, you don't need me. I can get on with dying."

Jim bit his lip. "We still do. You know things the rest of us never learned. Things we won't find in books."

"Not about electric," said the old bastard. "Can you get it going, Jim? It won't last forever but there's a lot we can do if we have that. There'll be fuel, but it is getting old, like me. Don't work properly. The diesel lasts a bit, but petrol don't."

Jim nodded. "Something anyway. The power station would need more diesel than we can afford to use. But there is the solar plant, and the lithium-iron batteries should be fine. Just the powerlines need work. And I am a linesman, after all," said Jim. "Never thought I'd work at it again."

"Reckon there's enough solar stuff to last a few years, until we get other things going," said the old bastard. "You'll be busy. No gas, no diesel, no petrol..."

"Excuse me, but we can make fuel," said the fellow from Prime Seal who had inserted himself into their conversation. "We can do alcohol, methane and even hydrogen. We probably can't transport it or store it, but we can make it and use it. It was an interest of mine, and I'll get it going for you." He'd decided he wanted to be part of the Roydon crew. Well. Most of them had. They'd suddenly discovered that what their lives were missing was an old bastard.

The old bastard shook his head. "Not for me. You get it going for you, and people will pay you—especially if you can make a way to cut wood and to power transport, as long as it lasts. Don't know what we'll do for money in the end, but they'll probably give you tucker. Or something useful. Ammo. Clothes. Be a while before we have our own wool, so clothes will sell," said the old bastard.

"Collect old clothes is about all I can do," said one of the women. "I was an accountant."

That got a laugh. "Well," said the old bastard. "There's always labor. People always need that. Or you could start a pub. That'll need an accountant, and the brewing part isn't hard. Good grog is, but people will drink rotten stuff until they can get something decent. And there's fruit and grapes in gardens I reckon. Those can be picked over, if you don't get shot in the process."

"I think that'll happen after the drinking," said someone with a grin. "And better to save the bullets for wallaby."

The old bastard said: "Get farming instead. I took my boat along the coast after you lot left with the cray boat. I saw cows. And at least one horse. There might even be sheep somewhere. Some of the islands had sheep. And every farmhouse is going to have some guns, some ammunition. I don't think this 'government' moved much away into the country. They looted the towns and looked for smoke to find people. There'll be other people on some of the other islands maybe. They might join us, if life is good here. Trade with us anyway. We need numbers, numbers with guns and some kind of communications before someone comes over to attack us."

"There's not a lot of people. Not here, not elsewhere," said Liz. "Humans are not short of land, for a long time. There's much more loot in the cities—what is left of them. Why bother to go conquering?"

The old bastard looked thoughtful. "Hmm. Not land maybe, but cultivated land? Our crops, our livestock? There's always going to be those who think stealing easier than working, Lizzie. And there's sure to be others wanting to make us do the work. Thing is, people always take the easy path. And if they got to choose between trading or working for something, it's going to be a long rocky road before anything but the bastards getting shot is going to change their minds to choose the hard way. They'll always pick on the soft target first. When everyone shoots back—they'll go elsewhere, or trade or work. And as for government, time 'straya learned what my people learned long back. Don't trust 'em: they're mostly thieves. Look, when we get big enough numbers of people, government is like the clap in dockyard whores. You end up getting it. But while every man and woman is armed they'll do some work instead of just stealing."

Jim touched the rifle on his shoulder. "It's something my forefathers should have learned. My kids are not going to forget it. And that the old bastard usually knows what is going on."

Let Freedom Ring

GRIFFIN BARBER

"Well, there went the neighborhood," Mao whispered as another of the Militia assholes popped into view about five hundred meters off.

"Nah, Stockton was always shit," James muttered, still tracking the first of the men to appear in his scope. He looked closer, saw the red bandana the lead man wore tied across the left bicep. He didn't need a closer look to know the red bandanas would have a thick silver thunderbolt marked on them. Little more than a big, militarized gang with delusions of grandeur, the Delta Free State Militia was a real threat to the smaller, less aggressive polities eking out an existence on the coast of Northern California. His Rangers had investigated the aftermath of one of the Delta Free State's raids a few months back. That shit show had proven the rumors of how the Militia had survived the Fall were true: ruthless amorality and lots of guns could force people to see things your way, at least in the short term.

"Two more," Mao said. "Ten, then fifteen meters behind the second. All armed with long guns."

"Copy," James said, cheek to his rifle as he maintained his watch. The first guy dipped out of view, popped back up with something in his hand. The other men closed up on the first, who showed it to them. They all looked around, started to fan out and move to the northwest. They weren't cautious of being attacked so much as alert to what was at their feet.

James gave mental shake of his head. With a lack of new infected to add to their ranks, exposure to wind and weather, a lack of easily accessible prey, and other diseases, the infected population had fallen off a cliff in the last year or so. Still, it wasn't so safe you could make a lot of noise without attracting attention from surviving pockets of the infected, especially around areas of freshwater and the population centers that made for easy living for the infected, and Stockton had both. James's team of Rangers were at the extreme northeast end of their planned scouting mission along the San Joaquin River and its sloughs. Any further upstream and the waterways were too controlled by pre-Fall engineering projects or too exposed to the urban centers where who knew what delights awaited an explorer.

James and the team watched for a few more minutes, making sure the Militia weren't going to change course. Once assured the Militia folks weren't going to come cross the Pixley Slough to get at them, James lifted his head from the sight and motioned for the others to pull out.

His small team rallied up a few minutes later in a shallow depression screened by a small wood sprouting from the soggy bottomland of the island they occupied. Just off the White Slough on a stretch of river called the Pixley Slough, the island had a good view of what James's map told him was the Trinity Parkway bridge.

Mao kept an eye out in the direction the Militia folks had gone.

"What are they doing this far south?" Jalen asked, directing his voice at the ground. James felt a surge of pride at his son's caution. The kid knew his business. Fifteen years old and pulling his weight like a man.

"Hunting, maybe?" Mao offered, equally quietly.

James nodded and added, "But what?"

Mao shrugged big shoulders. "That's the question, ain't it?"

"What we gonna do, Pops?" Jalen asked uneasily. The boy was fine with putting zeds down, far more comfortable than anyone not of his generation would ever be, but he was less sanguine about shooting uninfected. It spoke well of him, that hesitancy.

"Pull out and look for greener pastures?" Mao said.

"I suppose so. Didn't realize the Militia had come this far off the Sacramento." He shook his head, not really wanting to give up on the area, not least because they'd spent the better part of a week snooping and pooping their way up the delta and then the San Joaquin to get here, and the whole area had a lot of well-watered, viable land for agriculture that was also defensible. That land was the whole reason he and his people were on the delta in the first place.

"Probably had to, what with the fires and shit," Mao opined, taking his eyes from his binoculars. A giant of a man, he crouched down next to Jalen and took a sip from his camelback.

"Water's none too clean, either" Jalen added, looking at the muddy, sluggish water of the Pixley Slough as he slipped down to join his elders.

"Probably also a result of the fires," Mao agreed. "I know they did for the refineries I used to work at, and those tanks will be leaking dirty shit until the turn of the century."

James nodded. Forest fires had been a thing in Northern California even before the Fall, but after it, with no one minding the store, it seemed like the whole world had burned. He'd counted maybe five or six days last September when the air hadn't been a muddled, angry red that was hard to breathe. Probably going to kill them with cancer, all the shit they'd been exposed to, if the zeds or some nutter with a gun didn't do for them first.

James was on watch when the distant sound of gunshots rolled out across the water. He could see something he hadn't in a long time: a light shadow under the clouds. Someone was using spotlights to light up targets. He nudged Mao awake with the toe of one boot.

"Wha—?" his friend said, still half-asleep.

"Militia idiots stirring something up," James said.

Mao sat up, a darker shadow in the moonless night. They listened together for a minute.

From the number and varied timbre of the reports, James figured it for a bigger group than the trio they'd seen that afternoon. A lot bigger.

"They're gonna bring trouble on themselves, making that much noise," said Mao.

The shooting continued, the reports carrying easily across the water. As if Mao'd summoned it, the rapid-firing shots were joined by the distance-faded, dull, furious roar of a mass of infected on the hunt.

"Couldn't happen to a nicer bunch," James said, glancing at Jalen. His teenage son was sleeping through both the racket and the discussion his elders were having.

Someone over there went full auto, the sound like God tearing a tiny corner of the fabric of the universe.

"Damn, but they're blowing through some ammo."

"In for a penny..." James said. Infected ran straight at loud noises, ignoring terrain that would give a billy goat pause, and once one heard you, the rest who were within earshot of the first would be shortly notified by what survivors sometimes called "infected-phone."

The thought made James look over his shoulder. They'd made sure to clear the small island they occupied, but he hadn't survived this long being complacent. Well, there'd been that one time he'd forgot to check for traps, but that had been a lesson learned. His quick sweep didn't see anything changed from when they'd settled down for the night, and he heard nothing but the quiet lapping of the water around their island.

The shooting rattled on, rising to a crescendo before dying off. The roar of the howlers also faded away, which could mean they were feeding, but could also mean...

"Think they got overrun?" Mao asked into the silence that followed the shooting.

"We can only h—" James began.

Then there was one shot, followed a short while later by a pair.

"Nope," James finished. "That'll be them finishing off the wounded."

Mao nodded agreement, said, "Waste of ammo."

"Never been shy about poppin' off, the Militia."

"Nope."

"You're worried," Mao said after a moment.

James nodded, then, aware the gesture might have gone unseen, said, "I am. They're sitting on a lot of good land, and they don't play well with others."

"No, they don't," Mao said in his thoughtful basso rumble. "And the way they're living, sooner or later, they're gonna need to push south into the areas we control. That means we either fight or we pull out."

"We don't have any regular soldiers to fight them with. Sure, we do well enough against the infected, but we got almost no one trained to fight as regular infantry, against intelligent opposition."

"I know," Mao agreed. "But I also know they ain't the soldiers they pretend to be, either. Too many hunters, gangbangers, and weekend paintball warriors among them."

"Still shoot ours just as dead, and they carry a lot more guns to do the shooting with than we do."

"True." A quiet settled on the pair, Jalen's faint snores and the regular night sounds slowly enveloping them in an easy, companionable peace.

"I'll take the watch, brother," Mao said, a little while later. James let him take over, even though there was about an hour left on his shift, figuring he'd need the extra time to ponder what to do. Not that they were spoiled for choice.

He zipped up in his bag and thought through the problem.

The Treasure Island Cooperative, as his people had taken to calling themselves, boasted only about a hundred fighters. Sure, they had a few ex-military types, but most of those weren't trained tip-of-the-spear types, a fact they'd been happy enough with so far. Trying to survive without the technical skills most of the Navy, Coast Guard, and Air Force personnel possessed would have been next to impossible without adopting the kill-pillage-and-move-on methods the Militia used. Sure, there was a certain readiness to fight every person possessed if they'd survived the last couple years. But willingness and capability were two separate things.

The Alameda Axis had fallen a year ago now. To, of all things, a revolution: John Chou, the crazy megalomaniac who'd run Alameda like a personal fiefdom, *droit du seigneur* and all, had pissed off all the wrong people. The subsequent revolt had killed his chief lieutenants and, unfortunately, a lot of the rebellious survivors. The better part of the survivors of the rebellion had opted to try and join TIC. Try, because no one in TIC wanted shit to do with folks who believed the new world was reason to lord it over other people like they had done in the Axis. It had taken a while to get everyone vetted and worked through, but the end result had added a third to the population of Treasure Island and done the same for TIC's Rangers, Fighters, and

Mariners once they'd been trained in the way TIC did things. The Axis had even had a couple solar power technicians and a civil engineer who'd been worth their weight in beans and bullets. The rest had been put ashore on Alameda, a decision James had argued against, thinking they could have put the mothballed Air Force base and the marina to good use even if they hadn't reclaimed the entire island.

He'd been outvoted.

New Alameda wasn't doing well, at last report. Crops planted on the old airbase kept dying. Something to do with blighted soil, Sam's people thought.

There was another couple of small groups down San Jose way, but they had their own problems, the population of infected being that much higher to begin with and arable islands in short-as-shit supply.

The restored portions of the U.S. government might *want* to help, but they could hardly project power this far north along the coast, and most everyone but the pie-in-the-sky-dreamers at home were leery of throwing away their sovereignty in exchange for patchy, poorly defined, and inconsistent protections. No, these days, the laws didn't extend much beyond the reach of the men and women willing to enforce their own. That continuing failure of the rule of law was the reason the Delta Free State Militia types were able to operate with impunity.

Louis, before he'd eaten his gun, told the survivors he'd train them in modern infantry tactics, but the idea was lost among all the things that required attention in order to survive from moment to moment in the post-Fall world, and when he took himself out, no one else had pushed the idea. And now they didn't have the time to train up to face intelligent opposition. Not that the Militia were all that bright, but they were light-years ahead of the howlers. Shit, he might have suggested Sam and the Council negotiate with the Delta Free Staters, but the Militia had a reputation for using parleys to size up the opposition and, on one occasion at least, get in close enough to take out the leadership of the people they were supposed to be talking with.

James turned over, half an ear on the night sounds, mind clouded with thoughts nearly as dark as the post-Fall night, and eventually fell asleep.

∽ ⊖ ⌒

As he ate a cold breakfast, James decided to watch for any exploitable weaknesses the Militia indulged in. They would have to wait for the Militia party to decamp before leaving anyway and keeping the gang under observation should be easy enough. That in mind, the Rangers spent the misty and cold pre-dawn hours getting into position. As the morning mist burned off in the rising light of day, they got a long, good look at what lay across the water.

The U-shaped camp was sited on the opposite shore of Pixley Slough, about a kilometer east of where the Rangers had spotted their scouts the day before. Considerable effort had gone into its construction, too. He could see a small windmill and a pair of solar panels at the center of the camp. At the center of the camp was a big red fabric tent that looked like it might have been looted from some Renaissance Faire, the ersatz power station, and a low, loose-boarded wooden box about three meters on a side. Each corner of the camp had raised platforms, too short to call towers, where guards stood beside spotlights James had seen lighting the sky the night before. The Militia had set chest-high barricades on the perimeter, using a field adjoining the slough to provide clear fire lanes out to about two hundred meters inland, and the corpses strewn in clumps to show the site had been well chosen.

It looked as if the balance of the horde had charged along the shore, as there was a literal heap of dead about fifty meters short of the camp on that side, where a bend in the slough forced the infected coming from the ruins of Stockton to bunch up in order to get at their prey. The dead were a pitiful sight, even before death, with ribs showing and not an ounce of spare fat on any of them. Most had poorly healed injuries and sores, or other evidence of hard living, even before they'd been infected. Five or six looked much fitter than the rest. The Rangers had run across that before, too: newly infected people who'd survived in some shelter or the other, only to run out of food, hope, or will after a year and more of survival and simply decide to stop thinking—stop fighting entropy, Sam called it—and gave themselves over to the infected.

Carefully counting Militia heads, James came up with twenty, maybe twenty-three. Might be more of them out on patrol or something, but James didn't think so. He was encouraged when he saw they didn't bother setting watchers to look across the water at the island, their sentries all positioned to cover the landward side of the camp. Indeed, they had clear shots at nearly every part of the camp from across the slough. It seemed James's own Rangers weren't the only folks who lacked experience against uninfected opposition.

Beyond the attention of the sentries, though, the camp was all bad news: each militiaman was heavily armed, with a mix of ARs and AKs predominant. There was even a machine gun the likes of which James had first seen in Vietnam movies as a child, which James suspected was at least partially responsible for last night's full-auto mayhem. Everyone wore the red arm band that reminded James of old news reels of the lead-up to WWII or some shit.

James consulted silently with Mao and Jalen, who both confirmed his head count.

At midmorning nine men left the camp. Each man wore a large, mostly empty ruck across their backs, and each was armed with an axe or other heavy-bladed weapon suited to fighting infected at close quarters. One man in three had a crossbow in hand instead of the rifles the others carried. The men split into three groups before disappearing into town, each down a different road. The camp sentries remained on high alert while the looters were out, probably to be sure to cover for the looting teams if their nighttime clearance hadn't been sufficient.

It all looked quite systematic and moderately well-planned to James. Not a bad way to survive, even if it wasn't sustainable in the long term. That was the problem facing everyone, now: civilization required farming. Farming required arable land, reasonably clean water, and intensive manpower in the post-Fall era. That the Militia was doing this labor- and materiel-intensive looting seemed to indicate they were about to settle down to farms. But if that was the case, why were they laying claim to so much land on the delta?

Like some many things in life, the answer came only after a long wait.

James was starting to feel a little anxious, like they'd been sitting too long in one spot, when he heard a noise from downstream. There was a repeat of the sound, almost like a long splash, but he couldn't be sure what it was. He tapped Mao's heavily muscled shoulder and pursed his lips in that direction when Mao glanced at him.

All three Rangers made certain they were under cover from the approaching sound and settled in to wait and watch.

A few minutes later the head of a dragon appeared at the downstream bend in the slough. Not like a scaly western dragon, but a long-whiskered, Asian dragon. The dragon's "body" hove into view a moment later, and proved to be a relatively wide, shallow-draft boat manned by ten paddlers, five to a side, with a short, slender dude in the back with a longer paddle he was using to steer the whole show. All wore the red armband, and had rifles slung across their backs.

The boat covered the distance between the bend and the camp at a respectable clip, paddles moving in unison even without someone calling cadence. As the boat slid across in front of James's hide, the Rangers got a better look from above and down into the boat. From the length, there was room for twice the number of rowers they operated with at present. James made out a bright, heavy metal chain running along the center line of the boat from just behind the dragon-headed prow to just in front of the steersman or whatever.

The boat took a sudden turn toward shore, the paddlers increasing their pace as the boat swept toward the camp. A short while later and the boat was being pulled up on shore. Two of the crew, the steersman and one of the paddlers, didn't participate in the heavy work, instead moving to meet a short, broad-shouldered guy just emerging from inside the tent. The steersman had a ruck over one shoulder, and while it wasn't full, it was obvious from the way it hung that it was heavy.

Their conversation wasn't terribly animated, and their body language didn't reveal much beyond a casual familiarity. After a few exchanges, they were joined by two more of the crew, still carrying their long, broad-bladed paddles. The party turned and walked up to the wooden, boxlike structure. The bosses stopped on the shore side while the two men walked to the far end and stuck their paddles between the boards. They began to work their way back toward the other end of the box, slamming the paddles around inside.

The steersman dropped his ruck and the broad-shouldered fella from the tent dove into it, hands emerging with a set of shackles. The dude from the boat opened the near end of the

box and stood beside the gate. In a flash, a naked woman burst
from the box, only to be caught by the steersman, who threw
her gaunt figure to the ground as the other boatman slammed
the door closed behind her. The muscular guy dropped a knee
on her back while he hooked the shackles to her at ankles and
wrists. That done, he stood up, dragging the woman aside and
chaining her shackles to something on the ground. The whole
process took about ten seconds from start to finish. Less than a
minute later, all the men were back in position at the box and
the whole process started again.

"What the fuck?" James heard his son whisper.

"Ah, *fuck* no," Mao hissed as the first cries reached their ears.

James and his people returned to their camp just as the last
of the red sunset lay dying in purple-edged darkness.

"Fuck," James snarled, knuckles bone white with the grip he
had on his rifle.

"Yeah," Mao agreed, lead in the single word.

"Fuck," James repeated. He hadn't thought to see shit like that
ever in his lifetime. A bona fide, honest to God, *slaving operation*.
He imagined the smell of the branding iron and felt like puk-
ing. Might have, had his blood not been at a hard, rolling boil
that demanded he kill something, that curtained off awareness
of anything but the anger throbbing in his veins.

Jalen's eyes brought him back to himself after a while. They
were white all around, and full of fear. Fear of the rage contorting
his father's face, not some external threat. It brought James back
to himself, that fear. He needed to think, not rage. Think clear.
Think right. Think fast. He took a deep, shuddering breath, let the
rage simmer rather than boil over. Set it to fuel him, not rule him.

He reassured Jalen with a hand on his son's shoulder, the
gesture rendered stiff after the death grip he'd maintained on the
rifle. Jalen returned a smile that was uneasy, but no longer fearful.

"Need to think about what we're gonna do," Mao said, the
lead in his voice having heated somewhat.

"Yeah," James agreed with what he hoped was a reassuring
glance at his son. He released the youngest Ranger and sat back.

Jalen knew better, though. He looked from one elder to the
other and swallowed. Uncle Mao might be slow to rage, but he was,
if anything, more frightening when the fury had him in its grip.

James shook his head after a long moment, a brittle, angry wonder dawning in his mind.

He'd read a lot of history while a guest of the State of California and liked to think he'd learned a thing or two about slavery, both in its eventual American form and the practice of it under Sparta and Rome. Hell, some of his gamer buddies had been all into miniature war games with Spartans and shit. What they'd just witnessed went a long way toward explaining why the Militia were staking claims to so much land despite the manpower requirements of their survival strategy. A slave society could afford to free up manpower for military operations if they had efficient controls in place on the enslaved.

Or, in this case, if the enslaved were those infected who, for whatever reason, hadn't become the ravening monsters the vast majority did. TIC had been informed, of course, of the existence of betas. Hell, James had seen sign of them himself: infected who ran instead of immediately seeking a death match with whatever had impinged on their awareness. They were just as mentally impaired as the howlers, just not hyperaggressive like a fiend-on-the-fifth-day-of-his-coke-and-meth-fueled-bender impaired.

Some egghead from the remnants of the U.S. government had run the numbers and come up with a rough estimate of about eight percent of the total infected population having become "betas" when turned. From what he had seen, he felt that number was about twice as high as reality, but eggheads were eggheads both before and after the Fall, and arguing with them was most often an exercise in futility. And he had no way to seeing what data was used. As it was, the number, whether eight percent or four percent, was still pretty low. Their odds of survival in the aftermath were much, much lower, of course. Fifty percent die-off was considered unreasonable by those arguing the point. Of course, given the total percentage of the global population who'd contracted the virus in the first place, there were still a relatively hefty number of betas running about. About the same numbers as those who had survived the Fall uninfected, in fact. The Bay Area had been overpopulated to start with, and so it stood to reason the numbers would be high across the board.

"They'll be leaving tomorrow," Mao said, interrupting James's thoughts.

"Yeah?" James said absently. Numbers didn't come easy to him and thinking about this shit occupied a lot of bandwidth.

"They looked 'em over, and got them in the chains, ready for *transport*," Mao elaborated. He had James's full attention, with the emphasis he placed on the last word.

James thought about it for a hot second but shook his head. It was fucking suicide. "No way we can take eleven armed men."

"Not if they see us coming, sure."

James shot a significant look at his son he hoped Mao would understand.

Jalen caught the byplay before Mao could react one way or another. "Don't use me as an excuse, Pops. If we can, we gotta do something."

"Ain't something we can handle. Not those kinds of numbers. End of discussion."

"Man, fuck that," Mao said, softly.

"Three on eleven is flat out suicide and you know it, Mao."

"Might be, but then there's the five women—girls, really— who've been sold down the river. Down the mother*fucking* river, James. Never thought I'd actually understand where that term comes from, but Jesus, could I have done without learning it."

"They ain't—" James tried.

"Don't you fuckin' say it, man," Mao interrupted. Mao managed to look bigger even leaning back in the hollow. "That's the argument the motherfucking slaveholders used, and it was just as much bullshit then as it is now. Humans deserve to be treated like mother*fucking* humans."

"Man, fuck you, I was about to say they ain't being watched by a couple guys with single-shot muskets. This is eleven men armed with modern firearms who do not give a shit about their cargo. Not any more than the slavers operating out of Grand Po-po did. As soon as the shooting starts, the very people we're trying to save will get got."

Mao's face twisted in the last glow of the sunset. "Who?"

"Slavers. Slaves?" James said, unsure who Mao was asking about.

A gesture of negation from one of Mao's big hands, barely visible in the gathering night. "Where, I mean."

"Grand Po-po."

Jalen giggled. "Po-po, like police po-po?"

James snorted. "No, course not!"

"Jesus." Mao shook his head, the angry bubble between them bursting in the moment of confusion. His eyes glittered in the dark as he said, "And just where the fuck is Grand Po-po, you nerd?"

"West coast of Africa. Used to be called the Slave Coast," James said, trying to keep a snarl out of his voice. "And who the fuck you calling nerd? It was you got me into D&D in the first place." They'd always enjoyed the tactical, problem-solving aspects of the game. Story, too, of course. But man, the tactical stuff was a blast, and then there was the element of chance, too. Slaughtering goblins and such from ambush was always a good time and had already taught him the rudiments of what worked when the Fall started.

"True enough," Mao said with a soft, deep chuckle and open hands to acknowledge the hit.

A thought floated free of James's subconscious, triggered by something in those days of gaming. It hung there, just out of reach. He waited, knowing better than to try and grasp it before it had fully ripened.

When the thought refused to come fully forward, James focused on the present, instead. "Look, let's get the Kleppers prepped. I want to be on the water as soon as possible. If we can get far enough ahead of these pukes, maybe link up with the other Ranger team, might be we can figure a way to snatch the..." He decided against using the word "slaves" at the last moment, and said instead, "... the captives and get them out."

"Tear," Mao said.

"Shit," James said, pausing in his own efforts to lay his end of the collapsible kayak out. The frames were composite on the newer models, and tended to be pretty rugged, but the hard use and constant packing and unpacking the Rangers put the little boats through made for the occasional tear in the synthetic hull material.

A rustling noise came as Mao dug into his pack for the repair kit. "I'll get it patched. Just gimme a few minutes."

They had a lot of patching kits for Klepper kayaks, rich tech brats having been fond of the collapsible kayaks as a tool for showing their peers just how much more outdoorsy they could be than the next guy. Sam had said it had got pretty ridiculous there at the end, with tech weenies competing to show off their collections of, and accessories for, kayaks they took out maybe once a year, at best. Regardless of how often they had the use of them, the prestige hobby of a bunch of rich dudes had proven a godsend for the Rangers in their scouting. Silent, and low-profile, and able the kit for two Rangers up- and downriver or even in the Bay. Steep learning curve on paddling the damn things aside, the kayaks were light enough for one man to handle in a pinch, collapsible, and easy to portage. Indeed, the fact they were collapsible meant the Rangers didn't leave a telltale boat ashore behind them in potentially hostile territory.

A few minutes passed, and James had his end laid out and ready.

"Done," Jalen said from a few steps down the shore.

"Check," James said.

"Come ahead."

James moved over and started checking his son's boat for tears and frames lacking the proper rigidity.

"Check the pump for him, Jalen," James said. Damn hand pumps had a habit of going out at the worst possible time. So much so that the Mark One Plastic Milk Bottle, Capped, was used to bail water at least as often as the purpose-built tool.

"On it, Pops."

"Good man," James said, returning to the work at hand while his mind kept gnawing at the problem of how to save the captives. Hijacking seemed a fair option, until he considered how they'd disarm eleven men without exposing one of his team to being grabbed and held hostage or simply knifed.

"What are we gonna do, Pops?" Jalen asked as they put the kayaks into the water.

Taking out the map and his penlight, James gestured for Mao to join them. "I think we run west along White Slough to the San Joaquin. We didn't see any Militia on the way north along the southern branch, and I figure if we are gonna stand a chance of stopping them, it'll have to be on their way home."

"*If* they're going home," Mao said.

Jalen said, "We saw 'em making room for the captives."

"And that boat looked awfully heavy to run too far upriver with a short crew," James added. "The map has a few marinas and docks on the north shore of the Slough as we head west, and a marina might make a good spot to base out of, especially if it's on one of the no-shit islands that dot the slough."

"Sorry, man, but this just sounds like more reasons not to do the right thing."

James kept a tight rein on his temper. "If we don't know where their backup might come from, we can't very well count on getting away after we hit them. Especially with betas, who won't know us from Adam, and will likely try and escape us as much as their captors."

"Fair point," Mao said thoughtfully.

"And we didn't get a look to see if they had personal radios in the big tent or anything. Stands to reason they might have some. Can't see those lights using all the power they generate."

"You'd be surprised," Mao said. He snorted. "Sorry, brother, I'm just so...offended by this shit I all I want to do is murder some motherfuckers, you know?"

James could imagine Mao's expression. Glad the darkness hid his own, matching expression, he went on, "In any case, we're good with heading west on the White Slough?"

"Sure," Mao and Jalen chorused. James knew they were anything but happy, but that lacking a better plan, they had little choice other than to agree with him.

"What are we gonna do, Pops?" The question stuck with James down Pixley Slough and a good part of the way along the White Slough, which eventually joined the San Joaquin proper. A few kilometers as the crow flew, the White Slough bent and twisted like an accomplished stripper, drawing out the journey and giving him plenty of time to consider the questions writhing in his head.

About nine that evening, with the moon up and a foot-high mist rising off the waters of the White Slough, Jalen brought his boat in tight to James's and leaned over to whisper in his father's ear, "Lights through the trees. A little south of west."

James, who had been focused on both keeping course in the north braid of the slough and watching the southern shore of the mainland, peered in the indicated direction. The slough to the south was dotted with islands along this stretch, and sure enough, a light hung bright and artificial in the middle distance. Maybe a kilometer off, and partially screened by the trees of an intervening island, the light was the equivalent of a beacon in the post-Fall night.

"I see the Beacon of Gondor," Mao said, voice pitched to carry just so far and no further.

"Same," James confirmed, stifling an unprofessional chuckle.

Jalen either didn't get the reference or was too focused on the mission to comment.

"Snoop from the island between us?" Mao offered.

"Yeah. Let's find a place to pull the boats up and settle in for a watch."

"What about the rest of the Rangers?" Jalen asked.

James weighed splitting up but decided against it. If they'd already scouted downstream of the slough, he'd be all for sending Jalen on a quick run downstream. As it was, they didn't know if the whole of the White Slough from here to the San Jaoquin proper was dotted with Militia settlements or what kind of threats might be out there.

"Gotta scope this before we rush into things," Mao said.

James gave silent thanks Mao was down with keeping Jalen close. Sometimes the boy accepted direction from Mao more readily than his father. It was the way of things.

"Fuckin' plantation," James said as they climbed back up onto the deck of the house they'd cleared and claimed for their camp. Camp, because the floor-to-ceiling glass wall of the place was in shattered heaps on the deck and inside the living room. Thoroughly looted, the place had been some rich dude's retreat before the Fall, complete with vast sectional and easy chairs arranged around a big-screen TV, now forever dark.

"You were expecting something different?" Mao said, looking around in the rapidly closing darkness before descending on the long part of the sectional.

"No"—James hid a grin in the darkness as he continued—"but I have to say: I'm happy."

"The fuck?" Mao said, the sectional creaking protest as his weight settled on it.

"Pops has an idea," Jalen said quietly, taking position where he could watch the approaches to the house.

James smiled again as he sat on the other half of the sectional. "I do."

Mao made an impatient gesture James almost missed in the dark.

"What did we see today?" James asked, mentally reviewing the layout and situation himself. A big, plantation-style place, complete with white columns, dominated the landscape across the slough.

"That dragon boat showed up and dropped off its cargo with the bastards on the island across the way...and received a bunch of baskets of what looked like vegetables in return."

"Right, and how many men were there to receive the...new-comers?" James refused to call them slaves. Not ever.

"Six."

"Right, and that's a much better number for our purposes. Especially when they're dispersed over an island rather than eleven dudes in and amongst the people we are trying to save. Add to that they're on an island, not confined to a narrow boat, and a rescue attempt becomes a lot more doable."

"We don't know how many more Militia they have holed up in the big house," Mao said, not arguing, just thoughtful.

James cocked his head. "There's probably a couple armed folks we didn't see, not many more."

"How do you figure?"

"First off, the ones we did see didn't have any security out and looked bored as fuck until the...people they were looking over showed up all naked and such. Then they were all eyes on the prize.

"Secondly, the island ain't that big, and the fields don't require much more labor than what they just picked up.

"And lastly, did you see how the guys from the island didn't have armbands on?"

"They didn't," Mao said the words firmly, but his voice had a note of wonder in it, as if he just realized it was true. He snapped his fingers and said, "Fucking customers."

James nodded. "I think so."

"That would explain why they didn't show the same...discipline as the guys in the boat or the camp upriver, either," Jalen said.

"Then who the fuck are they?" Mao asked. "They'd have to pose enough of a threat to make the Militia see the benefit of a deal rather than a rip, strip, and run."

"Good question." James thought about it for a moment, added thoughtfully, "Did you see how some seemed to defer to the older fella that came down to the dock with that big guy? Bossman with the gray beard?"

James caught Mao's nod as the last of the light faded, leaving them in darkness. "A boss, though not to the guys in the boat. They didn't seem all that impressed."

"True. That guy, though, he had a tattoo. You see it?"

"No."

"Big thunderbolt on his arm."

A thoughtful silence stretched. "Retired Militia?" Mao said.

"I'd have thought their retirement would be like a street gang's: dead or locked up," James said.

"Ousted, maybe?"

"That'd make sense."

"If he was too powerful to kill out of hand and not powerful enough to take over," Mao said thoughtfully.

"May be." James thought about that for a little longer, then said, "Or maybe they tryin' to be all Roman and shit."

"What's that?" Mao said.

"Roman legionnaires were often given a tract of land in retirement. The smart legionnaires would try and time it so that any slaves taken as booty in their last campaign could either work the land for them or be sold to finance some other project."

"Fuck."

"Yeah. So..."

"So, we watch for a day or two, then get ourselves downriver and bring up the rest of the Rangers?" Mao said.

"And any Mariners we can enlist on it, yeah."

"Timing works," Mao said thoughtfully. "They're supposed to run us up some supplies this weekend."

"What day is it?" Jalen asked.

James smiled. What day it was had very little meaning for most of them. "Wednesday. Two days here, making observations, one to get down to the forward base, and then we come back in force. Assuming there's not another Militia base close enough to offer support in twenty minutes or so."

"Assuming," Mao said.

James shook his head, annoyed that Mao was less than completely supportive of the plan.

A few minutes passed in silence.

"Hey, man," Mao said, breaking the silence with a deep, rumbling, "you still a fucking nerd, but thank you."

James played dumb: "For what?"

"For keeping your head when we were all so angry."

"Oh, I'm still plenty angry, brother. Angry enough to kill every one of those fucks across the river there, living well on the labors of enslaved people."

"Damn straight." James could hear the feral grin in Mao's voice.

"There's about seventeen ways this goes sideways, James," Chong said.

James looked over and down at his fellow Ranger. "Ya think?" The shortest of the Rangers now Jalen was coming into his height, Chong was one of the guys who'd come over from the Axis. Indeed, he'd been one of the core members of the insurrection there. The most skilled gunsmith TIC had, he'd been forced to work the forward logistics camps like the one supporting the Rangers instead of ranging, a job he was at least as skilled as James at. So skilled and respected was he that he'd become James's second on the strategic side of Rangers planning and command, and his voice carried a lot of weight on the Council. That said, one of the hats he wore was that of devil's advocate, poking holes in any plan brought before him until it was as airtight as it could be.

"Yes, I do," Chong said, waving at the mock-up James had made of the target. Yet another gamer skill, making scale models of terrain with whatever materials were at hand. "Just how far away is their relief?"

"From upriver, it's two hours with muscle-powered boats. Half that for sail if they've got the proper wind. Twenty minutes, slightly less if they got a powered boat up there while we've been gone. From downriver, it's roughly twice that except for the powered option, which is maybe a half hour?"

Chong gestured at the unit markers on the model. "Tight timetable."

"It's based on their probable response time *after* they learn of an attack. We saw no antennas on the island, so it's not likely they've got backup on speed dial. Barring a smoke signal, or radio we didn't see with the range to reach the next camp, we should be safe on those margins, assuming it doesn't take too long to collect the evacuees up."

Chong ran the fingers of one hand though his salt-and-pepper hair as he considered the tabletop. "Seems like they've left themselves stupidly exposed. The dawn lineups in particular are pretty stupid."

"You know as well as I do how much those assholes think of

themselves. As to the lineups, we can't count on him doing one of them when we hit the place, and as to reasons, he probably thinks he's maintaining military discipline or some shit."

"Could be."

"Besides, they've got some justification for thinking they've intimidated the rest of the survivor groups in the Bay Area. They've certainly been throwing their weight around enough."

"What about prisoners?"

James gestured at the model of the plantation. "This is dangerous enough without us taking any additional risks to secure prisoners, so I don't expect there to be any."

"Still, that won't go down easy with the Council..."

"Man, *fuck* easy. These animals are enslaving their fellow man."

Chong studied him a long moment, then nodded. He then cocked his head as if considering something new and asked, "You give any thought to how our Council will respond to an act of blatant aggression against a neighboring power?"

It was James's turn to nod. "And I also thought about it in terms of the status of this particular plantation. If Bossman is an ousted political, then we might get away with it by removing a problem child from the Militia's playpen. If not... well, if I have to face charges for crossing the Rubicon, then so be it."

"More like Caesar's illegal invasion of Gaul, but I see your point. And, like Antony, I'll be in your corner should it come to that," Chong said. He took another long look at the mock-up, but eventually nodded. "Once we confirm all hostiles down, we call the Mariners in to transport the... evacuees and... any prisoners who surrender?"

"Assuming there's been no radio traffic from the target, that's the plan." James really didn't like how things would turn out if the plantation men surrendered. He didn't want to execute a bunch of assholes, and he didn't want to testify at a trial, the legality of which would be extremely questionable at best.

"What about..." Chong let the question trail off.

"What?" James said, barely keeping his tone even. Chong never hesitated to ask, normally.

"Look, I know this is something we gotta do... and I'm all in on it," Chong added in calm tones as he saw James's expression start to tighten. "What I mean to say, or to ask, is: have you guys thought this through?"

"You mean later?" James nodded. "Of course. Ain't gonna

be comfortable times, trying to both protect their rights and integrate the—"

"No, not that late," Chong said, interrupting. He stroked his beard, something he only did when he was anxious. "Shit, man. This is hard to—look, the Mariners ain't gonna allow the—the *evacuees* free run of their boat. That's a shit show on the go, guaranteed to drown everyone involved."

James shook his head again, not in denial, but in frustration.

"So, the thing is—well, there won't be a lot of difference in the way the people we save are treated, not before we get them off the island and somewhere where it's safe to deal with them being...themselves."

"Fuck," James said. He'd avoided considering the short-term issues inherent in controlling the flighty betas as someone else's problem. Sure, he'd thought it through enough to know they'd need bigger boats than the kayaks the Rangers used to get around, but he'd fallen into the habit of thinking the gas engine RIB was the solution for all that ailed the evac portion of the plan. And it would look bad. Possibly very bad, to his Rangers and the Mariners, too, to have the betas dragged aboard in chains.

Chong gave him time and silence to think things through.

"Right. I'll make sure everyone knows we can't afford to go striking chains and letting them run wild." He sighed unhappily. "And that it's a temporary measure, much as we might hate it."

Chong gave him another of those long, considering looks, then nodded and said calmly, "I can't emphasize enough how important it is we don't develop a morale problem over this. People get bent over this, they won't unbend."

"Right," James agreed. "Got it. I will make it clear we're gonna have to do what we have to in order to get them out before we can start treating them right."

Chong nodded. "Let's get everyone in here and on the same page, then."

"Fuck." James said the word with real feeling.

Six kayaks slid through the morning fog hovering about a foot above the waters around the plantation, the only sounds they made an occasional dip-slosh of their paddles in the White Slough. Faint moonlight limned the river fog, making it look as if they swept through a silver blanket.

Jalen and two of the other Rangers, better shots with scoped rifles, had snuck in the night before to keep the plantation under observation and report if things changed. The kayaks neared the point where they were to turn in and run toward the island or scrub the whole thing without James hearing a whisper from the team with his son.

Judging there wasn't going to be a better time, James gently slapped the water with the flat of his paddle.

At his signal, the kayaks turned as one and started toward the island. They made for the west shore, on the other side of the island from the dock they'd watched the plantation people use. The west shore had fewer spots to run the kayaks ashore, but also about twenty meters closer to the big house the plantation boss lived in, and the plan called for neutralizing him before he could organize resistance.

The shore was quiet, the shadowed trees rising from it pierced with narrow slashes of faint, silvery moonlight as he and Mao drove their kayak ashore. Debarking the kayaks was always a pain in the ass, but he and Mao were up and out of it in good time. They left their kayak for the rest of the team to drag further up as they moved inland to set up a perimeter watch. James was uneasy with the weight of all the weapons he carried. The guns were not a part of his usual Ranger load-out, being too noisy for the work his teams carried out against the infected. It made him uncomfortable, thinking that this might be the new task they were put to.

Putting away his unease for later reflection, James crept forward until he could see the grounds of the plantation, which was laid out along a gentle slope to the eastern shore.

The house bulked white in the moonlight, no lights from its windows at this early hour. Two outbuildings, one of which housed the prisoners and two guards, stood closer to the docks along a wide gravel path that shone whitely in the moonlight. The other building was some kind of storehouse or had been converted into one since the Fall. To the north and south of the path lay large fields planted with everything from corn to pumpkins. There was even a large pen with a dozen turkeys muttering in it. Down at the east end of the gravel path was the dock, the light burning above it a would-be defiant middle finger against the fall of civilization. Would-be, because no true civilization that James wished to be a part of would countenance slavery.

Everything was still and quiet and as expected, at least from his vantage point. As the radio hadn't alerted him to any change, he had to believe the pair of Militia sentries standing post at the front door of the big house were at their posts.

After a few minutes, he heard the rest of the team moving into position. Confident he and Mao only heard them because they were already aware of their Rangers' presence, he waited a full minute before tagging the transmit button on his radio twice and starting the countdown.

Beside him, Mao clicked his light on and off, twice, to signal the rest of the assault team. He, Mao, and four other Rangers moved forward in the pre-dawn shadows, weapons up. The remaining three of his Rangers stayed behind to cover the rear of the house, which, keeping true to colonial style, had only a single, solid-looking back door.

"Light on upstairs," Chong's voice was tight over the radio.

They stumbled once or twice on the way, but James's team stacked up quietly along the side of the main house with plenty of time to spare.

"Lights coming up all over."

James click-clicked confirmation, reviewing the plan. It was fifteen, maybe seventeen paces to the front door and the first of the guards. Push come to shove, he would round the corner and tag the near one, then the other. All he had to do was wait. Bossman would be handled by the shooters across the water.

Bossman liked to show his people he was in charge. Normally, that meant he did the rounds of his property at or just after dawn each day. James had even seen him, one morning, just after dawn, run what looked like a full inspection on his people. Lined up in front of the house, he examined each of them and their kit while they stood in front of a big brass mariner-type bell mounted for calling folks to dinner or something. The only exceptions had been those on guard duty, who stayed at their posts. James would have loved to hit them while most of them were all lined up, but there was no telling when the next inspection would be.

The first rays of sunlight began to slant across the slough, making it easier to see for those not facing into the sun like the guards at the front door. Or James, for that matter, though as soon as he went round the corner, that would no longer be a problem.

"Target on the move."

James raised one finger to shoulder height. Mao reached up from behind him and seized the finger in one huge mitt, signaling the stack was ready. Still nervous, James cracked his neck and settled his shoulders.

A moment later the front door opened, and he could hear Bossman's voice, a rich baritone, acknowledging his underlings. His two lieutenants or bodyguards would be with him, naturally. They weren't James's problem.

James socketed the shotgun into his shoulder and raised it to eye level. He could hear Bossman's voice move from the entrance out a ways.

"On the way," Chong's voice whispered.

A bell tolled.

It was a dull sound, that toll, nothing like the clear ringing expected from a brass bell like the one in front of the house.

James didn't have time to process anything but what was in front of his barrel, however, as he rolled around the corner and saw the near guard flinching away from something to his front.

The Ranger stroked his trigger. Buckshot slammed out of the barrel and downed the target. James dropped the bead on the next guard, stroked the trigger again. Buckshot caught the man high in the chest and low in the throat, tearing the latter out.

"Bossman d—" Chong began. Mao's AR cracked almost in James's right ear, the suppressor stepping the sound down from a vicious crack to a bearable cough that still muted everything else.

The stack followed James up the veranda and across it to the front door, where they made entry.

Someone must have had a rapid rush of blood to the head, because as soon as James was over the threshold, he saw the flash of gunfire from a doorway off the entry hall. Hot pain lanced across his cheek and brow.

Staggering, James returned fire, buckshot tearing a pair of useless holes in white wainscoting.

Mao's AR cough-coughed again, rounds creating small clouds of white splinters. The 5.56 rounds penetrated a lot better than James's buckshot, however, the proof being the corpse of the shooter appearing in the doorway, skull cracked open and oozing.

"Prison guards on the move," Chong's voice was strangely muted. "Engaging."

Some blood seeped into James's right eye. "Keep moving! Move!" he shouted, moving steadily down the hall in pursuit of a man dashing through a door toward the rear of the house.

Half his people went upstairs to clear it while he, Mao, and Kristene moved to finish clearing the ground floor.

The man he'd seen didn't try and escape out the back. They found him in the study, just picking up the radio mic as the trio made entry. The would-be radioman went down in a welter of blood, all three Rangers lighting him up.

James heard gunshots from upstairs—as well as a woman's scream—and then, in a sequence of instants that always seemed to take forever to complete, it was over.

James winced as Mike plucked another splinter out of his face. He was the only casualty, and his injuries weren't serious. They'd been lucky. The place had been full of weird Roman legion regalia and shit.

Mao appeared at the front door, helping a small woman down the front steps. She wore a shirt ten sizes too big for her and she was barefoot. Even from a couple steps away, James could see scars and fresh red weals at her wrists and ankles.

"Where is he?" the woman said, squinting into the morning sunlight. Her voice was hard, devoid of emotion.

"Who?" James asked, making several mental adjustments. In hindsight, it was foolish of them to think the Militia only enslaved betas. He stood, tried to shield her from the carnage in the front lawn.

"Jack Dean Angstrom, the pig fuck who—" Her eyes lit on Bossman, rage clotting her voice. Small hands turned to claws as tears welled in her eyes. She took a step forward. Mao let her go.

She moved unsteadily to Angstrom's side, knelt and raised her hands as if to strike. She was like that a long time, hands raised, before lowering them to her sides.

"How did he die?" she asked in a thin voice.

James walked around to stand in front of her, the corpse between them at his feet. Angstrom's chest had a neat, bloodstained hole in it. "One of my people tagged him from across the way."

"He never saw it coming?" she asked, squinting up at him.

"No . . . I'm afraid not."

"I heard the bell ring, and I thought . . ." She looked up, over her shoulder at the shiny brass bell on its pristine white stand. James saw a smear of red on it with a whitish mark at its heart where the jacketed lead round had gone through Angstrom's chest and struck it hard enough to make the ring James had heard.

"Thought what?" James prompted.

"He rang the bell when he had a new one."

"New on—" James started to ask.

"His 'new toys,' he called us, the women he took. Said he could never settle for them," she nodded at the betas being led from their enclosure down to the RIB. "Said the only way to know he was lord of all he surveyed was to see the knowledge in the eyes of his victims. Betas didn't give him that thrill."

"Well, there won't be any more of that," James said. The promise sounded hollow, even to his ears.

The look she gave him was weary, and skeptical.

Under that gaze, he resolved to make the promise real, to bring it about any way he possibly could.

"Evac is almost ready," Mao said, nodding toward the RIBs.

James looked at the woman, and at the dead creature that had wanted to be her lord and master, and said, "Go ahead down to the boats, but give me a few."

Mao looked at him. "What you gonna do?"

"This piece of shit liked the Romans so much; I think it only appropriate to leave a sign behind people like him will appreciate."

It wasn't easy, but prison had seen him trained as an apprentice carpenter, and there were plenty of stout fence rails on the property.

James and his Rangers left the island a few hours later, by which time everyone but Mao and Jalen had retreated downriver. He didn't ask for their help, but his son and his best, oldest friend pitched in without a word.

The hardest part was dredging up the proper spelling and grammar. He hoped he'd got it right as he paddled the kayak down the White Slough.

Behind him stood a new monument: a cross with a fresh corpse nailed to it. From the neck of the corpse hung a wooden plank with words burned into it:

CAVETE, TYRANNI DOMINI,
NAM VIVIT ADHUC SPARTACUS

Maligator Republic

LYDIA SHERRER

When Frank Oberman's mare finally plodded through the gates of Gallrein Farms' compound, all he wanted was a cold shower and a hot coffee. But based on the unfamiliar vehicle parked in the gravel lot and the angry voices coming from the mess hall, he had the feeling he'd not be getting either any time soon.

Being a twenty-plus-year veteran of the United States Marine Corps, though—and the father of a headstrong teenage daughter—he was used to not getting what he wanted.

"Teddy," he grunted to his mounted companion after giving his surroundings a careful scan, "look after Shadowfax. Me'n the dogs'll go see what the ruckus is about."

Frank's mare huffed a weary snort as if in relief that she, at least, was headed straight toward a good rubdown and some feed. The horse's name was courtesy of Frank's daughter, Maggie. He'd made the mistake of giving her naming privileges over their various animals, and a deep love of classic literature was something Maggie had shared with her mother—before her mother had turned into a zombie and tried to eat them both. He supposed the ridiculous names Maggie picked out were her way of remembering her mother.

Most days, he'd rather forget. But he knew enough to keep his mouth shut and let the womenfolk have their way.

"Sure thing, Frank," Teddy said, dismounting his own horse and shooting a nervous look at the unfamiliar SUV. The large vehicle was splattered with mud, but still impressive looking with sides and top reinforced by steel plates complete with what looked like firing ports. Underneath the mud splatter the letters N-W-O were stenciled across the steel plate sides in bright red paint.

"You sure you don't want some backup in there?" Teddy jerked his chin toward the mess hall.

Frank's lips twisted in a grimace. If he had his way, he'd never open his mouth but to give commands to his dogs. Dogs were far superior companions than humans, and the six currently surrounding him and Teddy were all looking at him expectantly, though their ears were swiveled toward the human commotion nearby.

Frank sighed.

This was his community. His people. He'd fought too hard and lost too much making sure they stayed alive to let little things like sweat, weariness, and dislike of humans in general keep him from doing his duty.

"Go get the horses took care of, Teddy," he grunted. "And keep your eyes open. Sentries were acting normal when we came in, but no sense not being prepared."

Teddy nodded and took Shadowfax's reins, then headed off toward the sprawling livestock barn.

"Fred, George." Two sets of ears perked. "Go with Teddy. Guard." He gestured at the retreating head mechanic of their community and the two German shepherds pushed to their feet and loped after him, tongues lolling in the late afternoon heat of mid-September. The mechanic was no expert dog handler, but along with select others in their farming community he'd been taught enough about operating with the three-dozen patrol and guard dogs Frank had trained since the zombie virus outbreak two years ago that he could send Fred and George back to Frank when they were no longer needed.

"Achilles, Odysseus, Huginn, Muninn." More ears perked. "Heel, alert."

That command would keep them close by and ready without putting them in attack mode—biting guests was generally frowned on.

Only generally, though.

Of the five percent or so of the U.S. population who had survived the Fall, there were always those happy to revert to rule by might. So far since the world went dark, four ragtag bands had attempted to intimidate or fight their way into control over the people of Maligator County.

None of them had survived to tell the tale.

Frank's remaining four dogs fell into their usual square formation around him as he tucked his 30-06 Springfield bolt-action hunting rifle under one arm and headed toward the mess hall, his lined and tanned face even grimmer than usual. He stank of sweat and horse and itched all over. He half hoped these "visitors" gave him an excuse to make them regret keeping him from his cold shower.

"—just calm down y'all. Yelling and hollering ain't gonna solve anything." Joe Gallrein's scratchy voice greeted Frank's ears as he swung open the mess hall door where they usually held community meetings. The old man's voice had been fuller once, but Joe had gotten a nasty bout of flu and pneumonia last winter. It'd been a miracle he'd pulled through with the rudimentary medicine they had left. But while Old Joe had been too stubborn to die and leave a gaping hole in the heart of their community, the ordeal had left him with a permanent cough. Even if his voice didn't carry over the noisy group, though, everyone saw his raised hands and stern scowl beneath the much-stained John Deere cap that was a permanent fixture on his bald head.

Achilles and Odysseus' appearance probably helped too. They'd stopped a few paces into the room and were staring, bodies stiff and hackles raised, at the group of strangers squared off opposite Joe Gallrein.

"Perfect timing, boy," Joe huffed at Frank, then coughed. As the old man recovered, Frank's eyes swept the room and noted the angry faces and hostile postures of his fellow farmers. Of those with weapons—which was almost everybody—most had them out and near at hand.

Then his eyes landed on the newcomers, noting first and foremost that none had visible weapons. That made him relax slightly, though it was also disappointing—he was unlikely to get to sic his dogs on them.

Pity.

There were four of them, two men and two women, dressed

like hipsters who'd raided an army surplus depot. They looked...
soft, lacking the tanned, lean appearance of Maligator County's
people after two years of backbreaking farm work, sunup to sun-
down, seven days a week. One of the men was fairly large and
had a dangerous, brutish look, but the other was pasty-skinned
and weasel-faced. Both the women had short hair, though the
furious-looking one in front had hair so short it was only a
dark fuzz, which did nothing to add to the appearance of her
pear-shaped figure.

"Our guests here were just fixin' to leave," Joe said into the
tense silence. "Mind giving 'em a proper escort out, Frank?"

The buzz-cut lady's mouth dropped open. "What? We're not
leaving, we just got here! And I haven't finished giving you our
terms—"

"Ma'am, you can take your terms and go have 'em for Sunday
lunch," said Joe. "We ain't interested."

"Well reconsider, old man! Don't think you can survive out
here on your puny little farm on your own. The New World
Order is rebuilding civilization from the ground up and either
you're with us or against us."

There were snorts and jeers from the crowd.

"Oh shut yer gob, crazy lady."

"Don't let the door hit ya on the way out!"

Joe nodded to Frank, so he stepped out from in front of
the door and jerked his head at the short, angry woman who
appeared to be the leader of the quartet.

"After you, ma'am."

She straightened and seemed to collect herself, though that
didn't dispel the pinched, sour look on her face. Instead of moving
toward the door, though, she pointed at Achilles and Odysseus,
whose eyes were locked on her.

"I'm not getting anywhere near those mutts. Make them go
away."

The angry muttering that met her words kept Frank from
strangling the woman, but only just. His dogs were a much-adored
mascot for everyone in Maligator County, affectionately titled after
the breed nickname of his Belgian Malinois dogs. He actively had
to work to keep people from spoiling them by slipping them bits
of scraps and venison jerky when he wasn't looking.

"They obey orders," Frank said, his words as hard and cold

as his expression, "and they don't have permission to bite you...
yet. Can't promise how long that'll last. If I were you, I'd move
it before I update their mission parameters."

The buzz-cut lady seemed inclined to get huffy at that, but she
moved all the same, only hesitating a split second before marching, head held high, between the gauntlet of watchful canines.

"Achilles, Odysseus, Huginn, Muninn. Escort," Frank barked
as the last of the four strangers passed between them. His dogs
relaxed slightly and trotted after their charges, spreading out to
either side of the group once they were through the door and
out in the open.

Unlike before the Fall, Frank didn't worry about training his
dogs using English phrases instead of the more common German
or Dutch. It made it easier for the other farmers to work with
them, and they were so isolated from any contact with strangers
that the dogs would never obey an outsider anyway.

His pack would make terrible personal protection or police
dogs, but they sure were terrific postapocalyptic guardians of
Maligator County.

Grasshoppers buzzed in the tall grass surrounding the gravel
lot as Frank and his dogs—and many of the mess hall occupants
who had followed them out, weapons in hand—watched the
strangers climb back into their vehicle. With a spinning of tires
that threw gravel and dust into the air, the SUV headed back
up the lane that led out of their compound and onto Vigo Road
that bordered the northern side of Gallrein Farms.

Once the sound of the vehicle's engine had faded into nothing, Frank stood his dogs down, slung his rifle over his shoulder,
and headed back into the mess hall. He passed through the mill-
ing crowd of his muttering fellows without comment. Inside he
found Old Joe in a quiet conference with his son Ben, general
manager of the farm, his granddaughter Sarah who was manager
in training, and Gary Gaines, their head of security.

"They give you any trouble?" Ben asked Frank as he walked
up to the group.

"Nope. The short angry one looked ready to spit nails, though.
Who were they?"

Ben sighed and Gary rolled his eyes.

"Some kooks out of Cincinnati," Gary said. "Called themselves
the 'New World Order' or something equally asinine."

Frank's brow wrinkled further. "Cinci? Long way to come for...what? And why in the world did you let them in the front gate? They coulda been armed to the teeth inside their vehicle."

"Give us a little credit, Frank," Gary said. "We searched them first, they weren't armed. And they said they had an important trade deal to propose. Claimed they had access to vital supplies like antibiotics and other medicine we've been desperate for."

"Likely a load of crap. How'd they know we were even here?"

"Comrade Coates"—Gary paused to chuckle at Frank's look of disbelief—"I'm not kidding, that's really what she called herself. Anyway, the short angry lady said she represented the 'new start of civilization' based out of Cincinnati. Claims they have a whole river trading system set up and had heard about us over the ham network. They seemed to think we're a poor, desperate hellhole of ignorant rednecks in need of their 'benevolent guidance' to turn our 'little operation' into something that will one day 'support civilization.'"

Chills marched down Frank's spine despite the warm evening air, and he swore viciously.

"The ham network? I thought we'd agreed on radio silence for all long-range transmitters after that last band of raiders tried to steal the beef cattle in the spring. Even before that we've been careful. How the hell—"

Ben held up a placating hand, and Frank cut himself off. He respected these men, but the safety of their entire community depended on drawing as little attention as possible.

"We don't know, Frank. And we have been careful. At least since the spring. Before that...well." Ben sighed and shrugged.

"Come on, Dad, you know JJ," Sarah piped up. "He's a growing teen and this isolation has been really hard on us younger people. He spends hours in front of that radio, listening to a world gone mad and trying to glean what he can. Remember we used to broadcast when there were still survivors to rescue in the area. Maybe these NWO people have known about us for a while and only now had the resources to come looking."

Frank shook his head, then removed his own sweat-stained ball cap and scrubbed his close-cropped head in frustration.

"Support civilization, huh?" he asked next, changing the subject to something he might be able to get answers for.

"Yeah-up," Gary replied, adopting a bit of a drawl for emphasis.

Before the Fall he'd been a big-time stockbroker from New York who'd moved to Bluegrass country to indulge in his gun and hunting hobby. They'd found him a few months after the world went dark, living off the land and hunting zombies for sport. He'd been instrumental in their "Operation Death Parade" of last August that had mostly wiped out the zombie population of nearby Shelbyville, enabling them to clear the roads, rescue the few remaining survivors in the area, and start scouring the city for usable supplies and parts. He'd suffered a leg injury during the operation, though, and without the necessary medical intervention available had been left with a permanent limp. After that he'd turned his full attention to the security and protection of Gallrein Farms as his new calling. Frank worked with him on mindset and tactics, drawing from his own years as a Marine MP, and in turn Gary oversaw the training of all able-bodied community members in matters of weapons and defense. The womenfolk could opt out after they'd mastered the basics of pistol, rifle, bow, and cross-bow. But all the menfolk were put on rotation to train regularly throughout the year. The only thing they couldn't do much of was firearm target practice, due to limited ammo. They'd scrounged quite a bit from Shelbyville after they'd cleared it of zombies. But they had no way of manufacturing more, and the fledgling U.S. government they heard talk of over the ham radio network was still focusing its efforts on the coasts and the more populous southern states, so they didn't expect any help from that quarter.

They were on their own, and they'd come to terms with that. Frank, in fact, liked it just fine.

"And what, exactly, did they envision 'supporting civilization' would entail?" Frank asked, voice dry as chaff in the wind.

Gary shrugged. "She didn't go into detail. From the tone of her little speech it sounded like she expected us to fall over ourselves in gratitude at their offer of 'benevolent guidance.'"

The words made Frank's nose wrinkle, and he resisted the urge to spit on the floor.

"I ain't never heard anything more crazy in all my days," Old Joe said, then reached back to one of the long mess tables and lowered himself onto its bench with a sigh. "She couldn't find her way outta a corn bin with the door wide open."

Gary and Sarah grinned, but Frank frowned. This was no time for humor.

"I heard some pretty heated voices afore I came in," Frank said. "Those crazies threaten you with anything specific?"

It was Ben who answered. "Nothing like that. She just kept going on about how we'd never survive without the New World Order and that we'd be sorry if we refused their help."

Frank grunted and stared at the opposite wall for a moment as he contemplated the situation. Odysseus, no doubt sensing his tension, gave a soft whine and nosed Frank's empty palm. Frank gave his dog an absent scratch around the ears, then huffed out a sigh.

"We should double the numbers on perimeter patrol and hold a general meeting to make sure everybody knows what happened and what to keep an eye out for. Other'n that, let's just hope those crazies go looking for someone more gullible to con."

Ben and Gary exchanged a look.

"Frank, we're not even half through bringing in the corn, and we've still got over three quarters of our other crops and vegetables to harvest, not to mention half our heifers are getting ready to drop calves in the next few weeks. We've got butchering to do, canning, drying, smoking, and planting the winter wheat. This is our busiest time of year. I don't know if I can spare anyone during the day, and extra night patrol will take away precious sleep we need to recover from fifteen, sixteen-hour days in the fields. This is all-hands-on-deck season. You know that."

Frank rubbed his forehead. He knew it too well. He'd taken precious time off tending his herd of Boer goats on his own little farm a few miles down the road to do this day patrol with Teddy. Though Maggie and Mrs. Rogers—an old neighbor who'd moved in with them after zombies killed her husband—could handle the goats, chickens, and dogs, only he and a few others were trained for long patrols with pairs of Frank's zombie-killing dogs.

He and Teddy had just returned from scouting out Bagdad, a tiny town about seven miles east and home to the Bagdad Roller Mill. The people of Maligator County had been forced to scrounge further and further afield to find parts for their cobbled-together farm machinery, and Teddy had wanted to take a good look at the mill before they dipped into their precious stores of biofuel to drive a convoy out. They'd modified their smaller gas-powered pickups to run off a mixture they distilled from corn, while the bigger trucks and farm machinery used a crude biodiesel made from soybean oil.

Being able to farm on the scale they were—nearly fifteen hundred acres plus maintaining multiple herds of livestock—was a miracle in and of itself. The only thing that made it possible was because of the Bulleit Distillery barely three quarters of a mile southeast of Gallrein Farms. It was separated from their main compound by part of Guist Creek Lake, but they'd built a ferry to get supplies across and the abundance of nearby water for livestock and crops made up for the inconvenience. They couldn't operate the distillery at full capacity, of course. There weren't enough parts and supplies to keep everything going. But with the help of good old Bill Tackett, a moonshiner they'd found holed up in the hills near Waddy, they'd been able to get a few of the vats working again and operating at a scale that could sustain their fuel needs if they were careful.

But they needed parts. They always needed parts. Thus, Bagdad.

The tiny town itself was devoid of life. The zombies in it had long since been hunted down or died from starvation and cold exposure, while the few surviving humans had been rescued and folded into their community. That didn't mean there were no zombies left. There were always those odd few that had managed to hide out somewhere and feed off rotting food or unfortunate wildlife. Those sorry creatures would take you down in a flash if you let your guard drop. But these days the main concern was other humans.

The only people who'd survived a zombie apocalypse and two years of civilization collapse were those willing to kill to survive. Whether bands or wandering individuals, they were all dangerous. The question wasn't if they were capable of slitting your throat and robbing you blind, but rather how much humanity and restraint they'd held onto—and how much of it they felt like showing you on any given day.

The Fall had made killers out of all of them. Even him. Maybe especially him.

"See if there's anyone you can spare," Frank said to Ben and Sarah, knowing the two would do their best. Then Frank turned to Gary. "In the meantime, double- and triple-check every radio. Make sure the patrol teams stay sharp. Up the frequency of check-ins and see what you can do to increase the coverage, even if it's just keeping the teams constantly moving instead of stopping at each station."

"Got it, boss."

Frank snorted but Gary simply grinned at him.

"Better you than me," Ben chuckled. "You at least understand him when he starts talking powder loads and moaning about all his precious guns he doesn't have ammo for anymore."

Frank ignored the good-natured jibe. "I'm headed to the showers, then I gotta get back to Maggie. Keep your radios close and remember to use the code we trained everybody on. It doesn't do us any good 'less we use it."

The others nodded, so Frank turned and headed off at last to find relief, his dogs following obediently after. The crowd outside the mess hall had dispersed, each man and woman going back to the tasks they'd been busy with before they'd been interrupted by visitors.

The communal showers were a crude affair: a simple tin-roofed cinderblock building between the two larger, but also simple barracks that served as the single men's and single women's quarters. There were set times before and after the workday for men and women to shower separately. Any other time the showers were up for grabs, but there were locks on the doors at either end of the building. Frank had all his dogs come in with him and gave them a brief spray-down before he took a quick wash himself. While they had enough electricity to spare on something as important as running water, everybody took military-style showers: two minutes, in and out. The cold water helped with that. They only ever had warm water—and lukewarm at that—available in the winter when they turned on the water heater.

By the time he was done and changed into his spare set of clothing, Frank felt considerably better. At least, until his radio squawked and a message came in on the frequency they'd designated for farm security. Frank kept his radio on that frequency by default, since he was often pulled in to consult or advise on dog handling.

"Alpha Team to Long John Silver. Lone hog, not tagged, not visibly angry, just turned onto Vigo from Cropper. ETA one apple pie. Over."

A few seconds later, Gary's voice crackled in reply.

"Long John Silver to Alpha Team. Stick to standard procedure. Headed up now. Break. Long John Silver to Devil Dog, you coming to dinner? Over."

Frank grabbed his radio. "Devil Dog to Long John Silver, gimmie two apple pies. You need a lift? Over."

"Long John Silver to Devil Dog. Pillion with your boney backside? Is that a proposition or a threat? Over."

Frank shook his head but couldn't keep his lips from twitching upward. "Devil Dog to Long John Silver, that's up to Shadowfax. Meet at the mess. Out."

Grabbing his things, Frank signaled to his dogs and they made a beeline for the livestock barn. He found Teddy tightening Shadowfax's saddle strap after having rubbed the mare down and checking her feet for rocks. Frank nodded thanks to his friend, then stuffed his dirty clothes into his saddlebag and slipped his rifle into its scabbard on the saddle. Shadowfax waited patiently as Frank swung up, then started off without complaint when he urged her out the barn door. He called to his dogs, including Fred and George who were lying on the straw nearby, and the six canines surrounded him as they trotted off to the mess hall. Gary was waiting by the door, and Frank slowed and offered him an arm to grab so the man could haul himself up and onto Shadowfax's rear behind the saddle. It wasn't a comfortable position to ride, but with Gary's bad leg it was vastly better than him limping the quarter mile up the gravel lane to Gallrein Farms' front gate.

Frank urged Shadowfax into a smooth canter, wanting to get to the front gate as quickly as possible. Functioning vehicles with enough gas to drive around were rare outside their community, and another one showing up so soon after the crazy NWO's departure put Frank on edge. The fact that it was alone with no visible weapons—the "not visibly angry" part of the front-gate guard's transmission—was only slightly reassuring.

By the time they arrived at the reinforced front gate flanked by two enclosed, fifteen-foot-high watchtowers, the new vehicle was already stationary outside the gate and a blond-headed, bearded man had his head out the window, conversing with one of Alpha Team.

While the gate guard instructed one of the newcomers to exit the vehicle and approach the gate, Frank pulled Shadowfax to a halt in the shade of one of the watchtowers. He and Gary slid down and he tied the mare off, then slid out his rifle, just in case. His dogs waited patiently on either side of him for their next command, tongues out and panting after their short run.

The man who cautiously approached the gate, unarmed as instructed, was not the one who'd originally hailed them from the vehicle. This one's dark face was clean shaven and he had a high and tight military cut to go with his alert and well-built bearing. He wore sensible cargo pants and a pocketed shirt, and Frank noticed an empty pistol holster on his hip.

"Evening, sir," he said, stopping a good ten feet from the gate and greeting Frank with a closemouthed smile, his hand held open and unthreatening at his sides. "I'm Terrance Jones, member of the United States Fifth Northeast infrastructure survey team. We've been assigned to the Ohio River Valley region and our job is to investigate and inspect the state of public and private infrastructure in this area. Our goal is to survey the general state of things as well as identify any critical pieces of infrastructure that are still able to be repaired and brought back online. We also try to touch base with any communities we meet on the way, since locals are best situated to know the area and can pass on valuable information on how the U.S. government can be of help rebuilding and reconnecting our great country."

The man smiled again and fell silent. It was obvious by his smooth delivery that he was used to repeating his spiel, and Frank raised an eyebrow, glancing at Gary. Gary looked thoughtful, but no less suspicious than Frank felt.

U.S. government. So, they were finally here. The question remained: was that a good thing, or a bad thing?

"Don't suppose you got any identification?" Gary asked, leaning one elbow on the gate and resting his opposite hand casually on the Remington 1911 on his hip. Frank listened in, rifle held in the ready carry position as his eyes flicked from their new guest to the man's vehicle, which was a dusty and unimpressive SUV.

"Sure do." Terrance reached slowly up to a breast pocket and extracted a flip wallet, which he flipped open and held out toward Gary.

Gary grunted, rightly concluding that no matter what the man did or didn't have, in their post-zombie world it meant little to nothing.

"We don't get a whole lotta news out in these parts," Gary said, his time in the Bluegrass smoothing out and mellowing the remnants of his New York accent. "Who's president these days?"

"Former Vice President, Rebecca Staba," Terrance responded promptly.

Gary grunted again. "What's left over of the government? Military? Cabinets? Legislature?"

"Not much," Terrance said with a grimace. "We've reformed a core of the federal government, executive branch mostly, but there's scattered members of the legislature that we're coordinating and slowly joining up with."

"SecDef?" Frank wondered out loud, though he already knew from various official broadcasts over the last year.

"The former SecDef didn't make it. It's headed now by Steven John Smith. You might have heard a bit about his daughters on Devil Dog Radio." One side of the man's mouth quirked upward, but Frank wasn't moved. All this proved was the man had a radio and paid attention. To be fair, that was a far step above the four previous groups of hungry, dirty, ruthless lowlifes who had tried in various ways to take what wasn't theirs. But it still didn't mean the man was official U.S. government—and even if he was connected to the government, that didn't mean whatever he intended was going to result in a better future for Maligator County.

"Who you got with you?" Gary asked, jerking his chin toward the SUV.

"That's my survey team. We've got two specialists, a mechanical engineer and a civil engineer, and then me and my partner are their security detail."

"That's nice," Gary said, sounding thoroughly unimpressed. "So what can we do for you, Mr. Jones?"

Terrance spread his hands. "As I said, we're a survey team trying to get a handle on what's left of our national and local infrastructure, so we can make accurate and timely plans to recover what can be recovered and rebuild what needs to be rebuilt. Obviously, we won't have the resources to completely reconnect our vast country for decades, but there are key facilities and resources that are essential to save now, before they break down even more, if we ever have a hope of rebuilding. Once lost, it could be generations before we regain the technology necessary to manufacture the advanced parts needed to get them fully functional again."

"Sounds like you have your hands full. What's that got to do with us, though?"

"Well," Terrance said slowly, looking around at the sturdy lookout towers and the tall fields of browning corn on either side of the gate. "It's obvious you all have done an amazing job of pulling things together out here. There's not many places where

I've seen crops growing on this scale. One of the key pieces of infrastructure we've identified as needing government protection and oversight is livestock and agriculture, though especially livestock. As you can imagine, between hungry survivors, wild animals, and bloodthirsty zombies, there's not a lot of livestock left. If we don't save what we have we'll lose their domesticated genes entirely. Same with crops, though they have a longer shelf life, so to speak."

Frank's frown deepened. Though he was more convinced that this group was from whatever fledgling government was attempting to put their country back together, the man's words increased, not lessened, the apprehension tightening his gut.

In his former life, he'd spent over two decades working for the federal government. He knew better than most what a bloated, wasteful, bureaucratic hell it was. Or had been, at least. That didn't mean he had any regrets about serving his country, far from it. But neither did he have any illusions about the government's capability when it came to stewarding precious, irreplaceable resources.

Maybe it was different now. Maybe the zombie plague had culled the useless bureaucrats and the new federal government was leaner, smarter, better. But even if it was, what was to stop them from sweeping in and taking over Gallrein Farms under some excuse that it was "essential to the rebuilding of the country"? It would simply be a more civilized version of whatever takeover those crazy NWO flunkies had probably been planning behind their greedy little eyes.

This was Maligator County, and the farmers here had owned and worked the land long before the zombie apocalypse. They'd survived on their own with nothing and no one there to back them up. What right did anyone have to take it away from them? Besides, a bunch of ham-handed, clueless bureaucrats with armed bully boys to enforce their decisions would likely run the entire farm into the ground in under a year.

Better to stay off everybody's radar and build cautious ties with small scale traders to get the few essentials they couldn't come up with themselves, like medicine.

Frank exchanged a look with Gary, and based on his friend's deep frown, they were thinking along the same lines.

"Well, we wish you the best of luck," Gary said, looking

back at Terrance. "There's not much here to see. We barely get by ourselves. We've been too busy surviving to do much poking around. I'd say go back toward Louisville or up north to Cincinnati if you want to find valuable infrastructure. We heard there's some kind of trade route up there along the river. Maybe they'll know more."

"I think you're not giving yourselves enough credit," Terrance said, gesturing around him. "This is exactly what we've been looking for: intact agricultural infrastructure. Those corn rows are too straight to have been planted by hand, which means you must still have functioning equipment of some kind. That means people with mechanical and agricultural knowledge, and we need to preserve that knowledge and find ways to multiply it so we can replicate it and scale it up. Supplies fit for scavenging are getting more and more scarce. We need to ramp up agricultural production if our country is going to survive the next five years, much less the next few decades."

"Sounds like a real pickle," Gary said, nodding sympathetically. "But like I said, there's nothing to see here. I'll bet there's plenty of functioning ranches surviving out west where there were hardly any people for miles around to spread the virus. I'd head that way if I were you. See what you can find."

Terrance pursed his lips, his gaze knowing. Frank tightened his grip on his rifle at the sight, hoping this nosey busybody would take a hint and go away. He had zero desire to hurt the man or his companions, but if it came down to him or them...

The distant sound of a revving engine floated across the still evening air, and Frank cocked his head, brow furrowing. It was coming from the opposite direction the government vehicle had come. From the direction of his own farm, as matter of fact.

Terrance heard it too and shifted his stance, looking wary.

"Friend of yours?"

"Possibly," Frank said, before Gary could speak. "Won't know till it's in sight. You might wanna go back to your car for a spell. No sense taking risks."

Terrance gave them one last look, then strode back to his SUV and hopped into the driver's seat. He put it in reverse and backed into the uncut grass beside the gate's entrance, aiming his nose at the oncoming engine noise and clearing the way to their gate.

When the vehicle in question came into view down the road, Frank's breath hitched and a surge of adrenaline shot through his limbs.

"Is that your truck, Frank? Who's driving it?"

"Maggie," Frank said, voice tight. "Cover me, I'm going over."

Gary pulled his radio off his belt and spoke some quick words to the guards in the towers on either side as Frank climbed the gate and gave his dogs the command to follow. Within seconds his old farm truck reached the entrance to Gallrein Farms and took the turn at highly questionable speeds, sending dust and rocks flying everywhere. Frank got to the side of the gravel drive and tried to calm his breathing as Maggie brought the truck to a sliding halt in front of the gate.

"What in the—"

"Dad! It's Mrs. Rogers! She fell and broke her leg and it's bleeding really bad. I tried to put a tourniquet on it but it's still bleeding and I don't know what to do. We've got to get her to Juliet!"

"Gary! Open the gate!" Frank hollered as his eyes took in Maggie's sweaty face and clothes smudged with blood and Mrs. Rogers's form slumped up against the opposite door, her skin deathly pale. He rushed to help Gary haul open the reinforced gate and barely registered the distant slamming sound of a vehicle's door. But the sound of pounding steps on gravel made him whirl and raise his rifle.

"Woah! Stand down, sir, stand down!" Terrance called out, hands raised. "I'm a former Army medic with three combat tours in the sandbox. It sounds like you've got an emergency on your hands and I have medical supplies." He plucked at the strap of a bag slung across his torso. "Please, let me help you."

Frank hesitated for only an instant. "Your men stay in their vehicle, clear?"

"Roger that."

In response Frank laid his rifle in the grass and sprinted back to the truck. Terrance joined him on the passenger side and caught Mrs. Rogers's slumped form as Frank carefully opened the door. Frank helped him lay the older woman gently in the grass, then followed the Army medic's calm commands to hold that and put pressure there while the man dove into his medkit and got to work. Within seconds Terrance had a proper tourniquet on Mrs. Rogers's leg, stopping the bleeding from the ugly break that showed bits of bone poking through skin. Frank breathed a prayer of thanks that his elderly neighbor was unconscious through it all, though her deathly pale and clammy skin made him follow up the prayer with a vehement string of mental curses that Maggie would have scolded him for.

Together they got Mrs. Rogers back into the truck with Terrance beside her, holding her steady. Frank slammed the door shut and Maggie sped off toward the compound and Juliet's rudimentary infirmary in the old welcome center. Frank grabbed his rifle from the ground and swung up onto Shadowfax as he called commands for Fred and George to stay with Gary and his other dogs to follow him. Then he was galloping after the truck as fast as his mare could take him.

A few tense hours later, Frank was holding a restless vigil with Maggie on the bench outside the old welcome center's front doors. Dusk was upon them and the quickly cooling air brought with it the smells of corn husks and freshly cut hay. Many community members had come and gone, expressing their sympathy and offering prayers of support. Frank really should have been busy doing something—anything.

But Maggie needed him there.

She didn't say it, but he could tell she blamed herself for Mrs. Rogers's injury. The older woman had become a mother figure for Maggie over the past two years, and Frank's heart—cold and practical as it was—couldn't take the thought of his daughter losing another mother.

He was swimming through dark thoughts and memories he'd long thought buried when his dogs' ears perked and their heads turned toward the doors. A moment later, Terrance came out of the old welcome center, his dark skin dully reflecting the lights within. Frank and Maggie rose as one, and Maggie's hand found his, squeezing it with bruising force.

"She's stable, for now, but she lost a lot of blood," Terrance said in a low voice. "My main concern at this point is whether or not her body will be strong enough to fight off infection. Also, there wasn't much I could do about the break itself, not with the meager tools at hand. If she does recover her strength and escape infection, I doubt she'll ever walk again, at least not without crutches."

Maggie choked back a sob and hid her face against Frank's chest. Frank wrapped her in numb arms and cupped the back of her head, pressing a reassuring kiss to her crown.

"You can go see her, if you like," Terrance said. "She's unconscious still, but I'm sure Ms. Dietsch and Mrs. Smith would appreciate some extra hands to help clean up."

"You go, Mags, and take Achilles and Odysseus. I'll come visit later."

His daughter hurried off with their two oldest and most loyal dogs following eagerly. All the dogs he trained obeyed him faithfully as their alpha, but they worshipped at Maggie's feet with pure puppy love. She'd always had a way with animals, and he often shook his head in chagrin at how easily she captured their affections.

As soon as the doors to the old welcome center closed, Frank's focus returned and his eyes swung to Terrance Jones.

"Thank you, for saving Mrs. Rogers." The words almost stuck in his throat, but he forced them out anyway. They were true and right, no matter what he thought of the man or his current errand.

Terrance gave a somber nod. "Just doing my job." Their eyes met, and Terrance's eyebrows lifted slightly. Frank sighed, mulling over the double meaning of the Army medic's words.

"You look wore out," he finally said. "Rest of your team is waiting in the mess. Come on over and get some grub. I'll gather a few people as might wanna hear you out. We'll talk."

Twenty minutes later, Frank entered the mess hall followed by Ben, Gary, Teddy, and Old Joe. He had Huginn, Muninn, Fred, and George with him now and he'd wrangled up some raw meat for their dinner. He plopped it down in four piles and gave his dogs permission to eat while Terrance shook hands and introduced himself and his team to the farmers: Owen Paltrow, their mechanical engineer; Daniel Thomas, their civil engineer; and Ethan LeMonte, former police officer and Terrance's security specialist. The two engineers seemed talkative enough, and both had inquisitive, bright demeanors. LeMonte was silent and watchful, which Frank could appreciate. He also appreciated the warm smile that passed over LeMonte's face when he saw Frank's dogs. Maybe the police officer had worked with dogs before. Or maybe he was simply a dog person.

Either way, it was a point in his favor.

As Terrance repeated his spiel, Frank listened silently. He'd already shared his concerns with Ben and the others, and they had all agreed: helping rebuild civilization was fine and dandy in theory, but their first concern was for their families, their second for their property and everything they'd built to survive.

Who could they possibly trust in this new dystopian reality they lived in?

By the time Terrance finished, Ben looked thoughtful and Teddy's eyes were alight with excitement, but Gary and Joe still had worried wrinkles across their brows.

"Young man," Joe said, "we're mighty grateful for what you did to help Mrs. Rogers. We owe you a debt of gratitude. But— well, let's just say us country folk've never had much reason to trust the government. I'm sure you can appreciate us wanting to keep to ourselves and look after our own families."

"Of course." Terrance nodded. "But I'm sure you can also understand that what you've accomplished here has massive implications for the rest of the country—possibly even the entire world. Your farm is a vital part of enabling mankind to rebuild a free, prosperous world instead of descending into warring tribalism and a dark age of technology. I'm sure you wouldn't want to keep all this to yourself when it could help so many. You might even say it's your patriotic duty."

Old Joe frowned deeply and if Frank had possessed hackles like his dogs, they would have bristled.

He'd already served his country and put his life on the line for decades. Was being left alone to farm their own land and take care of their own families too much to ask after what they'd already been through?

"This is our land and our resources," Joe said gruffly. "This farm has been in my family for five generations. I don't owe it to nobody."

Terrance's brows lifted. "So you're telling me there's not one vehicle, not one tractor part, not one piece of livestock or seed of grain that you didn't take from your neighbors after they went mad with the virus?"

This time scowls gathered on the faces of the farmers at the table.

"Don't be ridiculous," Joe said. "'Course we salvaged and saved everything we could. You think our neighbors, the people we knew and loved, woulda wanted us to starve and die over stuff they didn't need anymore?"

"Not at all," Terrance said, raising his hands placatingly. "I was simply trying to point out that what you've built here has depended as much on the wealth and resources of others as on your own private property. Everyone has had to do hard things and make hard decisions to survive. As they said in Wolf Squadron in the early months: what goes on in the compartment, stays in the compartment. But we're past that stage now and the only way our country has a hope of surviving is if we all work together. The first step of that is understanding what infrastructure we have left and what we can still save from complete collapse."

Old Joe huffed, which turned into a cough that he did his best to suppress as he waved a hand dismissively at Terrance. "Well y'all can leave us off your little survey. There's nothing collapsing here and we only got enough for our own families, no more."

Terrance's jaw tightened. "I'm afraid I can't do that. It's my duty to report everything we find. What's done with that information isn't up to us"—he gestured at his team watching silently from further down the table—"we simply pass it on to our superiors."

That statement made Gary and Frank exchange a look, and the tension in the room ratcheted up a notch.

"I think what my father is concerned about," Ben said, speaking up for the first time, "is lack of representation and legal recourse. Of course we want to help others, it's why we've worked so hard to preserve our community in the first place. But we don't know you, and this new government that has been formed, while it does hold some legitimacy in the form of the few surviving elected officials, well... who or what is there to hold it in check?"

Silence met Ben's question, though Terrance didn't flinch away from the farmer's concerned gaze. Ben looked around at each person at the table, then continued:

"You seem to think we've left the desperate times behind. But the way we see it, the desperate times are still ahead of us. We have nothing protecting us but anonymity, and if some government official decides 'the country' has a right to our land, our resources, our livelihoods that we need to survive, then what recourse do we have?"

There was another long silence before Terrance heaved a sigh and rubbed a hand over his face. "I understand your concerns,

Mr. Gallrein. They are the same thing many others are wondering, scattered across the country. But one fact I know for sure is that we are doomed if we can't figure out how to trust each other and act like a country again. I know the situation is still desperate, but it will get even more so if we don't act together. All your machinery and electronics, how long will they last before you need parts you have no way of scavenging or manufacturing? A year? Five years? A decade?"

Now it was Ben's turn to remain silent.

"Let's be optimistic and say a generation," Terrance said with a shrug. "We're already not sure how much advanced technology we can save. But it's a certainty that within a generation, if we don't get some kind of manufacturing back online and get energy and transportation resources flowing again, we'll be back to living in the preindustrial era. But it'll be worse than before, because even then we had huge amounts of science and technology information built up, and brilliant minds developing new things every day. Now? Barely five percent of the world population is left and so much of our information has been destroyed or lost. We could easily slide back into the dark ages. Who knows how many generations it would take to come back from that—or if we ever could."

A deep, somber silence descended over the group, and no one spoke for a long time.

Finally, Ben sighed and stood up. "Gentlemen, you've given us much to think about, and as my father said, we're very grateful for your help. But it's getting late and we rise well before dawn. Perhaps things will seem clearer under the light of day. We don't have much to offer, but there's a small cottage you four should fit in. Your team can stay the night with us and move on in the morning. We will, of course, be posting a guard outside the cottage for our community's safety. I hope you understand it's nothing personal, simply a precaution."

"I wouldn't expect anything less," Terrance said with a nod. Then he motioned to his men. "Let's get going so these good people can sleep. We thank you for the hospitality."

Ben returned the nod, then pulled Frank and Gary aside to whisper a few words. They both nodded, and Gary motioned to the survey team and led the way out the mess hall door, flashlight on, with Frank and his dogs bringing up the rear.

The cottage was at the very outskirts of the compound on the northwestern corner and bordered on two sides by cornfields. Several sheds and pens—the former petting zoo area from long ago—separated it from the main compound. Only the roof of the old welcome center and part of the mess hall was visible from the cottage, while the barracks and the buildings behind the welcome area like the machinery and livestock barns, dairy, silos, solar panels, generators, and more, were hidden.

It was an ideal place to isolate visitors they didn't want snooping around or seeing too much.

There was no bathroom, electricity, or running water, just a fireplace, a table and some chairs, and a single bed. But the survey team didn't seem to mind, and after driving their SUV over to it and getting out what supplies they needed, they said a polite goodnight and disappeared into the cottage with their own flashlights illuminating the way.

"Welp... you want first watch, or you want me to take it?" Gary asked Frank, his expression hidden in the near darkness.

"You better take it," Frank grunted, then stretched his arms out and yawned. "Me'n the dogs are tuckered out after that long patrol, and since your sorry ass is parked in a chair all day I know you're still fresh as a daisy."

Gary's snort sounded loud in the quiet night. "I wish my butt was parked in a chair all day. You'd think people would remember I've got a gimp leg but no, it's Gary this and Gary that all day long."

"Quit your grumbling, old man. If we didn't keep you busy, you'd go off looking for something to do, the more dangerous the better."

"It's not my fault sitting still is boring."

"Healthier, though."

"Not according to my doctor," Gary said and chuckled.

"Your long-ago zombified doctor? Or you talkin' 'bout Mrs. Smith who's been apprenticing under Juliet? You know I've been watching you two. You're sweet on her, aren't you?"

"Ooooh, I dunno. Maybe."

Frank snickered, hearing the embarrassed grin in Gary's protestations that no amount of darkness could hide.

"You can't resist a fiery lady with a gun in her hands, can you, Gary? And Mrs. Smith..." Frank whistled appreciatively.

"She's a vicious beast if you get on her bad side. Best of luck to you, my friend. You might wanna be careful what you wish for, though. She can shoot near as good as you, and with your gimp leg she could prolly whoop you in a fight."

"Don't I know it. And she's even more glorious for it."

Frank shook his head, his grin spreading wider at the dreamy tone in Gary's words. Then he headed off into the darkness to grab a spare sleeping bag from men's barracks, not needing a light to guide him on the familiar terrain. His dogs trotted silently with him, sniffing this bush or that barn door as they went along. When he got back, he unrolled his sleeping bag beneath the maple tree beside the cottage where they'd taken up a position. Then he called his dogs to him and gave them each a good petting, speaking quiet praise for a good day's work. Some dogs were food motivated and some were toy motivated. But the best dogs were driven by the deep bond they formed with their alpha, and hearing his praise was all they needed to reinforce their day-to-day training. Not that Frank didn't play with his dogs or give them treats at times. But those were the exception, not the norm.

Before bedding down, Frank put Fred and George on guard with Gary. Then he stretched out on his sleeping bag, rifle within easy reach beside him and his S&W Model 66 Combat Magnum revolver tucked under the fabric near his head. Huginn and Muninn lay down close by, heads on paws, though their ears were still pricked and attentive to the nightly noises.

Frank closed his eyes and did his best to clear his mind of worry. His good friend and patrol buddy Reggie Dale had volunteered to go to his ranch and spend the night there to feed the animals and keep an eye on things. Maggie was safe in the women's barracks. Mrs. Rogers was as well cared for as they could manage. And the worries of tomorrow could very well wait until tomorrow to be worried about.

He fell asleep to the noise of a breeze blowing through the drying corn and the soft chirp of crickets in the grass.

"Psst. Frank. Wake up. There's something fishy going on."

Gary's voice, barely a whisper of breath in the still night, brought Frank to abrupt wakefulness.

"Dogs are signaling danger, but I can't figure out more than

United We Stand

that. I think I heard footsteps on the gravel, though, down by the old welcome center. Don't wanna use the radio to check with the patrols, anybody could be listening in."

Frank nodded and rose to a crouch, holstering his pistol and then finding his rifle. With a barely audible sound through his teeth, he summoned his two pairs of dogs to his side. All four were alert, eyes and ears pointed toward the main compound.

"What danger, Fred. Zombie?"

The dog didn't move a muscle, so that was a no.

"Humans?"

Fred chuffed quietly, the sound more like a huff than anything else.

"Gary," Frank whispered. "What about the survey team? Could one of them have snuck out a window and got past you?"

"Past me, maybe. But not the dogs. I don't think it's them, Frank."

Which meant only one thing: intruders.

It could be anyone, but Frank had a sudden vision of the angry, spiteful twist of "Comrade" Coate's face as she'd stomped off to her vehicle earlier that day. It was the face of someone simmering in resentment, and resentment was a powerful motivator.

It also made you dumb as a rock.

Sloppy and foolish were probably more accurate terms, but "dumb as a rock" seemed more fitting for Comrade Coates.

Questions zipped through Frank's brain: How many were there? What was their goal? How long had they been watching Gallrein Farms? Had they killed the gate guards and come in the front? Or cut the electric fence and come in elsewhere?

"Gary, stay here with the dogs," Frank breathed. "I'm gonna get backup."

Quiet as a shadow and just as invisible in the complete darkness of the Gallrein compound, Frank slipped from the tree to the cabin and carefully opened the front door.

"Rise'n shine, fellas," he whispered to the darkness within. "It's another glorious day in the Corps. We got bogies outside and were wondering if y'all wanna join the fun."

There was a shifting as soon as he started whispering, and by the time he'd finished, a dark shape had joined him at the doorway.

"I didn't know you were Marine Corps, Mr. Oberman," said

Terrance, his white teeth faintly visible against the pitch blackness of his face. "If I'd known I would've been sure to give you more grief. After all, we can't let a little thing like a zombie apocalypse erase perfectly respectable branch rivalries."

"Save it for later, young'un," Frank grunted, though he, too, was grinning. "Dogs sniffed out some intruders snooping 'round the old welcome center, but there's been no alarm sounded, which likely means they snuck in or took out the guards. Earlier today we had an unwelcome visit from some loonies called the 'New World Order.' Ever heard of 'em?"

Terrance's white teeth disappeared as his smile turned to a frown.

"Yes, actually. We were briefed on them since they control part of our assigned area. They're a large group based in Cincinnati and they dominate trade up and down the Ohio River. We've been told they're fairly stable trade partners for anyone with enough firepower to defend themselves. But we've also heard reports of ruthless takeovers and some pretty crazy propaganda."

"Can't get much crazier'n calling themselves silly names like the NWO."

"You'd be surprised. But as best we can tell, they're just the biggest bullies on the block who use brainwashing and cultlike tactics to keep their rank and file in line. They claim to be 'for the people' while robbing everybody blind and subjugating those who don't go along."

Frank's apprehension deepened with each word Terrance breathed into his ear.

"I'm gonna guess this is a hostile takeover, then," Frank whispered. "They were mighty pissed we kicked them out earlier. Could be they've been planning something for a while, and that was the last straw. We need more intel, though. You'n your partner up for some recon?" Frank's eyes flicked to the second dark shape of LeMonte that had joined them.

"Affirmative," Terrance said, his white teeth showing again.

"The others?" Frank asked, noting that the two engineers had made no move to join them.

"They're too valuable to risk. You can teach anyone to hold a gun, but not many engineers left these days. Give us a sec to gear up, though."

Frank nodded and waited, then led the way back to the maple

tree and Gary. He went over the compound layout for their allies, then they assessed their supplies. He and Gary had their handguns and Frank's rifle, but not much in the way of spare ammo. Terrance and LeMonte were considerably better equipped with military issue M4 carbines, combat vests, and helmets. Even better? They had four magazines apiece and night vision monocular mounted on their helmets.

"Your superiors must really like you," Frank muttered, half in jealousy, half in jest.

Terrance snorted softly as he got his night vision monocular situated. "The world is a scary place these days. They wanted to make sure we came back alive."

For some reason the comment moved Frank in a way he couldn't put his finger on. What he did understand, though, was that these men didn't have to put themselves in harm's way. Yet here they were. And that was the very core of everything good about his beloved country—the country he'd fought and bled for.

The country he wasn't sure would ever exist again.

He shook his head and was about to signal their group to move out when shouts and screams shattered the quiet night.

Women's screams.

From the direction of the barracks.

There were more sounds of a struggle, yells, a few gunshots, and then suddenly a roar of engines in the distance.

"Move, move, move!" Frank hissed and took off bent low with Gary, Terrance, and LeMonte following single file. He could hear Gary's uneven, limping run behind him, but knew his friend could keep up, at least for a little while. His four dogs loped silently beside them, ears swiveling as they reacted to the cacophony of violence echoing through the darkness.

The darkness didn't last long, though. There was a screeching crash of metal in the direction of the front gate, and then four sets of headlights appeared over the crest of the hill, bumping up and down as the vehicles that they belonged to careened along the gravel drive at full speed.

Frank didn't slow. Even though his heart was in his throat and every instinct in him screamed to rush headlong toward the barracks where Maggie was, he kept his head down and led his team silently around the back sides of sheds and pens. Seconds before the invading vehicles reached the main gravel lot, the four men ducked behind the cover of the greenhouses on the east side of the old welcome center. Bright headlights splashed across the frontmost greenhouse and along the welcome center, the mess hall, and the pair of barracks with showers between them to the west.

By the time Frank and the others had circled the greenhouses and reached the rear of the welcome center, the gunfire had stopped, but the shouts had increased. Frank slowed beside a portion of the back wall where a ladder was affixed to the outside. He handed off his rifle to Gary, then dug in the holder on his belt for his spare rounds. Once Gary had everything he needed, Frank drew his revolver, motioned to Terrance and LeMonte, and took off again.

At the far corner of the building he slowed and peeked around it before advancing. He was about to come into sight of the back of the barracks when a familiar voice echoed through the night, amplified as if the person was using some kind of megaphone.

"Citizens of Gallrein Farm, lay down your weapons! We are holding your women hostage to ensure a safe and peaceful transition of power. They will not come to any harm as long as you offer no resistance. I, Comrade Coates of the New World Order, hereby take command of this facility for the good of the people and a brighter future. You will lay down your weapons and come out to the courtyard in order to swear loyalty to the New World Order and the good of your fellow citizens. Anyone who does not comply will be considered an enemy of the people, with hostile intent, and will be dealt with accordingly."

Ringing silence fell.

Rage churned inside Frank's chest. If those slimy, arrogant, imbecilic tyrants harmed one hair on his daughter's head, he would join his dogs in ripping them limb from limb.

Only one thought kept him functioning through the fear and anger clouding his mind: Maggie had Achilles and Odysseus with her. They were his smartest, most experienced dogs, and could rip the throat out of a full-grown man in seconds. They would keep her safe.

They had to keep her safe.

Frank tried not to dwell on the knowledge that Maggie was unlikely to consider her own safety but would send the dogs wherever they were needed to help others.

The eerie silence deepened further. After a minute or two in which it became clear no "citizens" were obediently dropping their weapons and meekly crawling out into the light to grovel at Comrade Coates's feet, the megaphone rang out again and the woman repeated her message in a decidedly more agitated tone.

Under the cover of that harpy's shrill demands, Frank motioned to his companions and they had whispered conference, then broke apart and started creeping forward toward the barracks.

Frank had no idea what had become of the front gate guards, but hopefully there was at least one if not two patrols out there in the darkness with rifles and a pair of dogs. There were also the married couples staying in the various cottages around the property, plus the Gallreins in their farmhouse behind the dairy. Lastly, the men's barracks housed nearly fifty single men from teens to old folks.

And all of them, men and women, young and old, had weapons of some kind or another.

All Frank had to do was figure out how to get into the women's barracks and deal with whoever was threatening the hostages. Then their people could start picking off these hooligans from the safety of the darkness and surrounding buildings.

After some careful creeping, Frank, Terrance, and LeMonte had their backs pressed against the rear of the women's barracks. On the way there Frank had gotten another glimpse of the gravel lot and confirmed that their enemies were still circled up in the middle of it, headlights pointed out, individual combatants set up behind the open, steel-plated doors of the SUVs. The headlights would make it difficult to pick off targets, but they'd cross that bridge when they came to it. He'd left his dogs sitting patiently in the shadow of the old welcome center, watching him like a hawk and waiting for their next command. The barracks had a back door, but it was shut and locked tight at night. Knocking or breaking it down would make too much noise and might prompt retaliation against the hostages.

If only he could get some sort of message to Maggie. Perhaps there was someone inside who could unlock it and let them in?

He felt a tap on his shoulder and looked to his right at Terrance. The man jerked his thumb and drew Frank's attention to the rear of the men's barracks thirty feet away. The back door had opened, and farm hands in various stages of dress were creeping silently out one by one, each of them clutching a weapon from rifles and pistols to bows and crossbows.

Frank nodded grimly, though the icy fear in his chest was as cold as ever. None of those men could help Maggie and the other women from out here.

"I'll give you ignorant pigs one last warning!" The angry screech of Comrade Coates's voice rang out again. "If you don't lay down your weapons and surrender right now, I'll—eeeeyyaaaagh!!!"

The rant ended in an abrupt and bloodcurdling scream, which turned into frantic sobbing overlaid with a familiar growl. In the background were shouts and sounds of fighting, all of it amplified as if the woman had forgotten to turn off the megaphone.

Frank froze in horrified fascination for only a second. Then he pushed off the wall and turned to his companions. "Set up on the corners of the building and give 'em hell!"

Terrance's teeth flashed in the dimness and the two men split, one to each corner. While they set up, Frank summoned his dogs to his side and tried to visualize the lock on the back door to the barracks, plotting how he could shoot it off or damage it enough to break through the door.

He had to get through. He had to make sure his daughter was still alive.

Just then, a panting voice rang out over the still broadcasting megaphone.

"We've got 'em handled in here, Dad! Now go show those bastards what us 'ignorant pigs' do to bullies and thugs!"

Hot, soaring relief swept through Frank's chest and he grinned at the echoing boom of his 30-06 rifle, held in the steady hands of Gary in his overwatch position on the roof of the old welcome center. Right on its heels the *crack-crack-crack* of measured M4 fire spat out as the gathered NWO forces scrambled to find targets in the darkness.

As if that had been some sort of agreed upon signal, suddenly the night was filled with the varied sounds of over a dozen different types of firearms spitting hot lead, while the return fire of their opponents sounded more like Terrance and LeMonte's M4s. The twanging of taught bowstrings didn't register over the gunfire, but Frank could tell by the occasional pained screams of their enemies and the clank of sharpened wooden points off steel that volleys of arrows and crossbow bolts were joining the hail of bullets.

Frank was preparing to try and shoot the lock off the barrack's back door when it suddenly opened, revealing the grim, blood-stained face of Mrs. Smith.

"Don't just stand there flappin' your mouth, you big oaf, go help your daughter!" The matron's stern voice snapped Frank out of his astonishment and he rushed into the barracks past rows of nightgown-clad women. Their expressions ranged from fearful to angry, but they were alert and the ones in the front were passing weapons towards those in the back. A few sharp words from him sent Huginn and Munnin back to guard the rear door while Fred and George trotted ahead, ears perked.

When he reached the common room at the front of the barracks, the first thing he saw were several women of their community hefting M16s standing over the bloody remains of their former captors. Two rough-looking men and a skinny woman with a mohawk lay sprawled on the floor, their throats gory messes that slowly leaked blood onto the concrete floor. He spotted several of their own women sitting on the floor or leaning against the wall nursing injuries, and Juliet was moving swiftly between them, checking their status. Then his eyes flicked to the center of the room and the sight he saw drew him up short: Maggie kneeling beside Comrade Coates, pressing a blood-soaked shirt to the unconscious woman's neck while Achilles and Odysseus stood protectively nearby.

Frank stood for a frozen second, hatred like he'd never felt before coursing through him.

"Mags, leave her," he said, barely recognizing his own grating voice. "Let her reap what she sowed."

His daughter's gaze flew up to him and tears swam in her eyes as relief transformed her face. Despite the tears, though, she scowled at him.

"Shame on you, Dad. We're better'n that, and you know it."

"She deserves it," he snarled.

"Of course she deserves it! But it's not our job to give people what they deserve. Love your enemies, remember? Or does that only apply to other people, not to you?"

"She tried to hurt you," Frank persisted, barely able to push the words past the anger locking up his jaw.

"Yeah and look what she got for her troubles." Maggie grinned savagely and the tightness in Frank's chest finally relaxed enough that he felt like he could breathe again.

Maggie was safe. She was alive. He hadn't lost her.

"Now quit standing there, Dad, and take over security so the other ladies can help us with the wounded!"

Belatedly Frank lurched forward, scanning the room again automatically for threats.

"Fred, George, guard door," he commanded, pointing at the front of the barracks. Then he holstered his revolver and nodded to the nearest woman, a middle-aged bank teller they'd rescued from Shelbyville, holding out his hands for her rifle. She passed it to him and rushed over to Juliet, asking how she could help. He was about to give the other two women guard instructions when a repeated shout became audible outside in between the rattle of gunfire.

"We surrender! We surrender! Stop shooting, we surrender!"

A booming call of "cease fire," rang out in Terrance's voice, and everything went quiet. The former Army medic continued speaking, ordering the remaining NWO members to throw their weapons away from their vehicles into the light, then to come out with their hands up and lie down on the gravel. There was a moment of silence, followed by a clatter of metal on gravel, a shout, and the sound of a struggle. Frank peeked carefully out one of the front windows of the barracks to see two figures grappling beside one of the SUVs. The shine of the headlights was too bright to see detail, but it looked as if one was trying to wrestle the rifle out of the hands of another, while the one with the rifle screamed obscenities and accusations of betrayal at his fellow. Then Terrance came into view, moving swiftly toward the vehicles with his rifle held high and tight to his shoulder in tactical firing position. Glancing the other direction Frank saw LeMonte mirroring Terrance's advance. The two men stepped over and around the bloody bodies scattered near the vehicles with practiced ease. To Frank's relief, the bodies he could see were wearing an eclectic collection of army-surplus-style clothing, not nightgowns or hastily pulled on jeans.

Terrance, who was in the lead, ended the struggle between the two NWO members with a powerful buttstroke to the back of the head, cutting off the ranting screams of the one who seemed to have a death wish.

After that it was all over but the shouting.

∾ ⊖ ᴄᴀ

Comrade Coates did not survive, despite Juliet and Terrance's best efforts. Frank couldn't bring himself to feel even the least bit sad about it but refrained from saying so to Maggie. On a practical note, the crazy woman probably would have been a useful source of intel, but they still had six other prisoners, five of whom seemed more than happy to spill every last bean they had about the inner workings of the New World Order.

The picture they painted was bleak: The New World Order was a dictatorship with a fancy name that required mindless devotion from its "citizens"—AKA those they subsumed by coercion or force. Those who did not toe the line were sent off to work at the "Peace and Education Camps" until the relentless brainwashing and backbreaking work of subsistence farming had sufficiently reformed them. In practice, of course, those who disappeared were never seen again, and there was an unspoken policy that any woman in need of "reforming" was free game to be used without consequence or punishment.

The New World Order purported to be "rebuilding a better world" and "fixing the systemic errors" of pre-Fall society. According to the prisoners, the NWO would not rest until the entire country had been "liberated" from the evils of the past. But for all its supposed utopian glory, the five NWO fighters who had surrendered seemed relieved at their capture. It would take significant work on their part to gain the trust of the people of Maligator County, but they were off to a good start.

The sixth one, well…it was a big farm with lots of livestock who made conveniently large piles of thick, pungent manure. Somebody had to collect all that manure to fertilize the greenhouse gardens, and Frank felt certain a few months on the shit list—literally—would soften him up.

All the intel was freely shared with Terrance and his team, and Frank could only wish them luck completing their survey mission of the Ohio Valley Region. He did not envy the job the U.S. government had cut out for it dealing with power-hungry factions across the United States like the NWO.

Of course, whatever the already strained U.S. military did or didn't do about the NWO in the distant future did not solve Gallrein Farms' immediate problem, namely, what would they do when the next wave of NWO fanatics came for their farm?

It was a pressing concern, and Frank was shanghaied—not

unwillingly but not exactly enthusiastically either—to remain at Gallrein Farms to help strategize on what was to be done.

"I've got good news and bad news," Terrance Jones said three days after Comrade Coates's ill-advised and disastrous invasion attempt. They were gathered around the dining table of Joe Gallrein himself with Joe, Ben, Sarah, Gary, Terrance, and Frank in attendance. "The good news is that I spoke with my superiors in Florida, and they are absolutely on board with sending whatever supplies and manpower you need here to fully support your efforts to preserve your livestock and crop lines. That would include zombie virus vaccines for everybody, significant security personnel, weapons, and ammo to keep the resources here at Gallrein Farms safe from incursion by hostile groups."

The farmers around the table exchanged glances and Frank leaned back in his chair and crossed his arms. "So what's the catch?"

"That's the bad news," Terrance said, his words belied by his spreading smile.

Frank's eyes narrowed.

The former Army medic's grin only grew, and he held up a hand in a "wait for it" gesture as he pulled out a bulky satellite phone from his cargo pocket and made a call.

"Yes, this is Terrance Jones of the Fifth Northeast survey team, calling to speak with Secretary Alvarado, as requested." The man listened for a moment, then gave a series of letters and numbers that Frank assumed was a security code of some kind. Then Terrance switched the phone to speaker and set it in the middle of the table. "Secretary Alvarado, may I introduce Joe, Ben, and Sarah Gallrein, owners and managers of Gallrein Farms, Maligator County. Also present are Gary Gains, the farm's head of security, and Frank Oberman, the trainer of their exceptional canine force. Gentlemen, you are speaking with United States secretary of the interior, Ms. Olivia Alvarado."

The looks around the table had gone from worried and confused to wide-eyed and awestruck. When no one immediately said anything, Old Joe cleared his throat.

"It's an honor to speak with you, ma'am, though I can't rightly say we're sure what this is all about. Us country folk are pretty plainspoken and straightforward, so would you mind returning the favor?"

A feminine sounding chuckle came over the sat phone, and Secretary Alvarado spoke:

"Of course, Mr. Gallrein. Mr. Jones has given me a complete report of the 'excitement' you had a few nights ago, and he hasn't stopped singing the praises of your people or your incredible accomplishments since. Word of your farm and everything you've kept going is a piece of good news we've sorely needed, and I intend to personally see to it that you get whatever you need to keep Gallrein Farms safe and prospering. All that we, your government, ask in return is your wisdom and knowledge to help our country organize our survivors and reestablish our agriculture base across the country."

Both of Frank's eyebrows rose, and he could tell the three generations of Gallreins were equally taken aback.

"Ben Gallrein, I heard you have a dual degree in agriculture and business from the University of Kentucky and have been running your family farm with your father for the last twenty years. That is experience we sorely need, and on behalf of the United States Government, I would like to appoint you as our new secretary of agriculture."

Stunned silence greeted Secretary Alvarado's statement, and Frank finally understood the Cheshire-like grin on Terrance's face.

His immediate gut reaction was denial, knowing in all likelihood that such a position would take Ben away from Gallrein Farms. But another part of him glowed with pride on Ben's behalf.

"I—I'm truly honored, Secretary Alvarado, but I really don't think I'm qualified for such a lofty position of authority. I don't know a thing about politics and I—"

"Oh hang all that," Secretary Alvarado said. "The last thing we need in the federal government right now is politicians. We need someone who knows how to build and maintain large-scale farming operations who also has the interpersonal skills to work with a diverse range of people, from everyday farmers to the President herself."

Frank looked at Ben and saw his friend's Adam's apple bob as he visibly swallowed.

"I, uh, still can't say that I feel qualified for such a heavy responsibility, ma'am. But...well...I certainly want to help my country if I can. Before you take that as an acceptance," he continued quickly, "I have to make it clear that my top priority is my family and my people here in Maligator County. I won't abandon them or this farm."

"Of course not, Mr. Gallrein, and I would be worried if you were eager to do so. When you do accept my offer," Secretary Alvarado said with an audible smile in her voice, "the appointment will still have to be approved by the legislature in Texas. President Staba, of course, has already expressed her enthusiastic support. In addition, your first job as secretary of agriculture will be to arrange for your replacement at Gallrein Farms and get everything situated with the new people and equipment we'll be sending you. That will take time, and I can assure you that your government is just as invested in the protection and success of Gallrein Farms as you are. You have the largest and most diverse group of surviving livestock we've found anywhere since the Fall, and I hear you've perfected using biofuels to keep your machinery running. These are stunning accomplishments considering the hell you've endured, and we count your farm as a critical piece of infrastructure to be protected at all costs."

"Th-thank you, ma'am," Ben said, glancing uncertainly at his father. "I would like to clarify, though, if you'll excuse my rudeness: Gallrein Farms and its resources belong to my family and the people of Maligator County, and we will decide what is done with them."

"I agree, Mr. Gallrein, with the caveat, of course, that when you become the secretary of agriculture, it will be your duty to build a plan for how to use all the resources of our great nation to help rebuild what the zombie plague destroyed. That will mean some sacrifices—time spent teaching others how to farm, maintain equipment, make biofuel, etcetera; seed and livestock sent to other locations to become the start of new farms; possibly even experienced personnel sent as well to organize and supervise the establishment of new agricultural infrastructure. All of that will be necessary, not only from you, but from every farmer across the nation if we have a hope of rebuilding what we've lost. Do you understand?"

"I do, ma'am. It's a massive job, one I don't think I'm cut out to spearhead. And you're asking a lot from me personally, as well. I hope you don't mind if I ask for a few days to think about your offer and discuss it with my family. It's not a decision I have a right to make on my own."

"Understood, Mr. Gallrein, and that will be perfectly fine. I look forward to passing on your acceptance to President Staba. Any more questions you can direct to Mr. Jones. If he doesn't know the answers he knows who to call to find out."

"Thank you, ma'am."

"I'll let you get back to whatever you were doing, Mr. Gallrein. I know running a farm is busy, busy work."

"That it is, ma'am. And thank you."

"No, Mr. Gallrein. Thank you. You make me proud to be an American. I look forward to working with you. Now, Mr. Jones?"

Terrance picked up the sat phone and switched off the speaker. As he walked to the other side of the room speaking quietly to Secretary Alvarado, Ben looked around the table where everyone was staring at him. He sighed and chuckled ruefully, "She doesn't make it easy to say no, does she?"

"Why would you say no, Dad?" Sarah asked. "Obviously it won't be easy, but think of the difference you could make? I thought the whole reason we were worried about getting on the government's radar was someone swooping in and taking over the farm, right? But if you're in charge, that fixes the problem! And you'd make a great secretary of agriculture, wouldn't he, Pops?"

Old Joe gave his son a half smile. "If anyone would, it'd be our Ben. Though you'll have a job and a half talkin' Barbara 'round. Her blood runs bluer'n the Bluegrass itself, and she'll have a thing or two to say 'bout moving to some southern swamp like Florida."

"I wouldn't even worry about that part yet. How can I leave you all, leave Gallrein Farms? Who would take my place?"

Old Joe sent a pointed look in his granddaughter's direction. "Ain't that what you've been training Sarah for these past years? She's a grown woman. Twixt the two of us, I figure we can manage."

Ben pursed his lips, brow furrowed in worry. "Gary? Frank? What do you think?"

Gary shrugged. "I'd be thrilled to get better weapons, more ammo, more security. The offer seems sincere, and it'd solve a lot of our problems, especially our most recent one spelled N-W-O. With you at the helm of the decision-making, I'd be hard put to come up with any reason to refuse."

Ben's gaze turned to Frank. "Well?"

Despite knowing the question had been coming, Frank didn't answer right away. His eyes flicked to Terrance, still in the corner speaking quietly on his sat phone. Images of the past few days flashed through his mind: Terrance and LeMonte, rifles raised, advancing unprotected towards hostile forces they'd had no obligation to fight. Terrance with medkit in hand, working for hours on end to patch up the wounded. Owen and Daniel, the engineers, shaking hands with Teddy and Old Bill Tackett, eagerly discussing the farm's systems and what replacement parts they were most in need of.

If these men were representative of the newly formed United States federal government, then Frank thought there was a good chance they might all survive the hell that had befallen their nation.

A curious feeling swelled in Frank's chest. It'd been so long since he'd felt it, he wasn't sure at first what it was. Then he realized:

It was hope.

"United we stand, divided we fall," Frank said, looking back at Ben and giving a firm nod.

Do Not Steal

MEL TODD

Kristy drove slowly toward the town. She'd heard about it over the ham radio, the only method of communication that was still reliable. The last two years had been hard, but most of the zombies were corralled in cities of the dead or in small roving groups. The information to create the vaccine had been widely distributed. She'd been living alone for a bit too long and figured she was ready for civilization—if they'd have her.

The town in the middle of what had been Nebraska was willing to accept new residents if you had something decent to trade and were willing to abide by the laws. Kristy didn't know what their laws were, and that was something she'd have to verify before she bought in. Some places were nightmares run by tyrants. You'd be better off getting bitten than going to them.

Trading with groups like that was dangerous enough, but if she wanted to keep moving she needed the diesel. Small oil-processing towns had sprung up as the stuff in the tanks was mostly worthless. Kristy survived off of scavenging houses that hadn't survived the outbreak. But after two years of sleeping with one eye open and worrying if she had enough ammo, food, and fuel to make it another week, exhaustion haunted her. This place at least let people leave, though she'd heard they had the death penalty if you broke their laws. That worried her, but only a touch. You didn't get second chances in this world very often. And she'd understand the laws before she agreed.

Her trade goods were in the back of her truck, which by itself was the biggest prize she had, but she'd made sure to bring valuable trade goods. Getting accepted as a charity case put you in as the lowest of the low. She wanted to be courted, encouraged to stay. Pulling up to the town, Kristy admired the walls surrounding it. It was surrounded by boxcars, creating a barrier that had to be at least ten miles across. She sat in her truck close enough that they saw her, but far enough away she could change her mind. This was a big step. If she made the wrong choice, she might regret not letting the zombies kill her.

One of the places she traded at had the vaccine, and she'd paid for it willingly, but that didn't mean you could afford to be careless. The vaccine didn't mean you couldn't die or wouldn't turn. Or worse.

Kristy shook her head. Those sorts of thoughts weren't helpful. The town looked healthy. She could see an active oil derrick a bit further out. That meant they had fuel. And they had fields with crops, which meant food.

To hell with it. If she stayed out here alone any longer, she'd make a mistake and die. This place was better than most, she hoped. Kristy shifted into gear and drove forward. There were two horses at the gate and a pair of mountain bikes. The guard, armed with a rifle and a hard look she recognized from the mirror, approached cautiously, scanning around the truck, under it, and behind.

"What?" His voice was gruff and unfriendly.

"Applying for entrance," she said, her voice cracking. It had been two months since she'd spoken to anyone.

"There's a quarantine period," he stated.

"Understood." That was only smart. No one wanted to let someone in that had been bit and didn't tell them. People lied all the time, something the apocalypse had proven again and again.

He nodded once. "Lock up your vehicle, then there's a trailer for you. Four days and full inspection required after."

Her eyes narrowed. "Who's doing the inspecting?" More than one group used inspections as an opportunity to grope, screw, or abuse applicants. It was a red flag.

The guard cleared his throat and looked away. "Wimmen get Mrs. Curtis. She used ta be a nurse. Men get Doc Boren. Swear."

"Okay." Fifteen minutes later she was in a large horse trailer, with a bed, chamber pot, blankets, and even a little solar shower with a curtain around it. The key to her truck was with her. Nothing was stopping them from killing her and taking it, but eventually you had to trust someone. And the lukewarm shower made her feel better.

The next three days were oddly nice. They brought her good food and water. And best of all she got to relax and read. She hoped from the hungry looks at her e-reader that her trade goods would be viable.

The morning of day three, a guard, with three others she hadn't met, pounded on her trailer.

"Miss Kristy?"

"Yes?" She was both worried and wary, pounding on doors or walls was rarely good.

The guard responded. "We've got zombies headed this way. You willing to help us take them out? It'll start your quarantine over and Mrs. Curtis will check you when you get back."

Kristy bit back a mental groan, but the idea of getting out and stretching sounded good, if dangerous. Zombies were always dangerous, but manageable if you knew how to deal with them. Most people still alive did.

The thought of another four days in here just hurt, though. Luckily it was late spring, so the weather wasn't bad, but she was already getting bored and restless. But if she wanted to live here, maybe seeing how they worked in the field firsthand was a good idea. That way she could change her mind about joining before she showed them her goods.

"Sure. I'll need my supplies," she said with a forced shrug. Everyone had their favorite zombie-hunting outfit and weapons. She'd taken her .45 into the quarantine with her, but she was only wearing light pants and a tank top.

The relief that flitted across the guard's face worried her, but he let her out and she headed to her truck, unlocking the cab. The bed with a camper shell had a lock on it. She pulled out a pair of bib overalls. They were hot, but the tough material plus quilted lining stopped knives and zombie teeth. She pulled those over her pants, then laced up her military-style boots.

"We sniping or close combat?"

The guard grimaced. "Sniping, I hope, but you never can tell."

Kristy nodded. This meant an exploratory search, not a defined place with sniper targets. So be it. She strapped an axe to her left hip, then her .45 to her right with the belt designed to carry both. She pulled on a long-sleeve shirt and one cut-proof glove.

"Can you fill this with water?" she handed a bladder flask to him.

He just nodded and took it over to one of their water towers, while Kristy continued to arm herself. After two years, getting dead at this stage would be stupid. She grabbed her AR-15, as well as five magazines. If they needed more than that, they would need to give her ammo or they were all dead anyhow.

She pulled a Carhartt jacket over her, sweat already dripping down her back. The guard came back, bladder filled. Kristy slipped it into the backpack, loaded up the magazines, and pulled the backpack on. She took a minute to make sure the jacket opened and closed smoothly. When they got to seeing the zombies, she'd zip it. The tube to her water flask slipped through the loops designed for it. She was as ready as she could get.

"Not bad. You might make it after all," the guard said, looking her up and down. Kristy didn't mind as there was nothing sexual about his gaze. Going out with someone who didn't know how to protect themselves put yourself at risk.

"We hunting or getting vaccine supplies? Anyone else coming?" Kristy jerked her head at the other trailers.

"They declined." The guard's tone was even, but it didn't take an emotional genius to catch the undertones. "Hunting and yes. There is a group spotted about two miles away. We think there're fifteen. We need to get them, get the spines, and get back."

"Sounds good." She was introduced to the six other hunters, but the names and faces didn't stay in her memory. And since most people wore some sort of headgear it was hard to remember the face under it. Everyone was very polite, careful, and gun-smart. All good signs.

She followed orders on the hunt, took her shots, and hit all five. The harvesting was as unpleasant as always, but that was an advantage to her cut-proof glove. It made that part go faster.

The trek back was lighthearted, but low key. Everyone was exhausted, and she was the stranger of the group.

A woman was waiting for her at a small building, standing outside. She had to be about fifty, and Kristy suspected she had once had curves; now she was lean with clothes that didn't fit right. But she had a friendly smile under graying hair and dark brown eyes. "I'm Martha Curtis. I'll do a quick visual, then we've got a hot shower and hot food waiting for you. Then back to your quarantine quarters."

Kristy blinked. "Hot shower?"

Martha smiled. "Boiling if you wish. Most of us inside have running water and Everhots in our houses."

The desire to ask questions bubble, but the lure of a hot shower was greater. "I'm up for that." Kristy stripped and rotated on Martha's command. For a hot shower, almost anything was tolerable.

"You look fine. A bruise or two." She handed her a towel. "If it helps, this is standard for all zombie interactions even after you become a townie. We always check everyone. If there is anything that looks like a break in the skin, we quarantine you. If you have blood on your face, same thing. We don't want any..."

"Wildfires." Kristy nodded. Wildfire was when someone in a town turned and then spread it before it was caught. The death tolls were horrid.

"Exactly. Enjoy. I'll have dinner brought to you"—Martha paused and looked back at Kristy as she stepped into the already steaming water—"and thanks. Safer to have more people on a hunt than less."

Kristy just nodded and then ignored everything as she had her first hot, really hot, shower in over two years. Dinner waited for her at her little trailer and the guard locked her in, offering her a rare smile. Kristy settled in with her e-reader and tried not to hope that this place might be as good as it seemed.

"Wake up. Today's the day," the guard, his name was Fred, said outside her trailer.

Kristy jerked up with a start, her heart racing.

"The interviewing is happening in about an hour after the evaluation."

She got dressed and braced herself, fingering her key and fighting insidious hope. Worst case, she'd had a week to truly relax, something that hadn't happened in years, plus a hot shower.

While it wasn't a five-star resort, if those existed anymore, it had been pretty nice.

A young woman walked out, or at least Kristy thought she was young. When she got closer, the slimness revealed itself to be body type, not youth. She had to be at least late thirties with dishwater blond hair, a pair of cutoff jeans, a vest that had a dozen pockets, and a wary look. Kristy just wanted to make her smile, because that seemed to be the expression she should wear, not this worry.

There were two other men there, the ones Kristy had seen when requesting admittance, but their quarantine should have ended days ago. She glanced back at Fred and jerked her head toward the two men with drawn brows. Fred just smirked and Kristy ducked her head so no one else saw her smile.

"We have petitioners to join Readton?" The young woman's voice was soft but strong.

"We do," someone called out, but Kristy didn't recognize the voice or see the person.

"Who vouches for the health of the petitioners?"

Martha stepped forward and looked at the woman. "I vouch for the woman."

A man that Kristy thought she had glimpsed stepped up. "I vouch for the men."

"Very well. Step forward and tell us who you are and what value you bring to our town."

One man, taller, with a lean body and a smile that Kristy recognized as a "crawl into my bed" smile, stepped forward. "Gacy Nelson. I'm a journeyman-level carpenter, or I was, and I have all my tools and carpentry books. My car is electric with jury-rigged solar panels good for two to three hours of charge. And I found a reloading set in an abandoned house with dies and shells for over fifteen different calibers."

Kristy understood the sudden interest. Ammo was getting harder to come by and having reloading equipment helped. You could at least make gunpowder and bullets if you had to. She shifted in sudden nervousness. What if they already had enough of what she had?

"Thank you. Next?" The woman didn't seem impressed but of the people gathered they seemed excited.

"Roy Barnes." He was stockier, held his baseball cap in his

hands. "I ain't got too much, but I grew up on a farm, so I know my way around most animals. My truck is old, but it means no electrics and I know how to fix or rebuild everything on it. Runs off diesel, though. I've brought reams of paper, fifty pounds of sugar—" He stuttered to a stop as a murmur of excitement went through the crowd at that. He cleared his throat and continued. "And I found a fabric warehouse. I filled my little trailer up with denim, cotton, and canvas fabrics."

The little U-Haul trailer she'd seen must have been his. It was a risky way to travel, but if he had slowly accumulated stuff, the trek here might have been worth it. Roads weren't so easy to navigate anymore.

"Thank you," the woman said, her tone even. She turned to focus on Kristy. "And you?"

"I'm Kristy Kenzie. I brought a few things. First, there is the truck. It's modified to run on railroad tracks. I updated the engine so it runs off biodiesel." Biodiesel was easier to make as rancid oil worked just as well as fresh. She swallowed and continued. "I have five buckets of garden survival heirloom seeds. I also brought five thousand rounds of .223, and a thousand .45 ACP." Even saying that hurt. She never talked about how or why she had that much ammo, but it should get her access to almost anywhere, hopefully. The back of a truck didn't have that much room, and she preferred to travel light. From the excitement rippling through the crowd and the few new people that drifted closer, maybe her trade was valuable. But this last one was the make-it-or-break-it. Once upon a time she'd been a data analyst and a bit of hacker.

Taking a deep breath, she started. "And I have a dozen twelve-terabyte drives, with solar chargers and cables for damn near any system. They are loaded with every book we could pull down from Amazon before it crashed, Project Gutenberg, and everything my friends sent me before I lost contact with them." It had taken some hacking, some time, but she'd saved everything on that drive as open-source e-pubs. "It includes science books, textbooks, nursing, everything." Awkward, feeling like everyone stared, Kristy babbled. "I had friends before the crash, they worked for Barnes & Noble, IngramSpark, Amazon, and other places. They opened it up and let us download everything and anything. We knew what was coming, and we figured knowledge and entertainment were going to be needed again someday. There were twenty of us. I don't know how many still live, but I don't want the data, these books, to be lost." Kristy cleared her throat and ducked her head, trying not to let her nerves get to her, but she was so tired of being alone.

She looked up but couldn't read people's reactions.

"Thank you. We will discuss."

A group of people, Martha and Greg included, clustered around the woman, leaving Kristy with the other men.

"Heya, cutie. I'm sure you'll get in. The seeds and the ammo alone are pretty valuable." It was Gacy, looming over her, a charming smile on his face. Kristy just wanted to sigh. A damn apocalypse and men were still jerks.

"My name is Kristy. I hope so. If not, I'll go somewhere else." She looked at Roy. "Animal experience is pretty cool." She didn't say anything else. No one needed to know her past.

"Thanks." He ducked his head and she sensed more than saw Gacy puff up.

"Don't worry. I'll vouch for you. Who wouldn't want a cute thing like you?"

Kristy gave him a hard glare and moved two feet away, focusing on the people still talking.

"Your loss, sweetie. You don't know what you're missing."

Kristy didn't say anything, just hoped and planned where to go if this failed. Worst case, she could fall back to where she'd been for the last six months, but the pickings there were getting slim and she really wanted some fresh vegetables and fruit. Scurvy was always a possibility.

There was movement and the group headed back, the woman in the lead. She stopped about ten feet away, her eyes locked on Kristy.

"We have decided. Kristy Kenzie, you are accepted. Roy Barnes, you are accepted." She turned to Gacy. "You are provisionally accepted. You have three months to prove your value to Readton."

Kristy wanted to whoop with joy, even as Gacy puffed up anger clear on his face. Before he could do anything stupid, the woman continued talking. "There are only two laws in Readton and you must follow them. Think carefully, because the consequences of breaking these laws are either expulsion or the death penalty, depending on the crime."

Kristy's excitement faded. Some places had weird rules, and there were some things she couldn't live with.

"Rule One: Do not steal." The woman's voice was clear. "Be very clear on this. Do not take anything that is not yours."

Kristy nodded in an unconscious response to the strength in her voice.

"Rule Two: Give more than you use. You are a part of a community here, not a charity case." Her eyes traced over the three of them. "If you agree to these rules, you will be allowed into Readton."

Kristy stood there for a long time, but she couldn't see an issue with these laws. She wanted to do something, be part of a community and the only way to do that was work.

"I agree," she said in a strong voice. Her words were followed by Roy and Gacy agreeing. With that, people started streaming toward them. The woman who had spoken to them headed toward Kristy.

"Ms. Kenzie, I'm Molly Laughlin, the assistant librarian. I want to talk to you about the books."

"And I want to see those seeds. I'm Jim Hince and I'm the head farmer for our town." The man who spoke was older, graying here, but a lean, tough build Kristy had always associated with cowboys in movies, back when there were movies.

She was hustled off to the side away from the glaring Gacy and quiet Roy. Kristy didn't care. She just prayed she wasn't making a mistake. The seeds were grabbed with much thanks. To her surprise the ammo was logged in as hers and she could leave at any time and get it back. Everyone was encouraged to keep a few hundred rounds in their dwelling as well as weapons. You never knew when you might need them. The rest were checked into an armory and she was granted ammo credit, minus what she used personally. Anything used on town missions, like the one she had helped with, were not counted. Part of her unraveled at that. While she might be down the seeds, at least she'd still have ammo.

Kristy didn't mention her extra stashes of various items. This was really what she could afford to lose or at least what she couldn't use herself. She just hoped they had the equipment available to make use of her books.

Molly bounced up and down. "Well?"

Kristy had unlocked the back of the truck's shell to get the seeds and ammo. She had clothes and basic camping equipment back there too, but everyone had that. Kristy went to the cab and opened it and pulled out the heavy metal suitcase.

Molly's eyebrow arched at that.

"I figured if they used nukes against the zombies, I'd keep them in this. I'm pretty sure it would act as a Faraday cage." Kristy wasn't positive, but it also made a good table when she needed one.

"I see. Well, come on. Looking at data-storage devices out here won't tell me anything." Kristy followed Molly into the town for the first time. For a minute Kristy felt like Dorothy in Oz. Everything seemed so normal. A few houses, a shop, government buildings, apartments. It was only as she walked that the difference jumped out. More bicycles, less cars; everyone had a clothesline; boutiques or coffee shops, and it felt so quiet compared to before the fall. Most of what she saw had sidewalks. There were roads through the small down. Red squares with big numbers in them painted in front of houses or buildings aroused her curiosity, but she just looked. A few buildings were obviously being either repaired or, in the case of a storefront, turned into apartments by a team of people.

Molly headed with an almost skipping gait to a building at the far end of town. It was a large brick building that looked too big for such a tiny town. Molly unlocked the doors and let Kristy inside. "Back here. I have the computers and e-readers set up."

Kristy followed with wide eyes. She'd thought almost no one had computers anymore, but there was a set of PCs and Macs that lined two tables, as well as a bunch of e-readers attached to a charger.

"Set the suitcase here."

Molly waved at a larger server tower that sat a bit away from everything with a table next to it. Kristy laid the suitcase down and opened it, pulling out the data storage and the cables that went with it.

"May I?" Molly all but whispered the words.

Kristy shrugged and handed her the drive. Molly connected it to the tower and then moved over to the computer screen and keyboard next to it. In a few fast strokes, she had the window open and had found the drive. Kristy held her breath as Molly opened it. There in a glorious list of files were thousands of e-pubs.

Molly sniffed, and Kristy shot her a worried look. The woman shook her head. "I'm just so happy. We've read almost everything and only a few of us had e-readers still by the time we got here. I've been prying information out of the Time Life books and Popular Mechanics magazines we had. But this. Are they organized?"

"'Fraid not. We just grabbed and dumped. Once one drive was full, we gave it to someone else to copy, and then we filled the next. It was a bit of an underground movement. We kind of agreed that if it turned out we were overreacting, we'd just never mention it and go back to buying books. But..." Kristy sighed and waved her hand around. "We weren't."

"You have no idea what this means to us, to me. It'll take me a few weeks to get everything copied to the servers and get the originals back to you. But then I'll organize and publish the updated library on the website."

"You still have Internet?" Kristy looked at her, surprised.

"No, we have intranet for the town. It lets us announce a few things or share books over it. Quite a few people still have smart phones or computers. They just connect to the Wi-Fi to get access, read-only. For those with e-readers they are going to be super excited. We're trying to make our world at least decent if not like the old one. Hopefully what you grabbed will get us books on building computers, though once our chips die we might have problems. I may have to look into other options, but we are good for a few years. Then all the extra ones you brought." She smiled a weepy smile. "I'm ecstatic."

Kristy shook her head amazed but let herself be led out of the library. It was locked up tight behind them. "It's only open a few days a week, from noon to four. People know this. The rest of the time I'm usually working on research requests." She looked up at a young man headed their way. "Ah, there is John. He'll show you to your assigned housing."

John took Kristy to one of the apartment buildings, handing her a key to the door. "The person here got married, so the apartment is open. The stuff in it is yours to use, but it belongs to Readton. If you don't need it or like it, put it in the recycle square out front."

That explained what those squares were, and she had to smile. "Okay. So then what?" No one gave stuff like this away for free.

John smiled. "Get your stuff. Get settled. You have three

days of getting comfortable here, then go to the courthouse for a work assignment or look at the jobs being posted. Some are Readton sponsored, others are barter, and some are opportunities like starting a business or a need the town has."

"Thanks. I'll look."

John continued, "There's a town store. Mostly stuff found on scavenging hunts, or from people coming in. Some of your seeds'll be there, as will some of the tablets you brought. All newcomers get a flat one hundred credits just to give 'em some breathing space. Then every time your items sell you get half that credit. Another quarter goes to the people running the store, and the town gets the last quarter. But you also earned a lot of credits for the truck. You could probably not work for a while if you didn't wanna. But you'll get a note with how many credits you have."

Kristy frowned. "What do they do with the credit?" She understood the need for taxes, but this didn't make much sense to her.

"So far we use it to purchase goods that other towns are in need of. Your seeds'll be a valuable trade. The books also are pretty valuable, especially if we find any that are about building or repairing things. Those we might print out. We then trade with those towns. That is about once every month or so. You'll see the announcement looking for guards and people willing to go. Depending on which town will depend on what they want or need."

"And we get paid in it?"

"Mostly. Renting the e-readers or tablets is only a credit for a week. We want people to learn." He flashed her a smile at that, but she was still trying to figure out these rules. "Otherwise yeah. Part of all harvests go to the store; you can build things, sell them there, etcetera. It's in the old grocery story. We try to have a bit of everything."

"How are the prices figured?" she asked, wondering what the seeds were worth.

"Well, scavengers tell us what they are willing to give an item up for and we charge double that. If it doesn't sell, eventually the owner—though that isn't the right word—and the town takes the hit and next time we will barter harder for those items." He shrugged. "It's a lot haggling and figuring out what things are worth to other people. Diapers, tampons, meds, those all sell for high credits. Canned food and whatnot is usually one to five creds depending. We have enough food here that it isn't as important as it once was. You earn credits for electricity too, though everyone gets a set amount each month, but it doesn't go far, so use sparingly."

That made her relax, but it provided a new mystery, figuring out the electricity. Being here a while would make her feel better and let her make the final decision.

"Anything else?"

"Lots probably, but for now, I think I'm good."

John smiled once more and headed out, leaving Kristy standing in an apartment. She looked around and everything looked like before the world ended. Before she lost her friends and everything else. She didn't know if she wanted to break down and cry or run away screaming.

It took her two days to get all her stuff moved in. Well, not that she had a lot. But she did need to switch out a few things and wash all her clothes. That was a blessing. Mostly it was looking at what the place had she didn't need or want, moving it to the recycle square and then make a list of what she did want. Her e-reader was fully charged, and she thought about spending the day reading. She had more books than she'd ever get to read, but instead headed out to actively pay attention to the town and the people.

Kristy headed through town, her .45 on her hip, and inspected her new home. She walked through most of the town. It wasn't that big. The walls that surrounded it were boxcars. Every so often, she'd see someone patrolling along the top. It wasn't an empty town, either. People were working, there were huge garden sections where people were tending to plants, a busy machine shop, windmills in the distance, and stationary bikes set up outside under a gazebo where a ton of kids were pedaling away. The place was neat, productive, and there wasn't anyone lazing about. It made her uncomfortable to not be working.

What was odd, especially for her as she grew up in the city, was how extremely polite everyone was. Even if everyone had a weapon, they nodded, said hello and at least three times people introduced themselves and they knew her name. Two people offered food if she needed it. They explained where the open cafeteria was if you weren't the best cook or didn't have the energy.

The place seemed like a dream. So where was the nightmare?

"Hey, Kris, where did you get placed?"

Kristy turned to see Gacy and Roy walking towards her. She kept her expression blank, but she really wasn't in the mood to deal with his attitude.

"It's Kristy. Apartments over there—" She jerked her head in the general direction of the apartment buildings.

Gacy frowned. His sharp bones and dark brown eyes on a fit body and a thick wave of hair should have made him attractive, but he just didn't do it for her. Kristy just wanted to figure out how to fit into this town.

"Wow, being a chick you get all the perks. I'm stuck in the bachelor's barracks until I either build or remodel one of the existing houses during my free time as my own." The bitter tone of his voice made her swallow.

"It isn't so bad. There are lots of places that were abandoned and just need to be redone. They set up the local elementary school as a barracks-type situation. It isn't bad and we have showers with hot water." Roy's joy at that made her grin.

"I know. Best thing I've had in a long time. But have you figured out where they are getting the power?" Kristy knew no one had consistent power here, yet this town did.

Gacy snorted. "Yeah. Believe it or not, between the windmills, scavenged solar panels, and the bikes those kids ride, they keep this whole place powered. Crazy green freaks."

Kristy just looked at him and turned back to Roy. "That sounds amazing. You should see the library. They have a huge server set up to store all the e-books, and even have a town intranet."

Gacy and Roy both looked surprised. "Does everyone have computers?"

Kristy shrugged. "I have no idea, but I donated tablets and e-readers and they already have a bunch. Molly was super excited about the one large-style tablet I had. But they seem to be very excited about books."

"Please. I doubt they have any good ones. I wouldn't mind a Penthouse or Playboy about now." Gacy didn't quite leer, but Kristy moved a bit further away.

"I'm headed to the courthouse to see what needs doing. Feels weird to be still for this long, especially after the few days in the trailers."

"Yeah. We had to sit there for eight days. Something about they saw a suspicious wound on us and wanted to make sure it wasn't a new strain. But it was a nice vacation, if boring," Gacy groused as he walked, but he didn't seem too upset about finding something to do.

Kristy thought back to the smirk from Fred and didn't say anything. They passed a few people as they walked. Without fail people looked them in the eyes, smiled slightly with a nod, and kept walking.

"Huh. Have you noticed that everyone here is extremely polite and considerate?" She turned, looking at the town. "And it is neat here. It reminds me of those old sitcoms in perfect towns."

"You call having your town surrounded by freight cars neat?" Gacy scoffed.

Kristy tried not to bristle. "There is no graffiti, the streets are clean, most of the buildings are maintained, and while there might be zombies, this almost feels safe." She didn't follow up with the "too safe" aspect.

Roy paused and nodded. "You're right. Maybe they're just making this work. Either way, I wanna see if there're jobs for me. We were told that how much we pull our weight'll go a long way to seeing if we can stay permanently." Roy had a muted smile on his face as he looked at his feet.

"I wasn't told that, but maybe they are expecting something else? I'm not sure, but either way I want to see what I can do. I'm bored." Kristy shrugged.

Gacy rolled his eyes. "Whatever. I need to prove how good I am. I want my own space again." He strode off toward the courthouse, leaving Kristy and Roy to follow.

Kristy still spent more time looking around than paying attention to either man.

"You enjoying it here?" Roy's voice pulled her out of her introspective survey of the town.

"Hot water is to die for. It was nice to have a door that locked and not jump at every sound." She still had but wasn't about to admit it. "I don't know enough yet to decide, but so far it seems like a miracle."

"Yeah. Was thinking that. It'd be nice to have a miracle." He gave her a shy smile.

Kristy just nodded as they stood looking at the huge bulletin board. It was almost pathologically neat. One area for jobs from other residents, another for items being requested, another offering a barter of skills, and the last section was for town-sponsored opportunities.

She stood there looking for a long time trying to make sense of it before it clicked. Most of the town positions were things that were either sporadic or rotating, though some were full-time. The other jobs offered goods or credit for the town store.

"What the heck is this: 'Electricity Needed, twenty creds per hour riding, plus twenty creds to your electric portion weekly'?" Gacy pointed at one of the town jobs.

"I think..." Kristy paused then smiled. "I bet it's the bikes near the library."

"Yeah whatever. Where is someone that can explain this stuff?" Gacy brushed her off. Roy gave her a sympathetic smile but didn't say anything.

Kristy growled but focused on the opportunities. The data-filtering request jumped out at her. She grinned. "See ya. I've got to see a woman about a job."

"Hey, want to catch dinner later?" Gacy asked with his normal charming smile. There was a small cafeteria that had basic food available to buy if you couldn't or didn't cook. She doubted the barracks had cooking facilities.

"No thanks. Bye." She heard a murmured "bitch" behind her, but ignored it, heading straight to the library after checking her watch.

The door stood open and an older woman was walking out. "Afternoon." She smiled and nodded at Kristy before heading over to the bike rack—real bikes, not the stationary ones.

Kristy watched her put an e-reader in the basket, then ride away. For a moment Kristy focused on the kids and a few adults riding the bikes. On closer inspection there was also a treadmill and all of them had cords running back to the library. "I was right." She cataloged everything she saw, all the "old world" tech that had been preserved. Running water, hot water, food, electricity, books, e-readers, even an intranet. With a smile Kristy headed into the library where Molly sat, sketching something on a clean sheet of paper.

"Hello?"

"One moment, I need to finish this multiple-furrow plow

design." Molly glanced up at the screen, then back down at the paper.

Kristy watched with awe as Molly's fast, accurate drawing took shape. It was like watching a blueprint appear.

"There, that should give Jonas what he needs to craft it. And it should help get more crops in." She looked up and focused on Kristy. "Hey. How can I help you?"

Kristy felt unsure all of a sudden; maybe this wasn't how they did it here? She swallowed and moved forward. "I wanted to inquire about the job cataloging the data?"

Molly's face lit up in a smile. "Excellent. I was hoping you'd apply. Do you have any idea how much data you have?"

"Not really. My friends were storing everything in cloud servers and we just grabbed and backed it up on to drives. I don't think there are lots of duplicates, but there should be a wide mix."

"Oh there is. You even have movies and TV series in here. The town council is excited about that and are talking about starting weekly outdoor showings when the weather is nice. Give people something to look forward to. The problem is I need them all logged and catalogued, and you weren't kidding about how much you had."

Kristy shrugged. "We thought the world was ending, and we wanted to save as much as we could." They hadn't known if it would work, but someday what they had saved might be valuable or it might not. "I know I filled my e-reader to bursting with anything I thought I might need or want. For the drives I downloaded gigabytes at a time and never looked at it until we didn't have anything left."

"And I can't tell you how awesome that is. But I need this catalogued and moved into our system. You interested?"

"Absolutely. Sounds like home."

"Come with me, I need to get this to Jonas, then I'll show you around and how to get everything cataloged." Molly rose with the paper in hand.

Kristy figured she probably knew how, it'd been her job once upon a time, but every system had its quirks. They headed out as Gacy and Roy were walking by.

Gacy's face lit up and Kristy rolled her eyes. "Hello ladies," he said as he pivoted on his heel to walk with them, sliding up to Molly.

Molly glanced at him, eyes widening a bit. "Hi?" The self-assured woman Kristy had been talking to disappeared as she flushed and focused on the ground. From an abstract perspective Kristy thought Molly was pretty, but really over the last few years, survival, not sex, had been forefront on her mind. Hell, Kristy wasn't even sure she wanted to deal with trying to be intimate. Safety was much more important.

"What are you two lovelies up to today?" He nodded at Kristy but turned his charm on Molly.

"Just going to the machine shop?" Again, Molly sounded as if she was questioning what she was doing.

Kristy frowned, becoming even more confused. Gacy was an overbearing flirt, but he wasn't that intimidating.

"Wonderful, do you mind if we come with you? I'm sure you'd feel better with two strong men walking with you."

Kristy glanced at the guards on the boxes surrounding the town and arched an eyebrow. Roy just shrugged and ambled along with them.

"Okay?" Molly almost stuttered the word.

Two men, one of them the guard Fred, were walking toward them, and they froze as they saw the four of them. Fred said something to them then pivoted and headed their way. "Miss Molly. Folks." He gave them a tight smile. "Gentlemen, I have some work you can do, if you'd come with me."

"Aww, we still have a day or so, and I wanted to get to know this little lady," Gacy replied.

Fred seemed to freeze as if torn between competing desires. "Miss Molly, did you want the company right now?"

Molly's eyes were wide, and she looked at Fred, then shook her head the tiniest bit.

"There you go, gentlemen; come with me now." There was something in his tone that had Gacy bristling, but Roy touched his arm. "Come on. Getting a few extra creds is never bad."

"Fine. Ladies, I hope I see you around, especially you, Miss Molly." He canted his words in such a way that it was both suggestive and promising. Kristy didn't know whether to smile or be creeped out.

"Gentlemen, let me tell you now, you don't touch the assistant librarian. If she wants your attention she'll ask, but we don't . . ." Fred's voice faded as the three men moved further away.

"Are you okay?" Kristy asked Molly as they walked away. The woman shook herself.

"Yeah, just...long story. So Jonas crafts most of the things we use around here, and we needed a double-edged plow, but he needed some specs." Molly waved the piece of paper. "Here they are. Now let me tell you about this place."

Molly kept talking and Kristy listened, but she still felt like there was an undercurrent she was missing.

Kristy was up early the next morning ready to start cataloging all the data on her drives; she'd wanted to know what she had anyhow and just hoped it wasn't all kid's books or something. Pulling on her shoes she heard a low wailing siren. For a minute she flashed back to the tornado sirens of her childhood, then it hit her—zombies.

Kristy grabbed her pants and jacket while switching to her boots. She grabbed her AR-15 and her .45 and ran to the street. Everyone else was doing the same and for a moment the town almost looked full.

An older man, hard bitten with a scruffy scalp, stood in the middle of the street. "Listen up. You know the drill. The number in front of your building is your box group. Get to it, see the lead for that group. Ladders are waiting. Move it, people. We have a large herd of zombies headed this way."

Kristy turned to look at her number. She hadn't paid it that much attention in the past. Then she started scanning the box-cars. Each car had a number painted on it about two foot tall in each corner. Her assigned box was across the town from her, but she could see it. She took off at a fast jog—most zombies weren't horribly fast, but still, if the alarm was going it meant *move*. That much had been covered in her orientation. That and the "do not steal" over and over. Everyone stressed it. It made no sense; how hard was it to not take things that weren't yours?

She pushed it out of her mind and headed up the ladder, which swayed a bit too much for her comfort. At the top she found a young man, though his dead look told her there was nothing young about him.

"Kristy, new gal, right?" He snapped out, not in a panic but not wasting time.

"Yes."

"You any good with the AR?" He nodded at her rifle in her arms.

"A headshot at four hundred yards," she replied promptly.

"Standing or prone?"

"Either," she said with a shrug.

"Good. Over there, your choice. Some idiot is running for us and has a horde on him. If they don't kill him, I might. Go." He snapped out the words and turned to walk the length of the box.

Kristy moved to her spot, but as she didn't see any zombies, took a quick look to check the layout. Each boxcar had three spaces with a blanket laid out and a box for casings. She took the one empty and then lay prone, sighting through her scope. It took her a moment, but eventually she found the dust and upset animals veering away from the ruckus. It looked like someone on a bicycle; it had to be a mountain bike to handle the state of the roads, and the crowd of zombies chasing the rider.

She looked up at the monitor for their section. "We harvesting?"

"Yes. I'd like to not kill the idiot, but don't let anyone get within a hundred yards of the boxes."

"Got it." Kristy settled down to wait. She was a good shot, but there was no need to rush it and at this distance she couldn't hit them anyhow. It took about ten minutes—the rider was slowing down—before they got close enough to start shooting. This was a large pack of alphas. "Where in the hell did he find them?" she spoke out loud.

"Shit. That's Jimmy Murphy," someone said. "He went out two days ago to check on some fishing traps with two other boys. They were expected back tomorrow." The stress in those words told her everything. Water was dangerous, but fish was good protein and populations had boomed with the lack of fishing and pollution.

"Tell me when," she said softly. This wasn't her problem; this was what the town council was for.

"Take them, fast headshots. We'll throw him in quarantine and have some vaccine on hand." The words were ground out and Kristy nodded, putting herself in a little box, and becoming nothing but the rifle and her target. They were just targets. She killed five before they were done, others had done more or less. But she'd only used five bullets, that counted as a win in her boat. As she headed down the ladder, she saw others heading out to harvest.

"Do I need to go?" she asked the lead; she still didn't know his name.

"Nope. You've got a job, go do it."

It was all so matter-of-fact that it creeped her out and made her want to cry with relief. The zombies were treated the same way as a blizzard. You dealt with it and moved on. She put up her AR, then headed to the library where an excited Molly waited for her. Kristy dived into organizing.

The days turned into weeks and Kristy started to settle in. The place was still odd, even the teenagers were super polite. She did regular guard rotations on top of the boxes, participated in one salvage run, and she was impressed at how serious and thorough they were. Any zombies found on the salvage run were harvested and the supplies run up via her truck to the hospital in the area that still had operative labs. Everyone loved her truck and the biodiesel additions made it much easier to fuel. Someone had bought a trailer that it towed when on the tracks and it moved faster than zombies could. Plus, the tracks were in better conditions than the roads.

She couldn't say she was happy or at peace, but she wasn't unhappy, and she felt safe. That was more than she had felt for years. Kristy avoided Gacy; he still annoyed her, but he'd upgraded to permanent resident and was apparently very good on the salvage runs and knew how to use the reloading equipment he'd brought. She'd seen him with one of the other women around town, to her relief.

Roy met her at the diner occasionally. He seemed nice, always lit up to see her, and they even went to the first movie showing together, *Speed*. It both went over well and hurt. Seeing how the world used to be, even with a mad bomber out to get you, just hurt. Everyone agreed fantasy and sci-fi from now on. The less like Earth the better.

Two months in, it still felt like a dream, but Kristy was making friends and growing into this life. But it seemed too perfect. She had seen people get up, get in each other's faces yelling, but they'd stop, take a deep breath, and back down. Every time. She could tell it left Gacy confused too, as the person would just walk away. It felt like one of the two worlds was a dream, the outside world where you were just as likely to kill someone you just met as help them, or this one where they had food, water, places to live, clean clothes, and everyone was polite.

"Walk you back to your place?" Roy said after dinner one night.

"Sure," she finished up, bussed her plates and they headed out.

"You're friends with the assistant librarian, right?"

"Molly? Yeah, she's my boss. She's pretty cool." Kristy walked into the cool night air. They'd have to start harvesting the gardens tomorrow and start the canning drive everyone had been prepping for.

"Gacy's annoyed we aren't allowed to bug her, but I kinda get it. Besides, I think he's found someone else. He was talking about moving out of the barracks the other day." Roy ambled along beside her.

"What do you mean you can't bug her?" Kristy had wondered, but Molly never talked about anything personal, not life before, not life now. It was all books, data, inventions, all the time.

"She's apparently who saved the town. She came up with the plans, the ways to create electricity, how to grow food, everything. I can't figure out why she's only the assistant librarian? Have you ever seen the Librarian?" he asked as they crossed over to her place.

"No. I never have. I assumed that person died or something. We all have things we don't talk about." They reached the foot of her stairs. "Want to come on up? I've got two brownies. One of the salvage runs came back with tins of chocolate powder."

A smile crossed his face. "Yes."

They headed in and Kristy flipped on the lights as she entered. "Let me get them." She headed to the little kitchen. It only had running water and a simple hot plate. Refrigerators and microwaves took too much energy, but cooking on a hot plate wasn't too bad. The cafeteria kitchen had refrigerators.

She looked up when she heard the dead bolt turn. "Roy?"

"I knew you wanted me. Gacy was sure of it. But now I know." He had his hands on her before she could react; the .45 was strapped to her thigh, but she couldn't get her arms free.

"Stop. Roy, stop. I'm not interested." Panic filled her voice as she fought to get away, but Roy had a foot and at least sixty pounds of muscle more than she did. His lips trailed along her neck as he ripped off her shirt.

The vague disconnected part of her mourned that shirt; it had fit and not been too worn. The rest of her fought. "No!"

"They all say that," he laughed as he pushed her down to the floor. "I love the squirming; it makes it so much more fun. Once they've had me, they never complain. They used to beg me."

"Oh fuck that shit." Kristy took a deep breath and screamed. It lasted for a second before his hand was placed firmly over her mouth.

"Moans are more fun. Let's hear you moan." He laid on her, held her arms with one hand as he groped and sucked on her breast, the other hand still over her mouth. "Hmm, I'm going to need my hand." He grabbed her torn off shirt and shoved it in her mouth.

Kristy fought and squirmed, tried to knee him, but on the floor with his weight on her, she couldn't get any leverage. His hands were at the waistband of her pants and even though she fought and yelled with everything in her, he had her pants down and she couldn't stop him.

Sobbing, she fought, but the act was over quick enough, painful, thrusting, and then a sigh of satisfaction from him. "I knew you'd feel that good. I'll see you again tomorrow." He pulled himself off of her and stood. Kristy struggled to roll over, her legs tangled in the pants, and her arms weak from struggling for so long.

"Bye, babe," he said with a smirk, reaching for the door.

Her hand wrapped around the .45, not even bothering to pull it out of the holster she swung it toward him and pulled the trigger. The sound of the gun firing echoed in the small apartment, but the bullet missed him as he pulled the door open.

Roy whirled around and glared at her. "What the fuck? Who do you think you are? You're mine now." He stalked toward her and Kristy tried to steady her grip, but her hands shook, the rag still in her mouth.

Before she could pull the trigger again, people flooded into her apartment: her neighbor next door, the one below her, more people, and they had Roy down on the floor before she realized what happened.

"Kristy," her neighbor started then trailed off. "Someone get Martha, and let the Librarian know."

The words made no sense: why would Molly be told? Kristy pulled the shirt out of her mouth and rolled over, struggling to pull up her pants. She'd survived zombie attacks; she could deal with the aftermath of getting raped.

Fred was suddenly there, but he didn't touch her, no one did and that alone made her want to sob in relief. She wanted to claw her skin off.

"I'm here. Everyone get out." Martha appeared and Kristy's apartment emptied, dragging Roy away too. "Kristy, listen to me." Martha reached out and gently pulled Kristy's face to hers. "Please tell me everything that happened."

The words tumbled out in a jumbled mess of anger, confusion, and shock, tripping her up as she worked through it.

"Okay. Do you mind coming to the clinic and being examined?" Martha asked.

Kristy shook her head. "No, but it's not like we have the ability to run a rape kit. It'll be my word against his, that I wanted it." That possibility died with the old world.

Martha smiled. "No. But I don't think you need to worry about that."

Kristy shrugged and went with it. She avoided everyone, slinking to the library, and refusing to talk. Gacy came near her once, looking like he wanted to talk, but she crossed the road almost jogging to avoid him. She needed to make plans to leave. She couldn't live some place that supported rapists.

"There is a community meeting tomorrow at two for everyone," Molly said the next day. Her voice was oddly flat. "Only a skeleton crew will be on the boxes. It's mandatory."

Kristy nodded mutely, she had barely said anything or eaten anything since it happened, though more than one covered dish or prepared meal had been left at her door. The day and the next dragged as she tried to figure out what the meeting was for, and how she could flee this place. The too perfect had a flaw she'd somehow expected. Or maybe she'd just been stupid. You were never safe anywhere. The question was which was worse, zombies or people.

A little before two the next day she dragged herself to the auditorium, any memories of watching a movie there forever sullied. Fred met her at the entrance. "Kristy, if you will come with me."

Kristy nodded dully. This would be where Roy got off, and she had to decide how much of her stuff she could get back. How far she could run. Living alone was the only thing that sounded safe. If you climbed a tree, zombies couldn't get you. Maybe a treehouse in a park.

She sat where Fred told her to and lost herself in daydreams of playing Tarzan in the trees above the hordes of zombies. Anything to avoid this reality.

"We are gathered here for judgment." The voice of a man she'd met once or twice, the head of the council, jerked her out of her thoughts. "The Librarian is called to hear and judge our case."

Kristy blinked, completely confused now, as everyone in the crowd, except for Roy who struggled against his handcuffs and gag, turned to stare at the stage. How had she ever thought he was vaguely cute or nice?

On the stage an old woman: white hair, a shawl, long dress, spectacles perched on her nose, and a staff with scales of justice on the top. Kristy stared at her as she stepped into the light and choked as she recognized Molly under the wig and dress.

"The Librarian stands witness." Her voice was low but filled the entire auditorium.

"Librarian, this man Roy Barnes stands accused of theft. Theft of choice. Theft of consent. Theft of safety."

"How pleads the accused?" Her voice didn't sound like Molly's, and Kristy wasn't sure, but there was a wild look in her eyes, something she'd never seen in Molly's smile. Then the words sunk in. Theft? He raped her and was charged with theft?

Roy's gag was removed, though his handcuffs remained. "She wanted it. She's been sniffing around me for months. It was either going to be me or Gacy, she just finally chose me. I didn't take nothing." He kept trying to speak, but the gag was put back in his mouth. Kristy felt the smallest bit redeemed.

Martha stood up. "Kristy Kenzie was found on the floor of her apartment with her pants around her ankles, gun in hand, gag in her mouth, with marks on her arms and face, along with bruising around her labia. She had tear marks on her face. There was no doubt this was not consensual."

"Councilors, do you agree?" The Librarian turned and looked at a group of men Kristy had seen at meals and while working, but she wasn't friends with any of them.

One of them stood up and nodded. "Yes, Librarian. Theft of choice, consent, and safety is agreed upon."

"Bring up the accused," she intoned as she stepped down to a lower area above a city drain.

Roy was dragged kicking and screaming while the Librarian

stood there, oddly calm. They forced him into a kneeling position before her.

"Roy Barnes, you are found guilty of Theft. There are two consequences for Theft, expulsion or death. The severity of the crimes warrants the second. You are judged guilty."

It happened almost faster than Kristy could follow. The Librarian twisted the headpiece of the staff and the scales of justice came off revealing a long blade or short sword. She swung it from left to right across his throat. The blood spurted out as he screamed into the gag. It faded to a gargle.

"Put him in the hogpen; they can use some fresh protein," the Librarian ordered. She looked out at the crowd, no one had moved or said a thing. "What are the laws?"

"No stealing. Give more than you use."

"What are the laws?"

Responses rung back louder this time. "No stealing! Give more than you use!"

"Remember that. We do not take. We have all had enough stolen from us; we will not tolerate anything else being stolen." The Librarian slammed her staff down on the cement next to the dead Roy then turned and walked away.

Kristy sat there stunned as people filed out, a few nodding to her, but no one approached her. Finally the dark side had been revealed. The consequences of breaking the laws were deadly. Kristy looked at the dead body being dragged away, then glanced up to see Gacy swallowing hard and standing up straighter.

All the politeness, respect, and general attitude of the town suddenly made sense. A slow smile spread across her face. Maybe she could live with this dark side.

Gonzo's Gauntlet

CHRISTOPHER L. SMITH

"God, I'm bored."

It was a statement that was half affirmation, half prayer.

For the last two months, Gonzo had been at the San Antonio Military Medical Center, under observation. What had started out as a case of the sniffles had turned into the worst case of flu he'd ever experienced in forty-five years. It had been bad enough to have him transferred from the Audie Murphy VA Hospital to the larger facility at Ft. Sam Houston. One of those months had been in an induced coma, according to his doctors. The last two weeks made him wish they had kept him under.

TV was not an option—the small flat screen only showed snow or a blank screen. Cell service was nonexistent, and the only reading material were magazines several years out of date.

He sighed, and picked up one of the magazines, wondering if the paper would make a good airplane.

A knock at the door gave him a slight start.

"Mr. Gonzales?" Lionel recognized one of the nurses, a petite young lady with light brown skin and curly black hair. "You have visitors, sir."

Gonzo sat up in his chair and waved her in as he racked his brain for her name. Collin? Coley? Cohen. That was it.

Nurse Cohen entered, followed by a man and a woman Lionel hadn't met before, both in standard BDUs.

"Mr. Gonzales," the woman said, "I'm Lieutenant Colonel Noe." She was fiftyish, short, with brown hair and an upper midwestern accent. "It's nice to meet you." It sounded like "meecha."

Gonzo stood and extended his hand. "Hello, Colonel."

Noe gave a slightly pained expression. "Mr. Gonzales, not to be rude, but shaking hands has become a health hazard. It would be best to break yourself of the habit, quickly."

He pulled his hand back, and glanced at the other Air Force officer, reading his name from the front of his uniform. Major Ferguson was a small mountain of a man, early thirties and in top physical form. With his shaved scalp and massive chest, he did a good impression of Mr. Clean.

And Mr. Clean looked like he had found a turd in his toilet.

Jesus, he thought, *guy looks like he could crush walnuts with those arms.* To the officers, he said, "Well, Colonel, Major, what can I do for you today? Come to free me from my antiseptic prison?"

"Mr. Gonzales..." Noe started.

"Call me Gonzo."

"MISter Gonzales, I'd prefer to keep our relationship on a professional level." At his shrug, she continued, "The U.S. government is practically nonexistent. The last month has been extremely difficult, to say the least. What do you know of the situation?"

"I heard a few rumors going around, but nothing I'd take seriously, to be completely honest. Biowarfare, breaking of the seventh seal, end of days kind of stuff. My favorite was zombie apocalypse, though." He chuckled, waiting for the other two to join in. When they didn't, he continued. "Basically, all I know is it that everyone thinks things are in the shitter."

"You should sit down, Mr. Gonzalez," she said, "Because it's all of the above."

Colonel Noe spent the better part of an hour getting him up to speed. At the thirty-minute mark, he'd noticed the sales pitch starting. At forty-five minutes, he'd wished he'd kept his mouth shut about being bored.

God has a wicked sense of humor.

As she wrapped up her briefing—he recognized one when he heard it—he held up a finger. Noe hesitated.

"Ma'am, I'm going to stop you right there. I know what comes next, and I have an answer."

"And that answer is?"

"No. No way," Gonzo said, shaking his head. "I did my time, got out. Not going back in. Period. Dot."

"I was out too, Mr. Gonzalez. Do you see me here? Am I in uniform? The phrase 'retired' means nothing to me at this point."

"And it means 'no' when I say it."

"You, Mr. Gonzalez, have the unfortunate luxury of now being fully immune to the virus. That makes you an asset that I can't afford to squander. However, I will make your life very difficult from here on out if you don't cooperate."

He snorted. "Like what? KP? Swab the decks?"

"No, what I will do is give you a sidearm and an escort. You will then be led to the gate, asked to leave, and we will terminate our relationship. No food. No ammo. No help, and no calculable chance for survival." She let that sink in.

"So my choice is to suit up, and go try to get myself killed, or you'll send me out to almost certainly get killed, is that it?"

"We need people, Mr. Gonzalez, and our resources are stretched thin, to say the least. This is where we stand—either you're with us, wholeheartedly, or you're on your own." She gave a sad smile. "Welcome to the way of the new world, Mr. Gonzalez."

Gonzo looked around warily as the gate closed behind him, searching for any sign of infected. He figured if he could stick to the highway, staying close to the cover of the abandoned cars, he'd be relatively safe until he got to the outskirts of town. The farms and ranches out near Selma would be more likely to have stockpiles, and less people.

Maybe one of these car—

"*Good luck, Mr. Gonzalez!*" He whipped around, mouth dropping open, as Noe raised the bullhorn again. "*I think you'll be safer if you stay close to the highway! And remember, the infected are attracted to loud noises!*"

Howls erupted from the distance.

"I'm standing right in front of you, Colonel. Is that necessary?"

Gonzo said, trying to keep his voice as low as possible. "Jesus, lady, you're going to get me swarmed!"

"I told you we'd escort you to the gate safely, Mr. Gonzalez, I didn't say we'd be quiet about it!"

The howls grew closer.

It was bad enough she was trying to get him killed to make a point, but the smirks and outright laughter of his former escort added insult to the situation.

A lone infected made his way across the highway, naked and covered in bites and welts. He spotted Gonzo and started running, his high-pitched cry sounding the dinner bell for any others in the immediate vicinity. Gonzo drew the .45 and took up an isosceles stance.

The cars dotting the interstate made the direct approach impossible, but the zombie bastard weaved his way in and out of the vehicles, closing fast, screaming as he came. Something moved at the far side of the asphalt.

"Colonel," Gonzo said carefully, "A little help would be highly appreciated."

"I'm sorry, Mr. Gonzalez, but you made your decision. I'm afraid we don't have the resources to assist a civilian outside the gate." She paused, to make her point, as if she needed to hammer it home, before continuing. *"If only we had more qualified and inoculated staff, we might be able to help those outside of the compound."*

More howlers came out of the scrub lining the highway, making their way towards the first. Gonzo lined the sights up and squeezed off a round, dropping the naked man as he climbed over a car. The other's pace quickened, fresh blood giving them all the incentive they needed.

This wasn't going in the right direction. In fact, it was going due south as fast as possible. More screams and howls joined the group in front of him, closing in from his flanks.

Shit. She's got me right where she wants me.

"Colonel," he said, "if it's not too late—" Gonzo took another shot, aiming for the zombie in the center of the group. If he could just distract them long enough...

"I've reconsidered my decision, and have determined I may have been hasty."

"Oh?"

Really? Do we still need the damn bullhorn? Bitch.

"Yes, ma'am, I believe so." Another shot, this time at the group approaching from his right. "After some careful consideration on my part"—he squeezed off another round—"I think your offer is very reasonable, given the circumstances."

"*I'm listening...*" A group of at least ten climbed up the embankment to his left, elbowing each other in their race to the top.

"Oh for Christ's sake! I'll do it! Just let me in, dammit, before I'm lunch!"

The Ma Deuce on the Jeep roared to life, sending half-inch rounds of flesh-pulverizing fury towards the approaching zeds. Gonzo backed up carefully, checking his six to make sure he wasn't crossing a line of fire. The chain link gate rattled slightly as his back made contact.

The three groups were down, but more howls came from far too close.

"Open the gate, Major Ferguson," Noe said, smiling. "Petty Officer Gonzalez, it is good to have you aboard."

"Yeah, yeah," he said as Mr. Clean let him pass. "I've got such a warm fuzzy about this relationship right now."

The gate clanged behind him, followed by the rattle of chains. He approached Noe's Jeep, using all of his willpower to stifle the urge to strangle the smirk from her face.

"Petty Officer First Class Lionel Gonzalez, it is my honor to reinstate you in the U.S. Navy, San Antonio Detachment. Please raise your right hand and repeat after me..." He did as instructed, and Noe continued, "I solemnly swear to uphold..."

Gonzo repeated the words, glaring at the colonel as he did. He finished the last sentence, adding, "No matter how truly fucked we are."

If Noe heard him, she didn't show it.

"So, Colonel, now that we're besties, why don't you tell me how you became such a manipulative cu—"

"I'd advise you not to finish that sentence, Petty Officer."

"—stomer?"

"I had four brothers, the smallest one towered over me." She shrugged. "I had to give as good as I got. I used my brain instead of brawn."

"Those poor bastards, ma'am."

Her smile, and the look in her eyes, spoke volumes.

∽ ⊖ ⌒

Gonzo glared over his book at the chirp of the radio.

"Chief Petty Officer, I need to see you in my office," Colonel Noe said.

He slammed the hardback closed and dropped it on the bed beside him, glaring at the black handset across the room.

Just getting to the good part, and OF COURSE she calls. I'd swear that woman has a camera in here.

He took a moment to compose himself, got up, and retrieved the radio.

"Ma'am, how urgent is this? It's my first day off in weeks."

"I realize that, Gonzalez, and I do apologize. But this is important."

He counted to ten, took a deep breath, and stifled the multitude of snarky responses he wanted to say.

"On my way, Colonel."

He sighed. It never seemed to end. He briefly considered changing clothes.

"Nah." He started for the main hospital, where Colonel Noe maintained her center of operations.

The last couple of years had been rough, but it seemed to be getting better. They'd been able to clear portions of San Antonio—near the base at first, then a greater and greater radius from there—but it had been a slog.

Some new procedures had become available after they'd swept the National Guard Armory just north of the hospital, thanks to the pair of Cedar Eaters they'd found. While the combination woodchipper and bulldozer made dealing with the infected hordes easier and somewhat safer, it also made it much, much messier.

With some help from the weather, in the form of several floods, they'd made good progress finding pockets of uninfected survivors, and had slowly expanded the number of people on base. While it meant that he'd had to go out in the field less and less over the past year, it also meant more processing and procedural tasks. He wasn't sure which one he despised more.

Going door to door in full bunker gear, in summer, had pushed the limits of his endurance. The constant grind of routine and boredom had pushed the limits of his sanity. Now, the colonel was pushing the limits of his civility.

By the time he reached her door on the fourth floor, Gonzo had a list of excuses ready to go. He paused, knocked, and waited.

"Come in."

Colonel Noe didn't rise from her desk at his entrance. She hadn't changed much since the first day he'd met her—just darker circles under her eyes, some gray hair, and the full bird on her uniform. She rolled her eyes at his clothes before gesturing to the chair in front of her.

"You wanted to see me, ma'am?"

"Thank you for coming. However, next time, please change shirts."

"Day off, ma'am. Not required to be in uniform, as per your rules."

"Yes, but the 'Have a Nice Day, Asshole' tee is a bit much."

"Feels appropriate, ma'am, considering the circumstances."

Noe sighed, apparently deciding that it wasn't worth the head-ache to argue. Gonzo fought to keep the smug grin from his face.

And failed miserably if the colonel's scowl was any indication. He placed one foot on the other knee, allowing his chancla to dangle. Noe's scowl deepened. Gonzo stayed silent.

After a few more seconds of silence, Noe laced her hands on the desk in front of her.

"Chief, we've got a bit of an issue." After a second's pause, she continued. "With the recent influx of survivors, our capability of creating vaccine is becoming dangerously stressed. Frankly, we can't keep production up to match the demand."

Gonzo sat up straight. Most of the survivors they'd found were military (or former military) that had the skills needed to continue clearance. Running short on vaccine meant their chances of progress diminished greatly.

San Antonio Military Medical Center had been the military's largest facility of its kind, capable of treating just about anything that came its way pre-Fall. The fact that it now couldn't maintain necessary production was both good and bad news. Good news because they'd found so many. Bad news, because now they couldn't keep them safe.

"Okay, what do we need?" Gonzo's day off would have to wait. This was important. "Raw materials?"

The best viable vaccine needed the spinal column of infected high-level primates to produce. As large apes like gorillas were in short supply, that meant people. Grisly work, and dangerous.

"Fortunately, not at this time," Noe said. Her gaze lingered briefly on the framed picture of her husband, eyes watering slightly. She regained composure and continued. "No, what we need is equipment."

Gonzo swore.

"Correct," Noe said, with a slight smile. "I'll need you to pay a visit to El Jefe."

He nodded with reluctance. There was no reason to argue about it again—El Jefe wouldn't deal with anyone but him. Any other personnel were turned away at the door, no explanations given.

"Time is of the essence, Chief." Noe handed him a list, then continued. "This should fit in the two Humvees waiting for you and your team at the ER entrance."

"Yes, Colonel." Gonzo stood. "I'll get the guys and head out within the hour."

"Thank you, Chief." She grinned. "Oh, and one favor: please keep that shirt on when you meet El Jefe. It'll let him know I'm thinking about him."

"Honestly, ma'am, I think he'll get a kick out of that."

His team was ready to roll as he approached the EMT bay, gear in rucks at their feet. As he approached, they came to attention. More or less.

"So much for your day off, huh, Chief?" Sergeant Adrian Cruz grinned as he spoke. Mid-thirties, stocky, Cruz had been with them for more than a year. He and his two kids had survived the initial infection period due to Cruz's prepper nature.

"Easy come, easy go," Gonzo said, turning to focus on the others.

The Martinez brothers, Jeremy and Matt, leaned against one of the Humvees, bickering about some minor plot point of a movie. As usual.

Jeremy, the younger of the two, was well over three hundred pounds, even after six months of limited rations. Despite his size, he was surprisingly light on his feet, and a formidable hand-to-hand combatant. Before the Fall, he'd been a bouncer in several of the areas' more disreputable biker bars.

Matt, in contrast, was leaner, older, and considered himself the intellectual of the pair. He had a knack for thinking outside the box, coming up with several unorthodox plans that generally worked when things got hairy.

The last member of the team, Chacho, was a bit of a mystery. Another large man, he out-massed Jeremy by at least fifty pounds, and had the strength and body shape of an Olympic level powerlifter. Generally quiet, he mainly spoke Spanish, with a small amount of English here and there. What little Gonzo had found out about him hinted at a shady past, heavily slanted towards the local illicit drug trade. Whatever he'd been involved with previously, Chacho was a solid member of the team, and had bailed them out of a few bad spots with sheer force of will and brute strength.

"All right gents," Gonzo started, "saddle up."

"What's the mission, Boss?" Jeremy asked, tossing his gear in the Humvee.

"Supply. Going to pay a visit to our friend, El Jefe."

"Sweet," Cruz said. "Milk run."

Everyone groaned, except Chacho. He just shot Cruz the finger.

"Dammit, Sarge, don't jinx it!" Matt flicked his cigar butt at the other man. "Remember the last time?"

"Hey now, how was I supposed to know there'd be that many Howlers in that apartment? It was barely five hundred square feet!"

"That's the point," Jeremy started in. "'This'll be easy,' you said. 'There's no way there's more than a couple,' you said."

"Well excuse me for being optimistic."

"How you survived out there on your own baffles me." Matt started for the driver's side of the Humvee. "You ride with Chief."

"Belay that," Gonzo snapped. He wasn't going to have both senior enlisted in the same vehicle. It was against regulations, or something. It surely wasn't because he believed in the jinx. "Chacho, you and Jeremy with me, Cruz, you're with Matt."

"Fine," Matt said, scowling. "But I'm driving."

Jeremy chuckled and got behind the wheel of the second Humvee. Gonzo and Chacho climbed in the back.

Their clearance gear, or "Zoot Suits" as Matt called them, were bulky, and would hinder movement inside the Humvee, so standard practice was to wait until they were in the hot zones to fully kit up, prior to exiting the vehicle. With a little luck, they wouldn't have to put it on at all.

"You figure out why El Jefe only deals with you, Chief?" Jeremy drove towards the gate casually, one hand on the wheel, the other digging into a bag of what had to be stale chips.

"Must be my winning personality," Gonzo replied. "You, uh, think that those things are good for you?"

"These days, if junk food kills me, I win."

"Fair enough."

Over the last year or so, the SAMMC teams had managed to open up I-35, moving the abandoned and stalled cars around to make a corridor. This made travel by Humvee and transports somewhat easier, and access to the multitude of service stations with viable gasoline and diesel possible. That had been one of Colonel Noe's first priorities—finding and stabilizing all fuel they could find. San Antonio was a fairly large area, and trying to clear sections on foot, hiking in and out, would have been a monumental task. Scavenging and transporting rations would have been nearly impossible.

The cars stacked two deep on each side of the highway kept most of the random infected at bay, though there was still the occasional roadkill. Their Humvee had sixteen stick figures painted on the driver's door.

"Ol' Jefe's still at the Dome, right Chief?"

"Yeah, he's settled in there, for now."

"Roger that." He keyed his radio and relayed the info to his brother.

Twenty minutes later, they pulled up to the barricades at the Alamodome back lot. The heavily tattooed guard behind the fencing didn't raise his AK, but neither did he open the gate.

Gonzo sighed. It was going to be one of those days.

"Pull up a bit closer," he said to Jeremy, while dropping his window. Keeping his voice just loud enough to carry over the engine, he addressed the guard. "Hey man, can you let us in?"

"State your business."

"Here to see El Jefe."

"Do you have an appointment?"

"You mean he didn't get the e-mail? Dammit, I'll make sure my secretary's written up when I get back to base."

The guard grunted.

"Why don't you tell him his old pal Gonzo's here and needs to talk business." He closed the window. "Kill the engine and keep an eye out for Howlers. Not sure how long this is going to take."

While he waited, he looked around at the improvements to the Dome complex. All ground floor windows had been removed and replaced with plywood. From prior visits, Gonzo knew that roughly two in five had gun ports, manned in shifts by El Jefe's "staff."

Some of that staff, he knew, had been found by SAMMC crews, and had decided to reject Colonel Noe's offer of joining the military. Others, like the guard, came from the city's criminal class. Gonzo recognized gang tats when he saw them.

Tracks bordered the north side of the building, and as luck would have it, two-mile-long trains had been parked when everything went to hell. They made an excellent primary barrier in addition to the chain link fencing to keep the infected out.

So far, SAMMC's dealings with El Jefe had been amicable, if not exactly friendly—something along the lines of "my enemy's enemy is not necessarily an enemy, for now." The unofficial arrangement between the two factions was tenuous at best, and dependent on the current situation.

"Check that out, Chief," Jeremy said, pointing at a wooden structure in the middle of the lot. "What do you think he's building?"

"Hard to tell with the scaffolding, but I'll be sure to ask. If we get in, that is."

"Looks like you'll get the chance." Jeremy started the Humvee as the gate opened. The guard waved the vehicles through, then motioned for them to stop after it had closed again. Gonzo dropped the window.

"Park next to the field inside." The guard returned to his post.

Jeremy eased the Humvee down the ramp, and into the Dome's loading and staging area at field level. There, they were met by another guard, rifle slung across his back.

"El Jefe will see you in his office." He pointed at Gonzo. "Just you. The others will stay here."

"Roger that. He still up in the VIP box?" Gonzo asked as he exited the Humvee. At the guard's nod, he turned to his crew. "Unass and gear up, so you don't get caught with your flies down. I'll be back asap."

What little power the building had, due to scavenged generators, was mainly for lighting. That meant taking the stairs to the fourth floor VIP suites. Ten minutes later, somewhat winded, he knocked on El Jefe's door.

"Come in, my friend!"

El Jefe stood as he entered, walked over, and enveloped him in a bear hug.

"Gonzo, it's good to see ya, 'migo!" His accent placed his origin in the Bronx, with his time in San Antonio giving it a slight Hispanic tinge.

El Jefe stood about an inch shorter than Gonzo's five ten, but possessed a wiry strength that belied his size. The man had almost every exposed inch of skin covered in black-ink tattoos, with the exception of a bright red pair of lips on the right side of his neck.

"Good to see you," Gonzo wheezed, "I can't breathe."

El Jefe laughed, gave one more hard squeeze, and backed off to arm's length.

"What do I owe the pleasure, Gonzo? Love the shirt, by the way."

"Unfortunately, business, not pleasure."

"Ah. So, Boss Bitch has you running errands again." El Jefe smiled, gold-capped eye teeth catching the light. He clapped Gonzo on the shoulder. "How is La Llorona?"

"As pleasant as ever." He took a seat in front of the desk as El Jefe poured them a drink. One thing about the zombie apocalypse, there was no shortage of alcohol. For now, at least.

"You know, I could use you and your guys down here, Gonzo," El Jefe said, handing him a glass. "That military *mierda* has to wear thin at times."

"Yeah, it does, but an oath is an oath."

"That's what I like about you, 'migo, you're loyal. To a fault, almost." El Jefe clinked his glass against Gonzo's then downed the shot. "Gonna get you killed one of these days."

"Tell me about it."

The other man took his seat behind the desk and leaned back, lacing his hands behind his head.

"So it seems we have to ramp up vaccine production, and need a few things."

"You mean more"—El Jefe made air quotes—"'raw materials'?"

"No, actually; thanks to you and our teams, we're good there." Gonzo pulled the list from his pocket, unfolded it, and handed it over. "What we're short of is the equipment."

El Jefe scowled as he read, nodding slowly.

Gonzo continued, "Your guys hit DPT labs and the nearby hospitals, right?"

The other man dropped the list and picked up a stress ball, squeezing it while leaning back again.

"Yeah, we have that stuff, but it occurs to me that I've been scratching your back more often than your boss has been scratching mine."

"Is that so?"

"It is, from my point of view."

Gonzo stood, walked to the windows looking over the arena, and crossed his arms. After a few moments, he turned back.

"SAMMC has provided you with fair compensation for your help. Weapons..."

"One fifty cal and a couple thousand rounds of ammo..."

"...people..."

"...that didn't want to enlist under duress..."

"...vaccines..."

"...that we provide the 'raw materials' for in the first place." El Jefe held up a finger. "Thing is, my friend, it's been our asses on the line more often than yours. Yes, you helped us clear this place, but let's be honest, it wasn't difficult. Meanwhile, we're collecting specimens for you regularly, at great risk to ourselves."

The man had a point—the Dome had been closed once the trouble started, and less than fifty Howlers inside when they cleared it. The job had had no casualties on their side and was probably the easiest large structure clearance to date.

"Okay, so what are you looking for?"

El Jefe smiled.

"Nothing big, really, just a symbol of your appreciation. In fact, it's nearby."

Gonzo grimaced. "Nearby" meant downtown. And downtown meant the riverwalk.

What they'd observed about the Howlers, was that they congregated near water. Downtown was the one place in the Greater San Antonio Area that had water in abundance, and plenty of resources. Hotels, restaurants, convention centers...you name it, it was there.

"And if we decide to look elsewhere?"

"Why don't you take another look at the field and tell me."

Gonzo turned back to the window. A single spotlight snapped on. At the fifty-yard line sat their Humvees, his team lined up against them. Ten yards away a Jeep had its mounted Ma Deuce trained on them.

"That's how it is, is it?" Gonzo felt the hairs on his neck rise. He turned slowly, not surprised to find El Jefe's gold-plated Desert Eagle leveled at him. The other hand continued to squeeze the stress ball.

"Unfortunately, yes." El Jefe gave him a small grin. "I don't feel there's a mutual respect between our groups. You ... you I like, but that can only go so far. A message needs to be sent to your boss."

"What's that line about shooting the messenger?"

El Jefe chuckled, but the barrel didn't waver.

"In this case, mi amigo, that *is* the message."

"Gotcha. So," he said, spreading his hands, "what can SAMMC do for you?"

His team looked apprehensive as Gonzo approached. Due to El Jefe's pistol in his back, he knew he looked apprehensive as well.

"Well, guys, there's a slight of a change in plans. Seems El Jefe here has been feeling somewhat neglected, and politely"—he gestured towards the Jeep—"requested that we do him a small favor, in return for the gear we need."

Matt and Jeremy both groaned, muttered "Jinx," and swatted Cruz on the shoulders. Cruz shrugged.

"Our mission, and we have no choice but to accept it, is to find and retrieve ..." He turned to El Jefe. "What, again?"

"A framed pair of 'Hattori Honzō' katanas from *Kill Bill*, signed by David Carradine himself."

Matt snorted. "So, what, these things are just hanging around in a closet somewhere?"

Gonzo glared at him.

"Yeah, how do we know these things exist?" Cruz asked.

"Saw them at the Fan Expo right before things went bad. In fact, it's where I met my two friends, Akari and Sakura." El Jefe raised his voice. "Ladies, come say hello to our guests."

Two young Japanese girls, no more than twenty, came around the Jeep. Twins, both wore BDU pants, boots, and matching T-shirts. Gonzo couldn't read the characters, but the crossed swords they framed gave him a hint. As did the sheathed katanas on their backs.

The girls bowed.

"Kon'nichiwa," they said in unison.

"Nice to meet you both," Gonzo said. "Where are the swords?"

"At the booth close to where we were demonstrating," said one of the twins.

"It was near the entrance of the convention center," said the other.

"Great." Gonzo turned back to his men. "There you have it—we'll get in, grab the swords, and get out. Any questions?"

Everyone but Matt shook their heads.

"Good, no questions." Gonzo ignored Matt's raised hand. "Load up and let's go."

"The trucks will stay here," El Jefe said. "Call it insurance."

"Fine. Gear up and let's go"—Gonzo turned—"if there's nothing else, that is."

"The twins will be accompanying you."

"No. I won't be babysitting two civilians while trying to sneak in and out of Downtown Howlerville."

"They know exactly where the items are, and I need to be sure you'll hold up your end of the bargain."

"That stings, Jefe." Gonzo shook his head. "I can't guarantee their safety."

El Jefe nodded at the girls.

As one, they drew their swords, faced each other, and took two steps back. El Jefe held up his stress ball, paused, and tossed it gently between them.

"Kiai!" Both swords swung, liquid silver flashing between the two girls. The stress ball landed in four pieces on the turf.

El Jefe grinned as the twins sheathed their blades and bowed.

"They can take care of themselves, my friend."

"Fine," Gonzo grunted. "At least they aren't wearing school uniforms."

"Only when we're at con..." one said, smiling prettily.

"...fan service," the other finished.

The five-minute hike from the underpass barricade to the convention center was fortunately boring. The summer heat and recent drought meant any infected had retreated indoors or were at least staying by the river.

Gonzo stood in front of the broken glass doors, shading his eyes against the late afternoon sun.

"So far, so good, Chief." Cruz's voice came through his earpiece.

He too was scanning the interior, further down the building. The others were spaced out, watching the streets.

"The booth was just to the right of those doors," Akari said, pointing. Gonzo had the girls tie different-colored ribbons around their arms, so he could keep them straight.

"Right," he said, trying the door. Locked, but the empty frame was just large enough for him to squeeze through in his clearance gear. From inside, he worked the latches, and opened both of the double doors. In case of a hasty retreat, he didn't want to get caught on his hands and knees.

"Jeremy, Chacho, you two post up at the doors, watching our six. Matt, Cruz, you come with the twins and me to cover our ass in the hall. Ladies"—he motioned toward the lobby—"after you."

It was quiet inside, neither a good nor bad sign. If there were Howlers present, they could be asleep, waiting out the heat until either dark, or a meal wandered through. Even though the full face shields they wore would muffle his voice, Gonzo used hand signs to direct the two men, then motioned for the twins to continue.

The main hall was huge, the floor covered in wrecked booths, overturned tables, and torn banners. Thousands of various memorabilia, toys, and other items were scattered everywhere, making it difficult to walk without stepping on something. What used to be neatly ordered aisles were now meandering paths through cast-off geek culture.

Sakura nudged him, pointing towards the center of the main aisle, where it had once been cleared into a fifteen-by-fifteen ring. A torn banner hung in two pieces, and he could make out the name "Ninja Sisters."

Akari, on his other side, jerked her chin off to the right, indicating a booth about ten feet away. What little was left of it showed various signed movie posters, promotional items, and actor's headshots, all signed and framed.

She started towards it, but Gonzo stopped her. Something had moved behind the still upright table, causing the framework display to shake.

He took the lead, making his way cautiously towards the booth.

Probably just a rat. Please let it be a rat.

As he got closer, he could hear a soft grunting. Another couple of steps and he could see inside.

It was a rat, in the process of being consumed by a male Howler, naked except for a filthy blue wig.

One of the twins gasped, the other placed a hand over her faceplate, retching.

The Howler stopped, saw them, grabbed something near it, and bolted.

The twins took off in pursuit.

"Shit," Gonzo broke radio silence. "We've got a runner, blue hair, heading towards the south entrance. Girls, stop!"

"He has the swords," Sakura shot back.

"Shit." They were acting recklessly, but he couldn't afford to lose Blue Hair. "Chacho, Jeremy, watch the exits. Matt, Cruz, cover the doors along the hallway."

Three "Rogers" and a "Si" came back.

He followed the girls, praying that the noise they were making wouldn't bring trouble. God apparently listened and no other infected appeared.

Bright sunlight blinded him as the Howler hit the door leading outside. Blinking, he could just see the naked man break right.

"He's outside, heading toward the street." The girls made the door, Gonzo three steps behind. They turned just in time to see Jeremy lunge for the Howler and miss. Cruz and Matt exited the building behind them as Chacho jogged up.

"Sorry, Chief, I almost had him." Jeremy picked himself up.

"Time for sorry later. Which way?"

Chacho pointed at the Marriott Rivercenter across the street.

"Christ. Of course. Let's go."

Clearing the Rivercenter Marriott had been hell. With thirty-eight floors, over one thousand rooms, offices, and suites, it took several teams working around the clock two weeks to finish. At the end of it all, they'd only found a handful of survivors, all of them in the kitchens. Gonzo still had nightmares of what they'd found on the upper levels. It had been his recommendation to burn the place to the ground. That had been ignored by the colonel, mainly due to the risk of the fire spreading to the rest of downtown.

In Gonzo's opinion, that was a feature, not a bug.

It had taken every ounce of self-control he'd possessed to not pull the pins on several Willie Petes and toss them over his shoulder as he walked out.

Now, here he was, running past the rotting chairs in the lobby, trying to figure out his quarry's next move.

Ahead, he caught a flash of blue disappearing down a corridor.

"He's heading towards the mall, Chief." Cruz's words were punctuated by panting.

As Gonzo made the turn, he swore. When they'd cleared the Marriott, the teams had boarded up the two mall access doors, as well as welding the stair doors closed. Since then, something had torn open a man-sized hole in the one in front of him.

"Chacho, you see that barricade?"

"Si."

"I don't want to anymore."

"Si."

The big man grabbed the edge of the hole, set his feet, and heaved. The splintering crack of the plywood was quieter than a rifle, but not by much. The team listened, only the sounds of their breathing coming over the radio.

"Sounds clear," Gonzo said, softly. "Let's move."

"Which way, Chief?" Matt came up beside him.

"There!" Akari started running. Ahead of her, Gonzo saw the telltale blue-hair turn west.

The team followed, scanning the shops as they ran. Their luck held—no Howlers. Even better, the wing their guy ran down was one of the narrower sections of the mall, and a dead end. Unfortunately, he was nowhere to be seen.

"Now what?" Gonzo stopped, staring at the stores in front of them. Behind him, he heard one of the twins giggle. "Something funny?"

"I bet I know where he went," Sakura said, still giggling. Gonzo followed her gaze. Three shops down, he saw the sign. "Anime Tokyo."

He shook his head with a sigh. She was probably right.

As they approached the blacked-out store, he could make out various items inside. T-shirts, action figures, and other things lined the walls, none of which he recognized. Pausing at the door, he clicked on his Maglite.

The beam caught their guy, clutching the case to his chest. Surrounding him were dozens of large pillows, each roughly five feet long, and featuring a female cartoon character. Most of the pictures were scantily clad, with large eyes, hair of various colors, and what he assumed were seductive expressions. All were covered in unrecognizable stains.

"What the actual fuck."

"Oh holy Christ," Matt said, behind him. "That's a lot of dakimakura."

"A lot of what?"

"Waifu pillows, Chief. I wouldn't touch them, if I were you."

"Of course you'd know that," Jeremy scoffed. "Fucking weeb."

"You're one to talk, Brony."

"Save it." Gonzo cut in before the brothers could really get going. "We need to get that case and get out of here."

"Pretty sure he's a beta, Chief," Cruz said. "Showing the regular signs. Nonaggressive, light sensitive, etcetera."

"Okay, so we kill it and bug out." Jeremy took a step, pulling his machete.

"No." Gonzo put a hand on the big man's arm. "Alphas are one thing. Betas are harmless. He's still an innocent. Let's try to coax it from him."

He looked around the store. The beta seemed to have some base-level instinct towards this stuff. He addressed the twins.

"Ladies, I need you to do something for me. Take off your helmets and face shields." At their confused looks, he added, "Look, you might be exactly what this guy is into. See if you can convince him to give us that case."

They looked disgusted, but complied, removing their helmets slowly, shaking out their long black hair as they did. With coy expressions, both girls strode towards the beta.

The beta cowered at first, but then showed at least one obvious sign of interest. He dropped the case and tentatively crawled towards Akari. He got within six feet when the man's smell hit her.

"Eww, no!" She flinched, took a step back, and tripped on a discarded action figure, breaking it. The beta pulled his hands back, grabbed one of his pillows, and began to scream.

His scream ended a second later as Sakura's blade pierced his throat.

Seconds later, howls erupted in the distance.

"Chief," Cruz said, "I've seen this movie. It doesn't end well."

Gonzo ran forward and grabbed the case, while the twins put on their gear.

"Weapons hot," he said, unslinging his rifle. Stealth was out the window. "Let's GTFO."

Cruz and Matt ran to the intersection, one on each side.

"Incoming," Cruz said, "They must've been at the food court below. Can't go back that way."

"Clear on my side." Matt waved them towards him, then joined Cruz.

"Take this." Gonzo handed the case to Akari. "Chacho, Jeremy, take hind tit and cover us. Matt, Cruz, start leapfrogging towards the nearest exit. Girls, you follow them."

The howling behind them grew louder, punctuated with gunshots as the two larger members of their group opened fire. Fortunately, the only way up was the defunct escalators, and a few corpses created a choke point.

Cruz and Matt took up position on a crossover, keeping the rest of the team out of their line of fire. Gonzo and the girls passed them, ducking around a corner.

"Fall back!" Gonzo took aim to cover the other men. The sound of breaking glass behind him told him the girls had taken care of their exit. He waited until his team caught up, dropped a few more Howlers, and followed them outside.

They'd exited the mall on Blum Street, a narrow walkway between two rows of shops, next to Alamo Plaza. This put the Dome and its relative safety to the north, behind them.

He swore. Alamo Plaza looked clear—for now—but that meant heading in the wrong direction. On the other hand, heading east—the more direct route—meant getting near the river, and by the sounds of it, swarms of infected.

They'd have to go the long way.

"Head west towards Crockett Street," he said, swapping mags. "Maybe we can cut back to Commerce."

"Contact, thirty yards and closing," Cruz reported. He began firing.

Crockett street was filled with cars, all smashed together at different angles. Most likely panicked drivers when the initial infection started. Trying to navigate that way could potentially trap them in between two groups of howlers.

"Crockett's no-go," Gonzo said, "keep moving west. We'll try Houston Street."

They ran, turning to fire behind them in an attempt to slow

the wave of infected streaming up from the river, and out of the surrounding buildings.

The plague had hit San Antonio in the height of tourist season, and downtown had been packed. Combine that with Fiesta in full swing, and it meant hundreds of thousands of potential Howlers.

And they all seemed to be coming for them.

"More coming in from the west, Chief," Jeremy said.

"How far?"

"Couple hundred yards."

"All right, we need cover, at least to catch our breath." He started for the Alamo.

"Oh, hell no," Matt groaned. "You can't be serious."

"Yeah, I am."

"I've seen this movie too," Cruz said. "It didn't end well either."

"Well, maybe the sequel will! Chacho, get the door open. Everyone else, cover him."

The big man ran up to the heavy door, drew back a boot, then paused before trying the latch. The door swung open easily. Chacho shrugged. The team rushed inside.

"Secure that door, and fan out."

As Chacho pulled the thick oak, several Howler arms reached in, keeping it from latching. He heaved, pinning them in place, the hands clawing at him and the other door.

They hit the floor, twitching, as Sakura wiped her blade on her sleeve, sheathing her katana. Chacho slammed the door, securing it with the thick iron bolt.

"Gracias."

"De nada."

Cruz and Jeremy checked the small church, signaling all clear.

"Now what?" Matt swapped mags.

"Take a breather, reload, and hydrate, while you figure out our next move."

"You got us into this, and now I have to get us out?"

"It's called delegation, an important aspect of leadership."

Matt said something in Spanish as he moved to the barred window. Chacho snorted.

Gonzo studied the others. Cruz and Jeremy were checking mags, consolidating any partials and dividing them equally. The twins looked at him, their seeming composure betrayed by the slight tremor in their eyes. Chacho's face was expressionless, as usual.

"Don't worry, ladies," Gonzo said, with what he hoped was a convincing grin. "We've been in worse scrapes."

"I got it, Chief," Matt said. "The way I see it, we have a better chance on the wider streets, like Houston and Bowie."

"Agreed. So?"

"So, we take advantage of the walls and fencing between here and the giftshop, cut north through the lot at Bonham, and get back to Commerce." He paused. "And pray to any and every deity you can think of."

Gonzo thought about it for a moment, then nodded.

"All right, folks, let's make this place a fond memory. Pack up and move out."

Matt cracked the exit door, scanning the courtyard beyond. "Clear."

The team moved into the open area, angling towards the northern wall.

Howls erupted behind them.

"Incoming, Chief!"

Chacho and Jeremy turned and fired, backpedaling. As soon as the others cleared the break in the wall, they covered the other two.

The team fell back down the paths, leapfrogging from cover to cover, using the bordering walls and trees. Howlers kept coming, tripping over the maimed and dying bodies.

"I'm out," Cruz said, slinging his AK, and drawing his pistol.

The city had started a renovation project prior to the Fall. The lot at the north edge of the Alamo Plaza was open ground, surrounded by low Jersey walls and wooden construction barricades. Most had remained standing in the years since the project had been abandoned.

The labored breathing of his team almost drowned out his own pulse, pounding in his ears.

"Not much farther," he gasped, clearing the first barricade. The twins fell in behind him. "Status check."

"Down to my last mag." "Out." "Still good." "Bueno."

"Keep moving."

Chacho's shout drew his attention. The big man hit the ground; ankle pinned in a small gap between two of the barricades.

"Cover!" Gonzo ran back, firing at the Howlers converging on his man, until the mag emptied. He switched to pistol and kept firing.

Chacho managed to free his foot but was quickly dogpiled before he could stand. Cruz, Jeremy and Matt had reached him, dividing their attention between the infected coming over the wall, and trying to help their teammate. For each one they dropped, two more took their place.

Scrums were bad news. Their gear would protect them as long as they could keep fighting. But it was only a matter of time before a person would tire out and succumb to the Howlers.

Gonzo's slide locked back. He holstered the gun and drew his machete as Akari and Sakura appeared beside him, katanas drawn. Each placed a hand on his chest, stopping him before he could move forward. The twins split, one on each side of the pile, and attacked.

Blades and bodies wove intricate patterns, a lethal dance that kept the twins out of reach of the Howlers. Katanas flashed and infected limbs dropped to the blood-slick pavement.

With a roar, Chacho burst from the pile, holding a thrashing Howler by the neck in each of his huge hands. He slammed them together, dropped one, and used the other as a club before tossing it over the wall. The pile of bodies had finally created a choke point, giving the team a much-needed chance.

"Fall back!" Gonzo's order wasn't needed—the others immediately turned and ran, Chacho limping slightly. Akari retrieved the dropped case, barely breaking stride.

They angled across the parking lot, weaving in and out of the abandoned cars, slowly widening the gap between the pursuing infected. Commerce Street was just ahead, and beyond that the gates leading back to the Dome.

They ran, angling across Bowie Street, dropping the few Howlers that had taken a shortcut. The main mass was still in pursuit but had been slowed down by the obstacles and broken terrain of the construction site. In minutes, the team made it back to the chain link fence of the underpass.

El Jefe sat behind the wheel of his Jeep, casually smoking a cigar.

"We got it," Gonzo said to him, "let us through."

"Show me."

Akari came forward and held the case against the fence.

"Happy?" Gonzo stared at the other man. "Now let us..."

"What's the magic word, amigo?" El Jefe grinned, took a puff, and blew rings.

The horde of Howlers had gained ground, joined by more from near the convention center. In moments, they'd be overwhelmed, out of ammo, and royally screwed.

"Now!"

El Jefe tsked.

"Remember our talk about respect, my friend."

"Chief..." Cruz was watching their back.

"Fine. Pretty please, with a fucking cherry on top."

"En Espanol..."

"Por favor," Chacho said. "Por favor podemos entrar."

"Now there's a man with manners." El Jefe nodded to his guards. The gate rattled open as the Ma Deuce opened fire. Howlers dropped only yards behind them as the team ran through the gate.

Gonzo, freshly showered and changed, knocked on Colonel Noe's office door.

"Come in."

He entered, crossed the room, and collapsed into the chair across from her.

"Please be seated, Chief," she said, scowling. "How is our friend, El Jefe?"

"He sends his regards, ma'am."

"Excellent. I expect your AAR by morning. You're dismissed."

"Yes ma'am." He stood and started for the door.

"Chief, one last question—I take it the mission went smoothly?"

Gonzo stopped, hand on the doorknob, choosing his words carefully.

"Better than it did in 1836, ma'am." He closed the door at her confused expression.

The Bride Wore Camo

MIKE MASSA

"Becky-Anne, the stripper tailor is here!"

Auguste Bertrand Boudreaux's clientele had once stretched from genteel Southern mansions to the densest thickets of the bayou. Titles and ranks mattered more in the South than any other part of the country. The pleasant labels were gracious and respectful. Some were insults shot like arrows into the heart of a man's worst insecurities. However, this rather obvious effort at the latter wasn't even in the top ten, so Auguste, with an upwards glance at the stout, stentorian matron, merely brushed past, forgoing any return snide comment about her heavy make-up or the strain she was putting on the waistband of her floral print, off-the-rack dress.

He'd been allowed to clean up, so his attire wouldn't have been out of place at one of Lady Dianne's famous French Quarter soirees, but it wasn't a natural fit for what was effectively a local feudal manor.

The only pair of Saint Laurent boots he'd been able to save elevated him three inches above his normal five feet two, and Auguste had repaired their shine during their time on the Mississippi barge. The olive riding breeches were salvage, but fashionably tight. The white linen shirt laced up the front, though he'd left the top open in a generous V, and the sequined, black toreador jacket was suitably camp. A red silk scarf trailed from one cuff, concealing the unfortunate stains one tended to accumulate on one's linens during these trying times. His customary pistol belt was missing, no surprise. The guards had been thorough so the throwing knives that normally lined his jacket were also out of reach. He wasn't completely unarmed. The eyeliner and beauty mark he'd freshened up would have to do.

Behind the door dragon, a neatly dressed blonde girl stood, a junior chambermaid or perhaps a younger sister. Auguste glimpsed smiling eyes before the girl ducked her head and curtsied prettily. The corsetiere swept off his black felt flamenco hat, and bowed en passant as he cleared the threshold and entered the room, only pausing to make a courtier's leg once he was a few steps inside. His glossy black bangs fell across his eyes, hiding them from the rest of the room while he snuck in a quick wink for the young maid just behind and to the rear. She'd been examining the fit of his breeches, and blushed pink.

"Good afternoon, ladies and gentleman," he said, slowly straightening.

Ahead, a collection of remarkably similar people were gathered on a somewhat less uniform set of furniture in a large, airy room. Most were blonde, wearing light but formal afternoon wear, including a suit jacket for the lone man. Like the functioning air conditioning, the clean, well-lit space reflected the family's status. The white paint was unmarred, the brocade upholstery unworn. A thick wool carpet covered most of the floor, leaving only a yard of polished honey-colored planks along the walls. Floor-to-ceiling bay windows showcased the perfect blue of a late summer sky. The medley of green hues of the half-acre truck garden which lay beyond wasn't just more practical than the pre-apocalypse lawn, but prettier too, in his opinion. Auguste could make out the familiar shapes of broccoli and peas. White roses still stood sentry along the edge of a three-meter-tall cypress hedge. He could make out the reason that all the adults in the room were unarmed: the distance-shortened figure of a sentry appearing to stride along the tops of the bushes, an optical illusion made possible by his path along the tops of the double row of shipping containers more than a football field away.

Why, the chamber even smelled nice! Auguste recognized

Chanel, which they must have salvaged in gallon amounts to keep the entire house so fragrant.

Perched in the middle of a family huddle of mostly female relatives and friends was his likely target, one Rebecca-Anne Caplewood, only daughter of the Caplewood clan. Dark blonde, college age or near enough as no matter. Broad in the shoulders, she was sitting stiffly, but her strained smile seemed genuine, unlike the tooth-baring grimaces affected by a few of the others. She was wearing a dreadful navy-and-white shin-length gingham dress of the same cut and color as the older woman, presumably her momma, at her side. Her quarter sleeves left her arms quite bare, showcasing a clear athleticism, somewhat at odds with the other, softer women and wilted male relative huddled on the couch and settees.

"So good of you to come," one of the older relations said, rising and moving to offer him her hand. If anything her smile yawned even wider, affording Auguste a view clear back to the molars. She was the older version of Becky-Anne, right down to the dress and hair color. Her low heels still amplified her height advantage, placing her bust at eye-level. It made her oversize blue enamel broach, decorated with a jeweled tree, unmissable. "I'm Dame Jeanette Caplewood. When our daughter told me she'd seen one of the most famous ladies' tailors of New Orleans and San Francisco in our little town of Natchez, I said to myself, I said, 'Jeanette, you just have to see if that young man is the real deal!' And here you are, Mr. Boudreaux! Are you truly from the Sable Jardin?"

As she spoke, Auguste could feel the various eyes surveying his outfit. A few lingered on the detail of his unlaced shirt. Auguste slightly angled his head to return their regard before he focused on the evident boss.

"It is my sincere pleasure to make your acquaintance, madam," he replied, allowing his French-Creole accent free rein, by way of presenting his own bona fides. As he raised her hand as to kiss it, he saw the faintest gleam of apprehension in her eyes. He was careful to brush his lips only to his own thumb. This was the South, after all, and no gentleman would kiss the bare skin of a newly introduced lady. "And yes, I can claim that honor. I journeyman sewed for Jardin for four years, and for five more after, rising to become a senior corsetiere. I confess I am a bit at a loss as to how your daughter recognized me. Your summons, though naturally welcome, was unexpected."

"Why you must have begun as a mere lad!" Dame Caplewood said, lowering her hand. It twitched in the direction of her skirt, but she didn't actually wipe it. "You hardly seem old enough for nine years of service. What was that fashion show called, Becky-Anne? The one we watched before the cursed disease ruined our lives and drove us into these poor accommodations? Ah yes, *Mega Runway Fashion Survivor*. You won, did you not?"

"Runner up, madam."

"Momma, you leave him alone," Becky-Anne said, shedding the circle of female relations and crossing to shake Auguste's hand. Her grip was warm and firm. She had an inch or two on Momma, and wore a similar brooch. "I'm so sorry, Mr. Boudreaux. I wasn't certain I recognized you, but then I saw the beautiful Sable Jardin corset your companion was wearing at the ferry landing. I knew it had to be you. We don't see too many corsets like that around here, and I'm, *we're* big fans of yours, Mr. Boudreaux."

"Please, my friends called me Auguste." Auguste favored her with a nod as he perched a fist on his hip. "I'm delighted to hear you enjoyed my work."

"Yes, my daughter was quite excited," Dame Caplewood said, the words barely escaping the smile which was trying to promote itself into rictus status. "You see, Becky-Anne is to marry in a few weeks. A wonderful young man, excellent family. The Montanaros are an old Southern family of the finest quality, and I must say our dear Becky-Anne hasn't been as enthusiastic as she could be."

"I see," Auguste said, though he definitely didn't see. There were nuances here, and he didn't yet understand the terrain. He arched one polite eyebrow just a fraction, and waited while it did the necessary work.

Becky-Anne folded her arms and looked daggers at her mother.

"I, for one, still think this is suspicious, Jeanette," the door matron advanced into the conversation, delivering a withering glance at the corsetiere, who returned it, looking upwards as sweetly as he knew how. "Someone *thought* she wanted a corset wedding dress. So, I offered her several designs, but no, only an authentic Sable Jardin corset wedding dress, which heretofore seemed impossible, would do. And now this...person has dropped conveniently into our lap."

"Aunt Catherine, I nev—"

"And apparently, that someone doesn't think her aunt, who's sewn every wedding dress in the family for a decade, is up to her *high* standards. This coddling is most unseemly."

"But—"

Dame Caplewood raised an open palm, shutting down both her sister and daughter, and returned her regard to the dapper figure to her front. Auguste looked up from the perusal of his manicure, and returned his overworked eyebrow to his toolbox, until it was again needed. Instead, he kept his smile natural and his posture relaxed yet subordinate.

"So you see, Mr. Boudreaux, we find ourselves in need of your services. We require appropriate corsetry for not only the bride but other members of the bridal party. Doubtless, there will be public talk over Rebecca-Anne's choice and our unconventional"—she very carefully looked Auguste up and down, mostly down—"style choice. However, if we are to indulge our young bride, it will be with family solidarity. None shall criticize her family. And our choice is to have the premier, surviving corsetiere from the world-famous Sable Jardin of New Orleans design and make our wedding attire. The wedding will proceed as planned."

"Mother, you're embarrassing me! Mr. Boudreaux—" Becky-Anne tried again.

"Miss Becky-Anne, do call me Auguste, please." Auguste gave the girl top marks for persistence. "I insist."

"—Auguste is not some beck-and-call-boy you just yank into our house with your guards when it suits you. Why would a tailor of his stature make me anything after getting snatched away by your goons from whatever he was doing?"

"I prefer to think of it as a firm invitation, Miss Becky-Anne," Auguste said, keeping his smile warm and relaxed as he turned to Dame Caplewood. "To be sure, the well-equipped gentlemen that scooped us up from the ferry landing could be considered... intimidating. Such capable types are doubtless a source of great comfort in these times. However, directly I can access my tools and my assistant, Miss Jonna, I would be delighted to proceed. I'm honored to be invited to provide my services. For a reasonable consideration, of course."

"I'm so sorry, Mr. Boudreaux!" Becky-Anne, wringing her hands. "I love your corset but I di—"

"I'm very glad to hear you say so, Mr. Boudreaux," Dame Caplewood overrode her daughter. "I would be positively wounded had you declined. That would have created an unpleasant tension with such a distinguished person, such as yourself."

Auguste surveyed the little group beyond. They had taken the cue from their mistress. What smiles remained didn't go as far as their eyes.

"I declare there's no need for anything but joy at the pending nuptials, ma'am," Auguste added. Since he was firmly *en rôle*, he blew an air kiss to Aunt Catherine, just to watch her jaw muscle jump. "I do love a good fais-dodo, but there is much work to do first. I would like to meet with the groom's family. I must also ask your indulgence to prioritize time dedicated to fittings since time will be short. Constructing the garments will require specialized materials, so I must beg your permission to access to whatever you have already gathered."

"I'd be happy to show you what we have," Becky-Anne offered. "It would be no trouble at all. The clearing and salvage parties have been working for several months, and the w—"

"Daughter, I am *so glad* you are once again firmly set on your duty to your family, but you have other details to finalize, dear, now that the matter of the corset dress is settled," Caplewood said, waving the younger blonde girl forward. "Invitations, seating arrangements, menu, meetings with the reverend, the list is considerable. Your sister, who will also continue to prioritize the family's needs over her own preferences, may act in her role as the maid of honor, and will assist the corsetiere."

The dame of the house firmly gripped the elbow of the slight blonde and pushed her an additional step forward.

"Mr. Boudreaux, this is my youngest, Priscilla-Jo. She will escort you to the Montanaro estate, on the other side of town. She can also show you the storerooms, and arrange for your quarters."

"Thank you, ma'am," Auguste said, bowing again before turning to Priscilla-Jo. "No time like the present, Miss Priscilla-Jo."

"I'll arrange a ride, sir," Priscilla-Jo said, shooting a slit-eyed glance at her older sister, who turned to stump back to the family group.

"This is certainly a step up from mules and my tired feet," Jonna Hayden said, surveying the sturdy golf-cart-sized vehicle toward which Priscilla-Jo and her guard were leading them. The gravel driveway had a few SUVs and trucks, but there were several rugged-looking golf-cart-sized vehicles with knobby tires. "But I'd rather have Betsy."

To Auguste's relief, his assistant hadn't broken composure when the armed men had accosted them and taken their weapons. It had been a nearer thing than those good old boys had realized.

"The Caplewoods were adamant, Jonna," he replied. "No long guns in town. It's fully cleared. Besides, you have the twins."

Auguste could tell she was slightly more relaxed now her double pistol rig was returned and hanging off her hip. Her beloved 1911s rode as a pair on the right side of her belt, which was supported with a baldric, Sam-Browne style. Fitted dark red leather trousers complimented the bespoke black-on-white brocade underbust corset which she was wearing over a slightly soiled, white men's collared shirt. Her sole concessions to travel were the sixty-liter Maxpedition bag hanging off one shoulder and the dusty Danner boots on her feet. Their rifles had been stored in the Caplewood family armory, and despite his misgivings, Mrs. Caplewood had been very clear on the need to adhere to the town rules. So Betsy, Jonna's scoped Model 70 in .22-250, was locked up next to his WASR.

"If someone dings her, or screws with the zero, I will not be consoled, Auguste Bertrand!"

She grudgingly yielded her pack to the male guard, who looked briefly consternated as he took the full weight of her pack on one arm. He sat it down and slung his rifle, freeing both hands. He squatted to collect the pack, and grunted on rising, before laying her gear in the vehicle bed.

"Jeez, did you pack the kitchen sink?"

"A corsetiere can't rely on finding adequate tools and compo-nents just laying around, can she?" she replied primly, mounting up and bouncing a little in the rear seat next to Auguste. The upholstery was generously padded with closed cell foam. She elbowed her boss. "Coulda used this when we were in 'bama. How do they keep this thing charged, solar?"

"Oh, no ma'am," Priscilla-Jo answered, pressing a switch on the dash while looking over her shoulder. "This area has always had natural gas, and now we're the new natural gas capital of Louisiana. That's how Daddy made his money, running a big gas company right here, downtown. You can't hardly poke a hole in the ground around here except gas will come out. His workers set up low-pressure wells to capture the gas and run it to one of the plants inside the Wall. We use it for everything, including the town generators and running the vehicles. One of his surviving workmen converted a bunch of off-roaders. This one is a Polaris."

As she spoke, she drove them out the big gravel drive and onto a paved road. The day was warm, but the roof kept the sun off the passengers, and Auguste enjoyed the breeze afforded by the open cabin. He surreptitiously gave Priscilla-Jo's bodyguard a good once-over. The prohibition on long guns didn't appear to apply to him, since the man riding shotgun was running a red-dot-equipped AR. There were also pistol-armed people in view going about their business, though mostly on foot.

"Why don't they have their own golf-carts?" Auguste asked. "If there's plenty of fuel."

"Well, Momma and the Montanaros, that's Dolf's family, are pretty much in charge—"

"Sorry, miss," Jonna interrupted. "Dolf?"

"Dolf is the only son of the Montanaro family. He's the one they're making Becky-Anne marry. And she doesn't even—" Priscilla-Jo stopped herself. "It doesn't signify. Anyhow, the Families decided it's more important to protect the town and look for other survivors and supplies instead of giving everybody a car. Even with plenty of gas, there's parts you need to convert to use it, and then tires, brakes and so on. No one is making more of those anything soon. Even though we only got about six hundred people left from Natchez now, that still a lot of vehicles if everyone insisted on having their own car and using it all the time."

"Sounds like your daddy was a smart man," Auguste said, watching the town go by. The streets were clear and in good repair. Signs of a large fire were visible, but most of the unoccupied buildings had either intact windows or plywood patches.

"Daddy was brilliant! He never minded when I asked questions, and always found time to talk to me. He taught me all about his plans for the town. Daddy cared what I thought. Momma is—well, she's Momma."

She took a deep breath and hunched a bit behind the wheel.

Auguste took a deep breath too, tasting the air. It was missing something. He could smell the exhaust of the little motor that whined underneath him. There were the usual floral scents, and the traces of woodsmoke. He inhaled again and looked around.

"Smells nicer than usual." Jonna was paying attention, as usual.

That was it. The usual familiar reek of rotting corpses was entirely absent. The locals had gone to a lot of trouble to get all the corpses belowground. The Polaris passed a work gang of a dozen men and women, dressed in gray coveralls, cleaning bricks and stacking them neatly under the supervision of a bored-looking man in jeans and a cowboy hat. Unlike other settlements where he and Jonna had traveled, this labor gang didn't appear to be betas.

"Are y'all using prisoners as labor, miss?" he asked, pointing towards the group.

Shotgun followed his gesture and grunted.

"Well, we do, but they're not prisoners exactly," Priscilla-Jo say, giving the workers a quick glance as they hummed past. "They can leave whenever they want, once they work off their debt. Daddy said everyone works and everyone eats. At first it was easy, everyone wanted the vaccine. Daddy's chemical engineers had enough know-how to follow the instructions the government broadcast on the radio. Later, people started expecting to be supported. Wanted fancy food, meat every day, their own cars, and air conditioners. But the Families made the rules. If you don't work, or you shirk your duties, you get judged, and after that, the lazy end up on supervised work details, if they want to stay inside the Wall."

"You mean the big line of shipping containers around town?" Jonna asked. "That's a lot of containers."

"Yes, ma'am. Even before New York went off the air, some folks around here organized to build it from the traffic in the river. Tens of thousands of TEUs were on the river during the Fall. We're—"

"Tews?" Auguste asked, watching as they passed another labor party and their "supervisor." "What's that?"

"Sorry, Mr. Boudreaux. Twenty-foot equivalent units— abbreviated tee-ee-you. Any given day, pre-Fall, there were better than thirty ships on the river, each one carrying as many as nine or ten thousand TEUs. We only needed five hundred double units to make the Wall, and New Natchez is on a peninsula, so really we only had to close off one direction and we're all set. It wasn't done before the zombies got real bad, but between the three families, we got it done."

Shotgun clicked on the radio, evidently bored with the conversation.

"Listen up, maggots! Drop your socks and grab your...equipment! This is Gunny Sanchez of the You-Ess Mareen Corps, coming to you from Guuaatanamo Bayyy!"

"Y'all can get Devil Dog Radio here?" Jonna asked, leaning forward to touch Priscilla-Jo's shoulder.

"We have a big tower for FM radio, and one of Daddy's men uses his ham radio to record the broadcast," she answered. "They report a lot about which cities are getting cleared. The music is okay, mostly old people stuff."

On cue, the radio started blaring the Marine Corps anthem and the guard clicked it off, harumphing disappointedly.

"My sister loves it, wants to grow up and be a Marine, she says, just like that girl, She-Wolf." Auguste saw Priscilla-Jo's grip on the wheel turn her fingers white. "Momma says her duty is to her family first. Becky-Anne tried everything. She asked for the impossible dress to stall the wedding. Then, jokes on her, you arrived. Now she has to go through with it. And *she* gets to marry Dolf after all."

Auguste carefully did not look at his assistant.

"Pardon, miss, but besides the groom's family and yours, who else is in charge?" Jonna asked. Auguste noticed the guard straightening from his slouch, giving them both some side-eye. He cut in.

"That is, if you don't mind us asking," Auguste said, with a frustrated nudge against Jonna.

"Well, it's long story, and Uncle Skip or Momma would know better. Besides, we're here."

"Here" seemed to be the parking lot of an ex-grocery store. The yellow-and-black sign had been painted over, but if there was one thing Auguste had seen a lot of as he moved about the South, it was Dollar General stores. The lot had a few cars, as well as several shipping containers, nearly lined up in parking spots. An inexpertly painted coat of arms covered the glass of the front display to the left of the door. The red shield wasn't perfectly symmetrical, and he had to squint a bit to discern three green hills in the middle, surrounded by three yellow stars.

"You sure about this, Miss Caplewood?" Behind Auguste, the guard spoke up. "Missus Caplewood call ahead?"

"Johnson, it's fine," Priscilla-Jo tossed her hair and went confidently to the door.

"What's that?" Jonna pointed out the coat of arms to their guard, who was bringing up the rear.

"It's a Montanaro salvage warehouse," he said, hooking a finger towards the tan plate carrier he wore. Auguste noted a pair of patches stuck to it, one an embroidered blue shield with the now familiar tree in the middle. "Ours have a blue shield. Theirs is red. We're all friends now, so share and share alike, Mr. Caplewood says. Used to be the reds and the blues didn't get along."

"But?"

"But nothing." Priscilla-Jo didn't even break stride; instead, she skipped ahead two paces, pulling the door open for Auguste. "We're friends now. Allies. And this is for the wedding. Besides, I've been dying to peek in here."

Auguste stepped into a relatively small foyer with a familiar cement floor, surrounded on three sides by waist-high tables that incorporated old checkout conveyors. Even though there were several lights, it took a moment for his eyes to adjust. He was jostled from behind so he shuffled forward a bit more. A heavyset man in camouflage trousers and a dingy red T-shirt appeared from the rows of head-high shelving that blocked further view in any direction. His lip curled.

"Caplewoods?" Auguste watched the man's eyes jump back and forth between the members of the party, finally pausing on Priscilla-Jo, who was fiddling with the latch on a hinged part of the counter. "Whatcha doin' here?"

A thirty-something brunette poked her head out, looking fearfully at Mr. Whatcha Doin' before scanning the foyer. She was better dressed, wearing clean blue jeans and a fitted red tank. It was no surprise she knew the Caplewood girl, but Auguste knew to the second when she recognized him. Her eyes opened all the way, and her jaw dropped.

"Dame Caplewood is coordinating the wedding with Mrs. Montanaro," Priscilla-Jo announced. Auguste noted that she didn't even bother to look up to look at the counterman. "I'm here to look for fabric for the wedding on their behalf. Open this thing, please."

"You'se gotta a letter from Missus Montanaro, miss?"

His workmate crept forward and tugged on his sleeve, but he yanked it away with an angry look. Auguste saw the man's hand come to rest on his belt, just above a holstered pistol.

"No letter, then? Best y'all move on."

"Are you a few minutes shy of a fully baked biscuit?" Priscilla-Jo had stopped fiddling, and her head snapped up. She saw where the attendant had his hand and lost her temper, dramatically throwing one arm towards Auguste. "This is an important guest! He's a Very Important Person, all the way from New Orleans, here to coordinate the wedding, and he's under Caplewood guest right. Hold him up, and the bride will personally stretch you out on the killing ground and leave you for the next hungry zombie that wanders by. Believe!"

"Him?" The man looked down uncertainly at Auguste, who had decided to stand a bit hip shot, and examine the nails of his left hand. It also left his right conveniently free.

"Do you not know who I am? My name is Priscilla-Joanne Constance Caplewood. My family saved this place! That isn't enough? Maybe you'd like to shoot the youngest Caplewood as a wedding gift to Dolf Montanaro? I'm sure he'd reward you—by making you eat your own eggs, you fool! Now open up—you're embarrassing me and this town! You will open up this instant or I will inform the Montanaros that you offered specific disrespect to the younger sister of the lady who's about to become the new Missus Montanaro! If you're lucky, you'll only end up outside the Wall. If I get my way, you'll be under it!"

"Yes, miss!" The man very nearly got all spitty in his haste to get the counter unlatched and swung up out of the way. "Sorry, miss, I didn't recognize you! I meant no disrespect, miss!"

Auguste sashayed through, Jonna on his heels, both following Priscilla-Jo's pointing finger. She followed them, nostrils flaring. Their guard stayed in the foyer, his weapon slung and a worried look on his face.

The lady attendant had skittered towards the back during Priscilla-Jo's outburst, but poked her head out again.

The aisle endcaps had inventory signs, but the organization was self-evident. Aisles of products extended into the darker interior. One of engine parts, another of tools, one of thousands of pairs of shoes. It was the work of a moment to spot the familiar shapes of bolts of cloth. These display units had been stripped of anything but the bottom shelf and one more, just about shoulder high to Auguste. Bolts had been stacked on end, leaning against the dividers. Unprompted, he walked over and began running his hand along the vertically stacked fabrics. There were a surprising number. Someone must have salvaged a fabric store. Several fabric stores? Everything was represented in quantity, from silk to upholstery.

"I know that Momma hasn't even picked out a final color plan yet, but there's plenty to choose from, isn't there?" Priscilla-Jo said, also running her hand along the fabric rolls. She appeared to have gotten over her indignation quickly. She unwound a length of white lace suitable for a bridal train and laid it across her arm. "Ooh, this one's pretty!"

The female employee crept up, eyes hungry and shining. She had added some lip gloss, unless Auguste missed his guess. Perfume was evident as well—something cheap and sharp.

"Excuse me, sir, are y'all—" she began.

"Yes, yes, Auguste Boudreaux from the Sable Jardin, but he's working," Priscilla-Jo said, flapping one hand at arm's length while she continue to look at bolts of cloth. "You can ask him questions later. He's designing a wedding dress and I'm helping."

"You looking for something specific, miss?" the female attendant summoned her courage. "We have a lot of fabric, but hardly any call for it. Not too many people are sewing yet. It's easier to salvage the clothes what they need. Even wedding dresses."

In the background, Auguste could hear the shop manager, if that's what he was, dialing an old-style wall-mounted phone. His voice began to gabble, almost inaudibly. Auguste sighed and turned back to the matter at hand, which was learning more about this place.

"Well, I do declare, we simply *are not* going to reuse a wedding dress," he said, smiling at the attendant. He touched the nearest bolt. "You have many lovely things, but I'm looking for something specific. This will be a corset dress. Structure will be everything. But it must be fine, as well. What we really could use for a start are some *charmeuse* and *batiste*."

Blank looks met his glance.

"Think double-layer satin for the first and a strong, sheer cotton for the second," he said, carefully *not* rolling his eyes. "We're going for a more architectural look, not a romantic design."

Both women listened carefully as his monologue became even more technical. The assistant began pulling out bolts and unfolding them along a long worktable. Jonna was stacking her own candidate rolls to one side and cutting swatches from a variety of earth tones. He looked more closely. All filmy selections. Tiger stripes, leafy green, mossy tree, various sorts of hunting patterns were represented. Trust Jonna to follow her instincts. He was diverted as Priscilla-Jo began listing everything she knew about her sister's preferences, although to Auguste, it sounded more like her own wish list. She held out a bolt of white satin for him to touch, and suddenly he was deep in *le espace créatif.*

That lasted an unknown time, until a sharp jab between his ribs staggered him.

The warehouse assistant gave a little scream.

Auguste looked up and kept looking.

The newcomer could have easily qualified for college basketball. Pro, even. He wore khaki trousers and a snug, red polo shirt. Auguste couldn't make out the pistol on his belt, but he had a great view of the AR-pattern rifle which was painfully tucked, muzzle first, under his own short ribs. At least Meathead didn't have his finger on the trigger.

Jonna didn't move, her eyes comically crossed on the muzzle of another rifle a few inches from her nose. Priscilla-Jo wasn't impressed.

"Do you know who I am!" Priscilla-Jo shrieked, enraged. "That's *our* guest!"

"Don't care, Miz Caplewood," the man said, giving Auguste another jab. "What I want to know is just who the fuck are you, little man?"

"My name is Boudreaux," Auguste replied, his voice cool. He turned, deliberately letting his jacket catch on the muzzle of Meathead's rifle, and coincidentally clearing his strong-side holster. "I am the designer."

"Yeah, that's what Missus Montanaro said you might be. None a y'all don't got permission to be here. We're going for a ride, pretty boy. The Montanaros want to see you."

The extent of Auguste's view was the inside of a black sack. Mercifully clean and itch-free, it nonetheless had kept him from seeing his surroundings for the last twenty minutes.

"Remove that at once!" the feminine voice was imperious. "This man is a visitor under my roof!"

"But, Missus Montanaro, you sai—" The familiar voice of Meathead sounded far more plaintive than Auguste expected, considering the previous rough handling. Over the nuclear objections of Priscilla-Jo, he'd been separated from his companions, then bagged, and bundled into another vehicle. Considerably higher off the ground, it felt like a proper truck. The ride had been altogether rougher and longer than the preceding trip.

Then yank—stagger—march, and blessed air conditioning again, he had found himself indoors.

"Shut your mouth, Jackson!" Unseen, Auguste winced at the whipcrack in that voice. "When I want your opinion, I will deliver it to you, ready to regurgitate. Remove that blindfold, unhand my guest and take yourself off."

"Ma'am, shouldn't I stay wi—"

"You're becoming quite tiresome, Jackson. You know what happens when staff take on that quality."

The ladies of this burg sure seemed comfortable giving orders. Auguste noted a bit of Commonwealth in the accent.

"Yes, ma'am."

The vise grip on his upper arm abruptly vanished, allowing Auguste to stand straight. The bag was whisked off, and Auguste blinked rapidly. He straightened the lapels of his jacket and gave his trousers a slight tug upwards. He missed the weight of his gun belt, but this didn't seem the opportune moment to inquire.

Auguste was in a big library. Tall ceilings accommodated the double-height shelving that lined the expansive room on both sides. Old wood and the scent of older books surrounded him. A wrought iron chandelier was off to one side, but the room was illuminated by a row of windows screened by gauzy drapery. However, all of it was secondary to the true focal point of the room.

She emerged from behind a large partners desk which took up a mere acre or two of the room. The lady was five eight or more, leggier than the exclusive merchandise his New Orleans madam used to hold back for special guests, and a spill of raven hair as dark and shining as his own swayed side to side as she strode confidently, like a lioness, to greet him. On a woman with weaker features, her strong Roman nose would have overpowered whatever good looks remained, but her high cheekbones and dark brows provided the symmetry to make her bold, not masculine. Her direct gaze spoke of confidence. She might have been forty or more, but the clean skin, bouncy stride, and taut figure spoke of a dedication to sport, the masseur, and self-discipline. Her legs, like her feet, were bare. She wore a loose, burgundy and white kimono-pattern robe over a black scoop-necked tank, and the visible musculature of her chest, shoulders and calves underscoring the sculpted lines of her face were due to athleticism, not an accident of diet. The ensemble was tied together with a wide sash. He noticed a traditional Japanese-style sword rack on the wall behind the desk, holding two black-lacquered scabbards of dissimilar lengths.

"Auguste Bertrand Boudreaux in the flesh! Love the beauty mark!"

"Lady Montanaro, I presume," Auguste bowed from the waist. His courtesies were getting a lot of practice today. Behind him, the library door closed, reluctantly it seemed.

"Please, call me Claudia," she said, advancing all the way, taking his hands in hers, and looking at him up and down. The air didn't warm, precisely, but Auguste felt her nearness like an animal presence, like the heat coming off a big cat, the machinery in perfect order and tensely sprung. "All my friends do, and I just know we'll become the very best of friends, don't you think?"

The rising inflection at the end of the sentence gave it away.

"Claudia, you'll pardon my presumption," he said, holding her hands and returning her beaming smile with one just as authentic. "Is that lovely accent of yours originally from Australia?"

"Well done!" she said, retaining one of his hands and starting to step across the room. He followed in her wake, if not enthusiastically, then at least obediently. "Most Southerners ask if I'm English. Such provincials. Met Georgio, that's Mr. Montanaro, during one of his fishing trips to Perth during his salad days. He used to be mad for fishing. His study has loads of mounted fish. Great, gaudy things. Dolf, Georgio's oldest, loves to hunt. Spends most of his time outside, like a beast."

"Not to rush your welcome, Claudia"—Auguste noticed he was being towed towards a nicely paneled door set to one side of the library—"but why precisely am I here? Are we to meet Mr. Montanaro?"

She drew him with her implacably. Open door, through door, close door. They proceeded along a long, interior hallway.

"Georgio hasn't been well enough to have guests in some time, Auguste. May I call you Auguste?"

"Certainly, Claudia." The carpet was thick, silencing their footsteps. "Mr. Montanaro is ill?"

"Georgio had a bad reaction to the vaccine," she said, turning a corner, still holding his hand. The new corridor opened to one side, windows brightening their path, while large portraits of the sort, painted over photographs, lined the opposite wall. "The Caplewoods supplied it, and while I don't think it was intentional, the product of their best efforts still created quite the side effects in a few. Georgio's fever didn't break for some time. I'm afraid it left some damage. Of course, he had what the CDC calls comorbidities. He'd run to fat, drank far too much and had a few minor heart attacks along the way. It's rather impressive he's still breathing, darling."

"So you *are* House Montanaro."

"I run the house. All of this is to please me."

A set of double doors opened from the inside. A slim, olive-skinned woman in a traditional maid's uniform stood to one side as they entered and then left at her mistress's nod. Auguste felt his hand released. He took the liberty of scanning his surroundings more closely.

He was standing in the nicest walk-in closet he'd ever seen. More specifically, it was a boudoir in proper Southern style. Matching settees and a fainting couch that would not have been out of place in the Sable Jardin took pride of place. An extraordinarily complete beauty station, complete with low chair and a neat array of cosmetics, occupied one wall. The inevitable four-poster bed was covered in a dozen satin pillows, it's expanse sufficient to satisfy a decadent French king. Interestingly, the bedside table held a tall stack of books. He barely refrained from walking forward to indulge his nosy habit of reading the spines. There were other things, custom pieces of furniture. They had the look of craftmanship but decidedly weren't something out of the Ethan Allen catalog. He decided not to notice.

Claudia Montanaro stood facing him, elbows akimbo and fists on shapely hips.

"My god, look at you! When my staff reported that the senior corsetiere from the Sable Jardin had not only survived but was in my city, I could not believe it. I had to see at once!"

"They were watching the docks, Claudia?"

"They were watching the Caplewoods," she said, throwing open a pair of double doors. "Amounts to the same thing."

He opened his mouth to reply, but she'd already stepped inside what turned out to be the actual walk-in closet. Several garments came flying out, and she impatiently unbelted her robe.

"I'd be happy to wait for you to change, Claudia," he finally said, giving her his back.

"Nonsense," she replied. "Ha! I have it. Be a love, help me."

He looked and saw her advance with a corset held to her chest. She managed to keep her girls covered, but she was unmistakably voluptuous on top, belying the absence of fat everywhere else. She rotated on the ball of one foot and presented the corset's lacings to him, incidentally displaying a pair of matching dimples just above her briefs.

"When I married Georgio, I was a good wife. I cooked, I cleaned, I bore his children, and I was a proper minx in his bed."

He somehow doubted she did much cleaning or cooking considering the house he found himself in. The minx part seemed about right, though. He busied his hands.

"His third marriage, you understand, so he was considerably older. Only one child at that point, Dolf, but I quickly produced additional heirs, which was what he was after. That, and a trinket to show off. I kept my figure but after a while his appetite faded while mine, if anything, grew. You understand? Then, two years ago, my children died from the virus."

"I'm very sorry for your loss, Lady Claudia," Auguste said, meeting her eyes in the mirror opposite. Sorrow shadowed her face for the span of an eye's blink. "Truly. This fallen land is sodden with the tears of those of us who remain."

"It hardly makes me unique, Auguste," Claudia said, returning her regard to the image of herself, running her hands up her flanks. "This a world of widows and orphans, grieving over the past. I'm firmly focused on the here and now. For the sake of my stepson, I'd largely refrained from sating my body's needs before the plague, but by God I did indulge my fashion-hunger. Which brings us to you, Auguste. You are my answer to interminable boredom."

"Indeed?" August said, his hands automatically straightening and snugging the lacing of her corset. He recognized it without having to check the tag. It was from one of his winter lines, a black leather overbust number from the year before the Fall, when the brand had really taken off following his appearance in *Fashion Survivor.* "I love your corset, by the way."

"I expect so," she giggled, her laugh husky. "I adore it! Let me brace so you can give it a proper tug. I've worked hard in the gym to ensure a much tighter fit."

She walked over to one of the custom pieces of furniture. He recognized she was waiting for him to comment on it.

Oh, chérie, a simple St. Andrew's Cross isn't going to shock me.

She took hold and nodded. He gave the lacings a firm tug, rocking her. Her underwear covered stern surged backwards a bit, so Auguste placed one hand in the small of her back, and tightened the lacings a final time, firmly pulling and causing her back to arch.

"Unlike her momma, I thoroughly approve of the Caplewood girl's choice of wedding attire." Claudia said, patiently waiting as he tied the knots. "However, I mean to have the best corset at the gala. Obviously, black will never do. So, you're going to fit me. And you're going to fit me *first.*"

"Delighted, of course," Auguste said, tucking the loose ends out of sight. "But my measuring tape, my assistant..."

She spun inside his arms and looked down at him with a proprietary air. Her hands established anchor points in suggestive places.

"Claudia, you're lovely as the dawn, but I confess I am a trifle overwhelmed. Aren't you going to ask me if I'm married or otherwise affianced?"

"A woman leaves her mark; she molds her signature into her things, whether they're furs, her home or a man." Her hands began to roam lightly about his person, and one grasped his right hand and held it up briefly to display an empty ring finger, before sliding back up towards his chest, leaving a trail of goosebumps. He stiffened as she grasped the vestigial bit of mammalian anatomy inside his shirt, which responded predictably, damn it. "It's a thing readily detectable to any other woman, whether there's a ring present or not. And mate, I find you unclaimed!"

"And your... underling? Jackson?" Auguste said. His hands weren't entirely still either. There was a lot of her to catalog, a sort of feminine index to savor. "I think I might have detected a mark or two there, no?"

"He's become boring. I think it's his turn to work for my son, who is happily away on a foraging party in Arkansas. Whatever will I do when he's gone?"

"I'm sure you'll manage."

This wasn't his first dance, or his twenty-first. Auguste had been expecting her to kiss him any moment.

He wasn't wrong.

Later, in the inevitably damp, tangled sheets, his breathing still returning to normal, he realized he'd been had.

Some days this job didn't, as the kids say, suck.

"Although this is as unexpected as you are lovely, my languorous Mrs. Montanaro," Auguste said, enjoying the slow passage of her fingernails up and down his spine, "why me?"

"Well, aren't you precious," she replied. Her hand dipped a bit lower, swirling a trace of hair at the base of his spine. "You are unattached, very attractive and frankly, you're available. A chance to indulge myself is rare. The selection here is rather dull, rather like my marriage. In the before times, and in an effort to help my husband address my needs, I made a study of, let's say, intimacy. I consumed everything I could get my hands on. Tantric exercise videos, Japanese pillow books, yoga, everything. Then I'd take trips to rehearse every combination I could think of. My budget was effectively without limit. Everything medically supervised, you see. Nothing sordid, only the most exclusive partners, venues and practices. I'm quite accomplished and sometimes handle two things at once."

"In that case, you won't mind if I ask some questions," he said, rolling onto his back. She lifted her hand off his tailbone as he did so, then replaced it in the corresponding location. "About this wedding."

"All questions are valid." Her hand became a little busier. "Not all answers enlighten."

"This town seems to be more than a bit feudal," he said. "Split between rival families, who are supposed to be sealing an alliance using a marriage. It's an arrangement well past your basic *tres* antebellum South! Convenient that there are only two families remaining in power."

He glanced down.

"Ah, my dear, I'll be with you shortly, but I do need a few minutes."

"Relax, my dear corsetiere, and let me try a little something…" She changed her angle and indeed, it appeared she'd accelerated matters. "Nothing unusual about it, the marriage, I mean. The reason hereditary and political marriages were so common was because they worked. They were a way to settle issues about land without violence. At the outset, there were several prominent businessmen in Natchez. Where we are is actually the ruins of Vidalia, across the border from what my husband charmingly labeled 'Mississip.' It was too small a town to hold itself together and was quite overrun. With enough people and proper leadership, it became defensible. So, we just moved across the river and made it our own. New Natchez, you see."

"You moved a state boundary, just like that?"

"Yes, just like that. Who was going to gainsay us, no? The zombies? We're more violent than them. Ah, there we go. Speaking of, a little gentle violence seems called for about now."

"Hello, darling, are you quite alright?"

"Jus—" Auguste, lungs pumping like bellow, tried box breathing to recover his mental balance. A few cycles later, he answered. "Just a moment."

She let him be for several minutes, passing the time tracing her finger about his chest, drawing little designs in their mingled perspiration.

"Well, what do you think?" Claudia perched over him on one elbow, her long, lovely length cuddling him from the side, the sheet discreetly rucked up over her hip. "Money and time well spent? If it's a mattress matter, I'm across it. What do you say? I must know. I collect the better comments, you see."

"Spung! I died happy," Auguste had begun to have a suspicion, and her last remarks provided the answer. He'd fallen into the hands of a genuine eccentric. The Commonwealth, and the gentry of the South seemed to breed them. Something about being possessed of both a surfeit of money and free time. When accompanied by an ache they couldn't properly describe, let alone fill, they sought something to assuage the gnawing feeling of loss. Some set out to be the Authority on obscure orchids, or the rarest of stamps, or archeology. Of course, the Fall had amplified everything. Greater loss, burning regret, more loneliness. Her need was correspondingly deeper. At least, Claudia had elected a more physical pursuit. It was...charming, in a way. And sad. Mr. Montanaro likely didn't know what he'd bargained for. "You are incomparable, beautiful Claudia. Magnificent."

"Here's something to help you recover—" She stretched towards the bedside table, retrieving a tumbler covered in condensation. He sat up to enjoy it. Ice-cold orange juice, and perhaps a little salt. "You can refresh yourself while you think of more boring questions."

"That's quite good." He sipped appreciatively, and considered what he needed to know. "How do you feel about the wedding, really?"

"Oh, it will be good for Dolf. He's an only child now, and he needs family. I won't be here forever. Old Battlewagon Caplewood is no spring chicken and she has only girls. Becky-Anne is the best of the bunch, which is why I insisted on her. Soon she'll be ours. Here, drink up."

He finished the juice while filling his eyeballs with the sight of her.

"The sheets are a bit damp, no?" she asked, flipping the sheet away. Her skin gleamed in the afternoon light filtering through the drapery. She was perspiring too, but her breathing was the long, deep rhythm of an athlete, quite prepared to continue. "I have this lovely couch we must try."

She half led, half tugged him to a couch in the shape of a shallow letter c, as if the letter had collapsed on its back and raised it forepaws and hindlegs in the air in surrender.

I know those feels, couch.

It was as broad as a twin bed, but one that had built-in headrests at either end. Anticipating her choreography, Auguste confidently arranged himself at one end. He might not be a sexual racehorse, but he had spent the last decade in New Orleans after all. He'd even seen this model couch before. He ran his hand along the super suede, moving the nap so that it slightly changed color as he did so.

Claudia strode a short distance to an end table. She looked, as they said in the Commonwealth, smashing, her glow complimented by an imaginary hum, full of improbable energy. She refilled his glass from a crystal pitcher that was soaking condensation onto a white cloth. It definitely hadn't been there at the start, so presumably her chamber maid was accustomed to visitors of his sort.

"Thank you," Auguste said, tossing off the entire tumbler in three large swallows. As he did so, he felt her hands move to his groin and busy themselves. "I'm delighted with your effort and—ahh—really feel—oh that's lovely—even for me, a short respite is in order, Claudia."

"Well, I'm sure you're right," she replied, a mischievous twinkle too apparent. "Still, I think that Parisian couple taught me a little something that might have bearing on this matter. Half-countrymen of yours, of a sort. But continue with the questions, as long as you don't mind answers that are brief. Or less intelligible."

Then she bent down.

"As you wi-ish," Auguste managed. Could his courting tackle already be stirring again? "The younger Caplewood girl played the government's radio broadcast for me. Eventually, they will come here. Have you thought about that?"

She seemed to think about it.

"Mm-hmm," she affirmed.

"Do you suppose the Caplewoods are aware of that, too?"

"Mm-hmmm..."

"An-and do you plan to share power with the Caplewoods when that happens."

"Uh-uh," she replied, far more tolerably.

"So, whenever the govern—" He paused in mid-conclusion. It had been awhile, but he was relearning what every boy found out in his early teen years. Too much, too soon after, was exquisite agony.

And suddenly it wasn't. His body responded most unhelpfully, or very helpfully. Matter of perspective.

He felt her chuckle deep in her throat.

Oh shit.

"Whrf immm duh ornng ju?" he asked, before his head fell to the couch's surface, his pillow abruptly removed.

"Come again, darling Auguste?" Claudia asked, thumping the pillow down on his thighs.

"What," he tried again. "Is in. The orange juice?"

"Well, oranges of course. Some electrolytes. And a teensy, tiny splash of very good vodka. Barely even there. Useful as a relaxant. Maybe a wee bit of sildenafil, in suspension."

He raised his head and stared at her, then plopped his head back down. He'd deal with it later.

"There are a lot of pre-wedding events," he said, gathering the skeins of thought that were more thoroughly tangled than the sheets on the bed where this had begun. "The Caplewoods mentioned a hunting reception. Will you attend in your husband's place?"

"Of course," Claudia said, swinging one thigh over and sitting on his upper thighs. She applied her hands to the well-defined muscles along his spine. Auguste felt paired thumbs spread and press on either side of his vertebrae, before being pushed upwards all the way to the base of his skull. Her strength still came as a surprise, even after the last forty-five minutes. Had it been forty-five minutes? Maybe twice that. Fuck, who knew. He was starting to float.

"The Families collaborate extensively, sharing responsibility for clearing infected—that's the proper term, right?—infected away from New Natchez in an expanding circle. We share alike in salvage, but maintain, by agreement, separate depots. Incidentally, the littlest Caplewood took a bigger risk than she knew. If I hadn't been so excited to meet you, there would have been considerable trouble for Missus Caplewood."

Some time went by before he could form the next idea, let alone speak it. She found knots just above his shoulder blades. He let her carry on, while he rehearsed what he wanted to say.

"The river is the key to recovering the central United States," he said. It was a strange twilight experience. His body felt alive, limber, even energized. His mind was foggier than he expected. "Controlling, or at least participating in the river trade will be to everyone's advantage."

"Oh my, yes."

"Could be enough profit and influence in it for the right people to have a significant leadership role in the state. Guv'nor, maybe."

"Certainly."

"Izzat somethin' you. Want?"

"Aren't you feeling quite relaxed, darling man?" Claudia asked.

"Maybe we can talk more about it later."

"Are you getting sleepy, deary?" She horsed him around a bit, so he was laying on his side, being cuddled by her from a sitting position. Suddenly, her activity changed.

"I think—what are you doing?" Auguste blurted. "Look, Claudia, I'm flattered, I'm replete, I'm beyond impressed. However, as a gentleman of some note among the boudoir set of New Orleans, I assure you that any new business will simply have to wait. A nap would be quite restorative."

"Are you totally worn out, then?" Claudia smiled. She didn't stop moving. He turned a bit, twisting to address her directly. Her open-mouthed smile conveyed a dark knowing.

That's funny, I can see the tips of her canines when I'm laying like this.

"The spirit is willing, but the flesh is bruised, and spongy. Yes, worn out is the correct turn of phrase."

"Well, ignore me. Just relax and if I'm wrong, I'll soothe you to sleep. But I rather think this will work. I adore the grand gesture, showing off, proving I'm right. Years I spent being dutiful, meek. No more. You see, not only did I study anatomy, neurology, even glandular function, I also spent time with Eastern medicine. I learned something from Su-Jin, my Korean maid. She brought it to LSU when she was a nursing exchange student. It's something that Korean women have known for thousands of years. So, I'm going to continue to have you, piece by piece, until there's quite nothing left to have, my beautiful corsetiere. We're not even halfway through my little program. When you get back to the Caplewood bitches, you'll be quite useless. Don't tense up! Ah, there we are."

Auguste felt her hands move into high gear, assisted occasionally by something smoother and slicker.

He tried to sit up, but she pressed him back.

"Tsk, tsk."

What on earth? Is she constructing a corset down there? Bend the busk about, careful, it wants to spring back on you. Leave room for the boning channels, ah, there's the fold for the modesty panel. Now insert the whalebone, handsomely, if you please. Test-fit the laces, nice and snug. Wait, is she whistling? What song is that? "House of the Rising Sun"?

The peanut bulb on the old sewing machine in Maman's fabric room blinked on. The creaky sewing machine made an almost inaudible electric whine. A little adjustment of the workpiece and the balance wheel was slowly beginning to come around. The needle bar eased down, then up and returned, like an old man nodding. The bobbin was threaded and the presser foot made contact with the dog plate. Suddenly the seam lined up and the full power surged through him. The stitching went from one-two one-two to a steady chuckle, like a train moving purposefully down the track, clickity-clack. The needle bar accelerated then, too fast to see, a smooth gallop, then a blur, the bobbin spinning and jerking, the whole machine straining towards the finish, straining, straining, straini—

The sun was very bright in the repurposed parking lot of a former warehouse hardware store, which the inhabitants of New Natchez had converted to long-term vehicle storage. The crowd was growing as the families, staff, and hangers-on assembled an ad-hoc bleacher to observe the impending celebratory hunt. The heat reflected off the macadam, making Auguste feel as though he was being broiled from two directions, flamenco hat or no. Located on the edge of the town, the space was bordered by the ersatz anti-zombie wall of shipping containers. Unfortunately, the metal boxes, stacked two high, simply created a hot, eighteen-foot-tall steel radiator. The riverside location offered no respite since the sluggish breeze was moving the air, sodden in the prevailing humidity, just enough to make him feel like the entrée in a sous vide.

He'd chosen to soothe himself by hiding his misery behind a pair of Versace mirrored sunglasses in rose-gold, acquired from the glove box of an abandoned Lexus. Standing with folded arms, his pistol on his side, at least he could observe the preparations in privacy. The arena in front of him took up a third of the generously sized parking lot. The chain link fence demarcated the fighting arena, with two additional shipping containers already in place, RV air conditioners on the roofs rattling away. The double doors were flush with openings to the enclosure. He and Jonna stood alongside the bleachers inside a further, larger chain link circle reserved for the families and their retainers. It kept the larger group of townsmen segregated from the Montanaros and Caplewoods.

"You look like shit, Auguste," Jonna said in a stage whisper. She was holding a stainless steel canteen, using it to cut the heat from the noonday sun. "I left the sewing room when I couldn't keep my eyes open any longer, but I didn't see you. What time did you finally go to bed last night?"

"I didn't. As soon as the wedding rehearsal was over, Dame Caplewood demanded another fitting, and elected to inform me in painful detail how every adjustment made her dress worse, not better, to the echoed refrain of complaints from her sister. Two weeks of nonstop fittings, sewing, fittings, more sewing, and she hates the color, the length, the fit, the collar—"

"Still hasn't forgiven you for your little tête-à-tête with the

Australian man-eater, has she? Well, relax. This assignment is almost over—as soon as the hunt is complete, we change for the evening wedding. Maybe then the Caplewoods will stop watching us like hawks and you can visit Chez Montanaro again."

"That nightmare," Auguste replied, withdrawing the red handkerchief from his sleeve and mopping his brow. "The only saving grace of the Caplewoods' anger is that the carnivorous, crazy, dangerous she-bitch hasn't found a time to sink her claws into me again. Speaking of time, did you get an acknowledgement on the radio?"

"Just that they got our message, and the cavalry is en route." Jonna watched the Caplewoods file into their box seats. "I couldn't linger and risk Caplewood security finding me. I still think we're overdoing the cloak-and-dagger business."

"Orders from the Boss," Auguste said. "Smith says we're spread too thin to police every aspiring baron or duke. We have to know who we're dealing with."

"There's Becky-Anne."

The scion of House Caplewood was dressed and equipped in light clearance gear. In place of rifle, she held a boar spear, and the handles of twin machete's jutted over her shoulders. Her bannerman was Priscilla-Jo, who kept the limp, blue pennant high.

"Quite the spectacle," Jonna observed. "You don't usually see armed brides at the wedding preparations."

"Becky-Anne insisted," Auguste said, pulling his shades down a touch, and looking over them. "She's got her own demons, and apparently she likes to kill them. If the demons aren't available, she makes do with the infected. That other corset I'm building is at her request. Ah, there's Lady Montanaro."

Auguste watched the beautifully dressed Claudia debark, but forbore any further comment. Didn't matter. Jonna spoke fluent Boudreaux.

"It's not often anyone gets the best of the Beau of Sable Jardin," Jonna said, watching the Montanaro boy hop out of his glorified golf cart and hurry to his stepmother's side.

"What can I say, Jonna? Claudia Montanaro knows her sexology, endocrinology—hell, her pharmacology. I don't care if we are the same height laying down. Unlike Sir Edmund Hillary, I have no more desire to climb any peak, let alone the tallest, just because it's there."

"Speaking of tall, isn't that guy with the groom the same one that took you to your assignation with Lady Exhaustion?"

Auguste followed her gesture, and sure enough, among the party wearing red, Meathead was shadowing Dolf Montanaro. The corsetiere had made the lad's acquaintance during the fitting process and he seemed nice enough. Tall, like his father, who was reported to be nearing the end. The town would be thanking their lucky stars if they understood he lacked his stepmother's grand appetites. The Montanaro scion was dressed and equipped much like his bride. He strode out with a red-shirted standard-bearer, joining Becky-Anne in the area.

Dame Caplewood and her house manager, a stout gray-haired man in a light suit, walked to shake hands with Lady Claudia, before they mounted the dais, and Claudia her private box. Caplewood began to address the crowd, her manager at her elbow, handing her pages of her speech. The theme was predictable.

Survival. Sacrifice. Rebuilding. Families coming together.

"This definitely ain't the average wedding-week event," Jonna said softly, after a while. "Whatever happened to 'we're not losing a daughter, we're gaining a son'?"

"Both families believe some sort of spectacle is needed to demonstrate the competence of their leaders to the people," Auguste replied sotto voce, gesturing to the spectators gathering. "It's the old cost-benefit of a titled landowner. The peasants work the land and trade their labor for security. The leaders make the decisions, collect the rents and protect the people, bleeding to do so, if necessary. Nearly Arthurian, I do declare. I admit the inclusion of the armed bride in the arena is a modern touch."

"Maybe," Jonna answered. "Becky-Anne makes it look good, but I'm not sure this is a legit wedding activity. I'm a simple girl. Where's the bridesmaids' party? What happened to male strippers?"

On the podium, Dame Caplewood was working up to the climax.

Mutual responsibilities. Obligations. Duty. She tapped her manager's shoulder.

He swung his hand towards the area. Dolf and Becky-Anne dipped their spearheads in salute, first to Dame Caplewood and then towards Lady Claudia in the other set of stands. Then the shipping containers swung open.

A pair of infected stumbled out. Someone had been taking

care of them, because they were a lot cleaner and better fed than the zombies Auguste had seen recently. The pair of infected oriented on the two meals-ready-to-eat and charged the bride and groom, who quickly spitted them for their trouble.

The crowd applauded loudly. A few hoots and catcalls were audible.

"See, as I understand it," Jonna said, "they're going to kill increasing numbers of infected to demonstrate their worthiness to each other and the hoi polloi. Whoever kills the most accrues the greatest honor."

"I'm interested to see how far this goes."

Four more zombies were released from the darkness of each container.

The combat was a little more frenetic, and Becky-Anne's spear was stuck on a ribcage, so she transitioned to machetes. She spun an infected's head free of its shoulders and the crowd screamed its enthusiasm this time. The screams from the Caplewood stands went on a bit longer than expected. Auguste looked towards the commotion. One of the party was down.

Holy bleeding saints, is that Caplewood on the ground?

"The fuck is going on?"

Auguste wasn't sure if those were his words, or Jonna's.

Dame Caplewood was cradling her house manager's bloody head and screaming. The crowd was just beginning to notice, when the containers disgorged not six or eight more infected, but scores. They weren't just in better condition, they were faster, jittery even. The seemingly unending pack streamed out towards the engaged pair. Auguste and Becky-Anne readied their weapons and stood back-to-back as the first of the infected reached them, and the screams of the surging crowd reached new heights. The packed family retainers of both sides were jostling, and Auguste began to lose sight of anything but what was immediately adjacent to him.

Over the screams, Auguste thought he heard laughter. Almost as an afterthought, he drew his pistol, muzzle down.

That's definitely someone laughing.

Auguste snapped his head around and saw the Montanaro woman laughing. Worse, she was looking right at him.

"What fuckery is this, Auguste?" Jonna asked.

"Heinous fuckery, my dear," Auguste said, considering the distance from his gun muzzle to the crazy bitch's skull. Through

the crowd, he saw Meathead and a few others in red shirts coming his way. "Fuckery most foul. 'Ware ambush!"

More firearms began to crackle around the arena. The roars
of infected were clearly audible now.

And then it all went for a ball of chalk.

*Mustn't shoot civilians, me lad. Boss wouldn't approve. Jesus,
Jonna, leave some for m— Oh shit, got you, you bastard. Shoot
and move, shoot and move. Wait, what's an infected, two infected
doing here? Oh, sweet burning beignets, the fence is down. I hope
those kids are okay. Okay, that's a red shirt—heh, perfect, the bad
guys are wearing redshirts. Ahahahaha—front sight, front sight,
front sight, HA! Got you! shitodear. Wait, why's my leg burning?
Where's that Montanaro bitch. She did this—fuck, infected. Mag
change, no, don't drop your mag in the scrum, need the bullet
need the bullets—no bitey bitey Mr. Infected, here EAT THIS! Is
Jonna screaming— Ohthankyoujesus it's someone else. Last mag—
where did all the infected come from? Oh, hello Meathead, okay
motherfucker, no fucking mer—*

*Ow. Oww. Blue sky? Why am I on the ground? It's not very
sanitary. What is wet? Oh, nasty, this naked fucker is leaking all
over me—shove this bastard off me, fuck me that's heavy. That's
a lot of shooting, let's see what's going on, nope can't move this
bastard. Who has machine guns? I don't have machine guns. Is
that "Anchors Aweigh"? Where's Jonna, I want my Jonna. Why am
I so cold? Mr. Boudreaux, you ask a lot of questions. It's getting
quieter, anyway. Now I lay me down to sleep, I pray the Lor—*

"Hey, Auguste," he heard. Auguste blinked blearily. "Hey,
Boss, are you tracking?"

He looked over, and Jonna's blood-smeared face swam into
view, swaying against a moving background. Then Auguste realized that she wasn't swaying, he was. He glanced down. He was
on a litter, about to be swung onto a pair of sawhorses.

"What the hell happened?"

"Oh, thank you God!" more of Jonna appeared, leaning over
him. "Look, you caught a round in the leg, not too bad, through
and through the meat. Something also fetched you a crack on
your Cajun skull, and you have a concussion."

"Help me sit up," Auguste said, struggling to get to his elbows at least. He looked at an IV line taped to the back of his right hand. "The hell?"

"Boudreaux, relax," a new voice said. This one belonged to a tall young man in ridiculous blue-patterned camouflage. Spiky black hair stuck out from under his red baseball cap, which read COMMANDING OFFICER. His name tape read CHEN. "I need you to lay back. The doctor is triaging casualties and you're definitely one of them."

Auguste squinted at Chen.

"Took you long enough to get here, college boy."

"Yeah, the cavalry got here just in time," Jonna explained. Behind her, two remarkably husky men in camouflage, helmets, and plate carriers trotted past with another stretcher. One looked down at Auguste curiously. "Lieutenant Commander Chen and half a dozen boats pulled up before your girlfriend could finish her plan."

"Help me sit up, goddammit!" August ordered. "You can help me or watch me fall over. And she's not m—you know what, fuck right off."

Together, they got him upright. Order was being restored, but the hubbub of activity wasn't quitting. An enormous number of naked, dead infected were in the middle of the area, and spilling outward in two directions, the chain link fence trampled flat underneath a mixed pile of bodies.

"Montanaro?" Auguste asked.

"Lady Claudia is in custody," Chen said, consulting a clipboard. "The Caplewood man is dead, but the boss lady is all right, except for the part where she's demanding I turn Montanaro over to her."

"The kids?"

"Well, see for yourself," Jonna said, motioning across the triage area.

A short distance away, two blood-covered persons stood talking to less be-spattered well-wishers. When he made out Dame Caplewood stalking up the little group, her face a mask of anger, the pair snapped into focus. It was Dolf Montanaro, with a pistol in his left hand, and Becky-Anne Caplewood, who was still holding a bent machete. While he watched, the couple saw the approaching storm too, and started laughing. They exchanged an overhand handshake, Weathers and Schwarzenegger-style, that was right out of the 90s-era action movies, before turning to face Dame Caplewood.

"I declare, that does not, *does not*, I say, look like a couple about to tie the nuptial bonds of matrimony," Auguste said, slumping back to his elbows. "And we still need a wedding to go with all my fucking corsets."

"You better not fall over, Mr. Boudreaux," Dame Caplewood said, her mouth pursed. Her icy expression matched the perfection of her pale blue corset dress. Though she wasn't taking any obvious care to not be overheard, the background jazz music provided some cover. "I do not care for posturing, and your recent wounds will not excuse you. I will not have this reception spoiled by a medical emergency."

"Madam, I assure you that falling over is entirely out of the question," Auguste said, swaying. "For the moment. Perhaps your sturdy daughter could lend me her strength so I can find my seat?"

Becky-Anne, the target of his initial mission, conveniently overheard and stepped over to place an arm around his shoulders.

"It's okay, Momma, I'll get him to a chair and you can make sure Priscilla-Jo is ready to cut the cake," Becky-Anne said, already guiding Auguste towards a round banquet table. "Mr. Boudreaux, you really shouldn't be on your feet. You're still mildly concussed. I thought a creative type like yourself would be above displays of macho."

"There is no one quite like me, darling, but it's true we *creatiffs* are mildly, I say, *mildly*, addicted to drama. Now, be a dear and get me to the friends of the groom table."

Jonna was waiting there, wearing one of her own creations. The overbust corset in green was accented by a very gauzy blouse, complimented by freshly conditioned leather trousers and boots. She was also armed. The combination of corsetry and guns was repeated throughout the room. As Auguste leaned on Becky-Anne's sturdy shoulder, he could see a stupendous amount of cleavage on display. He was glad to see the benefits of civilization in effect, because both the décolletage and weapons were spotlessly clean and holstered, as such things should be. He smiled at Jonna as Becky-Anne pulled out a seat. His assistant cum bodyguard had her hand on Zac Chen's thigh. His blue uniform was clean and pressed. A small, black handheld radio sat on the table for easy access, but the naval officer appeared fascinated with some detail on Jonna's corset instead.

"Zac, if you can convince your boss, I can come up with an improvement to that awful blue camouflage," Auguste said, calling Chen's attention to his arrival. "Something that doesn't scream blueberry tart."

"I don't think the secretary will accept a corset as a uniform item, and more's the pity," Chen replied, guiltily tearing his eyes away. He nodded towards Becky-Anne. "No matter how good a job you did on this one."

"I love this thing, it's perfect!" Becky-Anne smiled and ran a hand over Auguste's secret project. Her corset was a perfect match for the Marine-pattern uniforms that were scattered among the crowd, as well as the utility trousers she wore beneath it. It had built-in MOLLE loops, from which hung a flashlight, spare pistol magazines and a small first aid kit. "The overbust is deep enough to keep everything in place and the shoulder straps take the weight. I have the first tactical corset—a tactiset! Or maybe a mili-corse."

"If either of the Lieutenants Smith sees that thing, you can expect more orders for another ASAP," Jonna said, reaching out to straighten the flashlight pouch. "I'm just glad that your momma is relaxing into the new order."

"We were lucky," Chen answered, glancing to where the giggling bride and Dolf Montanaro had borrowed a Marine officer's Mameluke sword to cut the cake.

Auguste followed the look. The groom was wearing a black waist cincher under his tuxedo jacket, and the bride was radiant in a satin corset dress of brilliant white. The bustline dipped daringly, covered in lace and seed pearls, but panels below the bustline to the waist were semitransparent. Layers of skirts, split in front, flowed floorwards. It was decorated with still more matching seed pearls, and a two-meter train complimented the look of *another* Boudreaux masterpiece.

Auguste kept his sigh of contentment mostly to himself.

"If your sister hadn't been carrying a torch for young Montanaro, it would have been a real problem." Chen looked over at Becky-Anne. "His daddy was the popular one in the family, and there's a good chance the kid will turn out the same way. I've talked to him, and he's ready to support a return to a democratic system. Finding his daddy alive and drugged was the clincher. His ex was planning on cleaning up that detail directly the rest of her plan was complete."

"Hell, if those two weren't ready to tie the knot, I don't think Dame Caplewood would have settled for anything less than Montanaro's head," Jonna said. "Once we got Montanaro talking, it all came out. She never planned to allow her stepson to be in a position over her. Once the succession plan was eaten by the infected, and Dame Caplewood was out of the picture, she was going to take over. When the government representatives eventually arrived, they'd have to treat with her."

There was a low roar of approval from the cake cutting.

"Where is she now?" Auguste inquired, while craning his head to see what was going on. The newest Mrs. Montanaro had just smeared Mr. Montanaro's face with a palmful of cake. "The evil stepmother, I mean."

"Already shipped her downriver, in chains," Chen replied, returning to his perusal of Jonna's corset. She merely smiled indulgently. "Effing and blinding the entire way. Claudia Montanaro will end up at Guantanamo for trial. The days of 'what happens in the compartment stays in the compartment' are over."

"Speaking of compartments, those two need to go get one," Becky-Anne said, smiling at the scene where her little sister was being deeply kissed by her new husband. She raised her voice. "GET A ROOOOM!"

There was general laughter.

"I must say, Auguste, I'm surprised you didn't convert my tactiset to Priscilla-Jo's size, given how much Dolf loves hunting," Becky-Anne added, with a wink to Jonna. "It might have spiced up the wedding night."

"Auguste took care of it," Jonna replied, using her teaspoon to join the chorus of tapping utensils on water glasses. The happy couple embraced, again. "It is a truth universally acknowledged, that a bride wearing the fanciest, sexiest underthings will be shortly relieved of them by her groom."

"Oh?"

"I used some of that silk with a mossy tree camo print to make a pair of sexy, dainty panties for Priscilla-Jo," Auguste said, smirking knowingly. "Like my fellow corsetiere said, the nicer the underwear, the shorter the interval they stay on. Wouldn't be surprised if she had them on now, just to get some mileage out of 'em. But I do declare that tonight, when Dolf is finally alone with her, the bride will be wearing camo."

ABOUT THE AUTHORS

Editor **Gary Poole** has worked in the entertainment and publishing industry for his entire adult life. He's worked directly with John Ringo and several other authors on over a dozen novels and anthologies. He is also a film and television screenwriter, the managing editor of a successful alternative news website in Tennessee, hosts a popular radio morning show, and has voiced well over three thousand radio and television commercials. He lives in the burbs, worries too much about his lawn, and seems to attract every cat within a ten-mile radius of his house.

John Birmingham wrote features for magazines a decade before writing *Weapons of Choice*, working for *Rolling Stone*, *Playboy* and *The Independent* amongst others. He won Australia's National Award For Non-Fiction with *Leviathan: The Unauthorised Biography of Sydney*. Mostly though, he likes to make up crazy stuff.

Jody Lynn Nye lists her main career activity as "spoiling cats." When not engaged upon this worthy occupation, she writes fantasy and science fiction, most of it in a humorous bent. Since 1987 she has published over fifty novels and more than one hundred seventy short stories. She has also written with notables in the industry, including Anne McCaffrey and Robert Asprin. Jody teaches writing seminars at SF conventions, including the two-day intensive workshop at Dragon Con, and is Coordinating Judge for the Writers of the Future Contest.

Jamie Ibson is from the frozen wastelands of Canuckistan, where moose, bears, and geese battle for domination among the hockey

323

rinks, igloos, and Tim Hortons. After joining the Canadian army reserves in high school, he spent half of 2001 in Bosnia as a peacekeeper and came home shortly after 9/11 with a deep sense of foreboding. After graduating college, he landed a job in law enforcement and was posted to the left coast from 2007 to 2021. He retired from law enforcement in early 2021 and moved clear across the country to the Maritimes where he is now a full-time writer and part-time Foodie. Jamie's website can be found at www.ibsonwrites.ca, where he has free short stories available for download. He is married to the lovely Michelle, and they have cats.

Sarah A. Hoyt has written pretty much everything except Men's Adventure and Children's Picture Books. Those are unlikely, but she's not making any promises. Her first novel, *Ill Met By Moonlight*, was a Mythopoeic Award finalist. Her novel *Darkship Thieves* won a Prometheus Award, and her novel *Uncharted* (with Kevin J. Anderson) won a Dragon Award. She's still writing in her many series and starting new ones, when not herding her clowder of cats or going off on a cross-country adventure with her husband Dan Hoyt.

Brian Trent is the author of the acclaimed sci-fi thriller *Redspace Rising*, and his short fiction regularly appears in *The Magazine of Fantasy & Science Fiction*, *Analog Science Fiction and Fact*, *The Year's Best Military and Adventure SF*, *Daily Science Fiction*, *Escape Pod*, *Galaxy's Edge*, *Nature*, and numerous year's-best anthologies. His story "Descent into the Underworld" appeared in the Black Tide Rising anthology *We Shall Rise* and chronicled another episode in the life of apocalypse-survivor Silvio Cipriano. A winner of the 2019 Readers' Choice Award from Baen Books and Writers of the Future, Trent lives in New England. His website and blog are at www.briantrent.com.

Dave Freer is the author of some twenty-four novels and many shorter works. He lives a largely self-sufficient life on an island in the Bass Strait between Tasmania and mainland Australia, which involves a lot of hunting, fishing, diving and watching his plants die. His long-ago military past caught up with him, making him into part of his local Ambulance Service (he was a medic). He's been a finalist in the Prometheus and Dragon Awards. He reads too much and writes very slowly.

Griffin Barber spent his youth in four different countries, learning three languages, and burning all his bridges. Finally settled in Northern California and retired from a day job as a police officer in a major metropolitan department, he lives the good life with his lovely wife and needy, if tiny, Bengal. True to his eclectic background and tastes, Griffin has written stories across the SF&F field, from Hard SF, Space Opera, Dark (very dark) Fantasy, to zombie fiction.

Lydia Sherrer is the award-winning and *USA Today* best-selling author of the Love, Lies, and Hocus Pocus universe of books which has sold over half a million copies worldwide. Most recently she has published a GameLit series, TransDimensional Hunter, with *NYT* best-selling author John Ringo. Lydia subsists on liberal amounts of dark chocolate and tea, and hates sleep because it keeps her from writing. She is the mother of three, and due to the tireless efforts of her husband and her fuzzy overlords—i.e. cats—she remains sane and even occasionally remembers to leave the house.

Mel Todd has over twenty-seven titles out, her urban science fiction Kaylid Chronicles, the Blood War series, and the urban fantasy Twisted Luck series. With short stories in various anthologies and magazines, she hopes to keep writing tales that will capture your heart and imagination. You can sign up for her newsletter and follow her blog at www.badashpublishing.com.

A native Texan by birth (if not geography), **Christopher L. Smith** moved "home" as soon as he could. Attending Texas A&M, he learned quickly that there was more to college than beer and football games. His short stories can be found in multiple anthologies, including John Ringo and Gary Poole's *Black Tide Rising*, Mike Williamson's *Forged in Blood*, Larry Correia and Kacey Ezell's *Noir Fatale*, and Tom Kratman's *Terra Nova*. Christopher has cowritten two novels, *Kraken Mare* with Jason Cordova, and *Gunpowder & Embers* with Kacey Ezell and John Ringo. His cats allow his family and their dogs to reside with them outside of San Antonio.

Mike Massa has done a lot of traveling in uniform and out. He's visited ninety countries and lived in several large cities for protracted intervals. Big cities have a certain flavor and energy. This is especially true for New Orleans, where Mike spent some years growing up. The inhabitants of New Orleans have a certain, unique je ne sais quoi—and incorporating that flavor in a Black Tide story has been on Mike's to-do list for a while. Besides his writing, Mike works for an award-winning research university, integrating machine learning and artificial intelligence technologies into practical applications for cyber defense. Or, you know, Skynet. Whichever comes first.